Rules for Faking a Marriage
Katie King

Two Tree Birds

Copyright © 2026 by Katie King

All rights reserved.

No portion of this book may be reproduced in any form without written permission from the publisher or author, except as permitted by U.S. copyright law.

Contents

Dedication	1
1. Armpit Squelches	3
2. Aftertaste Of Manipulation	13
3. Fresh Air	22
4. Tire Shrapnel Trinkets	30
5. The Perfect Trifecta	39
6. Mr. G.P.	48
7. Operation: Crack The Scowl	55
8. Did I Just Say Girlfriend?	62
9. Shizzle Fritz	69
10. Emotional Whiplash	77
11. Peeing With The Door Open	86
12. Dowry Lists	96
13. Afternoon Pigeon	103
14. Breakfast Chaos	109
15. Happy Endings	114

16. Sweaty Cleavage — 122
17. Relationship Upgrade — 130
18. Nailed the Jealous Fiancée — 137
19. Very Different Algorithms — 141
20. It's Fake, Right? — 152
21. Gold-digging Whore — 159
22. Federal Paperwork Chaos — 171
23. Husband and Wife — 177
24. Truffle Nuggets — 187
25. No Ceilings — 193
26. Possessed Piñata — 200
27. Sunday Fun Day — 208
28. He's My Husband — 216
29. She Doesn't Need A Savior — 224
30. Korean Skincare — 231
31. Biofreeze Heats Me Up — 243
32. The Dark Lords — 250
33. Chicken Pot Pie — 257
34. Cheering Section — 267
35. Good Practice — 278
36. Defibrillator Needed — 287

37. Not Fragile	294
38. Bomb Shells	302
39. Six Months Later	312
Acknowledgements	316
About the Author	317
Also By	318

*For every Liz out there who pours her heart into lifting others up. Who always seems to be the one playing the role of the dedicated side character. You deserve a love story where **you** are the one everyone is cheering for.*

Chapter One
Armpit Squelches
Liz

"Mother Trucker."

I slam my forehead into the steering wheel after pulling onto the shoulder of a pitch-black Georgia backroad. I'm not usually an angry yeller. Excitedly loud? Almost always. A cusser? Never.

That said, this would be a really good time for the actual curse word.

I've got a flat tire. I'm in the middle of nowhere. This feels like a horror movie setup. Wonderful.

I lift my head, taking in the thick darkness stretching in every direction. Can I change a flat tire? Theoretically, yes. Actually, not a snowball's chance in Hades.

It'll be fine. Everything will work out just fine. I'll call AAA or the tire change people. Is there such a thing as tire change people? I glance around the surrounding darkness again. Are those eyes glowing in the woods?

Maybe I should call 911? I reach for my phone, but it doesn't light up. It died on set hours ago. I didn't have time to charge it, and totally forgot to plug it in when I got in the car. I've been singing my heart out to an old mix CD, trying to stay awake. I don't do well when I'm tired. I haven't seen another car for at least the last twenty minutes.

I guess this is up to me then. It'll probably be fine.

I grab a fistful of my floral-pattern skirt and climb out of the car, my bare feet hitting the cool pavement. A shiver runs down my spine. It's like Georgia can't make up its mind this spring. Desert temps by day, arctic temps by night. Tonight is one-hundred percent giving tundra vibes. I wish I had a sweater.

Good news first. Always the good news first. The spare tire is under the trunk mat, not strapped to the undercarriage. I am not built to crawl under a car. My brother calls me "eclectically girlie," which is code for *I dress like a hippie and act like a caffeinated border collie.*

Most of the time I am a glass half full kind of person. This is no different. This is a *challenge*, not a *catastrophe*. There will be no bad news tonight. Only good.

I will change this tire. I will crush it. I get to add "master tire changer" to my list of life skills. I will be so wildly competent that NASCAR will hear about how awesome I am and beg me to join their pit crew. There will be viral reels. Tire changing TikToks. All hail The Tire Changing Queen.

If I could just get these stupid round thingies off. Bolts? Nuts? Nubbins? Whatever, doesn't matter their name; I will make them my biz-nitch.

Twenty minutes later, I am still nutless. *Yes, I hear it. Don't make it weird.*

I wipe a streak of road grit off my face with my shoulder. Ick. It seems like my deodorant gave up the fight a while ago. I'm feeling defeat creep in, but I don't really have a choice. I have to change this tire. I don't want to sleep on the side of the road, but the stupid nubbins won't budge.

I throw my whole body weight into the tool thing. It's not a hammer or a screwdriver. I think it falls into the wrench category. *See, I know things.* I found it in the back of my trunk in an emergency kit that I'm sure my brother threw in there.

I'm so focused, I don't notice the motorcycle pulling up behind my car until the engine cuts off. A man swings off the bike with practiced ease.

The man takes off his helmet, but with his headlight blasting into my face, all I see is a broad silhouette backlit by shadows. He's tall. Built. Confident. My heart launches into my throat.

I casually slip my hand into my skirt pocket and tighten my grip around my keys. My thumb brushes over the little canister of mace my brothers and Dad insist I carry. Why did we have to film on location this week so far from civilization? Why didn't I stay at the motel an extra night like a normal person when we wrapped so late? Why did I think a two-hour drive home at this time was a good plan?

A few years ago I would've trusted this guy without blinking. A stranger stops in the dead of night, without a soul around to help me change a tire? Yup, that makes total sense. He's probably related to Mr. Rogers and wants to lend a neighborly hand. Everyone is kind and good. *Right?*

Now? Not so much. I jump when doors slam and flinch when strangers brush past me in the grocery store aisles. I carry scars. Some you can see, most you can't. And mace. Lots of mace.

Motorcycle man leaves his headlight on and walks toward me. The light illuminates me in all of my tire changing splendor, but he is entirely cast in shadows. The details of his face are hidden from me. I can't judge his intentions with the light blinding me like this, and my pulse skyrockets further.

"Need a hand?" His voice is rumbly and deep. It matches his motorcycle. Not something I should be focused on before I'm Ted Bundy'd to death.

"Um." I hesitate because I really do need help, but the thought of this guy getting close to me sets me on edge. "I think I can probably handle it. I'm almost done. Thanks for stopping by though." Lies. All lies.

He moves closer. I raise my hand to shield my eyes from the laser that is his headlight, but I still can't get a good look at his face. Although the way his body moves looks familiar.

My gut twists. I grip the tire iron tighter. I might not be good at fixing flats, but I can swing this thing if needed. I work out. Sometimes.

He's close enough that I can smell his cologne. I can see his features more clearly. His eyes shift to my hand, clocking the way I'm holding the tire iron.

His posture softens, and he raises one hand. "Easy there, slugger. Just want to make sure you're okay." His eyes squint, taking me in. "You left the set this late?"

My body relaxes a fraction. Maybe he was an extra today. Maybe that's why he looks a little familiar. I'm torn between giving him too much info and not answering at all. My desperation wins and I find myself word-vomiting on this man that I'm hoping is a Good Samaritan.

"Yes, I did! I'm trying to make it home so I can sleep in my own bed for once. We've been filming on location for two weeks, I'm just ready to be home. But my tire exploded and now the round knobby things won't come off."

I watch confusion wash over his concerned face. Was it the knobby things that threw him? Doesn't matter.

I charge on, "And the spare tire tried to murder me when I lifted it out of the back. I've seen other people change a flat tire. Really, it didn't look like it would be that hard. But, I've been working so much, and not going to the gym, I must have lost some of my muscle because the darn, thing-a-ma-bobs won't budge. How am I supposed to change a tire and prove to NASCAR that they need me on their pit crew if I can't get the old tire off?"

He walks slowly toward me with his hands outstretched in front of him like he's approaching an injured wombat, and cuts me off by gently taking the tire iron from my hand. "I've got you."

Three simple words. No comment on anything I just said. Just a casual, gruff *I got you.* The way his biceps bulge underneath his black t-shirt certainly looks like he can handle changing a tire. Alright, I guess this serial killer is going to help me before he murders me.

"I'm Liz, by the way." Always best to be on a first-name basis with those who may try to peel your skin off later. Makes you more human.

The farm next to our house growing up had baby cows. The farmer's wife, Mrs. Mary, wouldn't name them because it would make them too much like pets, and she wouldn't be able to sell them to the butcher. It's got to apply to people too, right? This stranger knows my name now, so he's attached; it makes him less likely to make me into a human sandwich. Logical.

He kneels next to my tire, doesn't look up, and grunts out, "Nate."

"Nice to meet you, Nate." As long as you don't cut my fingers off one by one later.

"You mentioned set. Are you an extra?"

He glances up at me. My eyes have finally adjusted enough to see his chocolate brown eyes.

"Something like that," he answers and goes back to fiddling with my tire.

Oookay then. I step back and let him work. Clearly, he isn't much for chatting. I, however, struggle to sit in silence. I try to hold my tongue while I watch his back muscles ripple through his shirt as he jacks up my car. *Yum.* Serial killer or not, he's good-looking. How long does it take for Stockholm syndrome to kick in? Do you have to actually be kidnapped first?

It's shocking I'm letting myself openly check this guy out. It's not that I'm immune to good-looking guys, I just don't usually let myself linger. I certainly don't daydream about how we'd look standing next to each other. Or how his strong hand might feel linked with my much smaller one. Or how his lips might...

Nope. Not going there.

The silence stretches, with just the clang of the tools and the insects as background music to my insanity. I can't take the silence anymore.

"So... where are you headed this time of night?"

He grunts while he tightens the knobby things around my spare tire.

I try again. "Are you headed home since we have a few days before we have to be back?" Still nothing. Cool, cool, cool. I'm fine with the silence. TOT-ally fine. Love the silence.

Maybe this is some sort of serial-killer tactic? Staying silent to throw the victim off? I haven't heard anything like that, but I've been so busy I'm not up on the latest serial-killer techniques.

"I live just north of Atlanta. I've been dying to sleep in my own bed all week. The hotel they booked for us is fine. I'm not, like, spoiled, but I miss my cat. And my bed. And my plants." I pause. Wow. That sentence sounded lame.

"I have other things in my life besides a cat and plants," I blurt. "I have friends. Lots of friends. I do. I have friends."

He glances up at me like I've sprouted antlers. I feel insane. Maybe I am, but I can't stop the verbal diarrhea now that I've started. "Friends that would miss me if I suddenly disappeared."

I fiddle with my mace keychain. I wish he would say something to put me out of my misery. But he doesn't.

"Like, real friends," I continue because there is no stopping this train. "Not made-up ones. I mean, okay, I *did* invent an imaginary friend in second grade, but that's because my parents wouldn't let me bring a friend on a family vacation. So I made one up and brought them along to have someone to talk to. Really that was just creative problem solving."

I take a breath but feel the need to add, "I don't usually talk to imaginary friends, but I do talk to Hulk all the time."

He's staring at me like I just escaped a padded room. I started pacing sometime in the midst of my monologue, my bare feet slapping against the pavement. Sweat pours from my pits, like a waterfall rolling down my arm and dripping off my elbow. I'm a real treat.

"Hulk is my cat. I don't try to talk to fictional superheroes." He's still staring. "Anyway, Autumn! Jenn! Those are my actual friends. You know them from set, right? See? Real friends. Totally real. Not imaginary. Not feline. Not a Marvel character."

Dear Lord, make it stop. I'm struck again that I'm in the middle of nowhere with a stranger. A strange man. A strange man who looks very strong. I take a not-so-subtle step backward.

Did I mention the mud puddle I've been avoiding stepping in all night? I avoided it successfully when I went to my trunk for my tire. I avoided it perfectly when I wrestled said tire out of the trunk and to the side of my car. It seems, however, that in my rambling and nervousness about being with a very strong-looking, silent man, the mud puddle slipped my mind.

Time slows. My arms flail like one of those inflatable car-lot advertisements. My body twists. My keys, with my beloved mace, launch into orbit. The mud puddle spreads out before me like it's saying, *Welcome home, child.*

Nate lunges, trying to save me, but his hand swipes the air where mine was a second ago. Props to him for attempting to get to me in time, though. A+ for effort.

Do I land gracefully? Of course not. Full-body mud pancake. Somehow, disgusting road water manages to make its way into my ear. Do I have to worry about brain-eating mud amoebas on top of everything else? Can muddy water give you permanent hearing loss?

I wipe sludge from my eyes and look into Nate's stunning brown eyes, now fully illuminated by his bike's headlight. The look on his face says he's regretting stopping, like he wishes he just kept driving into the night.

Falling into a puddle is one way to get me to stop talking. It's as effective as throwing a bucket of ice water on two teenagers necking. Necking? Does anyone say that anymore? I should bring it back.

"No. No one says that, and you shouldn't bring it back." Nate's tone is gruff. He's still staring at me like I'm crazy, but he's also looking at me like he's a little afraid of *me* now.

When I landed in the puddle, I guess I lost the few filters I do actually have in place. My thoughts are just tumbling out of my head without any warning or approval.

He rubs one large hand over his face and mutters something I can't understand. But, to his credit, he doesn't run away from me; he bends down and loops his hands under my arms to pull me out of the mud.

As soon as he starts to pull, my armpit squelches against his hand. I want the earth to swallow me whole. Maybe he didn't hear that? Maybe he thinks the swimming pool-amount of moisture, that's residing in my armpits, is from the mud puddle alone? Please, Lord, don't let him smell his hands anytime soon.

Once he has me upright, mercifully ignoring the armpit noises, I go to take a step toward him, but he holds up a hand. "Are you hurt?"

He steps closer to look over my face, his headlight illuminating us. Did I hit my head when I fell? I think I have a concussion, because I have no words. Wow.

It's a cliché reaction. I'm disappointed in myself for this completely run-of-the-mill response. But, this grumpy Good Samaritan is F.I.N.E. I numbly shake my head no to answer the question he asked me an uncomfortable amount of time ago.

"Okay." He points to the front of my car. "Stay put."

Standing still has never been my spiritual gift, but right now I'm determined to stand here like I'm training for a statue competition. He's irritated with me. I hate when people are mad at me. I don't want to cause him any more trouble, especially since it seems he really did stop to help change my tire and not murder me.

He slowly backs away from me like I'm a bomb he's trying not to set off, before he turns back to my tire without another word. I physically have to bite my tongue to keep from doing or saying anything to make this worse. It's a Herculean effort, but I'm determined.

I focus on the sound of the night bugs surrounding us. Whatever insect makes that sound, it's annoying. I switch my focus to the mud sliding off my body in small drips. Being soaked makes this chilly night feel even colder. I start to shiver.

Nate pauses his work and glares at me. I watch him close his eyes and take a deep breath like he's in a yoga class trying to find his calm. I bet he's never gone to yoga. Doesn't really strike me as the type. The image of him in a yoga pose is almost enough to make me break my silence, but I hold firm.

He tilts his head back, staring at the sky, and mumbles something that sounds strangely like, "Why me?"

He slowly stands and walks back to his bike, flips his bag open, and grabs something out. I haven't moved a muscle while I watch him. I don't feel scared anymore, but I still watch him closely.

He wordlessly walks up to me and thrusts a sweatshirt in my direction.

Mmmk? I feel confused, but I'm not about to take his gift for granted. I take it from him like I'm Smeagol and he just handed me the ring. *My precious.* He silently goes back to working the tire. I guess he noticed my shivering, or possibly he could hear my teeth chattering.

That was nice.

I weigh the pros and cons of slipping the sweatshirt over the top of my wet tank top. Nope. I need this off of me now.

He told me not to move, and I'm determined to listen, so I turn my back to him, whip off my tank top, and slide his sweatshirt over my head. Heaven. It's the only way to describe the warmth that envelops me. The scent that wraps around me is like a hug. I resist the urge to bury my nose and take a hit.

While I'm behaving like a crazed fangirl, Nate tightens the last bolt with a satisfying click, picks up the flat tire, and drops it into my trunk. He wipes his hands on his jeans and heads back toward his bike without a word.

"Uh... thanks?" I call after him, shifting my weight from foot to foot.

He lifts his hand over his shoulder sort of like a half wave. He doesn't even make a grunt. Doesn't glance back. He's silent 'til the end.

I gather my sweat-and-mud-stained skirt, and plop into my car. I'm dreading making the rest of the drive home with a soaked bottom half.

Never have I ever wanted to be showered and snuggled in my own bed, in my own space, more than I do right at this moment. I'm so tired. Deciding to drive home tonight is turning into one of the worst decisions I've made lately, and I don't have the best track record in decision-making.

I shimmy out of my skirt, toss it into the backseat, and blast the heat. I'll be driving home in my undies tonight, looking like a swamp monster. Not exactly swoon material. If tonight was the universe's idea of bringing me someone against my will, I want a do-over.

I pull back onto the road. A silent, broody man isn't exactly my dream version of a roadside hero. But thinking about his scowl while singing along to Britney makes me grin. He stopped. He helped. He handed me his sweatshirt like it was no big deal. Which, for the record, he's never getting back.

For someone like me, who doesn't trust easily anymore, his calm, quiet presence made me feel comfortable. Huh.

Chapter Two
Aftertaste Of Manipulation
Nate

I swing my leg over my bike and wait for her to get moving. I've never experienced anything like the last half hour of my life. She was like some sort of unhinged free-spirit that escaped from a music festival: glitter, chaos, and way too many words coming out of her mouth.

I watch her shadow moving around in her car. What is taking so long, woman? She tosses something into the back seat of her car. Was that her skirt? Is she driving home only wearing my sweatshirt? Why does that wake me up better than a cup of coffee could, and make me feel all sorts of possessive?

Her car lurches back onto the road, headlights glowing, a nineties pop song explodes from her speakers. Figures. Honestly, the music is the least surprising thing about this entire night.

I pull onto the road behind her, my eyes trained on the spare tire. It should hold until she gets home. I probably should've told her to get a new tire, but she seems like the kind of person who figures things out. Or doesn't, and somehow survives anyway.

I noticed her last week when filming started. The way she laughs with her whole body. How she hands out compliments like candy. People are drawn to her. I watched everyone in her orbit fall under her spell. There's something about her I can't pinpoint. I should be offended she didn't recognize me, but I tend to avoid the spotlight until necessary, so I'm not surprised.

Days on set can be long and mind-numbing, watching her made them go faster. Hopefully this whole three-month project will go quickly. I didn't want to sign on for this one because of who is working on the film, but with Liz around maybe it won't be as bad. She's beautiful, there's no denying that. I caught myself wondering what her hair would feel like if I ran my fingers through it, what it'd be like to pull her to me and taste her cherry-tinted lips.

Ridiculous. A grown man daydreaming. Completely pointless.

I don't do relationships. Don't want them. Don't need them. I shake off all thoughts of her, roll my shoulders back, and focus on the road.

Being a stunt double is starting to catch up with me. I'm beat. All I want to do is make it back to my condo and sleep for days. The older I get, the more I feel every hit, every fall, every stunt.

On paper my scene today was simple. Fall through sugar glass and roll into a combat scene. In reality, it was a three-story drop that'll ring in my joints for a week. My knee creaks as I shift gears. I pretend it's the bike, but it's me.

Even with my muscles screaming at me, it beats the alternative. I will gladly deal with the long days and the punishment I put my body through.

Lost in my thoughts, I follow Liz's taillights down the long winding road. I'm not *trying* to follow her. We just happen to be heading the same direction. One road in, one road out.

I smirk despite myself. She was trying so hard not to be weird that she made herself even weirder. Before she noticed me rolling up, she was something else. Focused. Determined. Fierce, even.

Then she saw me, and the fear kicked in. Understandable. She didn't recognize me. It's late. She's alone. But the way she gripped that tire iron? If I were a betting man, I'd say there's a story there. A bad one. That kind of white-knuckle fear doesn't come out of nowhere. It comes from surviving something. Her blue eyes were wide, her breathing elevated.

While I worked on her tire, I watched her from the corner of my eye. She fiddled with her mace the entire time. Even when she was spewing a thousand words a minute. So many fucking words.

Something in me flipped on at the sight of her hanging on to that mace like a lifeline. Not just protectiveness, though that kicked in too. I wanted to pull her into my arms, comfort her, assure her that I could handle whatever she couldn't. That thought stops me cold. That's not me. I must be more tired than I originally thought. I shake it off.

Thankfully, changing the tire was easy enough. The lug nuts felt like they were welded on. They probably hadn't been touched in years. It was tough, but straightforward. She would have been out there all night.

I huff a chuckle picturing her attempting to get them off. I've never met anyone that screams *complicated* louder than she does. At least I didn't need to talk; she covered that department for both of us.

I follow her almost all the way home. She turns taking the ramp north, and I go south. I feel an urge to make sure she makes it all the way home. Ridiculous. She's fine.

I open up the throttle, and let the wind drown out thoughts of her the rest of the ride home.

***

I CRASHED HARD when I finally made it in last night. I'm not surprised it's after eleven when I finally wake up. I force myself to stay in bed longer, counting the bricks climbing up the wall across from me.

Even as an adult, I don't have the ability to sit still for long unless I force myself. When I was younger, my parents used to drag me along with them to their studio for meetings. It was impossible for me to sit still and listen to them drone on all day. Eventually, I would wander off onto the sets and get into trouble. Climbing something I shouldn't. Making noise when silence was the expectation.

The memories roll over me as I reach the top row of bricks and start counting my way back down. When I was nine, they took me to yet another studio meeting. An action film was shooting on the lot, and I was itching to watch the excitement. Finally, my sighs and fidgeting got to be too much for my parents. I was dismissed with firm instructions to stay quiet, stay out of the way, and behave. Story of my life.

I remember tearing out of that room like a bat out of hell. That's when I stumbled across Joe for the first time. He was consulting on the film's hand-to-hand combat scenes. It was fascinating.

He noticed me and took me under his wing that day, let me come to his on-set classes, and trail after him, no matter the movie or how busy he was. He gave my restless body a purpose. An outlet. Freedom.

I sit up slowly, shaking off the memories. I'm sore. Still tired, but my brain won't allow me to stay in bed any longer. My inability to stay still is part of the reason why I became a stunt double.

I stumble into my kitchen and hit start on the Keurig before checking the fridge.

Fully stocked. Figures. After almost twelve years, it shouldn't still shock me *they* got my schedule again and knew I'd be home. Sending someone to clean my condo and restock the fridge is one of the least invasive ways my parents meddle. Believe it or not, this is them showing restraint.

I might seem spoiled complaining about a clean house and a full fridge, but they don't do it out of kindness.

Does it matter that I'm almost thirty? Nope. They'll always find a way to overstep, ways to try and control me. I pay the cleaning crew extra not to report anything they see or hear while they're here.

I wait for my coffee to finish dripping into my mug while I mull over my parents for the millionth time. They aren't all bad. I don't *think*. But their love comes with the strong aftertaste of manipulation.

My parents never planned to have children. They're Hollywood's *it* couple as far as production goes. My mother's family owns Sterling Pictures, a legacy studio that shapes careers, green-lights billion-dollar projects, and screams "you've made it." Everyone wants to work for or with George and Isabel Sterling. Yes, my father took my mother's last name.

I'm an eternal disappointment. They can't understand why I don't want to be one of the suits. I stay in the industry so they can't say I abandoned them completely. Thankfully, I'm doing something I love, but I'm far enough away that I can breathe. When I turned eighteen, I moved from LA to Atlanta and changed my name from Nathaniel Sterling to Nate Jones.

That might sound drastic, but believe me, it wasn't. I was always Nathaniel or Nathan growing up. Never Nate, until Joe scooped me up.

They were furious when I moved and changed my name. They didn't talk to me directly for a year. "Our legacy is one to be proud of." "Our legacy must be carried on." This, from the people who never wanted children.

They can't grasp that their world will never make me happy. The meetings, the pressure, the constant eyes on you. After one particularly brutal interview when I was seven, I swore off joining them in public ever again.

We'd been sitting through a rotating door of journalists for hours. I was tired, restless, ready to move. My fingers drummed on the table. The reporter noticed, and the next day the headline read: *Sterling Heir: Wild Child with No Interest in the Business.*

My fingers tapped the table. Tapped the table. I was seven. Of course I wasn't statue-still. It's ridiculous I was expected to sit at that table, much less show interest.

My parents were furious. Not at the reporter, but at me. I learned that getting noticed gets you in trouble. After that, I mastered silence. Faded into the background until *the Sterling Heir* disappeared like smoke.

My parents are still hoping that I'll grow out of "this phase." On our weekly call, they dangle my trust fund, the company, the whole empire like bait. But I don't need their money, and I sure as hell don't need their strings. I would have liked my parents to just be *my parents*, but I don't need that anymore either.

I hate that they treat me like a puppet. Lately, it's gotten worse. They changed the stipulations of my trust to include either coming back to work with them, or getting married. They think either of those options will put me back in their pocket. They have their reasons for their thought process. They are messed up reasons, but they have them.

If they really knew me, they'd know I'm never going to work for them. I'm never going to get married. I like not being tied to anyone or anything, that I can pick up whatever contract I want. But, even if I wasn't doing this, I wouldn't join their world again. I wouldn't settle down. I wouldn't marry whomever they deem appropriate. I wouldn't put on a suit every day like they are itching for me to do.

I have no need for the millions sitting in their bank, especially millions that come with lifelong expectations.

As I take a bite of the handmade pastry left in my pantry, I let out an appreciative groan. Maybe not *everything* they do is awful.

My mind drifts back to last night. To Liz.

I've come to appreciate the quiet life I've built. Usually people who talk a lot irritate me, but her nervous chatter didn't bother me. I'm curious about her, and that doesn't happen often.

I'm surprised I haven't been on a job with her before. I've been doing this a long time. I would've noticed her. I may not play well with others, due to my upbringing, but I notice everything. And she's impossible *not* to notice. I wonder how long she's been in the industry?

She seems very professional, minus the fact that she often kicks her shoes off and walks around barefoot, her long skirts trailing behind her. But, she puts everyone at ease. She was always smiling, no matter what the high-maintenance actresses threw her way. She's the exact opposite of me. Open, sunny, engaging. A damn spotlight where I prefer the shadows.

I've spent too much time thinking about her.

I finish my pastry and grab my gym bag. It's bugging me the way she has burrowed into my brain. Time to fix that. Basketball with the guys usually does the trick when something's gnawing at me.

When my schedule allows, I meet up with friends for a quick game. Most of them are stuntmen and crew members from past movies I've worked on.

We hit the court, beat the shit out of each other for a few hours, and pretend we're not getting old and falling apart. I push open the gym doors. It's an old school that has been converted into a workout facility. The school's old pennants still hang on the walls. No frills. No extras. But it has character and gets the job done.

Most of the group is already here. I've never felt more grateful for these guys as I do this morning. I would never tell them that though. We don't do feelings or small talk. We bond over trash talk and pulled hamstrings. My kind of therapy.

The echo of rubber on hardwood meets my ears. I already feel better.

"'Bout time you showed up, old man," my closest and oldest friend Lane calls, tossing me the ball. He's been calling me old for years, ever since I blew out one of my knees during a stunt, and had to walk with a cane for three months.

I catch it one-handed, and roll my eyes. "You're three months older than me, asshead."

"Yeah, but you move like you're ten years older," he shoots back, grinning.

I don't bother answering. I drop my bag, drive to the basket, shoulder low, and bank a layup off the glass. The muscles in my back bark their protest, but it feels good. We spend a few minutes warming up before dividing into teams for a game.

The guys talk plenty today, but not about anything that matters. Work stories mostly. All of us are married to the job.

After an hour, I'm dripping sweat, chest heaving, legs tired. My knee aches, but my head's clear. Mostly.

After I hit the showers, I make my way back to the old wooden bleachers where I know Joe is waiting for me. When he retired from stunt training in LA, he moved to Atlanta. He shows up every week, sometimes to heckle, sometimes to play. Even in his seventies, he can still kick all of our asses if he wants to.

Joe rolls a toothpick between his lips, massaging his calf muscle, while he eyes me in that special way of his. Sharp and steady, like he can see straight through the walls I've built.

"You're running on fumes, kid."

I huff out a laugh. "Haven't been a kid in a long time."

"Don't matter. You push too hard, body'll remind you real quick you're not invincible." He leans back, arms crossed. "Seen too many good stuntmen not take care of themselves, physically or mentally, and they burn out before thirty. You need something more in your life than the job."

His tone is rough, but the warning underneath shows me he cares. Sometimes it seems like he's the only one in my life that *actually* cares. He's been on my ass since he scooped me up at nine, made me one of his. I don't hate the way he quietly looks out for me. Even if he has a hell of a way of showing it most of the time.

"Yeah," I mutter, running a hand through my hair. "I hear you."

He claps me once on the shoulder, the way he used to when I was a kid tagging along on set. "Rest when you can, son. Keep up with your training. Keep your head straight. Don't let them get to you."

He doesn't have to clarify who *them* is. We both know. We never talk about it, but he knows the type of relationship I have with my parents. He has seen it firsthand for most of my life. He knows how I can let them get in my head and mess things up. I know he is also aware of the gala coming up. Everyone seems to keep better track of my calendar than I do.

The gala is one of my personal nightmares. There's an unspoken agreement with my parents that I attend every year if I'm available. The pressure and the expectations that come along with that night have me packing my schedule around this time of year in hopes I can get out of it.

I wish that was all that was on my mind today, but I don't feel like telling him about Liz. There's nothing to tell anyway.

"Rest. Got it. I'll pencil that in right after dodging fireballs and getting tackled through walls."

He chuckles, tapping me on the back to stand. I don't laugh with him, but the corner of my mouth kicks up before I can stop it. Joe has always had a way of dragging me back to solid ground.

Walking out to my bike, I catch myself wondering again if Liz made it home okay. I can't shake her. I can't figure out why I care.

Chapter Three
Fresh Air
Liz

I feel Hulk before I see him. My eyes are still firmly shut, even though I can feel the sun leaking through the drapes I forgot to close last night. I smile to myself, feeling him tiptoe his way up my body as he lies down directly on my chest before batting my hair around my face with his paws.

I got home later than I planned because of the tire fiasco. I was too dirty and tired to pay too much attention to my little man.

"Hey, Handsome."

I peel my eyes open and I'm face to face with the definition of cuteness. Hulk, my cat, is tiny for his assumed age. My little gray furball. I rescued him and he's been my shadow ever since I brought him home.

He gently purrs as I pet him and give him the attention he needs. He rolls onto his back and snuggles into the crook of my arm. "Did Auntie Chloe take good care of you this week? Hmm?" I snuggle him harder. "I'm sorry, my little love, if I could have taken you with me I would have."

Hmm. That's an idea. Maybe next week I'll break the rules and sneak him into my hotel room.

"Would you like to go on a little road trip next week? Want to be a little rule breaker with me?"

It might be silly to talk to a kitten like he's a real person, but I thrive on silly things. Plus, ever since I found him, he has brought me so much joy and peace. I missed having someone to love on and talk to. I don't do well with the quiet; my mind goes to dangerous places when the quiet settles in for too long.

Case in point: the way I spoke five hundred words per minute last night, compared to the less than fifteen words Nate spoke, or rather grunted the entire time.

I'll have to thank him somehow next week when we are back on set. Assuming he is more than just an extra. He made it seem like maybe he was. I'm not sure. I don't trust myself to read people or between the lines in conversations anymore. I used to be able to, but now I get in my head too much to feel confident I'm reading situations, or people, correctly.

Before I can spiral down a path I'd rather not travel this morning, my phone buzzes with a FaceTime call. Chloe. Of course.

My bestie and my brother spent months pining and pretending they were just friends. Now they're disgustingly in love and so cute. But being around them twenty-four seven? It's a little much for me sometimes. No matter how over the moon I am for them. It just reminds me how far I am from having someone in my life.

I swipe my phone to answer the call, her grinning face fills the screen.

"Finally!" she says, brushing hair off her forehead. "You survived your late-night drive back? James wasn't convinced you would make it back in one piece, but I knew you'd be fine."

"Thanks for the confidence in me, bro." I know he is somewhere just off camera. He's never far from Chloe. I try to glare at the camera, but it just comes across with a classic Harrison family smirk. "I survived one blown tire and falling into a Costco-sized mud puddle, but I lived to tell the tale."

Her eyes go wide. "Wait... what? Liz! Are you okay?"

"Perfectly fine. The tire was an easy fix and mud is all the rage in Hollywood, don't you know? It's exfoliating and rejuvenating for the skin. Ten out of ten would recommend a midnight mud bath." The tire *was* an easy fix, just not for me. I keep the tidbit about my scowling hero showing up at just the right time to myself.

Chloe groans, but she's smiling. "Only you could almost die on the side of the road and spin it into a beauty treatment."

"Almost dying is a bit dramatic, even for me. Although I do think I saw eyes glowing at me from the edge of the woods before Na..." Oops, that was close. I almost spilled the beans, but to be fair, I tell Chloe everything. I can't help myself. No filter, remember?

Chloe moved to town this past year and we hit it off right away. Then she *really* hit it off with my brother. These days she spends most of her time at his place instead of her apartment across the hall from mine. She isn't renewing her lease at the end of the month, so they will be officially living together soon.

I'm beyond happy for them. They've both had such rocky past relationships. Watching them love each other has been a bright spot in an otherwise really awful few years. I'm going to really miss having her right across the hallway though.

"Before what? Before who?" she presses, instantly suspicious. "You're making *the face*."

"I am not making *the face*." I am totally making *the face*. The one I make when I have information that I don't want to share, but probably will anyway.

I cave seconds later. "Just some guy stopped to help. Tall, broody, grunts instead of talks."

Chloe narrows her eyes as she examines mine through the phone. "Your whole face is turning red and you can't meet my eyes. Spill."

I scratch Hulk's chin with a little too much vigor and make sure I stare directly into Chloe's eyes. "He was nobody. Just a random passerby. I just embarrassed myself in front of him. But that's not too surprising. Nothing weird there. Case closed."

For some reason with Nate, I find myself being protective of our interaction. Honestly, it was such a tiny thing, it doesn't warrant talking about. Nate's grumpy face flashes in my mind. I resist the urge to lean into the collar of his hoodie for another whiff. *Yes, I slept in his hoodie, so sue me.*

She doesn't look convinced, but she drops it, her features smoothing out. "Well, whoever he was," she pauses and raises her brows giving me another chance to spill. When I don't, she continues. "I'm glad someone was there. I hate the thought of you stranded."

"Stranded? My sister is stranded?" My brother barrels his way into the frame. His face smashes against Chloe's. "You good, Lizzy Lou?"

Guess he hasn't been listening this entire time after all. "No big deal, just had a little car trouble, but all is well now."

My brother is the world's most protective sibling. Even more so after everything that happened last year. I love him for it, but sometimes I need a little breathing room. Chloe has helped him back off and I'm thankful for that.

"Need me to take it to the shop for you?" His face still looks concerned.

"I've got it handled, but thanks. You two go be in love somewhere else. Y'all are starting to make me nauseous with how you're hanging all over each other."

Chloe laughs. "I'm coming over later, I want the full mud-puddle play-by-play. I need details."

"You'll regret those words, my friend."

After hanging up, I force myself to get up and dressed in what I consider workout gear. Tie-dyed leggings and a bright glittery tank. Color makes me happy. I'm *really* leaning into things that make me happy these days.

I gather my hair into a bun on top of my head. It's probably time for a haircut. My unruly hair reaches past my waist now and when I wear it up for too long it gives me a headache. But haircuts are expensive, so I probably will put it off for a little while longer.

I walk around my apartment, checking all the things that were neglected while I was out of town. My plants hanging all over the house seem to be doing okay. I'm surprised Chloe hasn't killed them yet. If I have a green thumb, hers is black.

I'm still smiling thinking about Chloe and James, and the way they care for me, as I lean down to clip Hulk into his harness to go on a walk. Before we can get out the door, another call flashes on my phone. A call that makes my smile vanish and my spine straighten. I immediately send it to voicemail.

There are only two numbers that cause nerves to skate along my skin. I try to shake it off. I won't let that mess steal my sunshine today. I slam the lid shut on that mental box and head out the door.

Hulk and I make it about five steps out the door before he flops onto the sidewalk like he's been taken out by a sniper. Some days, he likes to walk, and some days I get an arm workout and carry him most of the way.

"Really?" I cross my arms, staring down at his tiny, fuzzy body sprawled like a chalk outline. "We talked about this. On walks we are supposed to be *walking*."

He blinks at me, then rolls onto his back, paws in the air, and wiggles like a dying fish.

"This is not helpful cardio, sir." I scoop him up for a quick snuggle then reposition him on the sidewalk to try again. He takes three very dignified prances forward before collapsing again. "How am I supposed to get in shape for the race Chloe signed us up for if my training partner can't make it five steps?"

Mrs. Downing, my eighty-year-old upstairs neighbor, is standing at the mailboxes, watching us with her head tilted like I've lost my mind. Which...okay, maybe that's fair.

I wave cheerfully. "Morning!" I throw a thumb toward Hulk. "Just taking the pussy out for some fresh air!"

Am I usually crude? Not really. Could I have said cat? Absolutely.

But Mrs. Downing's disapproval of everyone thirty-five and younger drives me nuts. It's like she's ticked off she has gotten older and didn't have fun while she could. She still could have all the fun but she won't. She doesn't want anyone else to have fun either. I watch her face scrunch up with disapproval like she bit a lemon, shake her head, and scurry back inside her apartment. I've made it my mission to shock the old broad whenever I can.

She probably already has her phone pressed firmly to her ear, informing her bridge club about the depravity of my soul and the circus I call my life because I dare to enjoy things.

"It's fine," I mutter to Hulk. "No one understands us."

He meows once, short and supportive.

"Exactly. Haters gonna hate. We can't help that we live life to the fullest."

In response, Hulk stretches his little body to its full length like he's about to curl up and take a nap. Looks like we aren't making it to the trails behind my building today. I think he is punishing me for being out of town this past week.

I sigh, crouch down, and scratch under his chin. "Alright, fine. You win. Let's snuggle and bedazzle something instead."

***

Hours later, I'm covered in glitter, glue, and other random bits from spending the afternoon making Nate's thank-you gift. I think he will like it. Actually, I have no idea what he would like, but it is a lot of fun. I carefully place it next to my suitcase so I remember to pack it when I head back to set next week.

I dust my hands off and return to the living room right as Chloe breezes through my front door. "Honey, I'm home!"

I rush her and throw my arms around her. Talking to her on FaceTime doesn't compare to the real thing. I miss my friend when I'm gone for too long.

"Careful, Liz, don't knock the pizza out of my hands!" She's laughing. I know she missed me too.

We settle into the couch, my throw pillows scattered between us with a bottle of wine, our pizza, and *Friends* playing in the background.

"Spill. I know you were holding back on the phone this morning."

I smirk at her. We know each other so well. Of course she could tell there was more to the story.

Glancing away, my telltale sign that I'm lying, I answer her. "I don't know what you are talking about."

I shove a giant bite of pizza in my face to buy time. Chloe is like a bloodhound on the trail. She's not about to let this drop. Her eyes narrow, roaming over my face before dropping to the sweatshirt I'm still wearing.

"Aha!" She declares like she just solved a murder mystery. She points a finger at me accusingly. "If there's nothing to tell, whose sweatshirt, pray tell, is that?"

Busted. We both knew I wouldn't last long, but I still feel protective over my grumpy savior. It's been a long time since I was in the presence of a man, alone, when I wasn't completely consumed with fear. Sure, when he first pulled up my pulse was so high I thought I was having a brain aneurysm. But, anyone would feel that way if a burly man appeared out of nowhere in the middle of the night on a very abandoned road. Not just someone like me. Someone with my past.

I cringe as I look down at the loudmouth sweatshirt. I should have taken it off, but it's so soft and it smells so good.

"Remember when I told you I fell in a mud puddle?"

Chloe takes a bite and points her pizza at me. "Go on."

"Well, it was freezing, and I was covered in mud and gross water. So the person who stopped to help me handed me this sweatshirt." Why am I so careful not to say *his* sweatshirt?

Her eyebrows raise. "And you are still wearing it because?"

Ugh. She's got me there. It's not like I *like* this guy. He was so surly, not someone I would ever consider for myself. I need someone full of warmth, light. That is if I ever decide to get back out there again. So far I've had zero desire to travel down that path.

There was something about the way he swooped in, scowls and all, and quietly took care of me. Well my car. Maybe I'm delusional that he was taking care of me, but it felt nice to have someone who wasn't family help me. Maybe he really was just a Good Samaritan. He probably would have stopped for anyone.

Per the usual I have built something up in my head that isn't reality, so I don't share any of my musings with Chloe.

"I was doing crafts, I didn't want to ruin any of my own clothes. I won't see this person again, so I figured, might as well ruin his sweatshirt instead of my own stuff." Lies. I was extra careful not to get anything on it today, but she doesn't need to know that.

I don't think she's buying it, but thankfully she lets it drop. We spend the evening catching up on the past week. Her coworkers, the trivia night that I missed, their co-ed flag football game from last Sunday. How she's already boxing things and bringing them over to James's a little at a time.

Her moving makes me so happy and so sad. Being able to pop over to Chloe's made this place a little less lonely. A little less scary. I would never share that with her, though. I'm a big girl. I'll be fine. Probably.

Chapter Four
Tire Shrapnel Trinkets
Liz

The set is bustling again after a few days off. I spent my time doing nothing but snuggling my cat and gluing rhinestones to anything and everything I could find. And of course, hanging out with Chloe whenever she wasn't sucking face with my brother.

I refocus on the task in front of me. Last week I was in charge of makeup for two of the actresses, but this week my specialty with wounds is needed on our main male lead and his stunt double. Which means I get to spend my days making people look like they've been blown up, flung off buildings, and run over by cars. My job is so cool. Every day is different. There are always people scurrying around. I love being surrounded by the chaos.

Today, however, my assignment is Becket Creed. I've never worked with him before. His questionable reputation precedes him and makes me feel hyper-aware. From what I've seen and heard, he's loud, arrogant, and a drama magnet. Thankfully, I won't be trapped in this trailer with him alone since his double is getting the same treatment. The thought of being alone with someone like that makes my skin itch.

I'm lost in my head, focused on settling my breathing, and setting up my equipment when the trailer door creaks open slowly. I take one last steadying breath, preparing to spend the next few hours with Hollywood's biggest d-bag, but when I turn around I'm pleasantly surprised.

"Nate!" A relieved giggle bubbles out of me. One second I'm lost in spiraling thoughts, the next, my grumpy-tire-savior is standing in front of me. I collect myself enough to squeak out a super cool, "Uh, hey. What are you doing here?"

His face is just as serious as I remember. "You're in charge of wounds today, right?"

It takes me a beat to process. He's not an extra. He must be Becket's stunt double. That's unfortunate for Nate, but my day is suddenly looking up.

He steps further into the trailer. *Woah.* The shadowed roadside did not do this man justice. Under the bright makeup lights, I see everything I missed the other night.

His dark chocolate eyes seem to convey all the words his mouth doesn't, and they are locked on mine. It feels like he is peeling away all my layers and seeing every secret I have tucked away.

My eyes trail over the rest of him. He's tall, but not crazy tall. I'm five-six. I have to look up at him to meet his eyes, but it's not neck-crick territory. He doesn't seem to mind that I'm taking my time looking him over. He lets me drink him in. Right at six feet, if I had to guess. Nice. Not that it matters to me how tall he is.

He has thicker scruff today, like he hasn't shaved since the last time I saw him. I guess that makes sense with the movie and what they are shooting today. The extra texture doesn't take away from the fullness of his lips or the sharp cut of his jaw, the angles of his cheekbones. Ruggedly beautiful. That's how I'll describe him to Chloe later. If I tell her about him at all.

Nate was the last one that said anything, but him showing up when I didn't expect to see him has yanked my brain's power cord and left me on mute. It's rare for me to stay quiet this long, but words are currently escaping me. I can hear the hum of the lights buzzing behind me.

I've officially crossed over from checking him out to staring like a lunatic, so obviously this is the perfect time to panic. I turn around, reach into my bag, spin back around, and shove my handmade thank-you gift at him.

I'm suddenly rethinking what I made him, but it's too late now. I wordlessly hold it out to him. He slowly drags his eyes away from mine and looks down at my hand without taking the gift. I can feel the word-vomit creeping up my throat. I try to hold it at bay. I really do, but I fail.

"So I made you this as a thank you. I know it's silly, but that's kind of my brand, I guess." I give a self-deprecating shrug.

"And that is..." He nods his head at my outstretched hand. His voice doesn't give way to any of his thoughts, but his wrinkled forehead conveys confusion.

To be fair, my gift might not be completely self-explanatory without taking the lid off.

"Right. An explanation."

I pop the lid off of the little contraption. "So, I used pieces of my blown tire, melted them together, and molded it into a candle holder. Ta-da! It's a manly tire candle. Don't worry, the actual candle inside isn't engine-oil scented. Unless you'd like that, I could probably switch the candle out. Actually, no, scratch that. The one I made you is my usual blend I make for my own house. An engine-oil scented candle is stupid."

Should I stop talking now? Probably, but instead, I barrel on with a detailed description of the essential oils I used before I lamely end with, "It gives off cozy vibes. Promise. The scent doesn't have an official name or anything. Maybe we could..."

I cut myself off before suggesting we co-name a candle like we're running an Etsy shop together. I'm struggling to keep my thoughts in order with his brown soulful gaze locked on mine. My arm has been stretched between us for so long the weight of the candle starts to drag my hand down.

"Listen, you don't have to take it if you don't want to. Candles probably aren't your thing, but I just wanted to say thank you for helping me the other night. When I was removing the tire out of my trunk, I decided to make lemonade out of lemons. Or in this case, a candle out of tire shrapnel."

Still nothing. The calm, safe feelings I thought I felt on the side of the road evaporate. I'm not scared of him, but my pulse is beating wildly in my chest. I power through the cold sweat that has broken out on my forehead.

"I love doing crafts. It keeps me out of my head, it's fun, and there's usually some sort of cool trinket at the end of the day. In this case, a totally unique, one-of-a-kind blown-tire-candle. Ha. Get it? Blow out a candle, blown tire."

Someone put me out of my misery.

His face has morphed from slightly confused to bewildered. It's not a bad look on him. I just wish it wasn't directed at me. "No? Okay, scratch that from your memory, that joke never happened."

The smallest, and I do mean the smallest, hitch of his lip, stops me cold.

I can't imagine what a full-blown smile would do to me. Heart-attack most likely. Someone should have the EMT warm up those paddles now. Thankfully, his micro-smile is enough to stop my word spiral.

He reaches out and takes the candle gently from my hand. It's cliché, I know, but our fingers brush and the contact makes me feel all fluttery. Not lightning-bolt cliché, not soul-mates-instant-connection cliché. Just... good. Settled. My pulse calms.

I want him to touch me again, but on purpose this time, preferably without repurposed Goodyear between us. Just his skin on mine and maybe some of that delicious scruff. Woah, where did that thought come from?

"Thanks, Liz." He tucks it into his satchel as he drops into the makeup chair like he didn't just fry my brain with a tiny smirk and innocent hand brush.

At the same time, Becket blows through the door, slamming it against the wall with a grand-entrance, demanding everyone's attention. I jump and involuntarily throw my hands in front of my face. I quickly drop them, hoping no one notices. I hate that I scare so easily now.

Becket strolls in like God's personal favor to the world. There is no ignoring him. He's the kind of guy that makes sure you notice him. He *needs* you to notice him. It's like he wants to make sure you know that you are in no way on his level. I have to fight my lip from curling.

I've known plenty of guys like him. Not who I like to regularly spend my time with. Not anymore.

Becket throws his sunglasses on the counter without a care in the world. I'm sure they cost more than a month's rent at my apartment. He spreads himself out in his chair, snapping at his assistant that trails behind him like a sad puppy to get his coffee.

Specifically his three vanilla pumps, no dairy, extra shot, one hundred and twenty degree latte with one ice cube dropped in right before she delivers it. What is she supposed to do? Just walk around with a melting ice cube in her hand until she reaches his majesty?

I take a deep breath to settle the nerves that men like him invoke in me. I catch Nate's eye in the mirror. He looks at Becket, and then back at me, and gives a subtle eye roll. It's so out of character I have to cover the grin and giggle that involuntarily bubbles up with a cough. That little eye roll snapped me out of my head and calmed my nerves.

Our eyes lock in the mirror and I'm grateful he's here. He gives me a subtle head nod, almost to say 'I'm not going anywhere.' It's comforting.

My hands stop shaking. I draw in a breath and turn around to get started working. One arrogant leading man, one grumpy stunt double, and me, armed with fake blood and latex scars. Today should be fun.

***

NATE

I watch Liz closely as she goes back and forth between myself and Beck, letting the layers of blood and injuries she's painting on our skin dry. To say him and I aren't exactly friends is an understatement. Unfortunately, I've known him most of my life. He's one of the few people on set who knows who I actually am.

He's a textbook nepo baby, coasting on his parents' fame. They were huge stars in my parents' movies. That smug entitlement rolling off him is exactly what I've tried to avoid being around my entire life.

It's interesting watching Liz work up close. I watched from afar when I was bored, but observing her right now, she doesn't remind me of the woman from last week at all.

Her body language isn't relaxed unless she's on my side of the trailer. That tiny fact has me both puffed up and confused. The chatter spewing from her bowed mouth dried up the moment Becket stepped in. She's as quiet as a church mouse.

I want to know why I've barely heard a peep out of her all morning. I want to know why she almost came out of her skin when Becket busted in. Why she threw her hands in front of her face. Like she was bracing. I've seen reactions like that before, and it never comes from a good place. That flinch made my blood boil. I want to know why she seems like a storm cloud is trying to snuff out her sunshine.

She's back on Becket's side, so I watch her closely. That homemade candle she made me really threw me for a loop. I was stunned she gave me anything for helping her. She didn't need to. I didn't expect it, but it was strangely touching.

Strange is probably the best word to describe her.

She finishes with Becket and he promptly exits the room, leaving her and I alone again. Her shoulders instantly relax.

I still have one more layer to go. She steps closer to me, her face lining up directly in front of mine as she puts the finishing touches on a particularly gnarly looking gash on my forehead. A little puff of air hits my cheek. She smells like something sweet and floral. It's distracting.

Today's call sheet hit my inbox early yesterday. I've had almost twenty-four hours to come to terms with the fact that we would be working very closely all week. Doesn't matter how much time I had to wrap my head around it, apparently. My skin comes alive every time she touches me.

I study her up close. Her blue eyes sparkle. They appear deep blue in this light, but I know they can be light blue when she's excited and chattering about.

She's concentrating so hard to get this last part just right. The tip of her tongue peeks out from between her teeth, her eyes squint, and she takes a step back to look over her work.

Damn. That's cute.

Her eyes hold me captive. The other night they were wide with uncertainty and fear. Now, squinting and taking in her handiwork, they are confident. Warm. Sparkling.

Her hair is piled on top of her head today, but I know the blonde waves reach all the way down to her narrow waist.

This is the longest amount of time she's gone without speaking and now that it's just us I'm curious as to why. "Where did your chatter go, Cricket?"

Her eyes snap to mine, confused, but a slow smile spreads across her face, making her turn from beautiful to devastating in a flash.

"Cricket?" She tilts her head, but holds eye contact with me.

I have to physically restrain myself from reaching out and grabbing her by the hips, pulling her closer to me. I don't know what it is about this woman, but she draws me in like a siren.

I shrug, keeping my face neutral. "You're always chirping. It fits."

I should stop talking. Usually I would, but I continue, "Plus, the other night all I could hear was your chatter and a chorus of crickets while I changed your tire. After a while, it all sounded the same."

She gasps and swats my arm. "You glass-hole. My voice is *not* the same as an insect's incessant rattle. Cricket is a terrible nickname."

Her voice pitches higher and higher. Her take on a swear word makes me fight a smile.

"Could've gone with Grasshopper, I guess." I shrug slightly.

That earns me another shove, light but playful. It's interesting that she was so careful with her touches with Becket. Only touching him to do his makeup. Careful to avoid him otherwise.

I like that she touches me easily. Without thought. I like that she's easy to rile up.

"Careful," I say, catching her wrist lightly before she pulls back. "You don't want to mess up my face."

Her lips twitch. "You do know you've got a four-inch gash across your forehead right now, right? Your handsome face is already toast."

My brow lifts and before I can stop it, I'm flirting with her. "Handsome, huh?"

She freezes for half a second, then scoffs. "Generic handsome. Like, Walmart-model handsome. A solid six on a good day."

"Generous of you." My mouth almost curves, but I hold it back.

Her laugh slips out, soft but real, and she ducks her head, turning her back to me as if that will hide the blush that's spreading across her cheeks. "That's me. Overly generous."

"Hmm." I wait for her to catch my eye in the mirror. "So, generic handsome?" I tilt my head in question.

She laughs. I like seeing her relaxed with a smile across her face. It's confusing that I'm the one who put it there.

"Just average. Very, very average." She turns back to cleaning her brushes.

Verbal sparring has never been my thing. Most of my life, I was told to be quiet, but I'm enjoying going back and forth with her. Pulling reactions from her. Before I can think of a reply to keep it going, she moves toward the door, calling for the next actor.

I stand, walking toward the door, closing the space between us until she has to tilt her chin to look up at me. My voice drops. "You don't look at me like I'm average, Cricket."

We are inches apart, our chests brush when her breath hitches. She covers the noise fast with a scoff, but I don't miss it, or the way her cheeks heat again.

I don't wait for her to reply. I trail my hand over her side, give her rib cage a gentle squeeze before letting my hand fall away, and throw in a wink, because apparently I'm doubling down on being reckless and acting completely out of character.

By the time I exit the trailer and the sunlight hits my face, I've already sworn myself back into line. No more flirting. I've got enough shit stacked on my plate without inviting her brand of chaos into it.

But damn if walking away isn't one of the hardest things I've done in a while.

Chapter Five
The Perfect Trifecta
Liz

Twelve hours later and I'm still thinking about that side squeeze coupled with that panty-dropping wink. Holy guacamole. That was hot. My skin still buzzes with the memory of his hand squeezing my side. That hint of a grin I caught on his face almost ended me. Bury me six feet under.

Who knew the man who only seems to speak in grunts and sneers could have a playful side? Dare I say a flirty side? Or maybe because he's shown me so little of himself it wasn't out of the ordinary at all. I can feel myself overthinking the morning. I'm sure it was a completely normal interaction. Right?

But I do know before today, he had been all frowns and snarls. That's a fact. Holy smokes though, one teeny tiny glimpse of another side, and I'm aching to pull that side out of him again.

I let myself into my hotel room and Hulk pounces from behind the curtains. I scoop up my little man, holding him to my chest, "Hello, my handsome rule-breaker. Were you a good boy today?"

I swear he understands me. His little paw comes up to bat at the hair that has fallen out of my bun and into my face. This sweet guy brings me so much joy.

I couldn't stand being away from him another week, and I hated to ask Chloe to watch him since she is busy packing. So, rules be damned, I snuck him into my hotel room. Hulk's my tiny partner-in-crime, hidden behind a Do Not Disturb sign like the cutest feline outlaw ever.

"Guess what happened today, Hulk." I set him down and kick off my shoes immediately. I hate wearing shoes. Toes were meant to breathe.

I stretch out on the bed and stare at the ceiling. "Mommy flirted with someone." Sort of. I think?

"Not just anyone." I roll to my side to scratch his belly. "You remember the man who helped Mommy with her tire? Him. I flirted with him. And let me tell you... Wow. Just, wow."

Hulk loses interest in my rambling and strolls over to his bowl in the bathroom to eat his dinner. I replay the whole interaction with Nate in my mind again and again.

I think about it from every angle. I can feel myself overanalyzing it, but I can't turn it off. After our flirty interaction, I thought I might see that side of him peeking out the rest of the day. Was it really flirty behavior though? Flirty-adjacent at best.

Every time I needed to do his touch-ups, I would say or do something just a little bit crazy to get a reaction out of him. There wasn't even a hint of his microscopic smirk. Sigh.

My phone dings, pulling me out of my head. The high from spending the day in Nate's orbit disappears fast as reality crashes back in. Half a dozen voicemails and a flood of increasingly worrisome texts wait for me. At some point, I'm going to have to stop shoving this problem into that little box in my brain where I store everything I don't want to deal with.

I sit up and scrub my hands over my face. In hindsight, signing paperwork with my douche-canoe of an ex without reading it first was one of my bigger screwups. Not *the* biggest, but definitely in the top two.

A few months after my ex landed himself in jail I found out I was on the hook for six figures' worth of debt from a so-called "business loan" he took out in my name from the shadiest banker alive. That was a fun surprise. And by fun I mean a complete nightmare.

I finally got to a place where I wasn't constantly fixated on his incarceration status when the bills started showing up.

I take a deep breath, reminding myself I'm safe before I go down a dark path. I usually try not to give him a single thought, but with these relentless calls from the debt collector, it's impossible to keep him out of my head.

A knock on my door pulls me out of my spiraling thoughts. Two of my best friends stand there with big grins. The knot in my stomach loosens. My girls are here. They're my constants, especially when everything else in my life feels less than certain.

Jenn is a fiery redhead with a killer body that she isn't afraid to show off. She usually has a new guy every other week that she has fallen head over heels for. It ends in tears every time, but at least she quickly moves on and doesn't fixate.

Autumn is a wisp of a human, covered in seemingly random tattoos that somehow all work together. She rocks combat boots like they're an extension of her body and wears dresses that look like they are made for a fairy princess. She's a walking contradiction, but it works.

Honestly, they are both pretty bad-a.

We went to school together and landed our first contracts on the same movie four years ago. We've been inseparable ever since. They've seen me through my lowest lows. While they know *almost* everything about the worst time of my life, they don't know *everything*. I haven't wanted to burden them with this debt thing. Knowing them, they'd go into debt trying to help me.

Autumn pulls a bottle of top-shelf champagne out of a purse that looks big enough for her to live in. "Ta-da!" she declares. "Change into your suit and let's go tipsy tubin'."

Did I mention that Autumn is the most Southern person I know? And that's saying something since I grew up in Georgia. Her words tend to leave off the last letter, or two, as the word fades with her twang. Her accent gets stronger the more she drinks. My little rocker-pixie is well on her way to being drunk.

Jenn laughs at Autumn, snags the bottle from her hands and tips it up before crashing down to sit on the floral couch. "Come on, Liz. We didn't get to see you all weekend since you went home. Come hang with us by the pool for a while."

"You're not allowed to be a hermit," Autumn adds. "We're revokin' your introvert card tonight."

"Since when have I ever been an introvert?" I laugh. I never turn down time with my friends. "I wasn't planning on saying no. Let me change real quick."

A few nights a week, when filming doesn't run too late, we hang out together. Sometimes just the three of us, sometimes with people from production or a few of the actors.

For tonight, it's champagne, friends, and bubbles. And for one more night, I shove my money problems into that little box and lock the lid tight.

After changing, we skip arm and arm across the parking lot to the pool area. This hotel is giving Motel 6 vibes with the outdoor fenced-in pool. Thankfully, the rooms are much nicer than the mystery stain energy of a roadside motel. And I'm all too happy to take advantage of the hot tub setup. My back and feet are screaming after standing all day.

It seems there's already a bit of a party going on, and we are late. Music is blaring. One of the younger actors just tossed someone in the pool. I can hear laughter ringing out from across the parking lot. The ominous vibes from my problems slide off of me. I love being in a crowd of people. It's fun. It's safe.

The girls and I beeline it for the hot tub. It's not too full. I lay my stuff down on a nearby bench, drop my cover up, and step into the blissfully hot water. I have to hold back a moan when the jets hit my lower back. Heaven. A little slice of heaven.

"God, this feels amazing," Jenn sighs, sliding in next to me. "I might never leave. Someone bring me snacks, a pillow, and a cabana boy with big hands."

Autumn snorts. "You mean *another* cabana boy. Don't think I didn't see you at our apartment pool bar this weekend batting your lashes at Mr. Six-Pack."

Autumn and Jenn live together in the city. Their apartment complex is very popular with the single twenty and thirty-something crowd. Even though it's early spring, their pool is heated, just like this one, so they can swim comfortably.

"That was networking," Jenn says with a grin. "He has a cousin who's a producer."

"Uh-huh. Networking with his tongue in your mouth I'm sure," I tease.

Jenn splashes me with a laugh. "Rude."

Autumn leans back, tattoos glistening under the water. "Don't listen to her, Jenn. Liz is just jealous she can't keep up with us. Last time a guy hit on her, and wanted something more, she practically sprinted to the bar bathroom."

"I wasn't sprinting away from him," I protest. "It was a brisk escape loo. I had to pee."

Jenn leans her head on my shoulder, champagne sloshing in her glass. "God, I missed you this weekend. Don't ever ditch us for family again. You're my emotional support blonde."

I roll my eyes, but my chest warms. "Fine. But only if you agree to stop making out with random production assistants in front of me."

"Deal. Maybe." Jenn says, already climbing into the lap of one of the guys across from us.

Autumn shifts closer to clink her glass to mine. "See? Balance. She's got loose morals, I kick 'em in the balls when needed, and you…you overthink everything when it comes to men. We're like the perfect trifecta."

I'm happy to cheers to that.

Autumn points a finger at Jenn and mock whispers to me. "As long as she doesn't actually fall for this one and we end up with alcohol poisoning from tequila shots again."

Everyone knows the score with Jenn. Her hook ups *usually* end with everyone walking away as friends. Except last year, when she thought she had something more with a guy from set.

It ended with us at a bar, most everyone having consumed too much tequila, posting a million pictures on social media to make him jealous, and finding her a rebound guy before the night was over.

That night wasn't all bad though. My brother ended up taking a very drunk Chloe home to take care of her. I feel like we helped them take another step out of the friend zone that night.

Jenn turns to us, waves her hand, nearly spilling her drink. I don't know how she can pay attention to what we are saying with this guy attaching himself to her neck like a barnacle. "Honestly, that was a great night for me. Even if everyone was hung over for days. At least it helped get James a little further out of the friend zone." She pauses for dramatic flair. "Dude, we totally deserve medals after surviving Chloe's 'I don't like your brother' phase."

Autumn groans. "Ugh, yes. Months of her pretendin' she didn't want your brother. I should've started a drinking game for every time she said, 'We're just friends.'"

"I'm glad you didn't," I say, grinning. "We'd all still be in recovery."

Jenn laughs. "Well, at least now she's disgustingly happy. Proof that even the most stubborn of us can find love."

Autumn waggles her brows at me. "Cheers to that."

I take another long sip of champagne to avoid answering. Love? Not in the cards for me. A random hookup though? Ehh, also not in the cards for me.

I don't know how Jenn does it. It would stress me out. My fear levels would be off the chart. Even before everything, casual hookups weren't my thing. I just don't think I can do the sideways tango with someone I don't have feelings for, or at least, sort of kind of like. Certainly not a stranger.

My friends have no problem with a one-night stand. I'm not judging, you do you; it's just not for me. I may be loud and crazy, but I need real relationship potential for anything more. And currently I can't even bring myself to consider going on a real date.

Watching Jenn get her neck mauled by her flavor of the week does make me feel slightly jealous. Not for a hook up buddy, but I'd be lying if I said I didn't miss having a guy. Someone to come home to and chat about our days. A best friend to do everything with.

Ever since my epic failure of a relationship, I've been gun-shy to put myself back out there. I enjoy going out with my girlfriends. Dancing with strangers. But the second it seems like someone is interested in more, I bail. Quickly.

Watching Chloe put herself out there after her past and fall in love with my brother makes me consider really trying. I want to be brave like her.

But like it always does when I think maybe I'm ready, the shadow of debt pops up in my mind like an unwanted thunderstorm. Squashing my dreams of putting myself back out there.

I lift my champagne glass to my lips and drain it.

All my focus needs to go to figuring out how to make more cash. I could get a second job? Maybe waitressing? Teaching makeup classes? I hear there's a lot of money in posting your feet online, but I can't bring myself to do that.

Suddenly my neck breaks out in goosebumps, pulling me from my worry. I whip my head around in search of what caused it.

Nate.

I watch as he swings his leg off his motorcycle. His head turns, his eyes locking on mine. Someone getting off a vehicle shouldn't be a turn-on. Nate's glare shouldn't be a turn on. I *should* feel afraid of how serious he looks. But I'm not.

Just when he starts to turn and walk away from our impromptu pool party, someone shouts his name. Not just someone, Becket. *Gag.*

He is currently set up in the corner of the pool, a harem of women and men surrounding him trying to get some of his Becket shine to rub off on them. Mostly it looks like they are kissing his rear end.

Hard pass.

Hanging with that crowd has zero appeal to me anymore. The children of Hollywood's royalty. They have everything handed to them on a silver platter. Or more accurately a diamond encrusted platter. They are the elite group, the ultimate "in" crowd. Not just the actors, but the producers and directors too. It's gross.

My eyes snap back to Nate's and I see him blow out a breath and reluctantly walk toward Becket's group.

I'm too far away to hear what Becket says to Nate, but the group cackles with laughter. Nate's face doesn't change. He looks annoyed, but that's not much different than how his face always looks. He saunters over to the cooler, grabs a beer, and plops down in a pool chair.

He looks wildly out of place in his dark T-shirt and jeans, surrounded by girls in string bikinis that leave nothing to the imagination. And men rocking their trunks so low I don't want to think about what's keeping them up.

He drags a hand through his wind-tossed hair and takes a sip of his beer, his eyes meeting mine again. I sink lower in the hot tub, all the way to my chin, to try and hide my embarrassment at getting caught staring at him.

A micro-smile flickers across his face, gone in an instant, you'd miss it if you weren't staring intently at his lips. Not saying that's what I was doing, but...

His gaze drifts to the chaos of chicken fights in the pool. It seems that it doesn't matter the age, the social standing, or how much money is in your bank account, alcohol, plus music, plus a pool, equals an inevitable chicken fight. I'm sure there's some sort of science behind it.

To keep my traitorous eyes from straying to where Nate sits by himself, I move to the opposite side of the hot tub, putting my back to him. I've learned that if I lack self-control in a certain area, that I should remove temptation altogether.

It's why I don't buy gummy bears. If they are in the house, I will eat the entire bag. I've got no will power. Absolutely zero self control when it comes to those tiny, gummy, delightful creatures. Ergo, remove temptation.

Come to think of it, Nate is kind of like a bear. Not a gummy one, but a grumpy one. He's big and burly, a little snappy, but maybe he could be a little cuddly too?

I'm losing it.

I tune back into the conversation happening around me, enjoying Autumn and Jenn's theatrics while they act out what happened in the club this past weekend. Apparently someone got too handsy with Autumn and didn't understand the word no. Our tiny punk rocker wasn't having it. She put him in his place by jamming her knee right into his manhood.

Jenn is currently sinking to her knees and screaming in agony reenacting how he went down like a sack of potatoes. Her boob almost pops out of her triangle top. She doesn't even bat an eye, completely comfortable in her body.

I missed them this weekend. My cheeks hurt from laughing. The combination of the hot tub, the champagne, and the giggles has me feeling overheated. So I pop myself onto the edge to cool down.

I feel eyes on me again. As casually as I can, I look over my shoulder. Nate is still in the same place. Still by himself. Still putting off hot broody vibes. Maybe it's the champagne or the incredibly good mood I find myself in, but I return his little wink from this morning with one of my own.

His eyes narrow on me, causing me to smile. I watch him bring the bottle to his lips, my eyes track his Adam's apple while he swallows his drink.

Oomph. Is it hotter outside of the hot tub? Heat curls low in my belly. Who knew watching a man take a sip of beer could feel x-rated?

If I don't get out of here soon, I'll march right over to him and prove that champagne and temptation don't mix.

Chapter Six
Mr. G.P.
Nate

I'VE BEEN SITTING BY the pool with the party dwindling down around me for an hour. Becket *requested* I hang for a beer. He's such an asshole. The guy's got me by the balls, he knows it, and he enjoys twisting.

I don't want everyone knowing who my parents are. I've known Beck since we were kids, so he obviously knows who I really am. He uses that to his advantage, gets me to do shit I don't want to, so he stays quiet. He doesn't really care if I'm here or not; he just likes the power he thinks he has over me.

The ache in my shoulder has me longing for a hot shower and bed. I planned to drink my one beer and get out of here. That was the plan. Then I heard her laugh, and the plan went to hell.

All the aches and pains fade to the background while I watch her hanging out with her friends.

Man, that laugh. It hits low, unexpected, like a punch to the ribs.

I'm almost feeling grateful that Becket and his pack of idiots yelled my name. I swore less than twelve hours ago that I was going to keep my distance from her. I spent most of the day being successful at doing just that after my brain went haywire in the trailer this morning and I attempted flirting with her. But now, watching her chat freely with her people, I feel myself being drawn to her.

A few people have wandered over to talk, but I have no interest in engaging in conversations with them. I wish I was close enough to hear what is being said in the hot tub.

She turned her back to me the moment my ass hit the pool chair, but now she's perched on the edge, water sliding down her body. She looks like she's glowing under the string lights above us.

Her suit isn't like the other women here. She's in a bright blue one-piece that somehow reads sexier than a string bikini. The low back, the thin straps. I don't know what the front looks like, and I don't need to. Unfortunately for me, the back is enough to make me fight to keep myself in check.

She doesn't seem to chase the spotlight, but damn it, if that doesn't make her stand out even more to me.

I watch her slowly peek over her shoulder right to where I'm sitting. She catches me staring, but I don't think I care. The noise of the pool fades when her smile spreads across her flushed face. She turns her head a little more and sends me a flirty wink.

My chest tightens. I feel that wink through my whole body. My mouth goes dry. I take another swig of my beer while we hold eye contact. I swear her face flushes more deeply before she turns back to her friends.

Whatever she says makes them groan in unison. Then she stands, grabs her stuff, and starts toward the parking lot and back to the rooms. I should let her go, but I don't. Every muscle in me snaps awake, and I'm moving before my brain catches up.

She's halfway to the exit when I fall in step beside her. Water's still dripping off her body.

"Couldn't take time to dry off first?" I ask. "In that big of a hurry to ditch the fun?"

A water drop slides off her hair, lands on her shoulder, and disappears into the towel. I track it like an idiot.

Her eyes spark, towel slipping off one shoulder. "Ditch the fun, huh?" She stops walking when we reach the gate and turns to me. "What would you know about fun? You didn't say two words to anyone all night and now you're pulling an Irish goodbye."

I don't have time to respond before she barrels on.

"Actually, do you think you have to be an active participant in a party for it to count as an Irish goodbye? Or at least grunt in someone's direction once or twice?"

I hum, low in my throat. "Your back was to me all night. I could have been deep in conversation the whole time."

"Watching me that closely, huh?"

Damn it. Touché. "Next time I'll change into trunks so I can hop in and join all the fun."

She snorts. "You? In a hot tub?" She taps her nail to her chin and pretends to think. They are painted bright pink. Happy. She continues, "I can't picture it. Too many bubbles and way too much fun for Mr. G.P."

"G.P.?"

"Mr. Grumpy Pants."

A sound that could almost pass for laughter slips out of me. It feels foreign. But laughing with her, I don't hate it. Liz looks entirely too pleased with herself for both the nickname and pulling a laugh from me.

Hell, she's not wrong. I am a grumpy bastard most of the time.

"That the nickname you're going with?"

"Seems to fit to me, and it's way better than *Cricket*." She beams and shrugs her shoulders. It snaps my attention back to her bare shoulder and the tiny droplets of water clinging there.

"So, you like your men bubbly?" I ask, forcing my eyes back to hers.

She tilts her head back and forth like she's actually weighing it, her grin full of mischief.

"I mean... yeah, bubbly's fine. But so is charming, quiet, cocky, mysterious, occasionally broody." Her smirk turns pointed, and she shrugs, giving my shoulder a playful nudge. "Variety's the spice of life, right? Keeps things interesting."

I drag in a breath, forcing it slow, controlled. The way she said *broody* like she's calling me out without actually saying my name. Is she saying she would be interested in someone like me?

"I've been known to have moments of charm," I say, keeping my tone even. "I just save it for the right people."

The wind rustles her wet hair. I look down and notice her feet are bare as well. She's got to be freezing. As if on cue, she tugs her towel tighter around her.

"Charming, huh? Well, maybe one day I'll get a glimpse of *that* guy."

I feel a hint of my real smile slip through. "Maybe so. But being a little grumpy is infinitely better than insufferable," I reply, tilting my chin toward Becket and his harem.

She laughs, real and loud with her head tilted to the sky. It shakes out of her like sunshine, lighting up her whole face, and I feel it burrow into my chest.

"And you think self-proclaiming how charming you can be *isn't* insufferable?"

I chuckle. "Fair."

We walk the rest of the way toward the rooms in silence; it's not awkward, but it is charged with something. I'm not sure with what though.

We come to a stop outside her door, two down from mine. She looks up at me with her eyes sparkling, water dripping. She's beautiful.

"Thanks for the escort, G.P. Next time don't just brood in the corner, come have some fun."

She pats my cheek like I'm five before slipping inside. I hate that I don't hate it. I watch the door click shut behind her, my jaw tight. I should've had a comeback, something to make her laugh again.

Instead, I'm standing here like an idiot, wishing she'd open the door back up. Get a grip, man.

***

Liz

Holy shiz balls. My heart is racing out of my chest, but I think I kept my cool.

Mr. Hot and Broody walked me to my door. On purpose. I guess he wasn't just in the corner slowly nursing his beer. He was watching and waiting on me. Is that creepy? I don't think so. My lady parts certainly don't think so.

Having Nate's attention on me lights me up. I don't want to hide from him or run away. It doesn't matter if his face scowls the entire time or if he hits me with one of those micro smiles. It is pure, dangerous magic.

Hulk stands up from snoozing on my pillow, "We might be in trouble, little man."

He lazily walks towards me where I'm planted right inside the door. My back rests against the cold metal. I sort of feel like I need it to hold me up. My brain just got scrambled from a simple walk across a parking lot.

Hulk reaches me and twirls around my legs. He pauses to sniff at the leftover water on my toes. He tosses his head in the air, totally unimpressed, and jumps back on the bed, settling back on my pillow like the tiny tyrant that he is.

"I hear you. It's way past our bedtime." I push off the door, shake off the lingering butterflies that appear anytime Nate is within five feet of me, and shuffle toward the bathroom. "Tomorrow I'll sneak you out for a walk, deal?"

He blinks at me like I'm an idiot and curls into a ball. Not impressed.

I rinse off and change into my rainbow, pin-striped pajamas and flop onto the bed beside him like I'm stretching out on my therapist's couch. I'm still not over Nate tonight. I pour my heart out to Hulk like he's a licensed professional instead of a three-pound ball of fur.

"Okay, fine, you don't have to say anything, but you saw him, right? That broody scowl. Gorgeous, serious eyes. Makes me feel giddy. He makes me feel safe, even though he looks dangerous." I sigh, my gaze drifting to the ceiling.

"That last part is the kicker. I don't remember the last time a guy made me feel safe. Heck, I don't remember the last time I stood side-by-side with just a man and I didn't feel like bolting."

The word echoes in my head. *Safe.*

Unfortunately, I don't have the best radar for men. All my relationships either fizzle quickly or end in a dumpster fire. The last relationship I had ended with dramatic flair that no one should have to live through. I almost didn't. So maybe I shouldn't trust how I'm feeling about Nate either. I let out a frustrated groan and roll into a ball.

Pretending the scars I carry don't affect me doesn't make them go away, it just makes them louder in my head.

Maybe it's time to book an appointment with my real therapist. It's been a few weeks.

I run my fingers over Hulk's fur, grounding myself. "But with Nate... he feels different." I chew on my lip, trying to put words to it. "He stopped the other night when he didn't have to. When he clearly didn't *want* to. He grounded me on set today when Becket freaked me out. His eyes on me tonight made me feel like the only girl in the world. And his laugh? Sure, it was barely there, but it was the sweetest sound I've ever heard."

Hulk flicks an ear, still not impressed, but I keep talking.

"He's given me zero indication that he's interested in me. In fact, he's been mostly silent and snarly. But that one tiny wink, that one half-smile, and now I suddenly *want* him to want more with me." I groan into the pillow. "God help me, Hulk. The last thing I need is to want anything with anyone. Especially a guy who looks like he could break me in half with one arm."

Hulk yawns wide enough to show off all his teeth, curls tighter, and promptly falls asleep.

"You are definitely winning therapist of the year, buddy." I turn off the lamp, but my mind still goes in circles.

I wonder how I would react if Nate and I became real friends. Does he have friends? Why does the idea of making him my friend sound so fun?

Chapter Seven
Operation: Crack The Scowl
Liz

THE NEXT DAY STARTS like the one before, with me in the make-up trailer waiting on the guys. Nate is scheduled to get here first *and* alone today. It will just be us for at least an hour. Becket's in a meeting with the director and script supervisor about blocking.

The thought of being alone with Nate makes my palms clammy. Not in a bad way. In a way I haven't felt in a long time.

Last night, my brain decided to replay every interaction I've had with him over and over. That micro-smile I've seen? That ghost of a half-laugh? That tiny crack in his grumpy armor? Utterly addictive.

In the last twelve hours, I've become a woman obsessed. If you blink, you miss those smiles, and now I can't think about anything except coaxing more out of him. So, today's the day.

Operation: Crack the Scowl.

I don't want echoes of laughs or smiles that you have to have a magnifying glass to see. I want his full laugh. His full smile. Surely those things exist.

I don't think being my normal self is going to cut it. Not that anyone has ever described me as normal, but his mask is cemented in place; nothing shakes him.

I'm planning on unleashing the unfiltered, full chaos, no apologies version of me. If I overwhelm and confuse him enough, maybe he'll forget to be broody. His smiles will fall like raindrops.

Is it healthy to be this focused on making a man I barely know smile? The clear answer is no.

Am I going to worry about that? Also, no.

I'm standing by the counter, waiting to pounce, when I hear his footsteps outside the trailer. The second he walks in, I beam.

"Good morning, Bear!"

My over-the-top cheerful greeting and his new nickname stop him in his tracks just inside the door. He eyes me suspiciously, taking his time to lift his coffee to his lips for a sip.

Over the rim of his cup he grunts out, "Bear?"

"Yup." I sing-song.

Before he can reply I add, "You don't mind if I call you Bear, right? Or should I go with Grizzly? Grizz? Teddy? Paddington?" I widen my eyes like I'm serious and tilt my head to the side. "You strike me as a Paddington guy."

He just stares at me. Mission accomplished. He's confused. Most likely contemplating if I sustained a head injury overnight.

I motion to the chair like a polite lunatic. He studies me as he moves carefully toward the chair, like I'm an unexploded bomb, and carefully sets his coffee down before lowering himself into the chair with a squeak.

I hold my silence. I will not break first. It's operation throw him off and if I'm chatting the whole time, that won't throw him off at all. The standoff is a huge exercise in self-control, but the sweetest win when he finally cracks.

"What happened to G.P.?" he asks. "What's with the bear thing?"

Victory.

I knew he liked my nickname last night. Maybe I should come up with a new one every time I see him?

"Because you're like a big, grumpy bear who got yanked out of hibernation early."

He grunts. Translation: *unimpressed but listening.* I'd like to think I'm already becoming fluent in his special caveman language.

That's not the whole truth. The truth is, I was lying in bed thinking about his micro-smile and craving gummy bears at the same time. My brain misfired and then all I could fantasize about was how badly I wanted to inhale an entire bag of those delightful creatures while Nate hit me with the tiniest hints of his smile at the same time.

Getting to have my hands on Nate for a few hours? Yeah, that's almost as good as housing a family-sized bag of gummy bears. I buckle down to get to work on the same injuries as yesterday.

We are quiet for a few minutes. He silently watches me while he sips his coffee. Black, I note. I want to stay committed to throwing him, but being this close to him is actually throwing *me* off.

He reaches up and touches my forehead, right along my hairline. "What's this from?" I love that he asked me a question unprompted. I didn't know what version I would get of him today. The version that squeezed my hip and gave me a flirty wink or the version I got for the rest of the day where he kept his distance. That is until the pool.

His touch is soft, comforting. I know the scar he is talking about. It's still slightly pink from the most recent time my head was busted open. I don't want to think or share about that particular time. But, the first time I cracked my head open right there is a safe enough story to share with him.

"I was four and I busted my head open." I pause to grab the next brush I need. He stays silent waiting for me to keep going.

"My gash wasn't nearly as gruesome as this will be when I'm done with it," I tap his forehead. His skin is smooth. I noticed yesterday he's got a great complexion. "I ended up having to get my head glued shut and a handful of stitches."

I smile at the memory. "That was one of the first times in my life I remember James." I glance down to find Nate watching me closely. "That's my brother. That was the first time I remember him really stepping up and being there for me."

I love my brother. We fought growing up like any siblings close in age do, but he always took the role of big brother and protector very seriously.

"We were supposed to be playing together, but the most beautiful butterfly went right past me, and I found myself following it." Nate scoffs.

"Next thing you know, I'm tumbling off a boulder and cracking my head on a jagged rock." I remember James felt awful. He cried almost as much as I did. Like it was his job to keep me safe and he failed. Nate is still quiet so I keep talking.

"I've always had a tendency to get lost in my own little world, chasing shiny things or new ideas. My dad used to say I was kind of like a beagle puppy. I just can't help but follow my nose. By the time I look up, I could be in a totally different time zone."

I stand back to observe Nate's forehead. "James shadowed me for two straight weeks after the-great-butterfly-head-cracking. He made sure I didn't tear my stitches or overdo it." I smile to myself thinking about how caring he was.

"So, what you're telling me is you have zero impulse control." Nate mutters, voice low breaking into my monologue.

I gasp and smack his arm with my brush. "Excuse me? I am a *free spirit,* thank you very much."

He lifts a brow, unimpressed glancing from my bare feet, up my flowy skirt, to my face. "Free spirit, huh? Sounds more like you require a full-time babysitter."

I try to give him my most annoyed scowl. He's the one that's supposed to be giving me smiles, not the other way around. But I can't stop the grin spreading across my face. "Are you volunteering for the job?"

His mouth twitches. He's trying to fight off a smile too. Come on, mister, hit me with that grin.

"Not in the habit of following insects around." His voice drops lower, like he's talking to himself and he runs a hand through his hair. "Or at least I usually don't. Seems I may be developing a bit of a soft spot." His grin is small and soft when he meets my eyes.

Is he talking about the butterfly from my story or is he talking about me? His mask is firmly back in place.

Abort mission, abort mission. I don't know what I'm doing. Is Mr. Broody being flirty with me? My hand is frozen midair like a mannequin, inside I'm short-circuiting. A soft spot. For *me*. My heart does this weird hiccup thing, and my stomach feels like I just slammed an entire bag of gummy bears.

I force myself to set the brush down before I accidentally paint blood across his eyebrow. Smile, Liz. Play it cool. Totally normal to be nose-to-nose with this man that won't leave your thoughts. Who has apparently decided you're his favorite. That's what he's saying, right? Too much for my brain to compute. I wish I could say I had something really cool to say, but then I wouldn't be me. Would I?

"So," I blurt, way too loud, "Uh... do you moisturize? Because your skin, yep, it's holding up great under all this fake blood." I give the top of his head an awkward pat.

Nate's mouth curves, slow and dangerously handsome. "My skin is good? Is that your professional opinion?"

I let out a nervous laugh that sounds suspiciously like a squeak. "Obviously. Very professional. Nothing but skin analysis happening here." I tap a finger to my temple. See? Super cool.

He doesn't buy it. Not for a second. His almost-smile lingers, and for one reckless moment I let myself enjoy how close we are, how his eyes catch mine and hold. I swear the whole trailer shrinks down to just the two of us.

Our eyes lock while I try and fail to figure him out. His eye contact feels meaningful, especially this close. One small shift and our noses would touch.

I forget about the chaos mission. Are we having a moment here? Or is it just me? I don't want to just crack his scowl anymore, I want to know what happens if all his armor falls away.

Then... the door slams open with a bang.

I jump hard and take a giant leap backward. I nearly stab Nate in the eye with my flailing hand as it comes up to protect my face. My heart rockets into my throat as Becket strolls in, barking into his phone about something I'm sure isn't half as important as he thinks it is.

"Mother-trucker," I mutter under my breath, moving my hands from my face, down my throat, taking deep breaths through my nose. One hand keeps moving and covers my heart, willing my heartbeat to slow, the other clutches the counter to steady myself.

Nate's chair squeaks as he shifts, all focus snapping from Becket to me. "You okay?" His voice is only loud enough for me to hear.

I watch his hands curl into a fist at his side, like he's keeping them from reaching for me. Maybe that's wishful thinking.

I nod quickly, forcing a smile that doesn't feel natural. "Yeah. Just got startled." I clear my throat. "No big deal."

Nate doesn't look convinced. His jaw tightens, his eyes tracking me like he's filing every twitch and flinch away to dissect later.

Becket finally hangs up and plops into his chair like he's a gift to the world, completely oblivious to my internal freak out or the tension swirling in the air. I try to shake it off and go back to work, but I can feel Nate's gaze on me while I work on Becket. It's sharp, protective, like he's already made up his mind about something I'm not ready for him to know. We don't talk anymore. Everyone stays quiet as Becket flips through the channels on the TV in the corner.

I finish with Nate before Becket, but he doesn't budge until I've finished with both of them. Only then does he stand to exit the trailer. Has he already figured me out? Does he know I don't enjoy being alone with men? He seems to be the exception to that. He gives my elbow a squeeze as he brushes by me.

Minutes pass as I try to figure out how I feel about him being able to read me so easily. I stand staring at the door he just exited, the spot where his fingers pressed against my skin feels like a secret meant only for me. No matter what he knows, or doesn't, him staying when he didn't have to means something to me.

And, that light squeeze he threw my way as he brushed by, feels more addictive than all his scowls and smirks combined. Shoot a fish. I can't deal with a crush right now, but it's official. I have one on Nate Jones, Mr. Grumpy Pants himself.

Chapter Eight
Did I Just Say Girlfriend?
Nate

I'M FEELING OFF-KILTER AFTER a full day of shooting with Liz by my side doing touchups. I decided there was no way to keep her at arm's length like I did yesterday. It only seemed to make her push harder.

Was she more today? More what? I don't know. Just *more* Liz. I mull over how she was even more excitable, more bold, a little more loud, a little more strange. She draws me in like I've never experienced. I thought I had her figured out, but I'm not so sure I do. She's a puzzle.

Walking into my room, I power up my phone. I've got a dozen missed calls from my mother and twice as many unread texts. Her persistence is an art form, and I know better than to think she'll let up. I'll have to call her back eventually or she'll make my life a living hell in her own special way.

I already know what she wants. The gala.

Even though my schedule is packed, someone on her payroll probably slipped my schedule to her. She must be aware that my next break aligns so that I can attend this year.

Every year Sterling Studios hosts a gala to celebrate their own inflated egos under the guise of an award ceremony. The charity tie-in is always an afterthought, whatever cause photographs best that season. A chance to pat themselves on the back and say, *look how kind and caring we are.*

Unfortunately, it's going to work out for me to fly out and show my face at their stupid party this year. Work is always my shield, my excuse. The few times they've forced my hand to attend over the years, it always turns into a pressure cooker. My role in the company, how it's time to step in and "do my duty."

If it's not career pressure, it's a constant parade of women. Fake boobs, fake frozen faces, fake interactions, but they all have one thing in common. These women come from money, they are in the right social circles, and most importantly, my parents deem them an acceptable match for *their son*.

It's the fucking worst.

Tossing my phone on the desk, I listen to it buzz against the wood until it falls silent. The thought of walking into that ballroom, wearing a tux, my hair slicked back, my parents' legacy weighing on me, makes my chest constrict.

Out of nowhere, Liz flashes across my mind.

Messy bun, streak of fake blood on her cheek, barefoot, colorful, crazy outfit surrounding her. Her grin firmly in place like it was this morning when she called me Bear.

She's full of color, chaos, unrestrained joy. The complete opposite of my buttoned-up, all-show, fake family. Nothing about Liz would fit in with their idea of who they want me to end up with. Which, I'll admit, is an appealing thought. One I shouldn't be having, but appealing nonetheless.

I run a hand over my face, scowling at the ceiling. Dwelling on Liz is a mistake. Letting her crawl under my skin even more than she already has is an even bigger mistake. And yet, lying here in the quiet, all I can think about is how big of a fan I am of her *more*.

I need to move. Clear my head before I call my mother back.

I head out the door and across the street to a small park. And there she is. Liz. With a cat in a harness of all things. Talking to it like it's the most natural thing in the world.

I walk slowly, observing the scene in front of me, until Liz turns, scoops the cat that's flopped itself on the ground up, and hits me with a lethal smile. It's a sucker punch to the gut. It's not fair that she's as beautiful as she is. Add in a kitten, and even my heart thaws a bit.

"What exactly am I looking at here, Cricket?"

She gives me a mischievous smirk and tucks her face into the cat's fur to give him a kiss. "This here is Hulk, Superhero."

She meets my puzzled face. I hate that I'm going to ask her, but I am. "Superhero?"

"Yup." That's it.

"Care to elaborate?"

"You rescued me the other night, and you are literally a stunt double for superheroes. Makes sense to me."

She shrugs and smiles at me like she is keeping a secret.

"Unless you prefer G.P.?" Before I can answer, that I do not prefer G.P. or any other nickname her mind comes up with, she continues. "Personally, I'm partial to Bear."

She's close enough now that I catch the scent of her shampoo. It's light and sweet. Almost the echo of a smell. It's gone before I can identify it. Her hair's still damp, she must have showered after work. I want to step closer and take a deeper breath.

"Makes no difference to me." I nod at the cat. "Why the hell do you have a harness on a cat?"

She snuggles him tighter. "He loves walks. He was so sad cooped up in the hotel all day."

"You're hiding a cat in your room?"

She ignores my question. "Do you think I should get him a sibling? Then he'd have someone to play with while I'm gone." She looks at me expectantly.

"Liz, I'm certain I have no opinion on if you should get your illegal cat *another* illegal cat to hang out with during the day."

Hulk yawns wide, his little tongue hanging out. Damn, that's cute. Against my better judgment, my lips twitch.

Liz catches it instantly. "Careful there, Bear. People might think you actually have a soul if you're caught smiling at baby animals."

Instead of hiding my smile, I let it happen. I feel it spread across my face. Just a little. Enough that her eyes go wide.

She gasps. "Stop the presses! Grumpy Pants smiles. Somebody call Guinness, this has to be some sort of record."

I huff a laugh, shaking my head. "Make a big deal about a grin and I might just not do it around you again."

"Ehh, sounds like an empty threat to me," she shoots back, smiling so hard it's contagious.

"You're ridiculous."

"Seems like maybe you like my brand of ridiculousness?" She looks up at me. Her eyes are happy, but vulnerability shines through.

That look, those blue eyes, they sear into my soul, and in this moment, I'd give her anything that she asked of me. I can't leave her hanging, but I can't bring myself to give her the truth. That feels a little too real.

"I tolerate it." I deadpan, then nudge her shoulder as we fall into step beside each other. "Fine, you're not so bad. You may even be growing on me."

The smile that breaks across her face is radiant.

For the next hour, I just let myself be. We walk the loop around the park together. She chatters about Hulk's favorite toys. She swears he loves to go on walks, but I end up carrying him after he flops himself on the ground one too many times.

She doesn't seem bothered that I'm barely contributing to the conversation. The occasional dry comment gets thrown in, but she folds me into her world, like it's the most natural thing to do.

Before we turn to head back to the hotel, Hulk suddenly decides he's part cheetah and leaps from my arms, bolting after a squirrel, leash flying behind him. Liz lets out a high pitch yelp and takes off after him, so I take off too. I watch Hulk's tiny jaw latch on to the squirrel's tail.

"No! Don't hurt him. You can't eat him."

"It's bigger than he is, Liz," I yell over my shoulder chasing the cat. "He's not going to eat him."

Her face scrunches while she puffs out of breath and amends her reprimand, "You can't kidnap forest friends, Hulk!"

I shake my head and pump my legs harder. I catch up to him first and snag the leash, stopping his high speed chase. His jaw relaxes, and the squirrel scurries up a nearby tree. When Liz reaches us, she's breathless, cheeks flushed, laughter ringing out.

She scoops Hulk up, panting. "Hulk. My sweet boy. You cannot eat the locals."

"That squirrel was twice his size. He wouldn't have actually been able to eat it."

She smirks. "And yet, he believed."

"Pretty sure he's delusional." He flops in Liz's arms, playing dead. "And dramatic."

She mock gasps and covers his ears. "Take it back. You'll hurt his feelings."

I arch a brow. "I wonder where he learned the dramatics from?"

She laughs again, still trying to catch her breath, the sound bright in the dark surrounding us.

By the time we reach the hotel, I feel lighter than I have in weeks. Maybe months. She gives me a "toodles" over her shoulder, tucks Hulk against her chest, and disappears into her room. She and her cat are chaos incarnate, and somehow I want more of it.

Back in my room, I pick up the phone, already bracing myself for my mother's voice. But I feel calmer and ready to stand my ground.

I barely get out, "Hi, Mom," before she launches straight into it. Her grand plans, RSVPs, details about the gala. She starts chattering about the different women she has lined up for my date options. Doesn't even ask if I'll be there, just assumes I'll jump because she says to. My back teeth start to grind.

I'm annoyed and irritated. And then Liz flashes across my mind.

Holding a cat, walking in circles, listening to the woman chatter about nothing and everything. It centered me. She made me completely forget all about my parents' world and the obligations they are trying to shove down my throat while we hung out.

Before I can rein it in, the words are out of my mouth.

"I'll be there," I hear myself say. "And I'm bringing someone."

The silence on the other end is sharp enough to cut through steel.

Shit.

"Nathaniel." My mother's disapproval is palpable even thousands of miles away. "Did you say you were bringing someone?"

I swallow down the urge to take it back. "Yes."

"This function is important, dear. It's best you let me set you up for the evening with someone appropriate. We don't need any rumors starting about you bringing an escort."

I can't hide my eye roll. I'm thankful we aren't on FaceTime. "I have never, nor would I ever, bring a hooker to an event, Mom. I'm bringing my girlfriend. I *am* allowed to have one of those, aren't I?"

Wait. Fuck. Did I just say girlfriend?

"Your..." She clears her throat. "You have a girlfriend?" she says, ice dripping through the phone. Is she irritated that I sprung this on her or that her spies didn't tell her I was seeing someone.

I could play it off and tell her I'm just kidding. Instead, my mouth keeps going. "Yes. I have a girlfriend."

"I see. How long have you been seeing this...person, Nathaniel?

"A while now. We are serious. We, uhh, we actually live together."

What. The. Hell. I wish I could stop, but apparently I'm pulling a page from Liz's book, and I keep talking.

"I've been looking forward to you meeting her for a while now." Nope. In zero universe would I be looking forward to that. My mouth has gone rogue.

There's no reply, and I pull my phone away from my ear to check if we've been disconnected.

"Mom, if she isn't welcome, then I'm not coming." There we go. Now we are talking, I can use this to my advantage and get out of the whole damn thing.

The ice thaws, her voice comes across smug and something else I can't figure out. "No, dear, that won't be necessary. I will take care of the arrangements. What is this girl's name?" Every time she says girl, or person, it's dripping with condescension.

A name. I need to create a fake person. I start sweating through my shirt. Even though I've lived on my own for twelve years, when I talk to my parents, I revert back to the hyper kid that was told to be quiet and sit still.

"Uhh, Liz."

"Hmm. How quaint. I look forward to seeing you and meeting this *Liz* at the gala. Talk soon."

There's a click, and just like that she's gone. I drop the phone on the bed, stare at the ceiling, and drag a hand down my face.

"Shit." I let out a short, humorless laugh. "Brilliant move, Nate. You now have a fake girlfriend named Liz. What the hell did you just do?"

Chapter Nine
Shizzle Fritz
Liz

I'M DISTRACTED THIS MORNING while I set up my supplies. I'm still thinking about my walk with Nate yesterday. Autumn and Jenn went on a double date last night, and I was feeling down and lonely until he showed up.

He may be a man of few words and many scowls, but the way he brightened my day just by walking beside me? I don't think I've ever had a person who makes me smile like he does. The way he just scooped up Hulk, carried him, and cuddled him for most of the walk?

Swoon.

Since I'm dreaming about a certain grumpy man, I don't check my caller ID before answering my ringing phone. What a mistake.

"Miss Harrison," a deep, oily voice slithers across the line, "how nice of you to finally pick up my call."

Well, shizzle fritz.

"Hi, Mr. Duncan." My voice comes out too high. Great. Might as well have guilty tattooed across my forehead.

"You've been a very difficult woman to reach."

"Yes, sir. I've been traveling a lot for work." Keep your voice even, Liz. Don't let him smell your fear. He's like a shark circling in the water.

"I see. And I suppose that's also why you haven't responded to the letters we've sent? The reason we have barely seen a payment from you?"

The accusation hits me square in the gut and makes me tremble. I hate disappointing people. Even sleazy people. But it's more than that. This man makes me feel real fear.

My fingers clench around the edge of the makeup chair. "Yes, sir. That's... that's why. I'll have another check in the mail by the end of the week. I promise."

He tuts, low and cold. "Promises don't pay debts, Miss Harrison. See that you do. Otherwise," he pauses. The silence kills me. "We'll be forced to consider other measures."

"Of course, you'll have the next payment by next weekend. No need to consider doing anything else."

He hangs up without a goodbye, like I'm not even worth the breath to acknowledge my lame promise of money. My skin feels clammy, my pulse racing.

I've had the displeasure of meeting Mr. Duncan once before. Once was more than enough. He certainly doesn't look like any banker I've ever seen, but he produced legal paperwork for a loan with my name on it. A loan I have zero memory of taking out.

I grab my forehead while the memories of how I got into this mess rush over me. A few months after everything imploded, the first envelopes started showing up. I thought it was junk mail at first. I just got settled in my shiny new apartment. Everything in it, I picked out specifically to bring me joy. I was moving forward, healing, happy, until the notices started piling up.

When I finally stopped shoving them into a corner and investigated the mysterious bills, I discovered they were in fact *not* junk mail.

Unfortunately, my former self was too trusting, too stupid, too battered, to question anything my ex ever did. I discovered my dill-weed of an ex took out a loan in my name. Certainly that wasn't legal.

I made a few calls and found out I *had* actually signed the paperwork for the loan. I racked my brain for days trying to figure out when I signed those documents. It finally dawned on me.

Occasionally, he would bring home papers from the studio and need my signature on things as a witness. I always just signed that stuff without a second thought. Turns out, I was actually signing loan paperwork and now I was on the hook.

I managed to get one free consultation with a lawyer over the phone. He barely let me finish before sighing and saying, "If you signed it, even under manipulation, it's enforceable unless you can prove duress. That takes time, documentation, and money." His voice softened, "I'm sorry. These cases are hard."

I remembered clearing my throat and working up the nerve to tell him about the abuse. It was still the early days and I had a really hard time admitting I was a victim of domestic violence.

I finally worked up the nerve and told the lawyer about everything. The hospital visit, the broken ribs, the concussion, he sighed and said, "I believe you. But unless you can prove that particular instance happened to force the signature, the loan is still legally enforceable." It wasn't. I signed those documents weeks before I was hospitalized. The money was probably spent the same day he got it.

I shove my phone into my bag like I can bury the whole mess with it. My hands are trembling, but when the trailer door swings open behind me, I force myself to take a deep, cleansing breath, paste on a smile, and steel my spine. I turn expecting to greet Becket, instead, I'm face-to-face with a now very familiar scowl.

Nate.

My insides loosen a bit. Dealing with Becket after just receiving that call would have been almost too much for me to handle. But Nate, he won't be a problem. Although he looks even more grumpy this morning. He looks like he's breathing hard. His fists clench at his side.

Even though he looks like he's ready to commit murder, I don't feel afraid. I feel a little better now that he's here. I'm shaken up by that call, but Nate being here makes me feel a little more safe. Like my problems can't touch me while he's with me.

"Morning, Boo-Bear." I try to sing-song, but if Nate's face is any indication, my greeting falls flat.

"Liz." He's watching my face closely. I feel like I'm under a microscope. It makes me feel squirmy.

"You're early today. I'm not set up yet, but you can go ahead and sit down." I gesture to the chair by my side and quickly turn around to pull myself together. I've never had a good poker face. I don't need Nate asking me what's going on.

He grunts at my back and I hear him drop into the chair with a hard thud, the vinyl squeaks under his weight.

I don't know why I expected actual words today. Maybe one of his almost smiles? A charming greeting? I just thought after our walk yesterday maybe he would be a little softer. I was wrong. If anything he looks less amused than ever.

I watch him in the mirror, his jaw muscles flex like he's chewing on concrete. I take a deep breath, turn, and hit him with a smile. "Did you sleep well, Sunshine?"

He takes a moment to blow out a slow breath before he answers. "Slept fine."

He doesn't even acknowledge my newest nickname. It's like we are back to that first night on the side of the road. Like our mild flirting didn't even happen. Ouch.

"Okay then. Well, let's get started." I try to infuse extra cheer into my voice.

"Don't you ever get exhausted," he asks, his voice low, but he continues at my confused stare. "Being," he waves a hand around like he's searching for the right word. "Perky? Being on, all the time?"

Exhausted? Buddy, you have no idea. For half a second, I want to sag under the weight of the pressure I'm under. Confide everything to him. But I force air into my lungs, smile bright, and pretend like everything is fine.

"On? This is just me, Bear. No switch, no batteries required."

"Sure, Cricket." His sarcastic response hurts my feelings and sets me off.

My morning has already been thrown for a loop with that money-hungry lowlife's call, I don't need this man making me feel bad about who I am.

"Well, pardon me for trying to add a little happiness, a little color to your grayscale life." I wrap my arms around my middle like that will protect me from all the big feelings swirling around inside of me. Fear. Exhaustion. Having my feelings hurt by a man I was starting to trust.

His shoulders are taut, his gaze locked on mine. The space between us feels too charged, like the air itself might snap. He looks at me like he can see through me, but he doesn't respond.

I'm not in the right frame of mind for this today. I move to my supplies, picking up a prosthetic piece that I slap onto his face a little too firmly, making him grunt, but breaking the tension swirling around us.

"Hold still," I mutter, voice tight. "Wouldn't want to mess up your perfect scowl."

I feel mad at Nate. Mad at myself. Mad at the sketchy loan guy. Mad at the scam artist that is my ex.

We don't speak a word as I work.

***

NATE

I'm silent and I'm angry while Liz applies the layers to my face.

That phone call I overheard approaching the trailer this morning had me stopping cold with my hand on the doorknob. The way her voice broke when she promised someone money. That tiny crack lit up every protective instinct.

I wanted to hurt someone. It didn't matter who. The way her voice trembled telling them they wouldn't need to *do* anything else. I want to know who she owes money to and why. Right now.

I'm off kilter. I planned to come in here this morning and figure out how to ask Liz to go to California with me to my parents' gala, but hearing her voice trembling threw me.

She's quiet this morning. Not filling the silence with her chatter. And I hate it. I want her insanity in full force. If for no other reason, than to prove that call wasn't as big of a deal as my mind is telling me that it is.

I keep my mouth shut, but my eyes are trained on her face in the mirror. I watch emotions flick across her face in rapid succession. Every once in a while, it's like she forgets I'm here, she's engrossed in her work, but her lips will move with a silent conversation I'm not privy to.

The trailer smells like latex, coffee, and whatever shampoo she uses. Normal things. The same things that have surrounded me all week. But today, they twist my gut. It's like I'm breathing through glass.

She's moving slower than she usually does. Her fingers are still trembling fifteen minutes after that call ended. It's a small thing. But the slight shake of her fingers when she reaches for a sponge is enough for me to break our silent standoff.

"Hey," my voice startles her and I hate that I made her jump. "I'm sorry. I was a jerk."

She freezes, her hand hovering over my eyebrow. For a second she looks down at me, eyes bright, but guarded. "It's okay," she says, a little too quick. "Everyone's entitled to an off day. I shouldn't have forced my cheer on you."

"You didn't. I was rude. It won't happen again."

She gives me a small smile. I can't stop myself. My hand reaches out circling her small waist. "You okay?"

I don't miss the goosebumps that break out on her arm before she glances off to the side, "Yeah, I'm okay. Just tired today."

Tired. I want to call her out on the lie. I want to press. I want to ask who the hell Mr. Duncan is and why she is so rattled by him.

But I don't.

I don't want her to stay mad at me. I don't want to terrify her more by interrogating her. Instead, I do what doesn't normally come naturally. I lean forward, moving my hand up and down her back in what I hope is a comforting gesture. I slide my hand to her wrist to keep her from spinning around away from me. Her skin feels cold under mine. She swallows, but holds my eyes.

I hope my expression says she can trust me. That she can tell me what's going on without me having to ask. I wait patiently. I've never had a problem with silence.

"It's nothing, Nate. Just… scheduling, bills, stupid adult things," she murmurs, and forces what I think she means to be a playful shrug and smile, but it doesn't reach her eyes.

Nate. She called me Nate. Not Bear, G.P., Sunshine or any of the other names she's come up with for me this week. It bothers me more than it should that she doesn't trust me with this.

"Okay, Cricket." I say, giving her arm a small, gentle squeeze before sitting back in my chair. "But if it was something more than just being tired, anything at all, if someone's hassling you, you could tell me."

It slips from my lips like a plea. Please, let her say she would tell me. Let me in.

Her laugh is brief, brittle this time. "Hassling me? What is this an old western movie?" she teases, trying to push the tension away.

At least her joking sounds a little more believable now. I look at her hands, the trembling has stopped. She turns to the counter for supplies. I watch her shoulders relax.

"Thanks," she says so quietly I almost don't hear it, but she quickly goes back to work.

Her motions regain a little of their usual rhythm. It's wild to me that I know what her rhythms are after such a short time, but I've always been observant.

When she finishes, she steps back and wipes her hands. She meets my eyes in the mirror, and for a fraction of a second, something unspoken passes between us. I nod toward her and leave quietly.

I don't know what happened this morning. How I went from telling myself to keep my distance to suddenly needing her to trust me and tell me all of her problems, but I know I'm screwed.

Chapter Ten
Emotional Whiplash
Liz

The pool deck is quiet when I slip outside. It should be, it's almost two in the morning. The chill in the air skates down my spine, making me wrap my towel tighter around myself as I cross the parking lot.

If anyone is peeking out their window, they'll see the ridiculous shadow of a woman tiptoe-running barefoot and slapping a hand over her mouth every time she steps on a pebble to keep from yelping.

Maybe I should have grabbed shoes.

Too late now, I'm almost there and I just want to get in the hot tub and relax.

I still feel on edge after that phone call a few days ago. Nothing sounds better than a long soak in the quiet. Well, not complete quiet. Silence and I don't get along, so I brought my portable speaker for background noise. A little calm before waking up tomorrow and doing it all over again.

As soon as I enter the pool area, I hear water lapping, bubbles bubbling, and I realize my plan is derailed. Someone is already enjoying *my* peaceful hot tub. Not just someone. Nate.

I consider turning back and leaving him alone for half a second, until my eyes snag on the line of his abs above the water and I freeze. Instead of turning around and heading to bed, I stand at the gate like a full-blown peeping tom.

Even though I just saw him a few hours ago when he met me to walk Hulk again, he certainly didn't have this much skin on display.

He's stretched out, arms along the edge, head tipped back to the stars, steam rising all around him. I think I can see the hint of a tattoo peeking out around his rib cage. Interesting. His trademark scowl is missing. For once, he looks completely unguarded and even more devastatingly handsome than usual.

He hasn't noticed me yet. I should probably stop perving on him. I half-turn to retreat, but his voice rumbles low across the water. "Coming in, or are you just going to stand there staring?"

His teasing tone surprises me, especially since he's been even more serious than usual these past few days.

His voice makes my shoulders drop a notch, and my eyes automatically roll. Of course he noticed me. "Don't flatter yourself. I was debating whether sharing bubbles with you was worth it."

He tilts his head to look across the pool at me. His browns meeting my blues, amusement bleeds into his voice. "Yes, I'm sure that's what you were doing for the five minutes you've been standing there ogling me."

I don't acknowledge the fact that I was absolutely standing here studying every visible inch of him like I was prepping for a final exam. Pretty sure there's drool on my chin.

The way he is watching me walk across the pool deck, makes me very glad I chose the swimsuit I did tonight. It's deep green and looks like a sexy version of an old-fashioned bathing suit.

From the front it looks like something a classy 1950s starlet would wear on a yacht. High neckline with a sweet bow at the base of my throat. At first glance it appears modest, but the keyhole between my boobs amplifies the girls and screams *hello, yes, these are real and magnificent.*

The bottom reads innocent with longer boy-short lines, right up until I turn. The back is anything but modest. Half my bum hangs out. Maybe more.

His eyes track me while I set my speaker down and connect my phone. I glance at him over my shoulder and watch his eyes flare when I toss my towel on a chair. I watch him sit up straighter as he gets his first look at my whole ensemble. His eyes roam from my toes, slowly lingering on some of my better assets, back to my face.

I slowly slip into the hot water opposite him, I'm not trying to put on a show, but I can't help that the water is too hot to plop right in.

When I'm finally fully submerged, it feels like heaven. I bite back a moan, but the sigh that escapes can't be helped as the jets hit my sore muscles. Nate shifts subtly across from me.

If I'm this sore from being on my feet all week, I can't imagine how sore he is. His job is extremely physically demanding.

Which is why his body looks like it does. Holy cheese on a cracker. It's hard to pull my eyes away from his sculpted chest and back to his eyes, but I do it. He gives me a knowing look, telling me he caught me checking him out. Again.

Honestly, I deserve a treat for keeping my eyes north of his pecs.

He breaks the silence first. "No Hulk tonight? I'm surprised you don't have him out here in a tiny pair of swim trunks."

The image makes me giggle so hard I snort, all pretenses of being sexy fly out the window with that, but I make a mental note to see if there is such a thing as cat swim trunks.

"He's not much on water. We are working on exposure therapy with the bathtub before I toss him in the deep end." My cheeks hurt from how hard I'm cheesing.

I love when Nate jokes with me. We've been walking every night after we wrap for the day. He's started loosening up more and more. Talking to me about his day, his life. Asking questions. Playing along with my bits. Yesterday, I said a pile of leaves was angry. Instead of looking at me like I was insane, he asked why. I'm slowly getting that scowl to melt and making him my bestie. He just doesn't know it yet.

Being on the opposite side of the hot tub feels wrong. It's too far away from him.

"Scoot over, Sour Patch, you're hogging the good jets." I bump him with my knee, before I swim across the small space.

Do I need to move to his side? No. The jets are the same all the way around, but I want to be closer to him. He calms me down, even when he's irritated or extra growly. It's weird for me, but even then, it's better to be closer to him.

He slowly scoots over making room for me, his head tilting slightly, that tiny twitch of a smirk tugging at his mouth. Once again, he doesn't acknowledge my newest nickname for him, how close we are sitting, or that I didn't really need to move to his side. I'm playing with fire, but I don't really care tonight.

Once I settle next to him, not close enough to touch, but close enough I can feel the water swirl when he moves, he leans his head back against the edge and speaks to the stars. "Well, what's the verdict, Cricket? Am I ruining your late-night spa experience?"

"Oh, completely." I can't hold back my smile. "I swear if your grumpiness infects me through the bubbles, I'll kick your rear, doesn't matter if you could bench press me with one arm."

He huffs a laugh. Small victory for me. "My rear?"

"You heard me. I could take you. Probably."

"I'm pretty sure that's not how hot tubs work, Cricket."

"Pretty sure you don't know the first thing about bubbles or hot tubs," I fire back, leaning against the edge, looking at him over my shoulder with a mock-serious scowl. "Bubbles are fragile. You, being in here, could easily contaminate them, transferring your dark cloud energy to me."

This time, his smile actually makes it all the way across his face, his eyes crinkling around the edges, before he shakes his head. "You're something else."

I turn my head into the crook of my arm, pretending to wipe water off my face to hide my megawatt grin. I'm a smitten kitten when it comes to his lighter side. I love it.

For a few minutes we just sit there, steam curling around us, the night air crisp. It feels easy. Our knees brush occasionally, making my pulse soar. I feel happy. It's a miracle, but I feel completely at ease, one hundred percent myself with him.

A content sigh escapes my lips as I lift my gaze to the stars. I can feel his eyes roaming over my face, but he doesn't say a word. Being a mind reader would come in handy with this man.

The air between us feels charged. Like we're both aware something is different, but neither of us wants to be the first one to acknowledge it.

This close to him, a slow country ballad playing in the background, the weight of his eyes on me, and our limbs brushing under the water, my silence doesn't last long. "This is perfect. My whole body hurts this week."

Nate grunts, but surprisingly actually answers. "It feels pretty perfect, yeah."

My eyes snap back to his over my shoulder. He's sitting closer. Our shoulders almost brushing. My stomach flip-flops. Did the hot tub temp just rise a few degrees? Are we having a moment? Maybe. So, of course I ruin it with my chatter.

"I, uhh, I really need to start working out again. If I was consistently working out maybe I wouldn't feel so sore." I pull my gaze from his. Sometimes when he looks at me like that I can't think. "My friend Chloe would kick my tush if she knew I've been slacking on running."

"Running?"

There we go, more comfortable territory.

"She signed us up to run a half marathon in a few weeks."

He whistles. Stretching his arms out. His fingertips brush my shoulder lightly. The touch is barely there, but my whole body reacts like he set off a sparkler under my skin. All I want to do is scoot closer, feel the weight of his arm settle around me, but I might be misreading this whole thing, so I don't.

"Sounds like a terrible way to spend a day."

"Tell me about it. I'm not a runner, but she is, and I love her. That clouded my judgment when I told her I'd do it with her."

I glance over at him. "Want to know a little secret?" I pause for dramatic effect, waiting for him to nod before I continue. "I'm a bit of a people pleaser."

He mockingly widens his eyes. "No, you don't say."

I laugh. "You did not know that about me."

"I could have told you that about you before even having a full conversation with you."

"Watching me that closely were you?" That makes me feel giddy. Even if he is uncovering things about me I'd rather keep secret.

He scoffs, but doesn't reply.

"Well, I don't know if you know *this* or not, but sometimes I can get in my own head and forget what's happening around me. Whenever Chloe asked me to sign up for this marathon I was kind of distracted and feeling guilty that I missed lunch with her, so I said yes."

"Why'd you miss lunch?"

I eye him for a second before I decide to give him the truth. "Swear you won't laugh."

He gives me that devastating full grin again. "Scout's honor."

I narrow my eyes at him, weighing if I think he's lying. "Fine. I missed lunch because I got into a very serious, possibly life-or-death debate at Target."

"A life-or-death debate at Target?" He echoes.

"Listen, I only went in for toothpaste and somehow ended up debating with a seven-year-old about whether sparkly unicorn notebooks are superior to narwhal notebooks."

His brow furrows, he gives his head a little shake like he's trying to get water out of his ears. "What?"

"We were in the notebook aisle. Gosh, I love that aisle. There is nothing like a brand new notebook. There were these two notebooks side by side. One had a unicorn, one had a narwhal. Both good choices, depending on what you are going for."

"Okay..." He says it slowly, like he's not sure if I'm joking or if he should call someone.

"And, the specifics don't matter," I wave my hand around in the air, "Unless you're someone who doesn't value mythical creatures."

He's staring at me without saying anything, so I go on. "We ended up taking our debate to the Target Starbucks. I think the kid's mom was embarrassed her child was arguing with an adult, but I didn't mind. I love to encourage a healthy debate with younger generations. Long story short, I lost. That kid had serious verbal chops, we debated for a while, which is how I ended up missing my lunch with Chloe. By the time I realized what time it was, she had already left the restaurant. Hence the guilty sign up for a marathon."

He actually laughs, an honest full one, and I'm a goner. "You're unbelievable."

"Unbelievably amazing you mean?" I hit him with the signature Harrison double eyebrow raise. "And don't even try to tell me narwhals win. That kid was wrong. If you have the choice between a mythical creature and a real creature, always choose the mythical creature. No matter how cool narwhals are, they lose."

He shakes his head, still chuckling. The sound is warm, real, I soak it in like sunshine after a storm. The warmth lingers only a beat before his voice shifts. His fingertips deliberately trace the water drops along my arm. Goosebumps break out across my arms, despite the hot water, I shiver. That feels so good.

But then he says my name. It sounds different. Weighted.

"Hey, Liz?" I'm instantly alert. Something is wrong.

"Yeah?"

"Will you tell me about the call you got the other morning?"

The question drops like a stone in water, sending ripples through the easy silence we'd built. A perfectly nice moment ruined.

I had a hunch he overheard my call, with how murder-y he looked, but I wasn't positive until now. I was hoping we wordlessly agreed not to go there.

"The call?" My brain goes into overdrive, scrambling for a way to brush it off. He didn't hear the other end of the call, how can I spin this?

His eyes don't leave mine. "I know I don't have a right to know who you were talking to, or why someone's demanding money from you," he says quietly. "But I want you to tell me anyway."

I force out a laugh, it sounds shaky even to my own ears. "Been eavesdropping, Mr. Stuntman? Didn't peg you for the nosy type."

He blows out a breath, jaw clenched, but his gaze is unwavering. He's not going to let this go. But I can't give him the truth. It's embarrassing. It's overwhelming. It's *my* mess. So I lift my chin, meeting his gaze head-on, lips sealed.

He doesn't say a word. He's good at that. Not saying anything, just waiting for me to crack. I don't want to play this silent game of chicken. If I stay here with him much longer I'll end up telling him everything, so I move to get out.

He reaches out, grabbing my hand to stop me, and pulls me closer. Our legs press against each other under the churning water. "I'm not trying to overstep. I know you don't know me well or trust me," his voice drops, softer, careful. He threads our fingers together, tightening his hold. "But, I just want to throw it out there that I'm here, whatever you need."

I wasn't expecting that. He *doesn't* know me, *doesn't* owe me anything, but his offer to help hits me square in the chest. Something in me aches with how badly I wish I could believe him, but I don't trust myself. Even so, I feel my walls starting to slip and that scares me. I stay strong somehow and hold my tongue.

His gaze bounces between my eyes. He nods once like he's made some kind of decision. Our eyes hold for another second before he lets go of my hand. "Alright, Cricket. We'll play it your way."

I clear the emotion that's lodged in my throat and try to joke. "Well, that was fun. Nothing like a late-night soak and an interrogation to really unwind before bed."

He shrugs, trying for casual but missing. "Yeah, well, sorry if I pushed." He pauses for a beat. "I'm not great at subtle."

"Yeah, I got that."

I stand, water runs off me in small streams, steam wafting from my skin. I feel his eyes drag slowly over my body. He shifts forward slightly, like he's going to reach for me again, but doesn't. My feet are still in the hot tub, I reach over to the plastic chair to grab my towel. I wrap it around me like armor.

Nate leans back, pretending he's relaxed, but I can feel the tension simmering between us. I'm just not sure what kind of tension.

It's like emotional whiplash. One second we are light and flirty, then he's asking heavy questions, the next he's looking at me like *that*. Curse him. Curse all good-looking men with shoulders like mountains and rare smirks that sneak under your skin.

I cinch my towel tighter around me like that will protect me from the attractive broody man and force my voice into something that resembles being breezy. "Careful, Boo-Bear. If you keep looking at me like that, I might start thinking you actually enjoy hanging out with me and all your snarls are just a front."

And just like that, we are back in friendly territory. "Wouldn't want to give you the wrong idea, Cricket."

Have I seriously decided I'm going to let him keep calling me Cricket? Dumbest nickname ever... except when he says it, I kind of like it.

He stands and grabs his own towel. We walk back to the hotel side by side, silence stretching between us. Not quite comfortable, but not quite as awkward as it was.

At my door, I tilt my head and force a grin. "Thanks for walking me home. Sleep tight. Don't let the bed bugs bite."

He shakes his head as he swipes his keycard and mumbles something under his breath. Pretty sure he said he wouldn't mind a few bug bites, but maybe that's just what I *want* to hear.

Chapter Eleven
Peeing With The Door Open
Nate

The week drags and flies at the same time. I don't bring up the call I overheard again, but I've wanted to. More than once.

We have one more day of filming at this location before heading back to the studio in the city. Liz and I have hung out every night. No matter how late we get done. It's become routine. Something I look forward to without meaning to.

We haven't met up in the hot tub again, but maybe that's for the best. If I'm going to ask her to be my fake girlfriend, it's probably best I don't blur the lines anymore than I already have.

She does my makeup every morning. She draws more words out of me every day. I keep telling myself when we are together that it's just casual flirting, but the truth is, I wake up looking forward to seeing her. Hearing the ridiculous things that come out of her mouth.

Every time she smiles, every time she bumps my shoulder, or laughs at something I didn't realize was funny, the lines smudge a little more.

I'm not sure I could handle another night in the hot tub with her without doing something monumentally stupid. Like pulling her into my lap just to see if she'd melt against me the way I think she would.

So yeah. Space is probably smart.

Even knowing that I need to keep some distance between us, when the day wraps, I head out the door to meet her. She's already across the street waiting, hoodie pulled up, leash in hand. When I reach her, we fall into step beside each other. We walk in silence for a while. Not too long. Liz never lasts in the quiet for long.

Right on cue, she bumps my shoulder. "You're a tough nut to crack, Bear. Do you ever willingly start a conversation, or do you just enjoy grunting in response to my verbal brilliance?"

"I talk."

She gives me a look, clearly unconvinced. "Mmhmm. Sure you do."

I grab the cat's leash out of her hand and bend to scoop up Hulk where he's flopped himself on the ground one too many times. He's so small he could fit in my pocket. "Maybe I just save my words for people who don't fill every second with noise."

She mock gasps. "You're saying my voice is noise?"

"I'm saying it's constant, Cricket."

She laughs, tossing her hair over her shoulder. "You would have been bored out of your mind on this shoot without me."

She isn't wrong.

Another minute passes, she nudges me with her elbow. "So why don't you say much? You hate the sound of your own voice?"

I think about brushing it off, but she's watching me, waiting. No teasing, just curiosity.

"I guess I got used to keeping quiet," I say finally. "Growing up, if I had an opinion, it was better to swallow my words than deal with the fallout. You do that long enough, it sticks."

Her voice softens. "Well, that's the saddest thing I've ever heard. You've been stuffing all your words down, holding them in. You seem calm all the time, but one day you are going to explode. You're like a human pressure cooker."

I can't help the short laugh that falls from my lips. "Something like that."

She smiles. It's not her giant grin, just a small one. Makes me want to reach for her, trace the lines of her mouth with my fingertips.

"Well, I like when you talk. Even if it's just to insult me."

She gives me a bratty look and changes the subject to her cat's Instagram followers, but the way she said she likes to hear me talk sticks with me.

The truth is, I've talked more to her this week than I have to most of my friends in the past year. She makes it easy to talk. The way she throws herself into everything, every story, every joke, every thought. It should be exhausting, but it isn't. I can't get enough of it.

***

THE NEXT MORNING, I beat Liz to set. An hour after we parted ways last night, I watched her walk across the parking lot and meet up with her friends and a pack of male extras in the hot tub. I watched from my window longer than I care to admit. After a while, I felt like a creep and forced myself to turn on the TV.

I wanted to storm out there and clear the place like a lifeguard at closing time. Which is completely insane. I know. But the way she's worked herself into my routine, into my head, has me off balance.

While I wait for her to arrive, I sip my coffee and think about how I still need to ask her to come to the gala. Every time I started to bring it up this week, I chickened out, or she launched into an insane story. I was all too happy to listen to her talk, to put off asking her to do this for me.

I've considered faking an illness to get out of the gala, but without a doctor's note, I doubt that would fly with my mother. She'd probably call the doctor herself to verify.

There's no way I can get out of it. I can only hope that she agrees to go with me. Pretending to be my fake girlfriend feels just crazy enough that Liz should agree without a problem.

Over the past week, I keep circling back to that phone call I overheard and the way Liz shut down when I asked about it later.

Sitting here now, slowly sipping my coffee and waiting on her, I can't stop wondering who she owes money to, or how much.

Maybe I could offer to pay her to pretend to be my girlfriend for the gala?

It's not a half-bad idea.

Liz busts in, out of breath and wild-eyed. She jumps when she sees I'm already there. "Holy snakes, Natey-cakes, you gave me a heart attack."

"Morning." Her reaction hits me again, the flinch, the automatic defense, and I clock it like I have every day this week. Not paranoia. Conditioning. It's another thing I need to figure out.

She's subtle about it, but her hand automatically reaches for her keys with the mace attached every time she startles. I keep my movements calm and slow until her breathing slows.

"I overslept this morning." I don't even try to hold back my eye roll. Maybe if she didn't stay in the hot tub for half the night laughing her ass off at whatever the stupid extras were saying, she wouldn't have overslept.

"Thankfully I heard you fire up your motorcycle this morning, or I would still be snuggled up with Hulk snoozing."

Well damn, that's an inviting image. Lucky cat.

I'm not sure when my thoughts about her switched from annoying me to death with her chatter, to craving her words, her touch, daydreaming about lying in bed with her and a stupid cat, but here we are.

She sets up her stuff and gets to work. Our conversation flows this morning. I don't know where Becket is, but I'm grateful it's just the two of us today. Once she's almost done, I decide it's time to man up and ask her to be my fake girlfriend.

I shift uncomfortably in my chair, wipe my palms on my pants, and clear my throat. I haven't been this nervous since I was a teenager, hoping to score second base with my crush.

"Hey Liz?" My voice squeaks on her name. She pauses and looks at me with a worried expression.

"Yeah?"

I clear my throat again. "I was wondering if you could help me out with something in a couple of weeks?"

Her shoulders drop in relief. "Of course, Bestie. What do you need?"

"Uhh, I was wondering if you would attend a gala with me?"

She freezes, meeting my eyes in the mirror with a ghost of a smile. "Like a date?"

"No." I wipe my palms on my jeans. They are tingling with nerves. That's not like me at all. "Well, sort of like a date."

I'm almost thirty, I shouldn't be this worked up to ask a girl to be my pretend girlfriend, but her answer means more than it should. She borrows a move out of my arsenal and stares at me, waiting for me to go on. No wonder she always keeps talking, having someone stare you down is a very effective measure to get someone to keep chatting.

"The thing is, my parents throw a big gala every year. Unfortunately, my attendance isn't optional if I'm not working. This year, our break lines up for me to attend."

She still keeps quiet with a mischievous smirk on her face, and nods for me to continue. "So, uh, my parents usually try to set me up with a vapid Hollywood type," I trail off, drop my head into my hands, and mumble, "But this year, I kind of told them I had a girlfriend I was bringing."

The trailer is totally silent. When I finally grow a pair and look at Liz, she's wearing the biggest shit-eating grin. "Well?"

"Excuse me, sir, are you asking me to be your fake girlfriend?" She looks way too delighted. "Can't find a real date for the event?"

"Just answer the damn question, Liz. Can you be my fake girlfriend or not?"

She gasps, fanning her fake tears with one hand and clutches her chest like she's been proposed to with the other. "Boo-Bear, this is just so sudden. I don't know what to say."

I grab one of her brushes and lightly throw it at her. She breaks out in giggles. I'm glad my misery is entertaining to her.

"You're lucky I love dressing up and don't mind a little public humiliation."

She walks over to me, stands between my widespread legs, and stoops so her face is inches from mine. She loops her hands around my shoulders, and slowly moves them up my neck to cup my cheeks. "My dear grumpy boy-toy, I'd be honored to be your fake girlfriend."

She laughs again before dropping her hands and going back to straightening her station. Damn it if I don't miss her touch.

"Seriously, just tell me when, where, and what the attire is, and I'll meet you there."

I hesitate. "Uhh, about that. It's kind of for the whole weekend."

She turns slowly back around to face me. "Boo-Bear?" That seems to be one of her favorite nicknames for me.

"Yeah, Cricket?" I sound sheepish to my own ears.

"Where exactly is this event?"

Might as well rip the band-aid off. "It's in LA, but I'll take care of all the travel, clothing, everything." I fight a grimace. "Actually, my mother has already booked everything and will have racks of dresses for you at our hotel." I run a hand down my face. This has already gotten away from me.

"Nate!" Liz practically screams my name in laughter. "Sir, what in the emotionally stunted nonsense is this? How long have you been planning this before you actually asked me?"

I hit her with what I hope is a smile that will have her saying yes even though my whole plan is more than a little crazy. Maybe she is rubbing off on me? "Over a week?"

"You chicken gizzard. You should have asked me before now. We've only hung out every single day."

"Chicken gizzard?" I shake my head, trying to make sense of that one. You know what? It doesn't matter. "I know. I should have. I was trying to figure out a way out of it all. I couldn't. So, will you do it?"

"A chance to be your pretend girlfriend, play dress up in fancy dresses, and potentially embarrass you? You couldn't keep me away."

She smiles down at me. "So what's our story? How long have we been dating? Are we still in the stage where we sneak out of bed, brush our teeth, then sneak back into bed to pretend we wake up minty fresh, or are we peeing with the door open?"

"Do people really do that?" I ask.

"Which one?" She waves her hand and keeps talking. "Doesn't matter. Yes to both."

"Well, in that case, probably the latter." I groan and lower my head again, but she carefully places her hands under my jaw. I like how that feels. She slowly lifts my face to meet hers. With her standing and me sitting, we are almost eye level with each other. It's distracting.

"G.P.? Why do I have a feeling there is more to this than you are telling me?"

She still looks amused. That's a good sign, so I power on. "My parents, they kind of think we live together."

Her eyes widen in delighted surprise. "Nathaniel! Is that your real name? Actually, I don't care. Nathaniel Davidson Jones, you big fat liar."

"Not my middle name. In fact, that's not my real name at all." That confession gives her pause.

"Explain that last bit."

If we are going to do this, she is going to find out anyway, so I might as well tell her now and get it over with. I blow out a breath and keep going.

"My parents are George and Isabel Sterling." I cringe as she steps back. "My name *is* really, Nate Jones. Now. I changed it when I was eighteen, but I was born Nathaniel Sterling."

"Holy fizzly shizz." She backs up against the counter and rests her butt on the edge like her legs are giving out, and keeps staring at me.

"Nathaniel what Sterling?"

"Huh?"

"What's your real middle name?"

"Oh, it's Hamilton. Nathaniel Hamilton Sterling."

She is silent. It worries me when she doesn't talk. It's out of character for her to be quiet for so long.

"Liz, baby, I'm going to need you to say something. You are starting to freak me out."

"*Baby*? Are we already practicing being a boyfriend and girlfriend who live together?"

I didn't even think about the term, it just slipped out. Felt natural too. The kind of slip I'd usually lock down hard, but with her I couldn't.

Before I can address her question she goes on. "Your parents are Hollywood royalty and you are hiding out here as a stunt double?"

"Their life is not for me. I don't want anything from them or their world." I pause before pushing on. "They would like nothing more than for me to join them at the company, but I want nothing to do with all of that. I like my job, my life. All they require of me is to go to this damn gala when I'm able, that I see them twice a year, and talk to them once a week on the phone. If I do those things, they stay out of my life, for the most part."

She is still staring at me like she doesn't know what to think. "Listen, I know it's a lot and you don't have to do this. It's a big favor to ask. Think it over for the night."

And then I make the mistake of continuing to talk. "I could pay you, to make it worth your while."

That finally snaps her out of it. She looks pissed. And offended. Great.

"You will not pay me to do this. I do *not* need your money."

Her sentence is sharp, landing like a knife in my side. Still pretending she doesn't have a money problem and still doesn't want my help with it. Got it. I give her a small nod, swallowing my argument.

"I'm just trying to wrap my head around the fact that there is a lot more to you than I thought. It's like if you find out your best friend is actually a werewolf at night. A whole new side of you just opened up and I'm trying to reconcile Nathaniel Sterling with Mr. Grumpy Pants, the cat carrying stuntman, that I've come to know."

I huff a laugh, shaking my head. "I promise I'm no werewolf. Still the same guy. Though I could do without the title you just gave me."

She smirks. "Yeah, well, you earned it."

Just like that, she's back to teasing. Thankfully she doesn't stay mad long.

She shakes her head, a full smile finally tugging at her mouth. "You know what this means, right?"

"What?"

"I get to raid racks of designer dresses and embarrass you in front of your stuffy parents."

My chest loosens, just a fraction. Trust Liz to not make a big deal out of my biggest secret. Instead, she makes my personal hell sound like fun. Every time I tell someone who my parents are, it changes something. I can see it happen in real time. Eyes widen, tone shifts, the questions start. Then the careful curiosity turns into calculation. I've seen it too many times to count.

When I was twenty, still wet behind the ears, I dated an up-and-coming actress. I thought she actually liked me. We spent a few months together before I realized she knew exactly who I was from the start and was just using me for introductions, trying to work her way closer to my parents. That one stung.

Since then, I've kept things surface level. Nothing serious. Never anyone in the industry, but even outside of it, no one sticks. Conversations go flat. No spark, no depth. I'm usually bored after the first date. It's easier to keep things surface level when I know things won't work out in the end.

It's easier to stay on the edge of things. Safer. At least until Liz showed up with her messy bun, loud laugh, and that ridiculous cat. Her chatter holds my attention. She keeps me on my toes. I never know what she's going to say next, and half the time I'm not sure she does either. But I find myself waiting for it anyway.

The way she didn't even blink when I told her who my parents are, that was huge to me and she has no idea. No starry eyes, no questions, no looking at me like I'm a meal ticket, no mental math about connections I could offer. Just that same mischievous grin and another nickname I didn't ask for.

It's refreshing.

Chapter Twelve
Dowry Lists
Nate

I drop my basketball bag inside the condo door as my pocket buzzes.

Liz: Hey, Boyfriend!!

Liz is a handful. I don't know what prompted me to tell my mother my girlfriend's name was Liz. There are about a hundred different ways this could go sideways on me. Ever since we exchanged numbers before coming home she's been hitting me with ridiculous text messages.

Nate: Yes?
Liz: Wow. Just *wow*.
Liz: The passion. The fire. The sheer romance.
Liz: Honestly, Shakespeare has nothing on you, Boo.
Nate: Sorry. Yes, Cricket?
Liz: Swoooooon.
Liz: Okay, question for you.
Liz: Don't panic. It's not about babies or matching tattoos.
Liz: But if you're busy being broody, I can wait.
Liz: Really, not a big deal.

I've learned Liz is a rapid-fire texter. Could she send all her thoughts in one message? Absolutely. I would prefer it. But why do that when ten messages in thirty seconds is so much more *fun*?

Nate: Hit me.
Liz: Do you think I should see where *we* live before we fly out to meet your rents?
Liz: Like, what if I gush about all the natural sunlight in our home...

Liz: ...and then find out you actually live in a cave.
Liz: Or worse. You live like a frat boy.
Liz: With bean bag chairs and like... three different gaming consoles.
Liz: And a mysterious smell no one can identify.
Liz: Or maybe you live in a bunker?
Liz: That seems like it would fit, actually.
Liz: OMG!! You do, don't you?
Liz: Tell me the truth.

I ignore her insanity, but it's not a half-bad idea. The more she's prepared, the less things we will need to make up on the spot. The less of a chance this ends in complete disaster. I don't see Liz being a very good liar, so I shoot her my address and tell her to come over at eight.

Liz: It's a date.
Liz: Can't wait to see our love nest.
Liz: See ya later, Snookums.

Yeah, this is going to be a dumpster fire.

***

Liz

Hours after I texted Nate, I find myself in a really nice part of the city staring at a large wooden door with the number seven on it. Lucky number seven. I could use a little of that magic.

I know I can act unaffected, or even slightly unhinged at times, but underneath the sparkly bravado, my stomach is doing backflips. I want people to like me, even my fake boyfriend's parents. I care, probably a little too much.

If I'm being really honest, and really dig deep, it's not about them at all. It's about him. I don't actually want to embarrass Nate. I want him to be glad that he asked me for this favor. I want to be someone he's proud to have standing next to him, even if it's pretend.

I wipe my sweaty palms down the sides of my dress and blow out a shaky breath.

I tell myself to relax. This isn't a big deal. It's just Nate. We've hung out for a couple of weeks now and I've been totally myself and he hasn't gone running.

After the disaster that was my last relationship, I promised myself I'd never change who I was for a man. That I wouldn't allow anyone to put me in a box or shrink me down. Yes, I am a people pleaser, but not at the expense of myself. Not anymore.

Nate has never tried to change who I am or asked me to be less. This is going to be fine.

I lift my fist to knock. One more slow, deep breath. Showtime.

Nate opens the door in a backward baseball hat, old T-shirt that clings to his chest, and gym shorts. Every ounce of tension I have reroutes itself straight to my pulse. His casual look works. It works so well.

Suddenly I feel silly that I was nervous at all. This is Nate. I've seen him quiet and reflective in the mornings. Slightly more talkative and caring in the evening. I've spent hours up close creating bruises and cuts on his body. Even though we haven't worked together long, I know this man, and I'm comfortable with him.

"Hi, Bear."

"Cricket." He pulls the door wider and steps aside.

Wow. The entry opens into a short hallway with a few closed doors that I fully intend to snoop through later, but the real showstopper is straight ahead. A wall of floor-to-ceiling black-framed windows set in exposed brick, framing the Atlanta skyline like a painting. Whoa.

It's hard to drag my eyes away to take in the rest of his space. The whole middle section of the condo is one big living, dining, and kitchen area. Sophisticated, but not magazine perfect. The couch sits low to the ground, but it's deep. I want to snuggle up with an art project right in the middle of it. A sleek high-top dining table that seats eight anchors the space behind his couch. Nate doesn't strike me as the dinner-party type, but it's gorgeous. Behind it, a chef's kitchen gleams, all clean lines and dark finishes.

His place is beautiful. Dark metals and natural woods woven throughout, gas lanterns hanging on either side of the TV, giving the whole room a moody, warm glow.

"Up to your standards?" Nate's voice comes from close behind me. I didn't even hear him move.

I glance back at him over my shoulder. He is standing there looking entirely too adorable for someone who also looks strong enough to murder you with their bare hands. He shifts from side to side.

Is he self-conscious about having me in his space?

"It'll do, I guess." I pause, tapping my chin. "I mean, if we knock out a wall or two and add a disco ball, we could really elevate the vibe."

"Disco ball?" he sighs.

"Don't knock it 'til you've danced under one, G.P."

The corner of his mouth twitches, and I swear it's a near-smile. Score one for chaos. Then, because I can't help myself I rub my hands together and add, "Now, let's see where the magic happens."

He throws his head back and mutters under his breath, "Why is this my life..."

When his eyes come back to mine, he tries for annoyed, but there's humor lurking there.

"After you, *Darling*." Oh my word, is he going to play my pet name game? I've died.

"Lead the way, Lovey."

I follow behind him through a wide, but short, open-air hallway into his room. No door. Interesting.

His room is masculine. Dark grays, more exposed brick, more black-framed windows. No coverings anywhere, so the view is just as jaw-dropping in here as in the main room.

I wander around his space, dragging my hand along the dark dresser. His closet is simple and meticulously organized. He looks like he suffers from a slight case of OCD.

But the real showstopper is the bathroom. He has a wet room. I've only seen bathrooms like this on HGTV. There's a tub that sits behind the glass of the shower, in front of floor to ceiling windows. Am I seeing this correctly? Not one, not two, but three shower heads.

When I die, this is basically what I picture heaven looking like. Maybe there is a basket of puppies in the corner and a unicorn butler, but basically, yeah, this is what I picture. A whimper escapes when I notice the floors are heated and there's a towel warmer.

A huff of a chuckle echoes around me, reminding me I'm not alone.

"I assume that moan you let out, means you like it?"

"When I found out who your parents were, I knew you were rich, but I didn't think about it practically. Like, I didn't think about the fact that your condo would be drool worthy."

He snags my shoulders spinning me so we are eye to eye. "My parents are rich." He pauses to make sure I'm listening. "My parents. Not me."

His voice is steady, but there's something hard in it. "I saved for this place on my own." He hesitates, then continues. "When I chose to walk away from the life they mapped out, I knew it meant giving up access to their money, giving up my trust fund."

My eyes widen. "They just cut you off?"

He blows out a breath bringing his hands to the bill of his cap in a nervous gesture. "They like to call it *strategic persuasion*. They are trying to get their lifelong investment to fall in line the only way they know how." His mouth twists. "By dangling money in my face. So yeah. Financially, they cut me off. Unless I come work for them, or get married, I don't get a dime."

"Get married?" I blurt, enraged for him. "What is this, the 1800s? Why is that a stipulation for your trust fund?"

He scratches the side of his face, looking embarrassed. "I overheard them talking about it the first time I came home after I moved here and changed my name. They think a woman would find out who I am, what I could be worth, the life I could provide if I wanted, and push me back into their world. They assume no one would want me just for me, I guess. Maybe they are right. They probably are."

My jaw drops. Nate is looking down at his feet like he's embarrassed. Like he believes that utter rubbish. "So basically they're out there hoping for a gold digger daughter-in-law? Very progressive. Should we start drafting my dowry list now? Because I'm thinking goats, a llama, and maybe one of those fancy espresso machines."

His lips twitch, but he still looks sad.

"Seriously though," I meet his gaze head on, crossing my arms. "You are a catch. Just you. Not them. If I see your parents trying to barter you off like you're in some sort of Victorian husband catalog, I will absolutely stage a movie-level-worthy rescue. Probably with disguises. Fake accents. Smoke bombs. The works."

He laughs, short and rough, like he didn't mean to let it slip out. The sound makes my chest warm. Mission accomplished. I smile up at him and he slings his arm around my shoulder steering me back to the living room. "Thanks for the support."

His arm feels heavy, comforting around me. His scent burrows into my soul. I fall asleep with that scent wrapped around me every night in the form of his sweatshirt, but it's starting to fade now. Maybe a mix of his soap and detergent? I'm not sure, but someone should bottle that smell, STAT. It makes me feel safe.

When we pass through the living room, I realize there's another comforting smell I didn't catalog earlier. My eyes scan the space and land on the candle I made him sitting on the coffee table. It's lit, flickering softly, the wax already burned down past the halfway mark. It's been used. More than once.

Something about that knocks the air right out of me. He didn't just keep it out of politeness. He's *used* it. In his space.

Something about that tiny flame feels intimate, like proof that a piece of me has already found a home here, even if this is just pretend. The scent weaving through his place isn't just wax and oil, it's me. And the idea that he wanted it here, burning, makes my chest ache in the best way.

I want to live in this moment a little longer. Snuggled into his side. I don't want him to move his arm from around me, but as soon as we make it back to the kitchen, he does.

The loss of contact makes me feel off-kilter. It's ridiculous, really, how something as small as a touch can undo me this much. But standing in his kitchen, surrounded by the scent of my candle and the echo of his laugh, I realize I don't just *like* being near him. I'm starting to crave it. His calm, his warmth, his quiet steadiness that's already made a home in my bones. It makes all the chaos, all the noise in my head fade.

"I figured we could order dinner and try to build our story so we are on the same page." He looks down at me. "That cool?"

"Yup." Now who's the one without words?

Chapter Thirteen
Afternoon Pigeon
Liz

THERE ARE FIVE DIFFERENT Chinese dishes and a dessert I don't recognize spread across the coffee table between us. I couldn't decide what I was in the mood for, so Nate ordered everything I mentioned.

We've had plenty of late-night conversations on our walks, but this feels new. He's relaxed in a way I've never seen. No set lights, no crew, no scowls. Just Nate, barefoot, comfortable, and openly chuckling at something I said like it actually amused him.

For how quiet and grumpy he can be on set, he's softer here. More open. Not *talkative*, exactly, but he's teasing me back. Asking questions. Smiling.

I found one of those cheesy online quizzes to help us learn more about each other. The title alone made Nate roll his eyes so hard I thought they were going to fall out of his head. *If you can answer these questions, you're soulmates.*

I put my chopsticks down and rub my hands together. "Alright, let's dive in." I curl into his couch, tucking my feet underneath my body, and grab the quiz we printed out. I love that he has a printer in his guest bedroom slash office. Very grown-up of him. I also love that he refused to read the questions from my phone. He's like my grandpa.

I grab the sheet and clear my throat dramatically. "Okay, number one: If your partner was an animal, what would they be?" I glance up at Nate. He's already smirking.

"Easy. Cricket. Next." His answer makes me giggle.

"It's like they wrote this question for us. Obviously you'd be a bear."

I pass the paper to Nate. He grabs a pair of reading glasses off the side table and slips them on. Backward hat *and* glasses. Holy Moses. Is this some sort of joke? I think my ovaries just exploded. He looks stupid hot.

He hums low in his throat before reading, "What's the weirdest thing your partner has ever done when they thought no one was watching?" He looks up at me. "Am I supposed to guess or are you just going to tell me? We could be here all night, Liz."

I gasp. "You calling me weird?"

He scrunches his face like he's in pain and runs his hand through his hair, his bicep flexing. "Weird might not be the right word. It doesn't fully capture everything that you are. You're... well," He hesitates. "You're a whole category by yourself."

I slug him in his perfectly sculpted bicep. He chuckles and rubs the spot like it hurt. Cute. "I like to think I'm not weird, I just don't fit the mold that was cut out for me."

He hits me with a micro-smile. I have to force myself to focus or I'll get lost watching him wait on me to answer.

I put a finger to my chin, pretending to ponder. "What's the weirdest thing I've ever done? Hmm. My brother would say the weirdest thing I did was when Autumn and I rescued a coyote puppy."

He slow-blinks and relaxes back into the couch. "I'm sorry? You what?"

"There was this little dog in an alley. Well, puppy. Covered in dirt. No mom around that we could see. It looked terrified. So, I took him home, bathed him, and put up posters."

He's looking at me like he's scared of me, so I go on. "Animal control saw one of my posters and called. Turns out I kind of adopted a wild thing. Long story short, animal control came and got him, and Clem went to a rehab wildlife center. No one was harmed in my twenty-four-hour adoption. Unless you count my houseplants and one armchair."

"What the fuck, Liz? You brought a wild animal home with you."

I sheepishly duck my head. "He wasn't wild, wild. Clem was just a little misunderstood." I can relate.

He's staring like I've grown a second head, so I yank the paper away. "Alright, moving on." I flip to the next question. "Number three: What's my go-to coffee order?" I look up at him. He still looks horrified from the previous question, so I answer first.

"That's boring. You drink your coffee black like your soul. Next." I shoot him a grin so he knows I'm kidding. Mostly.

"Pistachio latte, extra shot."

My eyes widen.

"Don't look so surprised. We've worked together for a while now. I notice things."

I shouldn't be this touched that he knows my coffee order, but I am. The bar has been subterranean with men in my past, so someone paying attention? It hits. Little things like this matter more than I'd like to admit.

I need to get my heart flutters under control. I look back down at the paper, forcing my focus back to the game. "Okay, here we go. This is a good one. What's your partner's biggest irrational fear?"

He studies me a second too long. "People not liking you. You play it off with jokes and your quirks, but you care. A lot."

Well snicklefritz. I guess we are really going for it. Our eyes lock. The air between us shifting. "Yours is becoming the person your parents want you to be." He grimaces, but nods once, small and quiet. I hand the questions back, pretending I don't feel the weight of whatever just passed between us.

"Is your partner a night person or a morning person?" He reads smoothly, shaking off our serious moment.

"Oh, that's easy, I know this about you. You are a night owl. You are quiet all the time, but you are more grunty in the morning time. I can coax more words out of you in the evening."

He gives my knee a squeeze confirming my answer. Wait, when did we move closer together?

"What about you?" He asks. "Early bird or night owl?"

"Me? I'm more of some sort of afternoon pigeon. I don't like waking up in the morning and unless I'm doing something super fun, I pass right out at night. What can I say? I love my sleep."

"An afternoon pigeon?" He asks flatly.

"It's a thing, Nathaniel." He passes the paper back, but I catch the hint of a smile tugging at his mouth.

"What's the one item your partner would grab in a zombie apocalypse?" I read, delighted. "This is fun. You're grabbing your motorcycle and getting the hell out of Dodge."

"A zombie apocalypse? What kind of list is this? Who thinks about these things?" He goes to grab the paper, but I move it out of his reach.

"Easy. Me. I think about these things. I know what I'm grabbing and it will save the world." I grin.

"Alright, I'm regretting this already." His face looks like he's bracing for the worst. "What is it?"

"A bag of flour." I puff up, proud.

"A bag of flour? You gonna bake for the zombies so they don't eat you?" He asks in disbelief.

"No, genius. I'll throw it at them." I demonstrate with a theatrical toss. "It'll coat them. Blind them. Buy me time."

He stares at me, incredulous. "You... what?"

"Think about it. They are zombies. I'm sure they are sticky, gooey, and pretty much all around disgusting. But if I have a bag of flour, I can throw it on them. It will stick all over their bodies, their faces, and blind them so I can get away."

He looks up at the ceiling like the universe is mocking him. He seems to do this a lot when I'm around. For some reason it brings me joy. "And this is who I chose to be my fake girlfriend? We are doomed."

I kick his hip, and he rips the questions away, grumbling under his breath that we're getting nowhere.

"Alright, serious one," he says, scanning the list. "How does your partner usually handle stress?"

My stomach tightens. Some of these questions don't feel so fun.

Nate doesn't miss a beat. "My partner pretends everything is fine. She tries to handle everything on her own and acts like she doesn't need help. Even when people *want* to help her, she won't lean on anyone." He looks at me pointedly. "How'd I do?"

I huff. "Fine. And my partner runs away when he's stressed. C-minus on healthy coping mechanisms."

"Fair," he says, voice low but with the hint of a smile. "At least we're self-aware."

He reads the last one: "What's something small that makes your partner really happy?"

I grin. "Oh, I can answer this one about you. Watching people trip and fall. You give off strong 'I thrive on the downfall of others' energy."

That earns me a quick, quiet laugh. "You're not wrong. That would probably make me smile. Especially if it was Becket."

That makes me cackle. Then he smiles at me. Soft and slow. Not the guarded smile he lets slip on set before he keeps talking. I'm done for.

"This is easy for me to answer about you too. You find happiness in everything. Doesn't matter if it's a dog sticking its head out of a car window or a stranger holding the door for you. Small or big, you find the good." He pauses, eyes still on me. "And you make other people want to do that too."

Heat blooms in my chest. I grin, stupid and giddy, which makes him look like he might roll his eyes, except he doesn't. He only squeezes my knee again, gentler this time. His hand lingers, thumb dragging once, slow and deliberate, before he pulls away. I wish I would have worn shorts so I could feel his skin against mine.

The weight of his words linger, warm and dangerous, fluttering around in my heart. I suddenly don't know how to act. I clear my throat and blurt, "Well, now that we've confirmed we're soulmates, and I'm ready to meet your parents, should I pick out matching pajamas or do you want to?"

His mouth twitches. "We are fucked if you think I'll be wearing matching pajamas with you."

"Don't you worry, me, you, and Hulk will be twining in no time."

Chapter Fourteen
Breakfast Chaos
Nate

I wake with a start to what sounds like a herd of elephants in my kitchen. And they're singing. Badly.

After we finished peppering each other with the world's most random questions, Liz insisted we watch rom-coms with the fake-dating trope "for research." Who knew that was even a thing? She made it halfway through *The Proposal* before she fell asleep curled up on my couch. I thought about moving her to the spare room, but honestly that bed kind of sucks and she looked comfortable. I covered her with a blanket and passed out in my own bed.

I scrub the sleep from my face, pull on a T-shirt and sweatpants, and head toward the noise.

Liz is in the kitchen, earbuds in, spatula microphone clutched in her hand as she watches bacon sizzle on the stovetop. She's still in her dress from last night, hair piled on top of her head, one strap sliding down her shoulder. Her hips sway to the beat, completely lost in her own concert.

It's not a bad way to wake up. Minus the screeching.

She spins mid-song and spots me, gasping like she's seen a ghost. The spatula goes flying, smacking me in the chest, while she hits the deck like I just lobbed a grenade at her.

"What the hell, Liz?" I swipe half-cooked eggs and bacon grease off my face and hurry toward her. She's sprawled on the floor, hysterically laughing as she yanks out one earbud.

"For a bear, you sure move quietly. I almost peed on myself."

I grip her elbows and haul her to her feet. "Could it maybe be because you were blaring music and singing at the top of your lungs?"

"Hmm, that could be it." She squints at me, trying not to laugh. "Or maybe you're secretly an assassin. You give off stealthy vibes."

Not five minutes after I've woken up she already has me laughing. It's odd. Not bad odd, just different. She steps closer and tilts her head. "Hold still." She reaches up without hesitation. "You've got something right there."

Her thumb swipes at the mess on my cheek, smearing it worse before finally wiping it away. She skates around the edge of my mouth, cleaning the last of the mess. I fight the urge to turn my head and playfully nip at her fingers.

"Smooth," I force myself to say dryly, and reach for a paper towel.

She grins, unbothered. "You're welcome. Breakfast and a facial, two for the price of one."

I glance around the kitchen, noting the dozen half-used paper towels scattered like confetti. "Liz, why are there paper towels everywhere?"

I walk around the kitchen, picking up all the litter. There's a balled up towel by the stove, near the trash, on the table. Some wet, some have food pieces on them.

I can't help myself. It's muscle memory at this point. Growing up, noise and mess were offensive to my parents. Everything had to be quiet. Neat. Perfect. My nannies and I used to spend hours cleaning up after a day of playing so no one got in trouble. Now, if my place isn't in order, that old anxiety crawls back up like it never left.

Our eyes lock as I nudge the trash bin open with my foot. I don't say a word as I drop them in. The lid snaps shut with a satisfying clang.

She lifts a brow, lips twitching. "Okay... guess we're not environmentally friendly here."

"Is that what you're going with? Environmentally friendly, instead of what's actually happening here. You used a paper towel, weren't close enough to the trash so you tossed it on the counter instead?"

"Hmm, that could be it." She answers back, smirking as she flips the bacon. Totally ignoring the crazy way I went on a mini cleaning spree.

I step closer, leaning over her shoulder to see what she's cooking. The smell of bacon and coffee hits me, warm and familiar.

"What exactly am I looking at here?" My voice comes out lower than I mean for it to.

She smooths a hand over her messy bun, suddenly sheepish. "Well, you bought dinner last night, so I thought I'd make breakfast before I go."

She says it like a question. Like she's not sure if she's overstepped.

The thing is, I don't want her to feel that way. I want her to feel like she belongs here. Like she can sing into spatulas and cover my counters in bacon grease and paper towels whenever the hell she wants. I want to pull her back to the couch, get tangled up with her, and waste the day on stupid movies.

Instead, I clear my throat, "Breakfast is perfect. The morning sing-along, though? That I could do without."

Her body relaxes and she hits me with a smile over her shoulder. "I can do that. Probably. I'm not the best cook, but one breakfast, sans happiness, coming right up."

I'm close. Too close for my self-control this early in the morning. My thoughts slow down and my pulse picks up. She smells like sugar and sleep, and it's doing things to my brain I don't want to unpack.

I roll my eyes to hide how much I want to pull her into me and move to the coffee pot to pour a cup. I grab plates and silverware before opening the balcony doors. I've got a small table out here, and I like having coffee outside when I'm home.

Heading back into the kitchen, I help Liz grab all the food she's made. Her music is playing through her speaker now, and she's quietly singing under her breath. She looks good here. Like she belongs. I've got to cut that shit out immediately. I can't be anything more than friends with her, I need to shut that line of thought down.

"Follow me." I grunt. She happily follows me.

"Oh my." She breathes out as she sets the food down on the table. "This was not part of the tour last night."

"I didn't think about it. I enjoy it out here in the morning best." She sits down and takes a sip of her coffee that I made for her. I didn't have her preferred creamer, but I did the best I could.

She moans, her eyes rolling back into her head, making me have all kinds of thoughts I shouldn't. I clear my throat and subtly reach down to adjust my sweatpants. "It's not a pistachio latte with an extra shot, but it's what I could manage with what I had."

"It's perfect." She sighs. "Sorry I passed out and became an uninvited house guest last night. Usually I can't resist Sandra Bullock and Ryan Reynolds' love story. I think I'm still wiped out from our schedule the last few weeks."

I take in her face with the morning sunlight highlighting her features. There are small, purple circles under her eyes that I didn't notice a few weeks ago. I wonder for the millionth time if whoever she owes money to is giving her problems. Keeping her from getting a good night's rest. She hasn't brought it up, and I haven't overheard any more conversations. I keep trying to push the whole thing to the back of my mind, but it hovers at the edge nagging me.

We finish eating out on the balcony, talking about nothing important. Movies she's worked on. Her siblings. The time she got kicked out of a spin class for "excessive enthusiasm." She makes even the most ordinary stories sound exciting. I find myself laughing more than I have in weeks. It feels easy.

I don't notice the minutes slipping by. By the time we've scraped our plates clean, the sun's high in the sky, and she pushes back from the table reluctantly.

"Well," she says, brushing her hands down her wrinkled dress, "I need to go meet my girlfriends. And I should probably leave before your neighbors think you've got a squatter. I'll let you get to whatever it is you do on your day off."

"You mean before my neighbors start asking why I have a crazy woman serenading the bacon and throwing cutlery around like a weapon?"

Her grin is quick, mischievous. My favorite one. "Exactly."

She heads inside to grab her bag, and I follow. At the door, she hesitates, shifting from one foot to the other, like she's not sure what the protocol is here. To be fair, I'm not sure either.

Then she steps in for a hug. It's quick, awkward, her arms loop around my middle. Mine hover in the air too long before I let them settle across her back. I breathe in her scent and squeeze her a little tighter. My head drops to the top of hers.

Then she's gone, bouncing down the hall with a wink, a wave, and a "ta-ta" tossed over her shoulder.

In a week, we'll be on a plane together, pretending to be something we're not. I should be dreading it, but I'm not. As the silence stretches through my apartment, I know I'm already in trouble.

Chapter Fifteen
Happy Endings
Liz

After leaving Nate's, I head directly to meet Jenn, Autumn, and Chloe. The girls want to do a spa day. We've all been working so much, we haven't all gotten to hang out lately. I miss all of us together, going out, dancing, gossiping.

Unfortunately, the kind of spa day they wanted came with a price tag that made my checking account cry. So I volunteered to plan our spa day instead.

I'm the last to arrive. Shocker. I jump out of my car and give everyone hugs.

"Liz, I thought we were having a spa day?" Chloe says as she embraces me and looks around the strip mall that we are standing in front of, completely confused.

"We are!" I exclaim and gesture to the sign above us. It reads *Foot Massages* in faded red letters. It's sandwiched between a tire change store and a wing place.

The girls all exchange looks.

I beam and say, more confidently, "We *are* having a spa day!" I quickly usher them under the sign and through the front door. The faint smell of rubber and buffalo sauce hangs in the air.

"I know it's not like the fancy spas in town, but I promise this is going to be even better. It will be the best massage you've ever had." I pull Chloe in for a side hug. "It's going to be great!"

I'm not sure if I'm trying to convince myself or her. I haven't been here before, but it came highly recommended by my pizza delivery guy. He said his girlfriend loves it here.

The front portion of the building is used for foot and head massages. There's a row of people in various states of undress scattered all around the room. Admittedly, that's a little odd, but we aren't here for those services anyway. If I'm totally honest, it looks a little worn, but I need to sell it.

"This place has the best massages in town. Hidden gem. Cash only, no nonsense, all these ladies have magic hands."

Autumn whispers to Jenn, "Magic hands sounds... ominous."

Jenn mouths, *What in the ever-loving fuck is this place?*

Before I can answer, a tiny woman with the posture of a ninja appears behind the counter. "Hello! Welcome!"

"Hi!" I chirp. "I have us booked for two couples massages!"

"Couples massages?" Chloe parrots, eyes wide.

"Trust me," I say, patting her arm. "You and me are together. You've been saying we don't hang out enough since you got together with James. This is quality bonding time, sister."

Chloe stares at me like she's questioning every friendship choice she's ever made.

"Just one minute while we prep your rooms." The ninja darts off toward the back, but comes to a halt when the door chimes.

A gentleman, I'm using that term loosely, walks in. He has dart-y eyes, a slicked comb-over, and sweat rolling down his temple.

The ninja woman beams at him and bobbles her head, "Oh, yes sir. All ready for you. Head right back. Last door on your left."

I can feel the girls shifting behind my back. Autumn kicks the back of my leg. "How did you find out about this place?"

Luckily, I'm spared from answering when the woman returns to lead us to our rooms. At the threshold, all four of us stop. The "massage rooms" look like they are being held together by sheer willpower. The walls have cracks down them and are so thin we can hear the guy in the next room moaning like he's Monica from *Friends* getting a massage from Phoebe. There are bars on the ceiling.

"What are the bars for?" Jenn whispers.

Autumn's pale skin goes a shade paler. "Oh my God. It's like a red room." Okay. We will be revisiting that later, but I cheerfully explain, "They walk on your back and use the bars for balance." Luckily, Pizza Pete prepared me for that one.

Reluctantly, Jenn and Autumn cross into their room, and Chloe and I walk into ours. There's a hip-level partition with a massage table on either side and not much else.

I can hear Chloe start to undress and slide onto her massage table.

"Liz," Chloe violently whispers, "The sheets are see through. Like negative fifty thread-count."

"They're vintage," I say, picking up the corner of my sheet. Sure enough, I can see Chloe perfectly through it.

She glares. "I don't want *vintage* sheets during a massage. I feel like things are crawling on me."

The door handle jiggles for only a second before our massage therapists walk in. I dive under the threadbare sheets like I'm sliding into home plate. Chloe is already on her table. I see her hesitate before stuffing her face in the hole.

Her therapist asks, "CBD oil?"

"Oh. Um... will I still be able to drive after?" Chloe answers nervously. I have to slap my hand over my face to physically hold back my laughter.

The woman answers impatiently. "Yes. Or no." I'm confident the woman doesn't speak English.

"Or *no?*" Chloe squeaks.

Thankfully I'm already face down on my table, because I lose it. "Chloe, it's fine. Your muscles will just feel extra relaxed."

Autumn's voice floats through the paper-thin wall. "Jenn, are we in one of those undercover sting operations? Like, are there cameras?"

Jenn hisses, "If a news crew busts in here, I'll die."

Chloe snorts into the headrest. "If this ends with our faces blurred out on *Dateline,* I'm disowning you, Liz." She ends that sentence with a moan.

"Sounds like you are really hating it over there," I mumble dreamily.

Twenty minutes later, I'm so blissed out I'm melting. Faint oriental music plays in the background, but even with that going, it's been quiet for too long. "You guys. We should say something we're grateful for."

"Liz, no," Chloe groans, voice muffled by the headrest.

"I'll start," I whisper loud enough that Jenn and Autumn can hear in the room next door. "I'm grateful for sketchy spas, girlfriends, and the fact that I still have underwear on."

Autumn snorts. "I'm grateful you dragged us here, against all reason."

Jenn mutters, "I'm grateful we haven't been murdered yet."

There's a pause, before one of the therapists chimes in softly, "I am grateful too."

We all lose it, half laughing, half crying, while getting the best back massages of our lives. They may be offering *questionable side services* here, but these women are like mythical creatures. The best massage of my life. My back has cracked in ways I didn't know were possible.

After an hour, we stumble out looking half-drunk and fully reborn.

"Okay," Chloe admits. "That was incredible. Sketchy, but incredible."

"I told you!" I pump my fist. "We're relaxed, rejuvenated, and I'm only mildly worried that we're accomplices to something illegal. Perfect girls' day!"

Autumn groans. "You're lucky I can't feel my legs right now, or I would kick your ass for taking us there."

"On to the next stop!" I pick up my phone to plug the next address, it's only a few minutes away. But I also have a text from Nate. I can't hold my smile back.

Nate: How's girl day?

Liz: You ever been to a spa where you're 80% sure they are giving happy endings, but your soul leaves your body in the best way so it doesn't really matter what they are doing in the back?

Nate: Can't say that I have.

Liz: You're really missing out.

Nate: Do I even want to know?

Liz: It's probably best if you don't.

***

THE NEXT STOP ON our day of pampering is waxing.

Again, I don't have the budget for the true Brazilian spa experience, but there's a beauty school around the corner that does them basically for free. I've never gotten one before, but the girls always do, so I figured they'd appreciate it.

They're hesitant, but after our last stop mostly worked out, they follow me inside with minimal grumbling. At least this place has solid walls and smells faintly of coconut oil instead of hot wings and regret.

The lobby looks promising, clean, bright, lots of inspirational quotes about confidence and eyebrows being "sisters, not twins." I sign us in and announce proudly, "Four Brazilians, please!" like I'm ordering coffees.

The receptionist blinks. "All four of you?" That should have been sign number one.

"Yep!"

We're each assigned a student and escorted to separate rooms. I'm feeling brave, borderline cocky, until my therapist, a.k.a. instructor, comes in trailed by what appears to be half the freshman class. That should have been sign number two.

"Do you mind if a few students observe?" she asks sweetly.

"Of course not!" I'm channeling false confidence. "The more, the merrier."

It's fine, totally fine. I'm just lying basically naked on a table, legs butterflied, lady bits fully displayed. I keep my eyes trained on the ceiling tiles and squeeze the daylights out of the stress ball they provided, while six wide-eyed students crowd around like I'm their own personal science experiment.

The instructor gives the class an overview that I tune out. I focus on my breathing. "Are you okay if Cheryl runs your appointment? She's one of our best students."

"Yep! No problem. Sounds perf!" By the time the first drop of hot wax hits my skin, I'm one deep breath away from a panic attack. I jerk so hard my back leaves the table.

"Too hot?" Cheryl asks while fanning my labia like she's trying to extinguish a candle.

The instructor peers down, nodding like a proud mentor. "Some clients have more sensitive skin. Try cooling the wax slightly before painting it on." They all nod and take notes.

Good ol' Cheryl slaps a waxing strip over what can only be described as molten lava on my hoo-ha, "Okay, deep breath."

"Oh my gosh," I squeak, dropping the ball and clutching the edge of the table.

My gaze drifts to the line of students, every single one of them looks like they just watched Bambi's mom die. Totally horrified.

And then she rips.

My life flashes before my eyes. Pain, white-hot pain sears my soul. I slam my knees closed, clipping the star student in the eyebrow. Two of the students cringe like they've just witnessed a crime. One girl's clutching her clipboard like a shield. Another's mouth is hanging open. The only male of the bunch looks so disgusted, if he wasn't gay before this, he is now.

I lower myself back to the table, the hygiene paper meshing with my sweaty skin, and against my better judgment slowly spread my legs again. "Everything okay down there?" I ask, voice strangled.

The instructor hesitates. "Uh... yes. It's just... she, um, used too much wax."

"What does that mean?" I try to keep my voice calm.

She exhales. "It means... this may take a minute."

Sweet mother of Mary, I was hoping it was almost over.

The instructor says, "You're doing great, sweetheart."

"Promise?"

She smiles. "Oh, I was talking to Cheryl. But yes, you're doing great too!"

"Is it almost over?"

"Mm-hmm. Trust me." She sing-songs as she taps Cheryl's shoulder, giving her the go ahead to continue.

She's a liar. An evil, soft-voiced liar. I should not have trusted her.

A ripping sound fills the room. I see stars. The clipboard girl faints.

When it's finally over, I wobble out into the hallway. What I've experienced can only be described as midevil torture. My soul left my body. My dignity packed a suitcase and fled. I'm pretty sure I'm bleeding. Chloe emerges a minute later, walking gingerly.

She points at me. "Never again."

Autumn limps past us. "We're never letting you plan spa day again."

"Fine," I say, wincing as I walk. "Next time, you plan." I'll take out another loan or something. Anything not to be in this sort of pain.

Jenn groans. "Next time, we're doing something safe, like manicures."

"Boring," I mumble. "No one ever passes out during a manicure." I wince. "Who is ready for the next stop?"

"No!" They shout in unison. Autumn grabs my hand, "We are going to our apartment to numb our pain with margaritas."

I wobble out to the parking lot. Sounds like a solid plan.

Liz: Pretty sure I lost a few layers of skin and my three best friends today.

Nate: Weren't you just having a spa day?

Liz: Spa day, going to battle. Tom-a-to – tom-ah-to.

Chapter Sixteen
Sweaty Cleavage
Liz

THE WEEK PASSES UNEVENTFULLY. I'm back to walking normally. Thank the Lord. We filmed at the in-town studio this week, but sadly Nate wasn't on my sheet. We still hung out, he even came to lunch with Autumn, Jenn, and me one day. He didn't say much, mostly just observed our insanity, but I think he enjoyed himself.

The girls were loving that I brought him along. I heard never-ending teasing about my new *boyfriend*. I didn't tell them we were dating. Fake or not. They just assumed since he came with us to lunch that we were. For once, I kept my mouth shut.

I just finished dropping Hulk off at their apartment. I would've asked Chloe to watch him, but since she's officially moved in with my brother, it's a no-go for them. James is highly allergic to my tiny best friend. He's taking allergy shots, so it's gotten a little better, but Hulk would still send him spiraling if he spent more than five minutes in their home.

My Uber driver pulls up to the curb at the airport. Am I nervous? A little. Should I be? Probably not. I don't think so. For how quiet and grumpy Nate is, he makes me smile more than anyone has in a long time. When we stayed up late quizzing each other and watching movies last weekend, it was the best night I've ever had with a guy friend.

And that's what we are, right? Sure, I have this undercurrent of attraction that hums along my skin anytime he is near, but I'm not sure if he feels it too. Sometimes I think he might. At the very least, he must like me enough to survive a whole weekend with me pretending I'm his serious girlfriend.

I have to admit I'm beyond curious about his parents. Of course I knew exactly who they were when he told me, but I'm around famous people all the time. So it didn't feel like that big of a deal, other than the fact that I had no idea they were his parents.

It shouldn't be too hard for me to see them as regular people. I'm more curious about them because of who they are to Nate, not because they are celebrities.

What kind of parents were they when he was little? What is their dynamic like now that he's his own person and out on his own? Do they hold his trust fund and the business over his head all the time? Is there going to be weird tension the whole time?

I stifle the small voice inside that rises up reminding my ex's parents were also industry royals and how badly that worked out for me. Nate isn't like my ex. And we aren't even dating for real. Nothing to worry about.

This weekend will be fun, or at the very least it will be interesting, but I live for interesting.

I can't deny I'm excited. The pampering, the shopping, the designer dress moment, it's giving *Pretty Woman*, minus the whole prostitute thing. A full day of being fussed over and pretending to belong among Hollywood elite without actually having to interact with them? Sign me up.

I grab my bags from the trunk, grateful I wore my cotton overalls. Less chance I'll face-plant or get tangled in a suitcase strap. I'm juggling a rolling bag, a tote, and a backpack that keeps sliding off my shoulder, scanning the crowd for Nate's tall, broody form.

Nothing.

I huff, pushing a loose strand of hair from my face. "Maybe he's late. Maybe he forgot. Maybe…"

"Maybe," a deep voice rumbles right behind me, "you should stop talking to yourself in public."

I yelp, spinning around, knocking my bags over at the same time.

"Geez, woman. What did you pack? We are only going to be gone for the weekend."

I can't stop the smile that spreads across my face when I meet his grumpy frown. "You know me, Pumpkin. Always be prepared."

"You look like you are *preparing* to move to LA." He grabs my roller bag and slings my carry-on over his shoulder without breaking stride.

Why is that hot? It shouldn't be hot. But it is. Maybe because the way he takes care of me seems effortless, like it's the most natural thing in the world.

I shake my head hard, trying to knock the thought loose before it takes root. I need to be careful not to blur the lines this weekend. This isn't Nate being sweet. It's Nate trying to move through the airport as efficiently as possible.

Still, I trail behind him like a lost puppy, grinning like an idiot the whole way.

We check our bags and join the security line. The slow crawl forward could test a saint, and Nate's patience is in short supply on a good day. I watch as his jaw ticks for the millionth time, his shoulders tight. I can feel the irritation rolling off him, and I have the sudden, reckless urge to lighten the mood.

"Hey, Honey-Bunny?"

He glances over, expression flat, but seems to convey "go on," without saying anything. Hmm. Not a fan of Honey-Bunny. Noted and absolutely will be using again later.

I lean in, but make sure my voice is just loud enough for the line around us to hear. "Babe, did you remember to take the handcuffs out of your carry-on this time? I really don't want to explain that to airport security again."

His head snaps toward me, growling out, "Liz..."

"Relax, Lover," I whisper, grinning. "Pretty sure TSA's seen worse."

The woman in front of us gives Nate a side-eye so sharp it could cut glass. She slowly positions herself between us and her adult child. I'm very much judging how she is coddling her man-child.

Nate pinches the bridge of his nose. "I'm going to kill you this weekend, aren't I?"

"Not in front of witnesses, you're not," I whisper back. "Even though your personality screams inmate, you'd be so mad at yourself if you went to prison for my murder."

We're in a stare down, me trying not to double over in laughter, him trying to give me his most stern look, when a TSA agent pulls him aside. "Sir, you've been selected for a random screening."

I bark a laugh and have to bite my lip to keep myself in check the entire time he gets patted down by an overzealous agent. He's wearing his perfectly beautiful scowl the whole time.

I can't resist, I take my phone out and snap a picture of him. When he shoots me a warning glare, I mime zipping my lips and drop my phone back into my bag. If looks could kill, I'd be a chalk outline by now.

When the agent finally waves him through, I'm patiently waiting for him on the other side, shoes back on, piles of our stuff at my feet.

"Don't." That's all he says. *Just don't.* I have to physically slap both hands over my mouth to keep from cackling out loud.

Nate grabs my hand like he's afraid I'll get lost in the crowd if he doesn't. Which, fair. We hurry to board the plane train to take us to our concourse, it's packed, per the usual. Atlanta's airport is one of the busiest in the world.

We make it just in time, Nate pulling me on board right as the doors close at my back. The car is standing-room only. There isn't even a pole to hang on to for balance. Honestly, I wouldn't touch it anyway. Have you seen those videos where people's butt cracks eat the pole while they lean against it? Hard pass.

The problem is, with how crowded it is, I can't spread my feet wide enough to balance. The train lurches forward and so do I. Right into Nate's back.

He stumbles, dropping our luggage, arms pinwheeling, and crashes forward, straight into a very well-endowed woman's bust. I watch in slow motion as his face disappears into her sweaty cleavage.

The woman gasps, clutching his shoulders. I can't tell if she's holding him there or pushing him away.

I choke down my laughter and reach to help him up just as the train jerks to a stop.

My hand misses his arm completely. Our carry-ons get tossed around the car like tiny pinballs, and I go flying, straight into the guy next to me. Who just so happens to be holding a scalding cup of coffee. The entire cup sloshes down Nate's back as he's still drowning in the poor woman's cleavage.

With scalding coffee searing his skin, his back arches, freeing his face from the woman's bosom with a suction sound.

He flails, trying to regain his footing, but slips in the puddle of coffee, crumpling in a heap at my feet. Nate jerks upright, red-faced and mumbling apologies while I wheeze into my hand.

"That was so smooth, Bear," I manage, tears in my eyes. "If you were interested, all you had to do is say. I'm willing to share. I would have given y'all some time alone."

He glares at me. "Not. Another. Word."

I can't contain my glee. My cheeks hurt from holding in laughter. When we finally reach our concourse, I stop him near the bathrooms. "Hold on. I have a shirt you can change into. You can't be comfortable."

I rummage through my carry-on. "Ah, here it is." I proudly hold up a spare T-shirt.

He looks at it like I've just pulled a live snake from my bag. "What are you suggesting?"

"Oh, I don't know," I say, still laughing, "that you change out of your sticky, coffee-covered shirt into a nice dry one so you aren't miserable the entire flight."

His eyes narrow. "And that's the shirt you're offering me?"

"It's the only extra I see being offered. So, yes."

It's a sparkly pink shirt that says *Hot Mess Express* across the chest in glitter. It was supposed to be my airport outfit before I decided to look like a semi-responsible adult.

He stares at it for a long beat. "You have got to be kidding me."

"I mean, unless you'd rather spend the flight sticky and smelling like burnt coffee."

He lets out a long breath, snatches the shirt out of my hand, and pivots toward the restroom without another word. I have my camera ready for his exit.

When he finally emerges, I find that I am in fact *not* ready. Seeing six feet of broody man poured into my sparkly shirt, tight enough to test the limits of cotton, is possibly the funniest thing I've ever witnessed. Even funnier than Nate unwillingly motor-boating the woman on the train.

He doesn't even look at me, just scoops up our bags, grabs my hand, and starts power-walking toward the gate like he can outrun the humiliation. We walk in silence through the terminal before he drops into a chair at our gate, legs stretched wide, arms crossed, giving off big *do not approach* energy.

I plop down next to him, grinning. "You look great."

He just glares at me.

"So, do I need to check you for third-degree burns or..."

"Liz."

I giggle and start scrolling my phone, trying to figure out how many different shots I can sneak of him in this shirt.

Then I come across the photo I snapped of him with the TSA agent.

"The perfect photo," I say, turning my phone toward him.

He groans when he sees his irritated face that fills my screen and a TSA agent kneeling before him patting down his legs. The angle makes it look like he's performing a personal favor, not a pat-down.

"That's not an appropriate photo for your phone's album. Delete it."

"You're absolutely right." I pause to admire the photo, "It's the perfect screen saver."

He exhales slowly, eyes closing like he's counting to ten.

I rest my elbow on our shared armrest, my chin in my hand, and stare up at him. "Never in my entire life has something even remotely close to what just happened back there happened to me."

He silently stares down at me before closing his eyes again. I can only assume he's pretending I don't exist.

"Come on," I nudge his leg with mine, "that was sort of fun, if you overlook the part where that woman's boobs almost suffocated you."

Still nothing.

"I think deep down, you sort of enjoy chaos," I say, leaning into his shoulder.

He cracks one eye open. "Deep down, I enjoy silence."

"Hmm. Then you really made a poor life choice inviting me along."

"Starting to realize that," he mutters.

Yup. He loves me.

I chuckle and stand to grab plane snacks. Nate waves me off when I offer to get him something. Trashy magazines, peanut butter M&Ms, and balsamic vinegar chips in hand, I make it back to the gate just as the agent calls our group.

Nate stands and grabs both of our bags before I can. "Cutting it close, Cricket."

"We're about to be trapped in a tin can for hours. I'm in no hurry."

He gives me a look. "Do you hate flying? I should've asked."

That's oddly thoughtful, if a little late. "No problems here, Boo-Bear. I'm the perfect flyer. I just love all the people you can meet when traveling. Learning where they're from, where they're going. I've made some great friends on planes."

"Of course you have."

When we finally board, the gate agent scans our tickets, pausing to glance at Nate's chest.

Her lips twitch. "Cute shirt."

I lose it completely, snorting as Nate clenches his jaw and keeps walking down the jet bridge like a man headed for execution.

Once we're seated, I lean over and whisper. "Are you a talk-during-takeoff or a headphones-and-ignore-me guy?"

He doesn't even blink. "What do you think?"

"Perfect," I say, buckling in and giving him my most mischievous grin. "Talking during takeoff it is."

He groans quietly as I launch into a stream of chatter about snacks, seatbelt signs, and why airplane windows are the perfect metaphor for emotional distance. But somewhere between the takeoff, turbulence, and complimentary pretzels, I catch him watching me. Not annoyed, really, just watching.

Eventually, my words slow, the hum of the engines and the soft buzz of conversation fill the space between us. His hand rests loosely on the armrest between us, fingers brushing mine with every bump of the plane.

I glance over. His eyes are closed, but there's a faint smile tugging at his mouth. The kind that looks unguarded, peaceful.

Without meaning to, I match his stillness and drift off.

Chapter Seventeen
Relationship Upgrade
Nate

Liz's head rests on my shoulder, her hand fisted around my forearm like I'm her personal anchor. About two hours ago, her words finally ran out and she passed out mid-sentence. I've been sitting here in the silence, pretending not to notice the way she fits perfectly against me.

I replay the whole morning in my head. It was like watching a slow-motion train wreck I couldn't stop. Even with changing into Liz's ridiculous T-shirt, my back's sticky from the guy's coffee, and I'm ninety-nine percent sure I need to disinfect my face from the woman's cleavage.

I almost let myself forget the kind of chaos Liz brings with her. Most days she seems *almost* completely normal. A little extra, maybe, but not totally unhinged.

If I had experienced this morning with anyone else, I'd still be fuming.

But Liz?

Her absolute delight over the entire fiasco made it worth it.

Sort of.

I stare out the window, watching clouds slide by beneath us, and for the first time since I came up with this whole fake-girlfriend charade, I start to wonder what the hell I've signed us both up for. A weekend with my parents, surrounded by people who measure worth by the size of their bank accounts and the headlines attached to their names.

I can't begin to imagine how my mother will react meeting Liz. Or how Liz will react meeting my parents for that matter. Maybe that's what I should be more worried about. I glance down at her again. Even though I feel concerned about the weekend, the idea of that gala doesn't feel like a cage this year. With Liz with me, it will be tolerable. She'll probably manage to shock half the guest list before dinner's served.

Still, I can't shake the feeling that bringing her into that world might be a mistake. My family eats people alive without even meaning to. And Liz, bright, messy, unpredictable Liz, doesn't belong in their world.

Then again, neither do I.

She shifts in her sleep, muttering something about snacks, and I can't help the corner of my mouth from lifting. Maybe this weekend won't be a total disaster.

I spend the rest of the flight lost in thought until Liz jerks awake the moment the tires hit the tarmac. She's blinking like she's not sure where she is. Her hair's a mess, one strap of her overalls hanging off her shoulder. Her big blue eyes blink up at me in confusion, and I reach down to brush the loose strands from her face. The smell of her shampoo drifts up, sweet and distracting.

"We made it?" Her voice is scratchy from sleep.

"Yep, Cricket. We're here."

She hums, half-asleep, and rests her head back on my shoulder like she's not quite ready to join the land of the living.

When we come to a stop at our terminal, I give her a nudge. "Come on, Sleeping Beauty, let's get you a coffee."

She unwinds herself from my side and stands to grab her luggage, but I beat her to it. She lets me lead her through the airport, to a coffee kiosk, then to baggage claim. Either no one notices my T-shirt or no one cares, because not a single person gives me a second look. Which is shocking, considering I'm a grown man walking through LAX in a sparkly pink shirt that says *Hot Mess Express*.

We snag our bags and turn to grab an Uber, but are greeted with a limo driver holding a sign that reads *Nathaniel Sterling and Guest*.

Subtle, mother.

Liz thinks it's hilarious and amazing, of course, and squeals like she's just spotted Santa Claus. The driver helps us load the luggage into the limo while she chatters nonstop, now wide awake thanks to the shot of caffeine. I give him the hotel address and sink into the seat, already fantasizing about peeling myself out of this sparkly skin suit parading as a T-shirt and standing under a scalding shower to erase the morning from hell.

I managed to beg out of the pre-gala festivities tonight, so Liz and I have the day to ourselves.

We make it to the hotel and approach the front desk. I already know what's coming, but I managed to block it out until now. I cringe before the words leave my mouth.

"Checking in for Nathaniel Sterling." Heaven forbid Mom use my legal name and let me live my life under the radar.

"Ah, yes, Mr. Sterling. Welcome to Los Angeles." The man's accent is heavy, but I can't place it. "We have you and your fiancée in the premier suite. I hope it is to your liking."

Yup, there it is.

I catch Liz raise a shocked brow, but mercifully she doesn't utter a word. I take our keycards and we head across the lobby, the bellhop trailing behind.

"Come on, future-husband." Liz tucks her arm through mine. "The elevators are this way."

We ride up in silence, and thankfully make it to our room without any more disasters. As soon as the door clicks shut behind the bellhop, Liz rounds on me.

"Boo-Bear?"

"Yeah?"

"Since when did we upgrade from living together in sin to being engaged?" I open my mouth to answer, but she barrels on. "The one hotel room, I could have predicted. I've done my fake-dating homework. This was bound to happen, but engaged?"

"Yeah. About that." I scratch the back of my neck. "My mom called a few days ago, still trying to push another woman on me, and I may have mentioned things had gotten more serious between us."

Her eyes narrow. "More serious?"

Even with her narrowed gaze, she doesn't look mad. That's got to be a good sign. "More serious, like I told her I proposed and we're getting married soon?"

It comes out like a question. I'm bracing for anger, but instead Liz collapses in a fit of laughter, flat on the bed, *our* bed for the next two nights.

"Are you having some sort of psychotic break?"

She sits up, wiping tears from her eyes. "It's just amazing how you continue to leave out *really* important information until the last possible second."

"So, just to be clear, you're not mad?"

"I'm not mad," she says, grinning. "You are absolutely insane. Maybe crazier than I am. You know we're going to have to bring our A-game tomorrow if we're going to convince anyone that you actually want to marry someone like me."

I open my mouth to respond, but she's already flopping back on the bed, giggling to herself. I'm annoyed that she added *someone like me.* Who wouldn't want to be with her?

Before I can say anything, Liz sits up again, pressing a hand to her chest. "Okay, new rule," she says, pointing at me. "If we're upgrading relationship statuses, I need to know beforehand."

I lift a brow. "A rule, huh?"

She hesitates, thinking, "Actually that's not a bad idea. We should come up with some rules. Just so we don't blur things." She swallows. "I'm not great when lines start getting smudgy."

"Okay." I settle beside her. "Rules like what?"

She immediately lifts a finger. "Officially, Rule one: no surprise relationship upgrades. If we're jumping from fake-girlfriend to fake-fiancée to fake-wife, I need a heads up. A sticky note. A smoke signal. A skywriter if you're feeling fancy."

I huff a laugh. "Deal."

"Rule two," she continues, warming up now. "No lying. Lying by omission counts too. I want to know all the things, so I'm not blindsided."

"Fair."

She nods decisively, then points at me again. "Rule three: no unnecessary touching or PDA."

My brows lift. "Unnecessary?"

"Yes," she says quickly, eyes widening. "If it's for the show, fine. But I need warning. Like, three seconds. Minimum."

My mouth curves before I can stop it. "Three?"

"Maybe five," she mutters. "I know myself. I'm a touchy-feely kind of person. If I have free reign to touch you whenever, things are going to get smudgy fast. And that's not what we want, right?"

I don't answer her right away. I'm frozen picturing her having free reign to touch me whenever she wanted. What would that be like? Her cheeks turn bright pink and she straightens, clearly embarrassed. My extremely long pause isn't helping.

"Right. That would be bad."

"Okay. Rule four," she says loudly. "No catching feelings."

I go still. Obviously I knew why she was creating rules, but does she think she's going to fall for me? Is she worried I'm going to fall for her and she's repulsed by the idea?

She acts like it is a joke, but something flickers in her eyes. It is small and fragile and she tries to cover it with a crooked smile. "Because that is how these things fall apart, right? Someone gets confused. Lines crossed. Bad decisions happen. And boom! Our brand new friendship is ruined. That is why we need rules in the first place."

There's a knot in my chest I don't know how to undo. Before I can think it through, I say, "Rule five."

She blinks. "There's a five?"

"Yeah." My voice comes out lower than I intend. "No more talking about yourself like you're the wrong choice. Like you're not good enough."

She startles, her mouth parting just slightly. "I was not..."

"You were."

Her gaze darts away.

"Someone like you," I echo her earlier words. "Don't say that again. Or anything like it. Don't imply that you are anything less than you are. Remarkable."

I glance down at the sparkly shirt I'm still wearing and pointedly look back at her. "Okay, remarkable *most* of the time."

She giggles, and the heavy moment breaks into something lighter.

She tucks her hair behind her ear. "Rule six," she says confidently. "We check in every night. Just to make sure we're still on the same page with our story and the expectations and... everything."

I nod. "Yeah. We can do that."

A beat passes.

"Oh, and rule seven. We can add or change the rules whenever we need to, as long as we both agree."

I squint at her. "Did you just use lawyer speak?"

She smirks. "I know things."

"That works for me."

"Okay," she says finally. She clasps my hand and gives it a shake, sealing a deal. "Rules in place. No confusion. No chaos. Totally clear."

I look at her. She looks back at me. Nothing feels clear at all.

"I am going to take a shower now."

***

Liz

While Nate showers, I settle in. The bellhop placed Nate's bag next to mine on the end of the bed. It's half open from him grabbing what he needed to bring into the shower with him. It's not snooping or breaking any rules if I'm helping him unpack. Right?

I clap my hands together in glee before I dive in. His clothes are meticulously folded and color coded. No fun surprises anywhere at all. Bummer. I carefully take his clothes and put them in the drawer next to mine. Yes, I'm an unpacker when I travel. I like to really settle in.

Our *premier suite* looks like something out of a magazine. The bathroom alone could fit my entire apartment. The sink area is separate from the shower area, so I line my toiletries up next to Nate's. It's oddly domestic to see our things together.

Steam curls out from the shower room, the sound of running water filling the space. I busy myself pretending to organize my makeup bag, definitely not thinking about him being totally naked on the other side of the door. That would smudge things for sure. When the water shuts off, I quickly swipe on a little lip balm like a lovesick idiot, hoping it'll somehow make me look more put together, and scurry away from the mirror. I'm definitely losing it.

He steps out in jeans and a T-shirt, with his hair still damp, and I melt a little. I swear the man has no right to look that good, but every version of him is better than the last.

"Unpacked already?" he asks.

"I always like to make myself at home when I travel."

He gives me a look. "You unpacked *my* stuff too, didn't you?"

I flash him my sweetest smile. "Just trying to be helpful, dear. Isn't that what good fiancées do?"

He mutters something about regretting everything, grabs his phone, and my hand, tugging me out the door behind him. Does grabbing my hand and pulling me along mess with our unnecessary touching rule? I think it's a gray area. Totally reasonable I think.

Chapter Eighteen
Nailed the Jealous Fiancée
Liz

We spend the day wandering LA. I've never been before. With the movie industry so prominent in Georgia, I've never had a reason to come. Nate humors me by hitting all the tourist spots. We've just finished at the Hollywood Walk of Fame, and now we are window shopping on Rodeo Drive when a high-pitched voice interrupts our conversation, "Nathaniel? Is that you?"

He freezes mid-step. Uh-oh.

A tall brunette in oversized sunglasses, a designer sundress, shopping bags dangling off her arms like trophies, waves at Nate like she's flagging down a taxi.

"Oh no," he mutters under his breath.

"Oh no what?" I whisper, already sensing drama. I. Am. Here. For. It.

"She's my mom's best friend's daughter. They set us up once."

Before he can protest, I plaster myself to his side just as she stops in front of us, all gleaming teeth and influencer energy.

"Wow, I didn't know you were in town!" She gives Nate's bicep a squeeze like she's checking the ripeness of fruit before her gaze lands on me. Her nose wrinkles. Apparently, I don't pass the Rodeo Drive dress code. "And this is...?"

Nate answers her. His tone harsh, but his frustration, for once, isn't directed at me. "This is Liz."

I beam. "Hi! So nice to meet you. I'm his fiancée." Instead of extending my hand, I run it up Nate's abs, landing on his chest for effect, and give her my best pageant-queen smile. This certainly qualifies as necessary PDA.

Her sunglasses slide down her nose. "Fiancée? I thought my mom said you weren't dating."

"Things change," Nate says flatly.

Okay, he could sell that line with more enthusiasm. I briefly consider going all in and kissing up his neck. That would *really* sell it.

She blinks and, because apparently I'm invisible now, turns back to him. "So, how are you? When are you moving back? My mom said your mom mentioned you might be coming home sometime this year for good."

Nate's expression shifts from semi-polite to I'd rather have all my nose hairs plucked out one by one. "I'm not," he says tightly. "I'm staying in Atlanta."

"Oh." She smiles. It's fake, just like her boobs. "That's surprising. Everyone always assumed you'd come back eventually."

She's completely ignoring me. First of all, rude. Second, she's clearly pissing Nate off. Third, I never let a perfectly good opportunity for drama go to waste.

Game on.

Before I can overthink it, I slide my hand from his chest to his jaw, turn his face toward mine, and plant a slow, smug kiss right on his mouth. No countdown necessary.

He goes rigid for half a heartbeat.

Then everything shifts.

His hand curves around the back of my neck, taking my pretend kiss and ramping it up. He deepens it, slow, steady, controlled like he's writing the rules now. Heat rushes up my spine. My brain forgets why I started it at all. The rest of the world blurs. Nothing exists except his mouth on mine and the steady, devastating way he kisses like he's got all the time in the world. The tip of his tongue swipes across my bottom lip and earns an indignant huff from Miss Rodeo Drive loud enough to register on the Richter scale.

It takes me a full second to register it, another to remember we are not alone, and a third before we reluctantly break the kiss.

Our eyes meet, his warm breath fans across my lips, my heart is sprinting.

Unfortunately, we have an audience and I can't figure out what exactly just happened. I spin in Nate's arms, my back to his chest. Standing on my own two feet without support feels impossible at the moment.

"Oh, sorry," I say sweetly, like I just remembered she existed. "He gets grumpy when people bring up moving. I've learned nothing pulls him out of a bad mood quicker than a little smooch. Isn't that right, Boo-Bear?"

She hums, clearly disgusted, like I'm gum on the bottom of her Louboutins. "So, how long have you two been together?"

My eyes widen and I panic slightly. We haven't rehearsed this. We both speak at once.

"Three months," he says.

"Six months," I blurt. I feel Nate's body stiffen behind me.

Her smile falters before it sharpens, sensing blood in the water. He wraps his arms around me tighter, pulling me more firmly into his body, like if he can cage my body in, maybe it will cage my mouth too.

"Feels shorter than six months," he says easily. "Time flies when you're in love." He sounds only mildly uncomfortable with that proclamation. It's probably for the best he doesn't have a job that requires saying scripted lines.

"Aw." I look up at him and grin sweetly. "Bear, that's so romantic." Then, for good measure, I trace my fingers up his neck to his ear. I'm aiming for flirty. Judging by how fast he swats my hand away, I landed somewhere closer to mosquito attack.

He looks down at me, eyes glinting. "You know me, super romantic."

"Yep, Lover, you certainly are."

The brunette clears her throat. "Well, it's been interesting to meet you. I guess I'll see you around, Nathaniel."

"Wouldn't count on it," he says, polite but firm.

She leaves in a cloud of perfume and attitude, her heels clicking on the pavement.

As soon as she's out of earshot, I drop the act and snort. "Three months? You couldn't even match me?"

"You said six!"

"Well, technically I'm not wrong if you count emotional months. It's like dog years."

He rubs the bridge of his nose. "There's no such thing as emotional months."

"There is now. Besides, it has to be believable. Who moves in together after only three months?"

He shoots me a look, half amused, half exasperated and ignores my question. "You know, for someone who just set a rule about limited touching and PDA, you sure did have your hands *everywhere*."

I grin, unbothered. "I commit to the bit."

"And the kiss?" His voice drops lower, rougher.

"Obviously part of the role," I say, way too fast.

He hums, clearly not believing me. "Good to know you take your acting career so seriously."

"Method acting," I say breezily, walking ahead of him before he can see my blush. "You should try it sometime."

My brain completely short-circuited. Method acting. Right. Sure. Totally. Except nothing about that kiss felt like acting. Or pretend. If that was acting, then someone needs to hand him an Oscar and someone needs to hand me a defibrillator because my heart is still doing parkour in my ribcage. I was supposed to rattle her, not unravel myself.

"If that was pretend, we're both in trouble." He whispers it behind me as he follows, like he's talking to himself rather than to me.

I don't know if I'm supposed to hear it or not, but I do. And it sends my pulse ratcheting higher, every nerve standing at full alert.

Chapter Nineteen
Very Different Algorithms
Liz

Hours later, my feet are sore from walking, my cheeks are sore from smiling, and my belly's sore from stuffing it full of ridiculously good food. Nate picked a restaurant that's quiet, tucked away, overlooking the harbor. The sunlight is turning the waves golden. It's perfect.

While we ate, we talked about nothing and everything. How I once tried to dye my hair pink and ended up looking like cotton candy, how he loves playing basketball, but never got the chance to play growing up because he was homeschooled.

He actually laughs, full and unguarded, while we polish off our dinner. I like that sound way too much.

By the time dessert shows up, I'm high on Nate Jones. The world feels small, warm, and good in a way it hasn't for a long time. All my worries fade when I'm with him. I don't think about the check that bounced when I tried to pay the debt collector last week. I don't think about what waits for me when we get back. I just think about how, when his gaze lands on mine, I feel like the most important person in the world.

When the check comes, Nate insists on paying. "Fake fiancé perks," he says.

I don't fight him on it. We linger over dessert a little longer and then walk back toward the hotel, side by side, not saying much. It feels comfortable. That is until we hit the elevator and I remember the fact that we are sharing a bed tonight.

Suddenly, all the tension in *one-bed tropes* makes perfect sense. We aren't really together. Nate hasn't shown any signs that he's interested in me beyond friendship. Unless you count that kiss from earlier. Which I don't. I initiated it. He was just playing a part. In fact, most of the time, it seems like he barely tolerates me.

This will be fine. Totally fine. I can ignore how hot he is and pretend we are just friends, and I want nothing more. Probably.

Nate swipes the hotel key, his forearm flexing.

Drool.

I need to escape. *Now.*

"Do you mind if I shower first?" I blurt, while I rush past him and into the room.

"It's all yours." He gestures with his hand and I sprint for the bathroom.

I take my time showering, brushing my teeth, completing a ten-step skin care routine. Anything to stall and shore up my defenses. Stupidly, I didn't really foresee the one room situation and didn't pack accordingly. Rookie mistake. All I have is a tank top with the words "Nap Queen" written across my chest in sparkly letters and tiny sleep shorts. Not exactly sexy, not that I'm going for sexy, but it'll do.

I tiptoe out, Nate's sprawled on the bed, one hand behind his head, eyes on his phone.

"Bathroom's all yours."

He looks up, takes in what I'm wearing. If he's surprised, he hides it well, and then he disappears into the bathroom. I climb into bed and try to figure out what I'm feeling. Was I expecting him to react to my tank top and tiny shorts? Maybe. Am I disappointed that he didn't react? Maybe.

I lie here in the silence listening to him move around in the bathroom, but my thoughts get louder than the sound of him getting ready for bed. It's too much for me, so I grab the remote, flipping channels until I find *Friends* reruns. My comfort show. Phoebe is my spirit animal. I love her so much.

Lost in the episode I barely register the sink cutting off. It's not until he's walking out in a gray T-shirt, flannel pants, and messy hair that's still damp that my pulse skyrockets. I immediately regret having eyes.

This is going to be fine, right? Just two platonic friends having a sleepover. TOT-ally normal. I slept over at his place just last weekend and it was fine. To be fair, I was on the couch a whole room away from him, and not feet away where I can smell his body wash drifting over to me like some sort of forbidden potion.

He slides into bed like we do this all the time. Completely unaffected. Since he's acting normal, I guess I'll force myself too as well. Or as normal as I get. I pick up my phone to doom-scroll and attempt to get a hold of my wild thoughts.

Soon I'm lost in the wonder that is social media. My body relaxes, my mind quiets. We lay in companionable silence, just the soft click of our scrolling and Monica and Chandler fighting in the background.

To my delight, my algorithm takes me down one of my favorite rabbit holes: famous musicians pulling kids up on stage mid-concert. Tiny kids. Brave kids. Teenagers who absolutely *own* it.

My chest tightens in the best way. This nine-year-old boy is shredding a guitar solo like he was born for it. My eyes sting, and I swipe at them quickly, letting out a happy chuckle.

"You okay over there?" Nate's voice rumbles low.

"Yeah," I sniffle, laughing at myself. "Sorry. I just love these videos."

He turns his body toward mine, propping his head on his hand. "What are you watching that's got you crying and smiling at the same time?"

Glancing at him, I see genuine interest on his face.

"Here," I say, scooting closer so he can see my screen. He rolls to his back and we end up sharing his pillow, our shoulders pressed together. I tilt the phone toward him and hit play again. On-screen, a young boy belts out the song like his life depends on it, every note raw and perfect.

"Rockstars that pull kids onstage during concerts. Look at him! He's crushing it. He's terrified and thrilled and completely unstoppable."

He watches the screen for a beat, then stares over at me and deadpans, "We definitely have very different algorithms."

I scoff, mock-offended. "Why, what's on yours? Let me guess. Motorcycles, workout videos, and..." I squint, pretending to think hard. "Half-naked chicks." If I'm honest, I can't picture Nate scrolling social media at all.

"You think my Instagram is half naked chicks?"

"Yep."

"That just shows you don't know me at all. We are screwed for tomorrow."

"Alright then, big guy, show me."

He picks up his phone and motions for me to come closer. Nate inviting me to snuggle in tighter with him? Yes, please! Rules? What rules?

I snuggle into the crook of his shoulder, his arm automatically wraps around me like second nature. I prepare to be unimpressed at whatever his phone populates.

Instead I'm hit with puppies. Lots of puppies. Puppies doing stupid stuff. Puppies with babies. Puppies falling asleep standing up. Puppies and baby ducks.

What the what? My mind is scrambled. My heart is complete mush.

"Holy mother of Mary. You *do* have a soul." I squeeze his side, causing him to squirm and he swipes my hand away with a grunt. Oh. Looks like Nate is ticklish. Filing that away for later.

"I'm going to regret showing you this, aren't I?" He swipes through to another video and a baby bulldog pops up chasing a toad. My heart can't handle the cuteness. I may explode.

"Why?" I don't have any other words, just why.

If he's uncomfortable, he doesn't show it. For once he answers without hesitation, without grunts.

"I don't use my social media. I don't want my parents knowing more about my life than they already do. I'm not going to make it even easier for them to interfere."

That breaks my heart for him. My relationship with my parents couldn't be more opposite. They are solid, they were great parents, good people. Sure, I overwhelmed them a lot when I was younger, and probably still do, but they never made me feel like I couldn't be myself. They always support me, and my siblings' dreams and encouraged us to chase them. They are salt of the earth kind of people.

For once I don't say anything. I pick up his hand and loop our fingers together. He looks down at our intertwined hands and smiles, not mentioning Rule Three.

"I always wanted a dog. I travel too much to make it happen right now. So instead, I enjoy them on here." He waves his phone.

"I love that this is what you do on social media."

He gives me a look. "You say that like I am doing something strange."

"It is a little strange. I mean, you look like the kind of guy who watches videos titled How to Survive a Bear Attack or Five Ways to Sharpen a Pocketknife."

He snorts. "That is oddly specific."

"Tell me I am wrong."

He pretends to consider it. "Maybe I do occasionally watch survival videos."

"I knew it. Meanwhile I am over here crying about brave children."

"So basically your algorithm is feelings and mine is puppies and hypothetical danger."

"Wow. We are really thriving."

His mouth curves slightly. "Apparently."

"You are full of surprises, Boo-Bear."

"Is that good or bad?"

"Good." I swallow. "Very good."

His eyes drop to my mouth for half a second, so quick I almost think I imagined it.

Then softly, "You surprise me too, Cricket."

My stomach flips like I am on a roller coaster. "Hope that's good."

"It is." His voice is warm. "It really is."

We waste another twenty minutes sharing videos with each other. Cute videos, funny videos, stupid videos, until I feel my eyes start to droop.

Nate gently takes my phone from my hand, plugs it in on his side of the bed, but doesn't let go. His arm returns, pulling me close, until my head finds its place under his chin. His heartbeat is steady against my ear, and it feels way too good for something that's supposed to be pretend.

"Hey, Boo-Bear?" I mumble into his shirt.

He groans softly. "I thought the talking part of the evening was over, Cricket."

"Just one question."

He sighs, resigned. "Shoot."

"Are we going to fall asleep snuggling?"

He clears his throat, "I figured since you were already over here, it made sense." He mutters, "Besides, it seems to have made your words slow down."

I turn my head into his chest, smile, and squeeze him a little tighter, "I guess if we are going to break the rules, we should go all in."

As I'm falling asleep he murmurs something low I don't quite catch, I feel the brush of his lips across my forehead. The sound of his breathing evens out, slow and deep, and I let myself completely relax before drifting off.

**

NATE

I wake up early to a cold bed and Liz's hushed whispers coming from the bathroom. Her tone instantly has me on alert. It's not her usual sing-song. This one's low, stressed. I slip out of bed, careful not to make any noise, and move closer until I can hear her clearly through the cracked door.

"Yes, sir, I know." A pause. I can hear the sound of her feet pacing on the bathroom tile. "Yes, I know I haven't met the minimum on the loan in months."

My chest tightens.

"I understand, but as I've told you, I didn't realize the loan was in my name until Colby was in prison for months."

What is she talking about? Who the fuck is Colby?

"Yes. I do understand." Another silence follows.

"No. I know the total now is nearing a hundred thousand, but as I've told you, I'm doing my best, all things considered."

There's a beat, then her voice hardens, "No, there won't be any need to send him by. I'll figure it out."

My stomach drops. *Send who by?*

I hear her end the call, then her exhale, a sharp, shaky sound that punches straight through my chest.

I try to process the pieces of what I overheard. A loan. Her name. Someone in prison. Someone threatening to *send someone by*.

Her footsteps padding closer to the door sets me in motion. I take off to the bed and slide back in, squeezing my eyes shut a split second before the bathroom door creaks open. The mattress dips as Liz climbs back into bed. She releases another slow and shaky breath, before rolling onto her side, facing away from me.

I keep my breathing steady, slow enough to pass for sleep, even though every muscle in my body is rigid.

A hundred thousand dollars. Some sort of a shady loan? Someone named Colby took out a loan in her name? My jaw grinds. I have no clue who she was talking to, but I know she's scared.

I lie completely still working over what I know. Again and again. The call I overheard weeks ago. The way she tenses when her phone rings. How she throws her hands in front of her face when she startles. The jokes that don't quite mask the exhaustion in her eyes.

And now this.

Rage simmers under my ribs. I want to roll over, pull her to me, force her to tell me everything. Promise I'll fix it. But if I push now, she'll shut down. It seems Liz only shows her cards when she's ready, and right now she's holding them pretty damn close.

My jaw aches with how tightly I'm clenching it to keep from raging. I want to storm out and make a few calls of my own. Find out who this guy that is threatening her is. Find out who Colby is.

But I won't. One wrong move and she'll build a wall between us.

So I lie there, counting her breaths until mine match hers, forcing myself to calm down. If she won't let me in, then I'll have to find another way to protect her, to help her. Whether she likes it or not. By the time the sun starts to creep through the curtains, I've made peace with exactly nothing.

The truth is, I don't have a hundred grand. I do okay, but I'm not that well off. There is a way I *could* get the money she needs, though. A plan starts to form in my mind. She'll be furious with me, but if it gets her out of whatever this is, it will be worth it.

Eventually, there is a knock at the door that forces us to both sit up and pretend we just woke up.

I open the door to find breakfast and a full glam squad waiting in the hall. In all my stewing, I forgot my mom arranged this circus. I step aside to let the room service cart roll in, followed by a man and a woman wheeling matching silver cases behind them.

"What's all this?" Liz asks, snagging a strawberry off the tray. She looks completely at ease, barefoot and bright-eyed. If I hadn't overheard that phone call, I'd never guess anything was wrong.

"My mother set up a glam day for you before the event tonight." I pause to really take note of her features. She doesn't look anxious, just a little tired.

A smile breaks across her face. "I'm always the one doing the hair and makeup, never the one getting to experience a real life *Pretty Woman* moment." She claps her hands together like a small child.

I don't even know how to respond to that, so I don't. Instead, I grab my clothes and head to the bathroom to change, already running through the plan I came up with, and what I need to get done.

When I return to the living room, Liz is grazing the breakfast cart, humming to herself while the glam team unpacks their gear. I step up beside her.

"I've got a few errands I need to run." I pull her in for a quick hug. She stiffens in surprise, nearly dropping her croissant.

"You'll be good for a few hours without me, right?"

I press a kiss to her forehead, lingering longer than I should. Long enough to breathe her in. To ground myself. When I pull back, her eyes are wide, brows scrunched in confusion.

I lean in close, nuzzling her ear. "They work for my mother. It's showtime, Cricket."

Do we actually need to put on a show for these two? Probably not. Do I usually go for public displays of affection? Absolutely not, but with her it doesn't seem so bad.

After that phone call, after hearing her voice break the way it did, I just needed an excuse to hold her. To steady the anger that's been simmering since.

She smirks up at me, eyes sparkling. "In that case, Bear," she whispers, "we should give them something good to report."

Her fingers slide into the hair at the nape of my neck, slow and deliberate, before she rises up on her toes and presses a kiss to the corner of my mouth. Just the edge of her lips brushes mine, and every muscle in my body locks up.

Yeah, no way I'm letting her control this. Who knows how many more of these I'm going to get.

My hands are still around her waist. I tighten my hold, pulling her flush against me until there's no space left to breathe, no thoughts left in my head but her.

The world tilts for half a second, just her breath mingling with mine, the faint smell of strawberry on her lips, the sound of her quiet laugh catching in her throat when our bodies collide.

"We can do better than that, Cricket."

She's surprised when I pull her mouth to mine. Her lips part on a soft gasp. The sound goes straight through me.

Our mouths come together in the sweetest battle. I nip at her lips, begging her to let me in. She swipes her tongue across mine, inviting me to play. It's a push and pull, heat and tenderness tangled together. I sink into the kiss further, getting lost in her scent, the way her body molds to mine.

Her hands slide from my hair to my chest, fingers curling into my shirt, as our lips come together again and again. She's no longer tentative. I wonder how far she will let this go. Then she tilts her head, begging me to deepen our connection, and I'm gone.

The kiss turns slow, but charged, a battle of restraint and want. I trace the edge of her mouth with my tongue, savoring the faint taste of strawberry and something that's just *her*.

Every point we are touching has my nerves on high alert. The feel of her hands as they slide back up my chest, the quiet sound she makes when I hitch her leg around my waist, pulling her tighter. It's equal parts promise and warning, both of us hovering on a line we shouldn't cross.

The reason we started this kiss is nowhere on my radar. For a moment, I forget everything else. It's just her and me.

A not-so-subtle lid slams in the background, reminding me we aren't alone. Reminding me why this kiss started. Right. A show. I reluctantly pull back to meet Liz's dazed eyes. Her leg slides from around my waist to the ground. Unsteady. Her lips are swollen, red from my scruff. She looks wild and perfect, and I'm a lost cause. I lean in and give her one more soft kiss.

"Have fun today, sweetheart." I wink, watching her expression morph into disbelief that I actually called her something other than *Cricket*. "I'll see you this afternoon."

With that I give her a light pat on the ass and head out the door. Her stunned face burned into my mind. By the time the elevator doors close, I'm grinning.

This weekend's going to be fun.

Chapter Twenty
It's Fake, Right?
Liz

Nate's form disappears with the slam of the suite door, and I'm left standing in the middle of the room, trying to process how the morning went from a total disaster to maybe the best thing that's ever happened to me. That kiss. Oof. One second I was running the game, and the next, he flipped the script and completely wrecked me.

What was that? Just part of the act? Because it didn't feel like acting. Not when his hands were on me, not when he said my name like that. Am I supposed to just pretend it didn't happen? Go back to normal?

Yeah, right. Normal left the building somewhere between his mouth on mine and my leg wrapping around his hip to bring us closer. The smart move would be to laugh it off, play it cool, convince myself it was all for show. The problem is, all I can think about is when I get to do it again.

I raise my fingers to my lips, still tingling from the contact. My pulse hasn't decided if it's going to slow down or completely self-destruct. That was hot. The rest of the world fell away while we made out like our lives depended on it. I can still taste him, mint and warmth.

I pace a few steps, trying to steady my breathing before I do something dramatic like faint or text Chloe a string of incoherent emojis. Which would be especially bad since she doesn't even know I'm here.

Pretending to be Nate's fiancée just got a lot more interesting.

I turn toward the whispers happening across the room to see the glam squad setting up like they own the place.

"Mmm. You've got it bad, honey." The man says when he notices me staring at them. The woman hits him across the chest.

"Oh hush. That's exactly the kind of kiss everyone dreams their lover gives them before they are apart."

"Oh, I'm not denying it's perfection. I thought for a minute I might combust watching it go down." The man steps forward, extending his hand and introducing himself as Rico and the woman as Maya.

Maya is all sleek lines, caramel skin glowing against a cropped black sweater and high-waisted pants that somehow make her look both professional and effortlessly cool. Her hair is a glossy curtain cut into a perfect bob that sways when she moves, and her gold hoops could double as bracelets.

Rico, on the other hand, is pure theater. Tight black jeans, a half-tucked vintage band tee, and a silk scarf knotted around his neck. His close-cropped platinum hair gleams under the light, and he smells like expensive cologne and has a truckload of attitude.

"So nice to meet you both. Thanks for doing this today."

"Oh darling, when Isabel calls and asks you to personally handle glam for her mysterious son and his *guest*, there is absolutely no way to say no to that." Maya sets her massive makeup case on the counter.

"Please tell me you're ready to be pampered within an inch of your life, while you spill all the tea."

"I was born ready," I say smirking.

Rico wheels over a cart overflowing with tools, brushes, and bottles. "And I was born to make you dangerous," he says with a grin that should be illegal.

I blink. "Dangerous?"

He gestures dramatically to my face. "You've got post-kiss energy written all over you, babe. Let's see if we can capture that glow and make it permanent. It will destroy him."

I can't help but grin. They're exactly the distraction I need after that kiss got dialed up to mach ten. The room fills with our chatter, the smell of perfume, the soft hum of blow dryers coming to life, and my heart rate finally starts to slow.

It's exactly what I need to take my mind off whatever that was. Noise, color, and laughter. They act like a shield against the echo of Nate's voice, his hands, the heat that's still crawling under my skin.

Hours later, I've been waxed, buffed, pampered, and styled within an inch of my life. My skin glows, my hair shines, and I smell like something that should come in a glass bottle and cost more than my rent.

Another knock sounds at the door, followed by a flurry of motion as a small parade of assistants roll in several racks of designer dresses and tuxes. I stand, towel still around my shoulders, watching the procession unfold. The tuxes are all timeless. Black, crisp, clearly tailored for Nate. Of course they are.

Then come the dresses. Two full racks of couture perfection. They are sleek, structured, every hemline whispering elegance. All black, all classic, all not me. Beautiful, sure, but soulless. The kind of dresses that belong in glossy magazines, not on a girl who uses drugstore dry shampoo.

And then another rack rolls in. Just one dress.

It hits me like a sucker punch.

You know the yellow gown Andie Anderson wears in *How to Lose a Guy in 10 Days*? The cut is exactly that, simple, fluid, heartbreakingly elegant, but this one... this one is something else entirely.

It's a blue so unique I can't describe it. Somewhere between sapphire and sky, with an iridescent shimmer that shifts when the light hits. The fabric is silk, weightless and alive, with an overlay of intricate embroidery. Up close, it's like a wildflower meadow captured mid-bloom. There are tiny blossoms, butterflies, and the faint glint of crystals that make it glow.

I reach out, but draw my hand back, afraid to touch it. Nervous I'll smudge the magic. For once, I'm speechless. Me. Liz Harrison. Professional talker, queen of all the words. Nothing. I've got nothing.

Maya's watching me in the mirror, a slow grin spreading across her face. "I think we have our winner."

Rico hums approvingly. "Oh, honey. You in that dress, you'll take his breath away."

I swallow, still staring and whisper. "This is the one."

***

THE SUITE IS QUIET now, the hum of the city below spilling in through the windows. Rico and Maya packed up a while ago, leaving behind a trail of perfume and bobby pins like glittery evidence of their magic.

The world's most perfect dress hangs on the back of the bathroom door, daring me to put it on. I slip inside, shoes in hand, my heart trying to beat its way out of my chest. I shouldn't feel nervous. This isn't a real date, but I do.

The silk slides over my skin like water, cool and impossibly soft. When I turn toward the mirror, I barely recognize myself. Maya swept my hair off my shoulders, exposing the low back of the dress. It hugs every curve like it was made just for me. The color makes my eyes look almost electric.

For a beat, I just stand there, staring at the reflection of a woman who looks like she belongs in a movie, not the woman behind the scenes working on the stars. I've never felt more beautiful.

Chef's kiss. No notes.

It's time to face the music and see if I can walk in these shoes without eating carpet. I take one last steadying breath, grip the doorknob, and push it open.

Nate is standing by the window, adjusting his cufflinks. The early evening light hits him just right, highlighting the hard line of his jaw and the way his tux fits him like it was stitched onto his body. He didn't shave this morning, the day of growth on his face makes him look dangerous and devastatingly beautiful.

He turns when he hears the door click.

The moment his eyes land on me, he goes completely still. His mouth parts, then closes again, but no words come out. The silence stretches. His gaze drags over me, slow and deliberate, like he's memorizing every inch, all the while heating my skin from the inside out, until it lands back on my face.

"Wow," he finally says almost reverently. "You look..." He swallows. "Incredible."

I can feel heat bloom across my cheeks, which is stupid because we're fake dating, fake engaged, fake everything. But there's nothing fake about the way he's looking at me right now.

"Guess the dress works then?" I manage, trying to sound casual even as my heart pounds hard enough to be heard in the next room. I do a little spin, showing off the back of the dress.

He blinks like he's pulling himself back to reality, then clears his throat and nods. "Yeah. It definitely works."

He steps toward me, and for a heartbeat I swear he's about to pull me into his arms. Maybe kiss me like he did earlier. I know we don't have an audience to perform for, but I find myself hoping that's what's about to happen. Instead, he stops right in front of me, reaches slowly into his pocket, and pulls out a small velvet box.

"Nate," my voice trembles in warning, as my eyes fly back to meet his. "Is that what I think it is?"

He opens it to reveal a ring.

Not flashy. Not showy. It's perfect. An oval blue stone set in a delicate gold antique band, tiny diamonds trail down the band like bubbles away from the main stone. It's dainty, feminine, unique. I couldn't have designed a more perfect ring if I tried.

"I figured if we're going to sell this, we should do it right," he says, voice gruff. "I wanted you to have something that felt like you, since I'm forcing you to do this favor for me."

Forcing me is a bit of a stretch, since I jumped at the chance to play his pretend girlfriend, and didn't bat an eye when that title leveled up to fiancée.

I reach my hand out slowly, like any sudden movement might shatter the moment. "Nathaniel Joseph, that better not be real." That's not his real name, but I can't think straight right now and I needed to hit him with a double name to show how serious I am.

He chuckles, lifting my trembling hand gently as he takes the ring from the box. The second his skin touches mine, a shiver races down my limbs.

"Only the best for you, Cricket."

My throat tightens as he slides the ring onto my finger halfway... then pauses and looks me dead in the eyes. Something soft flickers there.

"Be my fiancée?" he asks, voice weighted, vulnerable. His hand tightens around mine, like my answer matters far too much.

This shouldn't feel like anything. But my chest aches, tears prick hot behind my eyes, and his gaze is so earnest it steals the ground out from under me. Panic sparks, hot, confusing, too much, so I do what I do best: crack a joke before I combust.

"You sure about this?" I ask. "You're willingly signing yourself up for unpredictability, anxious rambling, and snacks I don't share."

He huffs a laugh and finishes sliding the ring home. He keeps my hand in his, firm and steady, as we both look down at the ring now resting against my skin.

"You could've just gotten something fake," I whisper. "You didn't have to..."

"I wanted to," he says, cutting me off. Our eyes meet again, and he lifts my hand to his lips. His mouth barely grazes my skin, just a whisper of heat, but it steals every bit of air from my lungs.

For a heartbeat, I wish this whole thing wasn't pretend. That the word fake wasn't implied in his question. Because the way he's looking at me? Feels real. It feels confusing.

He must see something slip across my face, because he clears his throat and steps back, the warmth between us cooling in an instant.

"We should go," he says quietly. "Wouldn't want to be late to our big fake debut."

"Right." I smile like the word *fake* doesn't suddenly make me want to throw up. I grab my clutch and follow him out the door, my pulse still pounding from something that has absolutely nothing to do with nerves about the performance we are about to give.

Chapter Twenty-One
Gold-digging Whore
Nate

WE'RE WALKING DOWN THE long corridor toward the ballroom, her hand tucked into the crook of my arm. The ring I placed on her finger reflects the light from every chandelier we pass under.

She was quiet on the elevator ride down. I had to remind myself she's just doing me a favor so I didn't hit the stop button and maul her. Show her how real I'm starting to want this to be.

She's talking now, something about how she can't believe how much people pay for centerpieces when they are thrown out at the end of the night, but I can't focus on a single word she's saying.

All I can see is her face after I said the word fake.

That split second when her smile fell and she didn't say a thing. No joke, no comeback. Just quiet. That silence said more than anything she could've thrown back at me.

The truth is, the reminder wasn't for her. It was for me. Because the second I slid the ring on her finger, I forgot every line we drew. Every rule we made. All I want to do is pull her to me, kiss the fuck out of her, and say screw it to this event and head home.

I spent all day walking around L.A. trying not to think about the kiss yesterday on the sidewalk and the second one this morning in our room. But I failed miserably. So, instead of spending the day obsessing over it and what she might be thinking, feeling, I focused on a task I could control. The ring.

I must've looked at fifty before I found it, the one that looked like it was tailor-made for her finger. Unique. Not loud or flashy, but impossible to ignore. A quiet kind of beautiful. The jeweler kept showing me diamonds, but none of them looked like Liz.

She's the kind of woman who deserves something that feels wholly her. One of a kind, without even trying.

I waffled on step one of my plan to give her the ring to really sell it. But, the moment she walked out of that bathroom, for a second, I forgot how to breathe. That dress. I thought it would look good on her, but I wasn't prepared. The way it clings to her curves. The way the dimples on her back show with the low scoop. She looks too good to be here with me.

Every thought I'd tried to bury all day long came roaring back to life and I knew there was zero chance I wasn't going to slip the ring on her finger. Make her mine, if only for a little while.

The brush of her body next to mine pulls me back to the moment. With every step it gets harder to fight the urge to pull her into an abandoned room, push her against the wall, and have a do-over of this morning. One where we don't have an audience. One where no one stops us.

But that's not in the cards. For now.

After walking what feels like miles through our hotel, we arrive at the ballroom my parents rented for the gala. It's decorated to perfection. Of course it is. I'd expect nothing less from the Sterlings. I'm sure the horde of assistants my mother keeps on staff have been working around the clock to make sure every chandelier sparkles just right. The air smells like money and pretentiousness. It sours my mood. It's too polished, too artificial, everything about this world makes me sick.

Liz inhales sharply beside me. "Holy buttered biscuit."

That declaration lifts my mood slightly, pulling a chuckle from me.

"This is insane."

"Only the best from the Sterlings," I say dryly.

We've barely had time to snag drinks from a passing waiter before I feel my mother lock on to us like a heat-seeking missile.

I lean into Liz, whispering in her ear. "Get ready, Cricket. Incoming." The scent of her shampoo wafts up to me, calming the anxiety that is bubbling up in anticipation of this interaction.

I take a gulp of champagne, secure Liz to my side, and look her in the eyes to gauge what mood I'm dealing with. She hits me with her signature smirk, runs a hand up my lapel, and boops me on the nose. "Let's play ball, hubby-to-be."

Dear Lord, let us make it through the night mostly in one piece.

"Nathaniel, darling, I had no idea you were already here! You should have come to us immediately." My mother's voice oozes practiced sophistication but lacks warmth you'd expect when greeting your only child. She pulls me in for an air-kiss, careful not to smudge her lipstick. My father follows, shaking my hand like we're business associates, not blood.

"Nathaniel," he says, tone sharp. "You look well. Keeping busy?"

"Always."

He hums low in his throat, dissatisfied with my response.

"We were just discussing you at our last board meeting. It's a shame you're wasting all that potential hiding behind a stunt double's helmet."

"Dad," I warn. My molars slam into each other to keep me from saying something I'll regret.

He smiles thinly, ignoring me. "You could be running the studio by now if you'd just..."

"Bear, are these your parents?" Liz interrupts, saving me from the lecture. Her smile is wide, bright, full of that spark that makes me nervous.

"Yeah, babe." I gesture between them. "Mom, Dad, this is Liz Harrison." I hesitate, but I'm more than committed now. "My fiancé."

My mother's smile flickers, polite and poisonous. "Yes, so you've said."

Liz steps forward, all sunshine and sparkle. "I've heard so much about you both. Thank you for having us tonight." She slaps on her brightest smile and tilts her head up at me. "We were thrilled our schedule worked out to attend your little party."

I watch my mother's expression tighten. *Little party.* It's a small jab, but it lands like a dart. Point one to Cricket.

Her eyes sweep over Liz's gown, lingering a beat too long. "Well," she says finally, lips curving in that polite, poisonous way, "I see you didn't go with one of the black dresses I had sent up. That blue is unexpected. Whimsical. Not exactly Hollywood chic, but I suppose it's memorable."

Liz hesitates. "Oh...uhh." Her gaze cuts to me, confusion flickering in her eyes.

I take a slow sip of champagne, saying nothing. Watching her wheels spin, putting it all together. The black dresses my mother sent. The blue one I sent. Just for her.

Her lips part slightly, the realization landing like a spark. She looks up at me, and for a fraction of a second, her smile softens. It's small, quiet, a secret just for us. It crashes through me like a wrecking ball.

"Well," she says, turning her entire body toward me and away from Liz, "You know dear, I was serious when I told you I had someone for you tonight. There was no need to hire," she pauses, letting her gaze slide over Liz again from head to toe, "a C-list escort."

My blood goes hot. Liz sucks in a breath, her hand grips my arm tighter.

"Mom," I warn through gritted teeth. It would be pointless to correct her, she only hears what she wants to. I'm already turning to pull Liz away. "It's been great catching up, but I think we see someone we need to talk to."

"I'm not finished," she snaps, stepping closer. "Be real, son. Do you honestly think my people wouldn't notice if you had a live-in girlfriend? How long are you planning to drag out this little charade?" She sneers at Liz, her voice dropping low. "You may have moved yourself thousands of miles away, but I still know everything that goes on in your little world you try to keep us out of."

Her voice sharpens, every word designed to wound. "Honestly, Nathaniel, it's embarrassing. You could have any woman in Hollywood, famous actresses, models, producers' daughters, women who understand our world, and *this* is what you bring home?"

My father hums, adding his quiet brand of cruelty. "Your mother is right." He looks Liz up and down. "She's interesting, but not the type of woman a Sterling marries."

"Exactly," my mother says, eyes locked on Liz. "Fun for a season, maybe. But not forever." She leans in slightly, voice soft but cutting. "Surely even you see that."

That's it. My restraint snaps. But, before I can open my mouth, Liz's voice cuts in, calm, steady, and lethal.

"If I may interject," she says, giving my arm a reassuring brush, "I hate to be the bearer of bad news, Mrs. Sterling, but you absolutely don't know everything going on in our lives."

My mother blinks, thrown off by Liz's sweetness.

"But you were right about one thing," Liz continues, her smile bright enough for a blind man to see from outer space. "I'm not the type of woman a Sterling would marry. But I *am* the type of woman a Jones would." She looks up at me, eyes fierce, and in a moment of absolute clarity, I don't want this to be temporary.

"If your spies, or even you, had been paying attention, you'd know that not only have we been together for some time now, we're actually getting married next weekend."

My mother gasps, the sound loud enough to draw eyes from nearby tables. I try to rearrange my face into something resembling a man who definitely knew he was getting married next weekend.

My father's brows lift, slow and skeptical. "Married?" he repeats, his tone dripping disbelief.

My mother lets out a sharp, humorless laugh. "That's rich. Oh, Nathaniel open your eyes, this is all so transparent," she says, voice smooth as glass. "I suppose we're meant to believe this is true love and not a strategic move on this one's part." Her gaze flicks to Liz, assessing, cruel. "Because we both know you aren't marrying him for love, dear. You're trying to marry up."

Liz's posture stays straight, but I feel her fingers tense against my arm.

My mother tilts her head, eyes glittering. "It all makes sense now. If you're even telling the truth. But the timing, the secrecy. You know once he's married, his trust becomes accessible. Well of course you know that." She looks at me, feigning pity. "Oh, Nathaniel. I thought you were smarter than this."

My jaw tightens. "That's enough." I start to put my parents in their place, but once again Liz beats me to it.

"It makes me sad that you don't know the man standing in front of you," she says, her voice smooth but razor-edged. "He's bright, intelligent, kindhearted, and a million other things. His trust fund doesn't even rank." She flashes my mother a grin so syrupy sweet it could cause cavities.

"We were going to invite you and Mr. Sterling while we were here, but since you think I'm a two-bit, gold-digging whore... I'm not so sure we need that kind of energy on our big day." She pats my mother's manicured hand with mock sympathy. "I'm sure you understand, right?"

The silence around us is deafening. My father's jaw twitches; my mother looks like she's swallowed a lemon whole.

I wrap an arm around Liz's waist. Not the most conventional comeback to my mother's controlling ways, but I expected nothing less. "Come on, Cricket. Let's get a drink."

She grins up at me. "Make mine a double."

My mother's stare burns into my shoulder blades, before she quickly walks away and starts whispering furiously in the ear of one of the event planners. Her face the picture of suppressed rage.

***

Liz

If there is one thing I learned tonight, it is that rich people can buy the prettiest rooms imaginable, but they still manage to fill them with the ugliest souls.

I can't believe those are Nate's parents. I would never dream of treating my child that way. I'm a little rattled, if I'm being honest, but holding it together for Nate.

We barely make it halfway to the bar when the music cuts and the lights dim. A spotlight hits the giant stage at the front of the ballroom, complete with a glossy white backdrop, and six stools. A host pops out from behind the curtain in a blazer so shiny it could pick up satellite signals. I wonder if they make that in my size?

"Ladies and gentlemen," he booms, "welcome to our annual Sterling Studios Charity Gala!" The room erupts in polite applause. "And this year, our amazing hostess, Isabel Sterling has arranged a little bonus entertainment for us."

Beside me, Nate goes still. His fingers flex around my hip. "That's not good," he mutters.

"Oh, come on," I whisper back. "Maybe it's a juggler. Or a magician. Or a troupe of dancing reindeer." I'm not sure if I'm trying to put him at ease or myself. I have a bad feeling about this.

His jaw ticks, but he stays silent like he's waiting for a judge's sentencing.

The host laughs into his mic. "You've all heard of the Newlywed Game." A murmur of recognition ripples through the ballroom. "Well tonight, for one night only, we're playing *The Nearlywed Game*."

I cringe. "Oh, shizzlefritz."

"Cricket," Nate says slowly, "how good of an actress are you?"

The host continues. "We'll be inviting up Hollywood's most beloved couples…"

Nate relaxes a fraction. "That can't be us. No one knows us here. Maybe she's got some other poor souls lined up."

"…and one very special surprise couple, handpicked by Isabel Sterling herself."

He tenses again. "Never mind."

"And now," Shiny Blazer crows, "please welcome to the stage, Nathaniel *Sterling* and his fiancée, Elizabeth Harrison!"

Well. That escalated quickly.

The spotlight swings and lands directly on us. A squeak escapes my throat and I throw my hands up like I've just been caught robbing a bank.

"She did not," he says under his breath.

"She did," I answer. My rage started to wane after walking away from his parents. I firmly believe in not holding on to anger, but it's been rekindled in full force, inferno-level, because I heard it too. *Sterling.* Not Jones. She didn't just throw him on stage. She exposed him.

"Looks like we're on, G.P.," I say through my teeth, pasting on my brightest smile, because what else are we supposed to do? People are starting to murmur. "Showtime."

The crowd parts for us as the spotlight tracks our every move. I squeeze Nate's arm, feel the fury humming under his skin. His parents stand near the front row politely clapping, Isabel's expression smooth and pleased, like she just did something generous. His dad looks mildly entertained, like this is all a corporate icebreaker.

"Deep breath," I murmur. "We've got this."

We climb the steps. The host meets us center stage, mic held out. "Let's give a warm welcome to the happy couple!"

The applause feels like a roar. People are ecstatic the long-lost Sterling heir has made an appearance.

"Elizabeth," he says, turning to me, "tell us how it feels to be up here tonight with the elusive *Nathaniel Sterling.*"

"Liz," I correct gently, smiling. "Only dentists and legal officials call me Elizabeth."

A ripple of laughter moves through the room. The host chuckles, amused. "Liz it is."

"And it feels wonderful," I continue. "I mean, who doesn't want to test their relationship in front of a packed room of strangers and a camera crew? Right, Nate?"

More laughter. Nate's hand finds the small of my back. His mother's smile twitches. Victory. I was tempted to say his full name sans Sterling, but I don't know if he wants people connecting his real life to his old one, so I refrain. The way I said Nate came out with a little bite though, so I feel good about that at least.

The host recovers from my tone with a quick laugh. "Of course, of course. Nate, Liz." He gestures to the stools. "Why don't you two take a seat?"

We sit back-to-back as two more couples join us. One recently engaged Oscar-winning actress and her director fiancé, and a producing duo who look like they would rather be anywhere but here. I wonder what they did to piss off the queen and get this punishment alongside us.

An assistant passes out whiteboards to each person as our oblivious and overexcited host explains the game. "Alright lovebirds," he says, pacing dramatically in front of us, "here's how The Nearlywed Game works. I'll ask a question, you both write down your answers secretly, and then, on my cue, you'll flip your boards to reveal whether your answers match."

He wiggles his brows. How badly does this man want to be hosting the *Price Is Right*?

"Wrong answers don't eliminate you, but the couple with the most points at the end of the evening wins an evening with George and Isabel. And, of course we will be able to tell which couple is the strongest."

The audience laughs. The host turns toward the crowd with exaggerated flair. "Let's start with something simple." That tone says it will definitely not be simple.

"Question one!" the host declares. "Women, what was your man's first impression of you? Men, write down what your actual first impression was."

I freeze, not because I don't know what I want to write, but I wish I had chatted with Nate for thirty seconds before we started this so we could be on the same page. I can hear his marker moving across his board. I guess I need to stick as close to the truth as possible.

The host moves down the row of couples having us reveal our answers one couple at a time.

When it's our turn, on three, we flip. My board says: **"He thought I was way too much."** His says: **"Words. So many words. But also fierce."**

The crowd loses it. The host confers with the judges and they deem our answers to be a match. I do a little shimmy in my seat and I can feel Nate's chuckle against my back.

The host wipes imaginary sweat. "Oh, we're playing for real I see."

The scoreboard updates. We are tied with the Oscar-winning couple.

"Question two," he announces, "Where was your first kiss?"

When he gets to us and we reveal our boards they both read: **On a sidewalk.**

The Oscar-winning wife claps for us, they also had matching answers. The producing couple looks irritated and mildly threatened, since they haven't gotten one correct.

"Question three: Who would survive longer on a deserted island?"

My marker moves instantly. When we flip, it's unanimous again. Mine reads: **Nate. Obviously.** My board also features a badly drawn palm tree and a crab wearing sunglasses. His reads: **Me. No question.**

"And why do you both think Nate would survive longer?" The host shoves a mic in my face.

"Easy," I jump at the chance to answer. "Nate watches survival videos for fun and probably knows how to make fire with his bare hands. Meanwhile, I require snacks, crafting supplies, and toilet paper made by the same people who knit clouds. I don't think a deserted island can meet those needs."

The audience finds that hysterical. Nate leans just close enough for only me to hear. "For the record, I'd find you snacks."

My stomach swoops. If he keeps saying things like that, it's going to be increasingly difficult to pretend that I care about our rules. Apparently the way to my heart is snacks.

"Alright," the eager beaver host declares, "let's raise the stakes." He reads the next question dramatically. "Which of you is more likely to adopt a stray animal and bring it home?"

Neither of us has to think about our answers. I doodle a whole zoo's worth of animals with me and Nate in the middle.

When it's time to reveal, Nate's answer simply says: **Liz.**

Mine reads: **Absolutely me. He'd pretend to be mad but secretly he'd love them all.**

The host steps closer, the Oscar couple is one point behind us, and strangely I really want to win this stupid game. "Final question, and this one's worth double bragging rights."

A hush spreads.

"Write down the song that best describes your relationship."

Oh boy. My heart kicks. This one feels a little more personal. I chew the cap for half a second, debating how to play this. We've never listened to music together.

There's a pause before the host calls, "Reveal your answers!" All three couples flip.

The Oscar couple misses. One answers: **"Lover"** by Taylor Swift, while the other answers: **"Perfect" by Ed Sheeran.** They are nauseatingly cute. The producer couple may want to look into getting a divorce lawyer, he answered, **"Highway to Hell."** And she looks like her head is about to explode.

The host makes his way to us. Mine says: **"Like Real People Do by Hozier."** The line, *Honey, just put your sweet lips on my lips. We should just kiss like real people do,* has been echoing in my brain since yesterday afternoon.

There's a soft, romantic murmur through the crowd. It's a vulnerable pick for me. Secretly telling Nate what I'm thinking without actually telling him.

His says: **"I Don't Dance by Lee Brice."** Under it, in small handwriting: "**...but I would for her.**" I've never heard the song, but my stomach flutters anyway. Nate was vulnerable too. I can see it in his eyes when we stand up. His chocolate stare has me feeling like I'm striped bare on this stage.

The host grins like this is his peak career moment as he hands us a crystal trophy breaking our eye contact. "Even though they missed their last question, it appears we have our champions."

The spotlights sweep, applause swells, and before I can fully process what just happened, Nate's hand finds mine, linking our fingers together. We face the crowd, but I feel like we're the only two people in the room. He leans down, just enough for only me to hear. "That was a good choice, Cricket."

My voice barely works. "Yours too."

Chapter Twenty-Two
Federal Paperwork Chaos
Liz

People stop us on our way off the stage. Congratulations, questions, jokes about how we should watch our backs because the other couples are coming for our crown next year. Cameras flash.

Nate's parents walk toward us to give us their obligatory congratulations. His dad looks stunned. His mom looks like she just got a whiff of something rotten.

Her sneer sneaks through for half a second before she quickly smothers it with a big smile for the camera and leans in to give Nate a hug and an air kiss. She can't ignore me with so many eyes on us, so she repeats the same process with me.

I can't help myself. When she leans in, I whisper, "Pretty good for a C-list, gold-digging whore, right?" I hear her suck in a sharp breath, but she doesn't react otherwise.

Another point for team Liz and Nate. We really need a relationship name. Lite. Lizte. That's not pronounceable. Niz?

Yeah, that's the one, team Niz.

Winning that game and putting Nate's mom in her place makes me feel slightly less like punching her perfectly plastic face, but only slightly. The way his mother spoke to him earlier, like he's a misbehaving child, not her grown son. The tone she used, icy, clipped, condescending. I can't imagine using that tone on a loved one, much less my child. And then throwing us on stage. Using his real name. Trying to humiliate us, to prove we aren't a real couple.

You're done hurting Nate. Not on my watch, lady.

Nate slams our trophy on the bar and orders us each a drink.

Between the rage his mom sparks in me, the bomb I dropped telling her we are getting married next weekend, and the giddiness of surviving and winning a live relationship pop quiz, my nerves have morphed into a strange cocktail of adrenaline, tenderness, and what-the-heck-are-we-doing.

Announcing our upcoming wedding maybe wasn't my most measured move. I sneak a glance at Nate beside me, trying to read his face, but as usual, he's unreadable. Calm. His control right now makes my nerves start working overtime. My stomach twists.

"Nate..." I start but trail off when he looks down at me. His mask slips and his face is pure adoration.

"Thank you."

"For what?" I stutter out. The way his eyes are locked on mine feels like he's saying more than thanks.

"For being here with me. For being completely you back there. For not backing down from them. For playing that stupid game. For choosing me."

"Of course I choose you, Bear." I roll my eyes to hide how warm his declaration made my chest feel. "Honestly, I don't know how you came from those two. Even if you only grunt for the rest of your life, you're leagues above them."

"Noted." His eyes sparkle with amusement that I'm starting to see more and more of.

I take a small sip of my drink, replaying the last hour of this insane night. The high from the game dips, replaced by a familiar low thrum of panic as I remember all the things his mom spewed in our conversation. The trust fund. The way she accused me of using Nate. I felt like my debt was a giant billboard on my forehead in that moment.

I had totally forgotten about the trust fund. Nate told me about it the other day, how marriage would make it accessible. I hope he doesn't think I suggested getting married thinking we would *actually* get married. I'd never want him to think I was using him.

The call he overheard weeks ago looms in the back of my mind. Oh shizz, what if he thinks I *am* a gold-digging whore?

"Nate," I say, hesitantly. "I didn't mean it." He looks at me perplexed. So I continue. "Earlier, talking to your parents when I said we were getting married next weekend. It just slipped out because I was seeing red and wanted to shock them. I do that sometimes. Say things for shock value."

His expression shifts, thoughtful, unreadable again. "I know you didn't." He pauses, takes a slow sip of his drink, pulls me close, his hands running up my bare back. I hold back my shiver because he's looking at me like he's about to detonate a bomb. "But I think we should follow through with it."

Record scratch.

Excuse me?

Are my ears working correctly?

Did he just say we should actually get married, to piss off his parents?

My mouth drops open and I jerk back but his arm is firmly looped around me so I don't go far. "I'm sorry, what now?"

He takes another slow gulp. His Adam's apple working like he didn't just casually suggest the most insane thing I've ever heard. And I've heard a lot of insane things. In fact, most of the time, *I'm* the one suggesting the insane thing.

"I think we should follow through with it," he says again, in a maddeningly calm tone.

"Follow through as in... actually get married?"

He nods once, completely unbothered. "Yeah. Why not?"

I blink at him, waiting for the joke. "Why not? Uhh, because it's *marriage*, Nate. You don't just," I wave my hand between us, "get married to prove a point. That's insane. That's chaotically insane."

He smiles faintly. "You like chaos."

"Yeah, not federal paperwork levels of chaos!"

He leans one elbow on the bar, one hand on my hip, thumb moving slow circles, watching me with that steady, thoughtful look that makes my pulse jump. "It's not just to prove a point. Your suggestion, it shuts them down for good. Locks them firmly out of my life."

I feel my eyes bug out of my head. "You're crazier than I am. You do realize this weekend started with, 'Hey, Liz, want to be my pretend girlfriend?' and now we've escalated to, 'Let's legally bind ourselves together for eternity?'"

He doesn't say anything.

I stare at him, trying to read the space between his words. "You're serious."

"Completely."

I huff out a disbelieving laugh. "You're seriously crazy."

"We have the ring," he interrupts smoothly. "We worked well together just now." He gives a head nod over his shoulder to the stage. "And I know a guy at the courthouse. It's open 'til midnight."

I choke on my drink. "You're suggesting we *elope* tonight because we crushed a silly game?"

He doesn't blink. "Not because of that, no, but why wait?"

Oh, he's lost it. Full-out cosmic-level insane.

"I...Nate...this is..." My hands flail uselessly. "You don't even like people. Now you want to be someone's husband before sunrise?"

His mouth curves just enough to make me nervous. "No, not just someone's." He teases lightly. "Yours."

My stomach does an entirely unhelpful flip. "You're ridiculous." I am sure there are other words I should be saying, should be thinking, but my mind is blank.

"Maybe," he admits, "but hear me out."

He straightens, placing his drink on the bar, turning to face me fully, the teasing edge fading from his voice. "Didn't you say your apartment lease is up in what, three weeks?"

I blink. "Two."

He nods, like he's been keeping track. "You said rent's going up, so you were going to have to find a new place anyway. You said it yourself the other day, you've been stressed trying to figure out what's next."

I narrow my eyes. It's annoying how well he listens and retains information when I'm babbling. "What's your point?"

"My point," he says, lowering his voice, "is that if we got married, we could move in together. For real. It'd solve the lease problem, you'd save money, and it gets my parents out of my life, for good. Win-win."

I stare at him. "Did you just *pitch* marriage to me like a business deal?"

He smirks. "When enough time has passed for the trust money to come through, and you've saved what you need, we can get a divorce. I like practical solutions. I'm giving you one to solve some of the problems you're facing *and* that I'm facing."

I press my palm against my forehead. "I thought you didn't care about the trust money?"

"I don't. Not really, but it would be one more jab at my parents."

"And how long would we need to stay married for the trust money to come through?"

For the first time since suggesting this insanity, he looks sheepish. "The money will be in my account as soon as I present our marriage documents. For it to stay in my account, we have to stay married...for at least a year."

"Nate!" I whisper shout. "A year?"

He looks around to make sure no one is listening in, "I know it's not ideal, but it would be easy for us. Just look at it as having a roommate for a year. I don't mind spending time with you."

"High praise." I interrupt.

"You know what I mean." He continues. "We already work together, why not just spend even more time together? When the money hits, I'll split the trust with you."

"Absolutely not. I don't want any of your money."

"You may not want it, but as my wife it would be yours. I'd want you to have it."

My mind whirls with the debt I'm in. I could use part of it to pay that off and donate the rest to worthy causes, I don't want any of Nate's parents' money.

"I can't tell if this is starting to make sense or if I need to be checked into a mental institution."

"Both?" he chuckles and leans in slightly, eyes softening in a way that steals the breath right out of my lungs. "But think about it, Liz, you'd never have to worry about anything again."

There's something in his tone, something warm and dangerous and too careful, that makes my chest constrict. Is he thinking about my debt or something else? He doesn't know the full story, but he knows enough. This feels an awful lot like him swooping in to save me, not me saving him.

"Nate..." I whisper, because I can't bring myself to ask if my debt is factoring into this. I don't want him to just play hero and save me. I find myself wishing that he wanted to marry me, just for me.

He smiles, slow and sure. "So what do you say, Cricket? You and me, courthouse, tonight?"

I stare at him, searching for the lie, the joke, *anything*.

My ex flashes through my mind. How we moved in together so quickly, how he isolated me from my friends and family. How his *love* turned into control, and his control into bruises you couldn't always see.

Nate isn't him though. There have been no red flags, nothing but care and respect from him. I should be nervous that history is repeating itself. I search his eyes, looking for what, I'm not sure. A warning sign. A shadow. Something.

But all I find is certainty. Steadiness.

Mother-trucker. Looks like I'm getting married.

Chapter Twenty-Three
Husband and Wife
Nate

I wake with a start, Liz pressed against my side like a small heater. Last night feels like a distant dream, but one glance down at the ring on my left hand tells me it actually happened.

The evening couldn't have played out more perfectly if I'd orchestrated the entire thing myself. I spent most of yesterday not only searching for a ring, but also calling in a favor to an old friend at the courthouse to get a marriage license.

I wandered aimlessly trying to figure out a way to get Liz to actually marry me so I could use my trust to get her out of trouble. Some people might ask why I feel a responsibility to help her. I tried to figure it out myself, but all I came up with was that I do.

I didn't ask her to be my fake girlfriend, or upgrade us to engaged, with the thought of marrying her to solve her debt, but once it occurred to me, it's all I could think about.

The thought that she is walking around scared or that someone is harassing her has me seeing red, and if there's something I can do to fix it, I'm going to. Sure, we haven't known each other for a long time. And yes, she talks too much sometimes, but I'd be lying to myself if I said I wasn't attracted to her. Drawn to her. Every day we spend together hasn't felt like enough.

When she told my parents we were getting married, the stars aligned. I knew I needed to lock her down right then or I might miss the opportunity. Liz is just spontaneous enough that it worked.

We left the gala and got to the courthouse just before it closed. Me still in my tux, Liz still in the dress I picked out for her. It wasn't a traditional white wedding gown, but I've never seen a more beautiful bride.

We stood before a judge, exchanged ridiculous vows that no one but us would understand, and sealed it with a kiss. A damn good kiss. A photographer was on hand to capture the moment. Two strangers signed as our witnesses. Then we celebrated by getting greasy burgers, fries, and a milkshake.

Only the best for my new bride.

We stayed in the booth, high on life and each other, until exhaustion caught up with us. Liz was slap happy and could barely make it back to the room. I removed her shoes before we both crashed hard. Sharing a bed isn't new; we already slept tangled up the night before. Luckily, last night wasn't weird or uncertain. It was familiar. Like our bodies already knew where to fit, even if our brains haven't caught up.

Just with the addition of a wedding license on the nightstand.

We didn't talk about what this means for us. Are we still pretending? Does Liz actually like me? I feel like a girl wondering all of this, but it's suddenly very important to me.

Did last night mean something to her, or was it just another one of her wild, spontaneous adventures?

I know we have insane chemistry after that kiss yesterday afternoon and the wildfire she lit inside of me kissing me again at our wedding. If we weren't both exhausted from the emotional hoops my parents put us through, last night might have ended up differently. Maybe. I can't figure out if this is one-sided. Admittedly, feelings and talking things through aren't my strong suit.

I'm in uncharted territory here.

Liz releases a little snore that makes her hair puff up and her nose scrunch. I hate to wake her while she's sleeping so peacefully, but a glance at the clock says we need to get moving to make it to the airport. I'd rather not be in a rush and have a repeat of our experience on the way here.

I lean in and kiss her gently on the forehead, taking a deep breath of her intoxicating scent. "Liz."

Her voice comes out muffled against my chest. "No."

That pulls a chuckle from me. I brush a piece of hair from her face. "Cricket, we have to get up now."

"No. No, thank you." She tightens her arms around me, voice sleepy but defiant. "I have no interest in that."

"We have to head home now."

Her nose wrinkles. "As my husband, you should already know that I am not a morning person."

I grin. I like the sound of that and that she wasted no time acknowledging what we did last night. "We can stop and get you a latte on the way to the airport. You can sleep the whole way home if you want. I won't even complain if you drool on me, but we have to get up now."

She cracks one eye open, studying me like she's trying to decide if the promise of caffeine is enough to move. "You drive a hard bargain, Bear."

"I'll take that as a yes."

She wraps her arms around me a little tighter. If I expected things to be awkward with Liz this morning, I shouldn't have. It feels like we've woken up this way for years. Like she's carved herself into a piece of my soul already.

She slowly unwinds herself from me, sitting up, hair sticking everywhere. I lie back against the headboard and take her in. She stretches her arms above her head, making her T-shirt ride up and expose the skin along her stomach. She lets out a little squeak. It's stupid adorable. I have to fight the urge to drag my hand along her exposed lower back. To pull her into me. Miss our flight for a whole different reason than sleeping in.

Self-control wins for today, and I jump up to get dressed.

She groans dramatically and flops onto her back, staring at the ceiling like getting out of bed is a personal tragedy.

"Fine," she mutters. "But I want an extra shot in it today."

"Deal. I'll even throw in a muffin."

That earns me a sleepy smile, the kind that hits me square in the chest. I move around the room, gathering our bags while she sits up and stretches again, her shirt riding even higher. I swear she's doing it on purpose this time.

"Do we have time for showers?"

I glance at the clock. "You do if you're fast."

She narrows her eyes. "So, no."

"Exactly."

She sighs, dragging herself off the bed and shuffling toward her bag. "Fine. I'll just do the traveler's special, extra deodorant and a prayer."

"Very glamorous," I tease.

She shoots me a look over her shoulder. "Don't judge me, Bear. Not everyone wakes up camera-ready."

"Can't imagine you ever not being camera-ready."

Her mouth curves in that little half-smile I'm addicted to. "Careful. That sounded dangerously close to something sweet. Almost flirty."

I pull the zipper on her suitcase, barely getting it closed with how much she has stuffed in there. "Must be the newlywed bliss going to my head."

"Or lack of sleep." She laughs, twisting her hair up into a messy bun before rummaging for her makeup bag.

I should probably stop staring, but watching her move around the room feels different this morning. I feel different this morning.

I'm married. To Liz.

I married Liz Harrison last night. Technically Liz Jones now.

I have a wife.

***

Liz drops into the window seat like she is boneless, pulls the strings of my hoodie tight around her face, and tries to get comfortable. I noticed the hoodie in her drawer. My hoodie. The one I gave her the night I changed her tire. I forgot about it, but when I saw it mixed in with her things it made my chest do funny things. Picturing her wearing my clothes around her house makes me want to beat my chest and then rip it off of her. I don't call her out on what she's wearing, but I love it.

She looks tired in the prettiest way a person can look tired.

She buckles her seatbelt, then glances over at me. "This week is going to fly by," she says. "I can feel it."

"Yeah?" I tilt my head toward her. "Why's that?"

She lowers her voice dramatically. "Because I'm a married lady now, well, technically married now, and everyone knows time goes faster when you're married."

"I don't think that's a thing."

"Sure it is. Like when you are a kid and every year feels so long, but now as an adult the years go faster and faster. Now that we did a very grown up thing by technically getting married, time will speed up again."

I hate that she keeps saying the word technically. She laughs after she says it, but the sound wobbles enough that I know she is still trying to make sense of all this. Can't blame her. I am right there with her, but I wish she'd just say married because that's what we are. Married.

As the plane pulls away from the gate, she tucks her legs under her and shifts closer until her arm brushes mine. "Okay," she says. "We should talk about all the stuff. Everything."

"Everything," I repeat.

"First," she says, lifting one finger like she is about to present a school project, "what are we telling people?"

I shrug, "For now, I guess not much. We can keep it quiet at work if you want. We don't need a big announcement. But one thing we have to agree on is no one can find out it's fake, or we won't be awarded the trust money."

She nods, then groans quietly. "James is going to have a conniption."

"Your brother?"

She nods again, eyes big. "He is very protective. Painfully protective. Overly protective."

I want to ask what he is protecting her from, but the way she shifts in her seat tells me not to push. So I don't.

"We can take it slow," I say. "You don't have to tell him today."

She blows out a breath. "Okay. Next topic. Moving in. When am I bringing my stuff to your place?"

The question punches a strange mix of nerves and anticipation. "Soon," I say. "I can come by tomorrow after work. See what we are dealing with."

She snorts. "Brace yourself. My apartment is... not minimalist."

"Never would have guessed."

"It is part craft store, part glitter explosion, part thrift shop graveyard." She lifts a shoulder. "And Hulk has claimed every surface as his personal kingdom."

"Looking forward to it."

We go quiet while the plane takes off. She pulls the blanket over her lap and leans her head against my shoulder like it is the most natural thing in the world. I like that she doesn't seem to think about touching me. She does it freely.

"I still cannot believe we actually did it," she says softly.

"Me either."

"But it was kind of perfect," she adds. "Burger grease and all."

"Very romantic."

"It really was," she insists, then hides her smile behind the blanket.

A flight attendant rolls past. Liz watches her, then tilts her head toward me. "Are you freaking out yet?"

"No." I glance at her. "Are you?"

She thinks for a long second. "I'm not freaking out," she finally says. "Just overwhelmed I think." She scrunches her nose, a hint of vulnerability sneaking into her tone. "And also trying to understand what this means."

"What do you want it to mean?" I ask before my brain can stop my mouth.

Her eyes flick to mine, surprised. She tucks her legs closer to her chest. "I don't know yet."

I do. Or at least I am getting close. I liked waking up with her curled into me. I liked that she drooled on my shoulder. I liked her ridiculous, sleepy one-word refusals this morning. I liked all of it way more than I should.

She shifts again, sinking deeper into my side. Her hair tickles my jaw.

"Wake me when the snacks come," she mumbles.

"Sure."

She is asleep a minute later, mouth parted, breathing slow and steady. Her hand inches across the armrest until her fingers hook around mine. I stare down at our hands like an idiot.

I have a wife.

And I am not panicking.

Not even close.

***

Monday morning comes fast and early. Too fast after our weekend away.

Thankfully, yesterday's travel day was uneventful. I don't think I had another airport disaster in me.

Our call time's later today, but I still left the condo early. Unfortunately, that means I hit peak rush hour traffic. It's better than sitting in my bed after waking early, alone.

With nothing but time on my hands, I replay parts of that plane ride in my head. Liz kept talking about how this week was going to fly by, how weird it was that she's technically married now. *Technically.*

I'm not sure what I expected when I asked her to go through with it. Panic, second thoughts, maybe her telling me I was insane. Instead, after the initial shock, she said yes like she was saying yes to grabbing lunch. No hesitation. Just that wild, reckless kind of faith that's equal parts impressive and terrifying.

We talked through logistics on the flight after she woke up. What we should tell people. When she is going to move in. The sooner the better, I think. We decided I'd help her move in after her race with Chloe this weekend. I saw the relief in her eyes. I think she's tired of carrying everything alone.

I'm looking forward to going to her place after work. Seeing another glimpse of her world. We need to decide what needs to be packed, and what can go in storage. I can only imagine what her apartment looks like.

I'll get the guys I play basketball with to help me move her. They will be surprised that I'm married, but not really. We don't share a lot of details with each other anyway. The only person who will really be shocked is Joe. I tell him everything, so me getting married will come completely out of left field for him. A problem for another day.

The only thing Liz seemed uncomfortable about was lying to her family, especially her brother. I don't get it, not really, I don't have siblings. But the way her face scrunched when she mentioned telling James and Chloe, told me she was worried about it.

With time I hope she trusts me enough to open up.

I should probably feel guilty for pulling her into all this. Instead, I feel settled. Like I finally took control of something for once. I keep telling myself this whole thing is practical, a way to access my trust and help her out, but that's not the full truth, and I know it.

It's more than that.

I grip the steering wheel a little tighter, catching my reflection in the rearview mirror. Married. The word still sounds foreign in my head.

It's supposed to be temporary. Convenient. But, I'm not so sure I want it to be. By the time I pull into the lot, I've cleared my mind of all Liz-related thoughts. Or at least I tell myself I have.

The guard at the gate waves me through, and I flash my ID badge like always. "Morning, Jones," he says, grinning. "You're in early for a late call."

"Couldn't sleep," I lie.

Truth is, I slept fine. Better than fine. I just woke up earlier than usual. After only two nights of having Liz in my bed, it felt too empty without her.

Inside the studio, the air smells like coffee, sawdust, and metal. The scent always settles me. The crew's already moving in rhythm: carts of equipment roll by, camera ops checking gear, someone yelling about continuity. Feels normal.

I'm halfway to the stunt room when I hear a familiar voice.

"Jones!" It's Marcus, one of the riggers. He's built like a linebacker and has the subtlety of a marching band.

I turn. "Yup?"

He pauses, studying my face. "You look different. Did you take a vacation or something?"

"Something like that."

He whistles low. "Whatever it was, keep doing it. You usually look like you want to throat punch me."

"Appreciate the feedback," I mutter.

He grins, undeterred. "Seriously, you get lucky this weekend or something?"

I give him a flat stare. As if I would ever answer that question.

He raises both hands in surrender. "Kidding! Just saying, you're practically smiling. It's weird, man. Creepy, even."

"Good to know."

He laughs and heads off, shouting something about resetting the crash pads. I shake my head, but I can't stop the faint curve tugging at my mouth. Maybe he's right. Maybe I do look different.

I drop onto a crate, resting my elbows on my knees. The warehouse hums around me, metal clanks, saws buzz, people shout, but it all feels muted compared to the noise in my own head.

I feel happy. Relaxed. Words that don't usually belong to me.

Chapter Twenty-Four
Truffle Nuggets
Liz

Filming went late. It's after midnight, but Nate still insisted on coming over tonight. I'm running around straightening up a little so I don't completely overwhelm him.

I picked Hulk up from Jenn and Autumn after our plane landed yesterday. I lasted all of two minutes before I told them I got married. As soon as they accused me of being weirder than usual, I spilled. I didn't tell them it was all fake though, so that's something at least.

They've seen Nate and me around the set and hanging out a lot after we get off. They were shocked, but not surprised. They are used to me doing crazy stuff all the time. I asked them to keep it quiet until I could tell Chloe and James myself. Hopefully they do. I'm not looking forward to that conversation.

All day Jenn and Autumn made kissing faces behind Nate's back like they are five years old. It both delighted me and horrified me that he would see and know I already spilled the tea.

His knock on my door echoes through the apartment and brings my speed-cleaning session to an end. I scoop Hulk up on my way to let him in.

"Daddy! You're home." I wave Hulk's tiny paw at Nate's bewildered face.

"We aren't making that a thing." He walks past me and into my space. His head swivels back and forth, taking it all in.

It can be a lot if you don't know me, but this has been my safe place. A place that makes me happy. I try to look at my apartment through his eyes.

I bet he will say it's too loud. I have bohemian couches and pillows, a living green-wall behind it with vines stretching to kiss the top of the couch. Shelves of trinkets and knickknacks decorate my walls. In my kitchen there's a high top table made from a dozen different types of wood. It's a freeing space. I love it here. I brace for his disapproval, but that's not what I get at all.

"I like it," he says finally. "It feels like you. But the cat can't call me Daddy." He pauses. "Nor can you make your cat voice and call me Daddy. In fact, no one should ever say that word again. It's giving creepy-porn-star vibes."

I blink, stuck on the fact that he didn't criticize a single thing about my space. My ex always told me I was too much. Too loud. Too bright. Too lively. I spent so long stuffing myself into a box for him. I didn't realize I was nervous that Nate would do the same until he walked in here and accepted me, and my space, without hesitation.

He walks into my bedroom and back out. "Okay, I think we'll need to put your bedroom set in storage. There's not room for all of it in the guest room, but we can switch my couch out for yours if you want." When I don't answer, he keeps talking. "I like your high-top table. We should bring it in and see if it fits by the prep counter. Drilling into the brick walls for your shelves will be a pain in the ass, but we'll figure something out."

I just stare at him. He doesn't want me to *fit into* his life, he wants to blend ours together.

"Liz?" He snaps his fingers in front of my face. "Are you having a medical event? You've never been quiet this long."

I shake myself out of my shock. "I love that."

"What part?"

"All of it. All of it sounds perfect. Except we should keep your couch. I've had dreams about it since the last time I was there. I can't wait to curl up and veg out in those deep-set cushions."

He looks at me like he's not sure if I'm serious, but doesn't comment. "I've got a U-Haul rented for Saturday. Me and a few buddies will come over and load everything. Need me to grab boxes for your personal stuff?"

Who is this talkative, organized, take-charge man? Swoon.

I drop Hulk and walk straight to Nate, throwing my arms around him. His body freezes at first, then he relaxes and wraps his arms around me.

I feel seen. Protected. Safe. And ridiculous for getting teary over a man talking about moving and storage logistics.

"What's this for?" He asks softly.

I laugh up at him, blinking away the sting behind my eyes. "Well, Boo-Bear, most people call this a hug. It's what two people do to express a multitude of emotions. Including, but not limited to, being happy, being grateful, being overwhelmed..."

He studies my face, taking in every emotion flitting across my face. I'm suddenly very aware that I've molded my entire body to his and the fact that we are very, very alone.

He doesn't scare me. I've never been afraid for my safety with Nate. He scares me in a whole different way.

His hands settle a little lower on my back. Not inappropriate. Not even intentional. Just familiar. Comfortable.

We shouldn't be standing like this. I shouldn't feel like this. We just made rules two days ago about lines and smudging and not catching feelings. And here I am. Smudging everything.

He clears his throat, but he doesn't step back. Not right away. His gaze flicks to my mouth for a fraction of a second. A tiny flicker. Barely there.

I feel it like a spark down my spine.

Oh, truffle nuggets, I'm screwed.

***

As expected, the week flies by in a blur of work, training for the half marathon, and packing my apartment. I thought I might feel sad boxing everything up. This apartment was where I learned to stand on my own two feet again. Where my mind and body healed. Where I remembered how to be myself.

But instead of sadness, all I feel is nervous excitement.

I know this isn't a real marriage. Obviously. But I can't help the flutters that hit every time I talk to Nate. Every time I think about the fact that we're about to *live together*. Sure, it's technically a roommate situation, not a love interest, but I'm still excited.

We hung out every day this week. Both at work and then Nate would come over at night and help me pack.

Tuesday afternoon was different though. The sky opened up on set and everyone scattered. I was trying to save my makeup kit from turning into a swimming pool when my shoe caught on a lighting cable. Before I could face-plant in front of the entire crew, Nate's arm was suddenly around me, steadying me. Strong, warm, close enough that I got flashbacks from snuggling him in LA. His scent wrapped around me, and I suddenly didn't care if I was getting soaked. I just wanted to hang out in the moment for a while.

Luckily, his brain wasn't misfiring like mine. He released me slowly, looking me up and down to check for injuries.

We ended up trapped under a canopy until the rain eased, just talking. Not about work. Not about the fake marriage. About everything else. Small things, big things, childhood dreams. He told me his first stunt was jumping off a shed with a garbage bag for a cape. I told him about my first makeover, when I shaved part of my little sister's head. It was fun. Lighthearted. I just enjoy being *with* him.

I've avoided thinking about our kisses in LA. If I do, it's all I'll think about. Kissing him completely consumed me. I wouldn't be mad if we had to do it again, you know, to convince people this thing is real. For the cause.

I've also avoided talking to James and Chloe all week. They've both called to get together, but I don't trust myself not to blurt out *I'm married* the second I talk to them.

I'm getting ready to head out and meet them for the half marathon now. Hopefully, the early hour and all the running will keep my big secret from slipping out.

It's stupid early, the sun isn't even up yet. I'm grumpy, running on fumes, and dangerously low on caffeine. I hit snooze one too many times, which means no time to make coffee. I know I shouldn't drink it before a long run, my stomach wouldn't be happy with that, but the shoot went late again last night, and I need coffee like I need oxygen.

I want to cry.

"See ya, Hulk-baby." I blow him a kiss, hustle out the door, and run straight into a very *chipper* looking Nate. Why is he grinning so big? Is the world ending?

"Morning, Sunshine."

Well, that's new. It's then that I notice he's holding two cups in his hands.

"Gimme!" I make grabby hands at the cup, and he chuckles, actually chuckles. It still blows my mind every time it happens.

I take the first glorious sip of the heavenly nectar he offered and realize it's a latte made to perfection, and let out an indecent moan.

"Sweet caffeine, take me now."

He shakes his head, eyes on my mouth, throat bobbing.

I flash him my sweetest smile and pat his chest. "See something you like, husband?"

That earns me a quiet huff of laughter before he steps back, offering me a bottle of electrolytes.

I blink at him. "You got this for me?"

He shrugs like it's nothing. "I've seen you training this week. You're going to need this for after."

I squint my eyes and purse my lips, like I'm annoyed at him, but I'm secretly pleased he thought to bring me this. Before I can say anything, he nods toward the curb where a few of his buddies are waiting beside a truck. They're watching us with way too much interest.

"Go run your race," he says, his voice low and steady. "We'll have you moved in by the time you're done and you can just meet me at home."

Home. The word lands warm and heavy in my chest. "You don't have to do that, Nate. I said I would help after my race."

"I know." He takes a step closer, and for a second, it feels like the rest of the world falls away. "This way you don't have to do anything but recover after your run."

That's the kindest thing. The way he takes care of me in every small detail. It's thoughtful. I'm not used to it, but I could become addicted quickly.

"Good luck, Cricket," he says, leaning down just enough that his lips brush mine, his knuckles brush gently under my chin tilting my lips to his for a quick goodbye kiss. I'm sure it's supposed to look casual, for the guys watching, but it leaves me breathless all the same.

I climb into my car. I can't resist glancing back to find him. I find him still watching me, coffee in hand, expression unreadable. I'm suddenly very motivated to run as quickly as I can so I can make it home to him.

Chapter Twenty-Five
No Ceilings
Nate

Liz's apartment is a minefield of plants, pillows, and enough knickknacks to open her own flea market. If you'd told me a month ago that I'd spend my Saturday hauling furniture and houseplants for a woman who can't go ten minutes without shutting up, I'd have said you were insane.

But here I am doing it and I don't even mind. In fact, I'm secretly really happy about it.

Lane and Joseph, the guys I play basketball with, showed up this morning right on time. We may not share every detail of our lives with one another, but we show up for each other.

I picked up the U-Haul last night, it came with moving blankets and straps. Everything is in order. I want today to go smoothly. She deserves that. It's weird how easily I've slipped into this role, thinking about someone else. Making sure everything is planned out perfectly for her. Feels good. Feels right.

By lunch, her apartment is empty except for Hulk, who's been perched on the counter for hours supervising like a judgmental little foreman. His eyes tracking us every time we walk past, tail flicking in what I'm pretty sure is disapproval.

"Dude," Lane says, pointing, "that cat's been mean-mugging me for two hours."

"That's his face," I mutter, carrying another box toward the door. "Don't take it personally."

Joseph snorts. "You sound like you actually like the thing."

"I don't dislike him," I say, setting the box down in the truck, thinking about the many miles I've walked holding that cat. That's information the guys don't need to know. "He makes Liz happy."

They exchange a look, and Lane grins. "You're already whipped."

"Shut up and grab the dresser."

By the time we unload the last box into my place, I'm sweaty, starving, and weirdly satisfied. Even though nothing is in its spot yet, her stuff already makes the house feel warmer, more inviting.

The only problem? Hulk. He rode over here in my truck, tucked firmly against my leg, wearing his harness, but now...

I could've sworn I saw him jump into one of the boxes in the living room earlier. That box now sits empty. The front door's been open all afternoon. Shit.

"Lane," I say slowly, scanning the room. "You seen the cat?"

He's taking a swig of Gatorade. "Uh, not lately."

My heart drops. "Not lately, like in the last thirty seconds?"

He shrugs. "Maybe sometime in the last thirty minutes."

Thirty minutes. "Son of a bitch." I run a hand through my hair, already searching. "Hulk!"

I snatch his food and start shaking the box.

Joseph looks up from unstacking boxes. "What's wrong?"

"The cat's gone."

He freezes and then cringes, like he knows the deep shit I'm going to be in if Liz comes home and doesn't have a cat. "Gone where?"

"If I knew that, I wouldn't be saying he's gone, dip-shit!"

Lane starts laughing, which earns him a glare.

"This isn't funny. Liz loves that cat. Like, will probably name our firstborn after the damn cat, level of love."

"Relax, man," Joseph says. "We will find him. He's probably hiding."

"Yeah? Well, if he's hiding outside, he's road kill." He loves going outside. Liz walks him every day. He isn't afraid of the outdoors. I live in the heart of the city, so many terrible things could happen to the little guy.

I should've gotten a damn carrier.

My phone buzzes in my pocket. I pull it out and feel my stomach drop.

Liz: I survived!!! Just finished the race! I'm headed your way.

"Fuck."

Lane glances up. "What?"

"She's on her way."

They both blink at me.

"She can't come home to no cat, guys. I can't start our marriage by killing her cat. That's not the vibe I'm going for."

Joseph whistles low. "Never thought I'd see the day you panic over a house pet."

"It's not about the cat!" I snap, crouching to look under the couch. "It's about Liz!"

Nothing. Just dust. I check behind the curtains, under the bed, inside the laundry hamper.

"Hulk!" I call, trying not to sound desperate. "C'mon, buddy. I'll buy you the expensive tuna."

No answer.

"Maybe he got into one of the boxes," Lane says helpfully, cracking open another one by the kitchen.

He's wrong. I know the cat isn't in a box. We search for another ten minutes before we hear it.

It sounds like scratching and we all freeze.

It's faint, but it's coming from the kitchen. I drop the box of cat food on the table, hit my knees, and open the cabinet under the sink. Two gray eyes blink back at me from behind the cleaning supplies. He's curled in an unraveled roll of paper towels.

Relief slams into me so hard I almost laugh. "You've got to be kidding me." Hulk blinks once, stretches, and lets out the loudest mewl I've ever heard.

"How did you get the cabinet open to get in there?" I mutter, half scolding, half laughing. "You little jerk."

Lane leans over my shoulder. "Wow. He really had you sweating."

"Don't tell Liz," I say, scooping Hulk into my arms before he can disappear again. "She doesn't need to know I almost lost her favorite thing in the world."

Joseph grins. "Man, you sound like an actual married guy."

I look down at Hulk, who's now purring against my chest like nothing happened. "Good thing, since I *am* an actual married guy, idiot."

The guys grab their stuff and head out with the promise of beer and pizza this week, just minutes before Liz arrives. I'm grateful for their help, but even more grateful they are gone. I couldn't trust them not to tell Liz we almost killed her cat.

***

Liz

Houston, we have a problem. Not only have I never been so sore or so tired, but I have an even bigger problem.

Usually, when you train for a distance run, you work your way up to the longest distance. Well, I never ran farther than seven miles in my training. Those last few miles? Brutal. Made worse by the intense need to go to the bathroom. I drank Nate's coffee down in record time and stopped to get another one. Two lattes. Twelve miles.

I've kept it together, but if I don't make it to a toilet in the next five minutes, I'm screwed.

I park and sprint to the elevator to take me up to Nate's place. It's moving at a glacial pace. I might not make it. Sweat beads across my forehead. My phone rings, and I answer it just to distract myself.

"Make it to your friends yet?" Chloe asks. She knew I needed to find a bathroom or else. She suggested I just go at the race, but I couldn't bring myself to use a port-a-potty. I'd rather go in my pants. Honestly, it might come to that.

"Not yet. Almost." The elevator doors open, and I sprint for Nate's door. Do I want to blow up his toilet thirty seconds after moving in? No, no I don't. I'd rather die, but my options are limited.

I burst through the door like I'm on fire to find a startled Nate sitting on the couch, *snuggling Hulk*. He looks up, wide-eyed, a beer paused halfway to his lips. I'd love to stop and melt over how cute the scene is, but the situation is dire.

"Hi! Don't get up. I'm just going to pop into the bathroom real quick."

"You can use the main bath..."

I cut him off while ducking into the guest room slash office.

"No need, the guest bath is fine!" And by fine I mean it's closer and I can't imagine using Nate's toilet right now.

"Sounds like you got there?" Chloe's still on the phone.

"Yeah," I pant, fumbling at the waistband of my compression shorts. "Holy shnikies, Chloe, I can't get my shorts off."

She chuckles nervously. "What do you mean?"

I throw the phone onto the desk, switching it to speaker.

"I mean I'm tugging with both hands and they won't budge. Maybe my legs are swollen from the run? That, coupled with the sweat, must have superglued them to me. Chloe, I'm panicking."

"Calm down. Take a breath and try to slowly tug them down."

"It's not working!" I grunt. "Oh no. I can actually see the toilet. My brain is telling my stomach it's go time. This is it. This is how I die. Covered in my own poo, trapped in a pair of shorts that have fused themselves to me!"

My stomach clenches in betrayal. Nope. Not now. Not here. I feel the first trickle of what can only be described as liquid diarrhea exit my body.

"Chloe, it's happening!" I shriek.

A panicked Chloe screams back. "Liz, what do you mean it's happening?!"

Another trickle. My shorts are so tight it has nowhere to go. It's trapped.

There's a knock on the door, and I freeze. "No..." I whisper-hiss.

"Uh, Liz." His voice is way too loud.

"Everything's fine! Be out in a minute!"

He clears his throat. "Liz, you should know, the bedrooms don't have ceilings. The only closed-in rooms are the actual bathrooms."

I look up to see the tall ceilings, and the beautiful exposed duct work that I admired the first time I came over. The bedroom wall stops five feet from the ceiling. It reminds me of a shower stall in a bathroom.

"What kind of crackhead designed this place?"

My stomach lurches. I clench my cheeks together as hard as I can, willing the waterfall that has now started to stop.

"Chloe, I gotta go."

"Liz, I'm coming in."

"Please, sweet baby Jesus, do *not* come in here!"

He cracks the door open. I can only imagine what I look like, dead tired from the race, disheveled, panicked, with my shorts rapidly expanding with my own feces.

He walks in calmly, grabs a pair of scissors from the desk, and crouches beside me like he's preparing for a high-stakes medical procedure.

My eyes go wide. "What are you doing?"

"It sounded pretty serious in here. I'm getting you out of these."

"Nate. I have a high threshold for mortification, but you are absolutely not cutting me out of my own shorts." I rip the scissors out of his hands.

"Got it," he says, trying to hide his amusement, hands raised in surrender.

I quickly run into the bathroom, slamming the door behind me, and I waste no time freeing myself. I slide the blade under my shorts, and like sausage packed too tight, the fabric *explodes* off my legs.

I should be mortified, but I don't even care.

I yell through the bathroom door. "Nate, if you care about me at all, you'll leave that room, put on noise-canceling headphones, and we will never speak of this again."

"Copy that," he says, voice tight with restrained laughter. "Good luck, champ."

Once the entirety of my stomach has been emptied, and my pride along with it, I've showered and scrubbed the bathroom from top to bottom, I have nothing left to do but exit this safe haven and face the music.

I quietly open the door and peek my head out. The apartment is quiet, except for faint music coming from the kitchen. On the desk sits a folded pile of clean clothes, the sweatshirt I stole from him, and an empty trash bag.

My heart squeezes. He just saw me lose a battle with my own digestive system, and his first instinct was to take care of me. I don't know what to do with that kind of kindness.

I swiftly empty the trash in the bathroom, including my clothes from earlier, before pulling on his T-shirt and sweatpants. They hang loose and soft against my skin.

I know all my clothes must be here somewhere, but I love that he left me his instead. It feels intentional, like a quiet act of care. And they smell like him. Clean. Warm. Safe.

Chapter Twenty-Six
Possessed Piñata
Nate

It wouldn't be Liz if we started living together any other way than pure chaos. I could hear her clearly from the living room, obviously panicking about getting her shorts off and getting to the bathroom. Shit happens. Literally.

I hide my chuckle behind a cough when I see Liz emerge from the guest room. She pauses at the end of the hallway leading into the living area. She's wringing her hands together. She peeks up at me like she expects me to flinch or laugh or run for the hills. My chest tightens, because I know someone in her past probably made her feel foolish for being human. Not here. Not with me.

I don't know exactly how she's going to react to everything that just unfolded, but I already decided if she came out embarrassed, I was going to nip it in the bud.

"So, you shit your pants."

A laugh bursts out of her, bright and unrestrained. She tucks a strand of damp blonde hair behind her ear and walks farther into the room. She left her hair down after her shower. It hangs in loose waves almost to her ass.

"Yeah. That happened." She folds herself into a pretzel on the opposite end of the couch from me. Hulk immediately abandons me in favor of her. Traitor. I thought we bonded today.

"When I was fourteen, I was at a stunt camp," I start, leaning back against the couch. "It was the first time my parents willingly let me go instead of me sneaking off with Joe. I didn't have a ton of friends back then. Most people thought I was socially awkward since I tend to go quiet in large groups."

"No, you? Quiet? Shocking," Liz teases.

I toss a pillow at her, relieved she's teasing and smiling.

"It was the second day of camp. There was this girl I thought was really cute. I woke up not feeling great, but there was no way I was missing that day. Around the time we broke into groups for live-action rig work, my stomach turned. Sweat ran down my neck, my mouth was watering. All the warning signs were there, but I was partnered with the girl, so I tried to tough it out."

"I'm nervous for you," she says, hugging the pillow, half-laughing, half-cringing.

"I was hooked into a harness. She was supposed to fake kick me, then the line would pull me back through a fake wall and into a crash pad. The second her foot touched my stomach, I blew chunks. And since I was strapped in, I couldn't even move."

Liz's hand flies over her mouth. "No! Did she...?"

"She screamed. And then the guy running the rig yanked the cable, because he didn't realize what was happening, and I went flying backward mid-puke. There's video footage. It looks like a horror film. Like I'm vomiting so hard it propels me backward through a wall."

Liz explodes into giggles. "No! All I can picture is a miniature you. Not yet all muscle-y and manly, wanting to impress a girl so bad, but turning green and totally ruining any chance you had."

"Oh, it gets worse," I say, grinning now. "I was dangling in the harness, still retching, spinning like a possessed piñata from hell. The girl was a sympathetic puker. She started throwing up. Which set off another kid. Then another. Joe had to shut down the whole workshop. He was furious. Didn't talk to me for a week."

Liz wipes tears from her eyes, laughing. "Poor, Bear. That's bad. Almost as bad as pooping your pants in your fake husband's house before you're even unpacked. Then having to cut yourself out of your shorts. Almost that bad."

"Nah," I say, smirking. "It's no big deal. Like I said, shit happens.

Her shoulders drop, and she visibly relaxes. Mission accomplished. I nudge her knee with my foot. "We won't talk about it again. It never happened. Tell me about the race instead."

She groans dramatically and pets Hulk. "Don't ever let me sign up for another race again. That's Chloe and James's thing, not mine. After mile nine, my feet went completely numb. Which, honestly, was a blessing. Before that they felt like the skin was peeling off them like an orange. I lost five pounds in sweat and regret."

"Come here." I shift closer and pull her feet into my lap. She lets out a small whimper.

"What are you doing?"

"Rubbing your feet."

I pick one up gently, thumb brushing along the arch. Her toenail polish is chipped, her feet red and swollen from the miles. "I bought you Epsom salt so you could soak," I admit, "but... after everything, I forgot about it."

She sinks deeper into the couch, throws her wet hair over the back, and her eyes flutter closed as I work her foot. A soft sound slips out of her, somewhere between a sigh and a purr. My brain short-circuits. I am absolutely not thinking about kissing her damp neck so I can feel the vibration of her moans and not just hear them. Nope. Not even a little.

"Oh! I almost forgot," she says, lifting her head slightly. "I told Chloe and James I'd meet them for trivia night on Tuesday."

I tilt my head. "Okay? You don't need my permission to go out with your family or your friends."

She throws the pillow back at me, aiming for my head. "We wouldn't make it if it was that kind of marriage." She smirks at me. "I figured you could come, and we could tell them that we got married."

I blink at her. "So let me get this straight. Your plan is to spring me on them and tell them we got married all at one time at trivia night?"

"Right."

I groan, dragging a hand over my face. "Liz..."

She grins wider. "Relax. It'll be fun. You like trivia, right? We'll just slide the marriage thing in somewhere between rounds."

Her optimism is ridiculous, but somehow contagious. I can't help the laugh that escapes me. "You're lucky I like trivia."

"It'll be the best night of your life, besides marrying me." She shoots back, smirking.

I grunt a laugh. Life with Liz will always be entertaining, at the very least.

"Soup'll be here in twenty. There's another bottle of electrolytes on the table." I toss her the remote. "Pick whatever chick flick you want."

Her lips curve into a lazy smile. "You're the perfect man. Marry me." She cracks one eye open. "Oops. You already did."

I shake my head, but I cannot stop the stupid smile tugging at my mouth. I married her to solve a problem. Now I'm starting to think she might be the best thing to ever happen to me.

***

Liz

It's been the perfect afternoon. We rotated from the couch to unpacking and then back to the couch. I fell asleep for a little while and woke up to a craft corner Nate set up in the corner of the living room. I couldn't stop the tears that welled in my eyes and fell down my cheeks. He was visually uncomfortable with how touched I was, waving my praise off, but the fact that he built me a corner to do the things I love. Stick a fork in me. I'm done.

He excused himself and took the last of my boxes to the dumpster. It gave me time to get my emotions under control.

Today was the most productive lazy day ever. Now we're cozied up on the couch, eating leftover soup and watching *Special Forces*.

Nate hit his romcom fill about two hours ago, but this show is perfect for both of us. They take celebrities and make them complete military training for two weeks. It's TV gold. We're taking bets on who will be the last to complete a challenge or the first to tap out. Our banter has an easy rhythm, like we've done this a hundred times before. It feels like this is always how we spend our Saturday nights.

The day should have been awkward after how it started, but he immediately put me at ease. Every time I started to overthink, he'd crack a joke, brush a hand along my shoulder, or refill my drink like it was second nature.

I've been ridiculously comfortable in his clothes all day long. Now I'm tucked into his side, my head on his shoulder, his hand resting lightly on my thigh. It's the kind of casual touch that shouldn't mean anything, but feels like it does.

We haven't talked about our rules for our fake marriage since last weekend. Maybe we should? I know it's not real, but today has felt incredibly real.

I don't want to burst whatever bubble we're in, but it's inching toward bedtime, and I don't know what he expects. Do I say goodnight and disappear into the guest room? Or would that make things weird now that we're married on paper? Do we sleep in his bed? Would he even want that? Would I?

My pulse ticks faster just thinking about it. I know we aren't actually husband and wife, but how far do we take it?

"Alright," Nate says, breaking into my thoughts as he switches the TV off. "You look like you're falling asleep sitting up."

I blink, realizing my head's been resting on his shoulder longer than I thought. "Oh. Yeah. Probably should, uh, head to bed."

He gives me a look, the one where one eyebrow arches and his mouth barely tilts, like he knows exactly what's going on in my head, but he's too polite to call me out.

And before I can stop myself, I start rambling. "I mean, obviously I can take the guest room, right? I don't want to, like, invade your space or anything. Not that sharing a bed would be invading, I mean, we are technically married. Legally. And we already have shared a bed before, well, not that we have, you know, *shared a bed*, shared a bed. Nothing is weird. I'll just take the guest room and you'll sleep in your room like you always do. However you usually sleep. Naked? Or not. It doesn't matter how you sleep. We are just two totally normal married people, doing our bedtime routine. Oh my gosh, why am I still talking?"

He's fighting a smile and losing. "No idea. It's impressive though."

"I'm shutting up now," I say, throwing my hands up. "Just point me toward the couch or guest room or wherever and I'll..."

"The guest bed's small," he cuts in easily, like it's no big deal. "And the mattress is garbage. You'll wake up with your spine shaped like a question mark."

I blink at him. "So, the couch it is then?"

He leans back, totally calm. "Or," he says, voice low and steady, "you just sleep in my bed with me. It's a big bed. I don't bite."

"That's debatable."

He laughs quietly, and the sound does something dangerous to my heart.

"I mean, if you're sure," I start again, words tripping over themselves, "because I don't want you to think I'm assuming we're, like, bed-sharing people. We could totally be like Lucy and Ricky and sleep in our own twin beds. Maybe we could go shopping tomorrow? Or maybe we could even get bunk beds. I always wanted those as a kid and getting bunk beds in my late twenties with my fake-real husband seems like the perfect time to fulfill that childhood dream."

"Liz."

"Yeah?"

"Go get ready for bed. I set all your stuff on my sink already. Tomorrow we can go shopping."

I raise a brow. "Bunk beds?"

"No. We can go pick out new sheets and new comforter. Something that fits us both."

I stare back at him eyes wide. "Now go get ready for bed." He says it gently, but there's no room for argument. It's not an order, it's reassurance. I nod, trying not to overanalyze the way his voice makes me feel, and head toward his bathroom.

As I pass him, he gives my backside a smack and I get moving. That's normal, right? More like a good game between bros?

When I'm done in the bathroom, the lights are dimmed, and he's already in bed, one arm tucked behind his head, hair a little messy, looking unfairly comfortable. He glances over at me and lifts the blanket in silent invitation.

My brain short-circuits for half a second, but I slide in beside him.

It's quiet in here. The kind of quiet that hums with energy. The kind where everything unspoken fills the space between heartbeats. Hulk jumps onto the bed and settles at our feet.

"See?" he says softly. "No big deal."

Easy for him to say. My heart is currently trying to tap-dance out of my chest.

We lie there in the dark, both staring at the ceiling, like the two old people in the Notebook waiting to die. The silence stretches. I count the seconds, then the minutes, trying to slow my racing thoughts. The sheets are too warm. My brain's too loud. I shift once, twice, trying to find a comfortable spot. Then again.

Finally, a quiet sigh from his side of the bed. "You always this squirmy?"

"Yes. No. Maybe. I can't sleep," I whisper. "My brain won't stop, my body is sore, I can't get comfortable."

He doesn't say anything for a second. Then I hear the soft click of his phone unlocking, the glow lighting up his face. I roll onto my side to find him scrolling, his brow furrowed in concentration.

"What are you doing?" I whisper.

He glances over, one corner of his mouth lifting. "Finding something to quiet that brain of yours."

I blink, confused, until I see what's on his screen. Instagram. Videos of little kids being pulled on stage to sing with their favorite rock stars. My favorite rabbit hole.

"You remembered!"

"Of course I remembered." He scrolls again, then tilts the screen toward me. "Come here."

I hesitate, but he pats the spot beside him, and I scoot closer until I can see the phone. Our shoulders brush, and the contact makes my pulse skitter.

He presses play. A little girl, no older than twelve, sings her heart out beside a guitarist twice her height. The crowd goes wild. I feel my throat tighten the way it always does with these.

"She's amazing," I whisper.

"Yeah," he murmurs, tilting his head down to look at me.

I glance at him, but his eyes return to the screen.

Another video auto-plays. Then another. We fall into an easy rhythm, him scrolling, me reacting, our whispers and quiet laughter filling the dark. At some point, my head ends up against his shoulder again, and I can feel his slow, steady breathing.

When he finally sets his phone down, the room goes dark.

"You good now?" he asks quietly.

"Yeah," I breathe, half-asleep already. "You're dangerous, you know that?"

"How so?"

"You remember all the things I love and then do them."

He huffs a quiet laugh. "Go to sleep, Cricket."

Chapter Twenty-Seven
Sunday Fun Day
Liz

I WAKE UP EARLY wrapped around Nate just like last weekend in California after having the best night of sleep I've ever gotten. The combination of moving, running myself into total humiliation, and breathing in Nate's calming scent must really do it for me. I try to unwrap myself from him as slowly as I can so I can make us coffee. There's somewhere I want to take him today. Some people he needs to meet.

I'm moving slowly, my muscles are sore, but when that first drop of coffee hits the pot it's like smelling salts to my veins. I haven't even had a sip yet, and I already feel more alive. I pour my first cup and open the fridge to see my creamer options. I'm not expecting much since Nate drinks his black. Hoping for at least some milk. There, next to some Mega Man drink, certainly going to make fun of him for that later, is pistachio-flavored cream. I've never found it in a store, I don't know how he did, but it makes me feel fluttery. All over.

I take my first sip. It's perfection. I pour Nate a cup of black coffee with plans to put it on his side table until he wakes, but when I look up he's slowly walking into the kitchen. His hair is a mess, he's shirtless, sweatpants slung low, wearing glasses, and holding my cat. I'd say he's adorable, but he's too sexy to fall into that category. Adorably-sexy? New category unlocked.

"Morning." His morning voice is rougher than I remember it last weekend. He hasn't shaved in days and it only adds to his sexiness factor. How is this my husband?

"Morning! Sleep well?" My voice sounds breathy and it annoys me. I need to rein in my body's reaction to him, but it doesn't want to cooperate.

"Like a rock." Nate sets Hulk down gently and he wanders over to me and rubs against my leg in a figure eight. Nate stretches his arms above his head making the V next to his lower abs stand out even more. Blurry. Things are getting very blurry for me.

"Great!" I thrust his cup of coffee at him to give myself something to do. "Do you have plans today?"

He eyes me skeptically over the rim of his cup while he takes a slow sip. "Not really. Why?"

"There's somewhere I want to take you today. Some people I want to introduce you to."

"Okay." It was more of a grunt than an overwhelmingly enthusiastic YES, but I'll take it.

"Cool. Great. I'm going to go shower and we can head out?" All I can think about is escaping the room from this man before I do something really stupid like get some of my crafting glue and stick us together for forever. I turn and head toward the guest room, but his voice stops me.

"Liz." I look at him over my shoulder and cock an eyebrow. "I put all of your stuff in our bathroom. It's yours to use."

Our bathroom. I guess last night wasn't a fluke. We will be sharing a bedroom and bathroom. Full-on married life.

"Great. Thanks!" I make an about face and walk to the master, clipping my shoulder on the wall, because spatial awareness has left the building along with my self-control. "I'm fine. Everything is fine!"

***

AN HOUR LATER, NATE is dressed in jeans and a white T-shirt. My hormones have calmed, but only slightly. He pulls into the parking lot of my favorite place on earth. I pull a pair of muck boots from my bag and slip them on.

"Welcome to my home away from home."

He gets out of my car, shields his eyes, and looks around at the fields surrounding us. A baby colt is kicking up a storm in the field to our left and I see a smile spread across his face.

"Where exactly are we, Cricket?"

I come to stand next to him and point across the lake, "See that white house through the woods over there?" He squints to see where I'm pointing and nods his head.

"That's my parents' house," I pause, looping my arm through his so I can turn him toward the big barn, "And this is my favorite spot on the planet."

We walk into the barn and I breathe deeply. I may be a girly-girl, but the smell of animals, hay, and the outdoors will always center me. Mrs. Mary pops her head out of a stall.

"I thought I heard someone chattering. I should have known it was you, Lizzy-girl."

"Hey, Mrs. Mary! I hope it's okay that I popped by this morning?"

She wipes her hands on her jeans and swallows me in a hug. "It is always okay for you to be here. You know you don't have to ask." She releases me and turns to Nate. "And who is this cowboy?"

I smile at the gleam of appreciation in her eyes as she takes Nate in. She may be nearing seventy, but she isn't blind.

"This is Nate, but I might just start calling him cowboy. I like that." He gives me a dirty look when I reach back for his hand and twine our fingers together. "My husband."

It's the first time I've introduced him as my husband. A thrill runs through me. That felt nice to say. I feel proud to introduce him this way to one of the most important people in my life.

"Well, well, well. Seems like you've had some big life changes since the last time you stopped by, Lizzy-girl." She turns to Nate and takes him in with a new eye, she must find him worthy because she steps forward and gives him a big hug.

I fight my giggle at Nate's frozen face. "Congrats to the both of you. Nate, I hope you know what you've signed up with our girl here. You'll never be bored with our Lizzy."

"Yes ma'am, I'm learning that."

"Mrs. Mary, we'd love to do the morning feeding if you haven't already."

"Free labor? You know I'll never turn that down. Made the bottles, but haven't fed the goblins, you know where the stuffs at."

I grab Nate's hand again and we walk to a little barn down the hill. His face is as unreadable as ever. If he's surprised my favorite place on earth is a farm, he isn't showing it.

"Goblins?"

"Don't worry, hubby, I'll protect you."

We walk into the barn, a perfect tiny replica of the giant barn on the hill, and hear the first moo. Nate's face is confused for half a second before he peeks into a converted horse stall and sees five calves. I walk behind him and take the bucket down from the wall that holds five giant baby bottles. Think if Bigfoot had a baby, that's what a cow bottle looks like.

I set the bottle holders over the fencing inside the stall and drop the bottles in. It's a rambunctious crew. They all head butt each other trying to get to the first one. It makes me giggle. "Calm down, you'll each get one!"

When I get to the last bottle, the smallest baby is the only one left. I hold the bottle out to Nate. "Come here."

I give him the bottle to hold and feed the little one. He steps over to the baby and holds the bottle down for her to latch on to. She makes happy little grunting noises as she eats. Usually I can't tear my eyes from the babies, but today my eyes are locked on Nate as he smiles down at the tiny little cow. He runs his other hand over her head, between her ears. I can't help it. I take my phone out and snap a picture. The peaceful look on his face is not something I want to forget. His face looks how I feel every time I'm here.

"So you grew up here?" He asks and looks around.

"Yeah. James and I spent a lot of time helping Mrs. Mary out when we were growing up. Her husband was in the Navy and was gone a lot. She's run this place for decades almost completely alone. Even if she didn't *need* the help. It would have been hard to keep me away. It's my happy place."

The baby cow snorts snot all over Nate's leg. "I can see why."

I punch his arm. Not hard, just playful. The babies are finishing, so I round the bottles up and we spend time loving on each one before washing the bottles and walking down the path away from the barns.

"Thanks for bringing me here."

"Of course, but the morning isn't over yet."

We make it to my parents' front porch just minutes later. The home I grew up in looks like a miniature farm house. I try to see it through Nate's eyes. It's painted peach with maroon shutters, sounds weird, but somehow it works. The front porch is covered in plants of all shapes and sizes. I get my green thumb from my mom. If my dad is in the doghouse, all he has to do is stop and get a plant for her and all is forgiven.

We toe off our shoes and walk in the front door without knocking. It's unlocked, like always. I don't think it's ever been locked. Nate trails behind me. If he's nervous he doesn't show it.

"Mom? Dad?" We walk further into the house and see my dad on the couch, the same one they've had since I was little, cleaning his hearing aids. Mom pops her head around the kitchen door.

"Liz? That you sweetheart?"

Dad notices the commotion and looks up. A big grin spreads across his face. My parents were older when they had all of us. They were always the oldest parents among all my friends. I hated it when I was younger. They never tried to be the parents that were friends with their kids. They were always just our parents. Steady, dependable, hardworking. Trying to raise us all to be successful adults.

They suddenly look fragile to me. I know I'm the cause of more than a few of the gray hairs that grace their heads. I wrap them both in big hugs. I may not have been friends with my parents growing up, but the smell of fresh bread wafting off my mom gives me comfort, peace. Her hugs always make me feel small again. They make me feel like everything will always work out and be okay when I'm wrapped in her hug.

After our greeting, they look behind me and see Nate standing by the door. My dad pops his hearing aids in.

"Young man?" My dad holds his hand out to shake Nate's hand before knowing anything about him. Nate steps forward and shakes my dad's hand. His stance makes my dad's shrinking form stand out even more.

"Sir."

"Mom, dad, this is Nate." I hesitate only for a minute. I know they won't freak out. I know they won't even bat an eyelash after everything I've thrown at them, but I suddenly feel nervous. I want them to love Nate as much as they loved Chloe when James introduced her. "My husband."

My mom stutter-steps on her way to wrap him in a hug, she reaches his mid-chest, but that's the only hiccup I notice with my proclamation.

"Welcome, welcome. Come on in, let's get you something to eat and you can tell us all about your young man." I smile at Nate who looks bewildered at their reaction. Mom leads us into the kitchen and starts plating a freshly baked pie.

"Tell us everything."

So I do. Sort of. I leave out the fake bit. And I play up our whirlwind romance a little. I tell them how we were so in love, we couldn't wait another day without getting married. I never wanted a big wedding, so that plays in my favor with our whole story. By the end of telling them our love story, we've polished off our pies and dad is asking Nate to help him with something in the garage that he isn't strong enough to do.

As soon as they walk out mom comes over and sits next to me taking my hand. "You're happy Lizzy?"

I stop to think before answering her. I don't want to give her lip service. "Very."

"And he treats you well?"

"Very. I've never felt so cared for. He's a really good man, mom." I squeeze her hand. "I know you didn't get a chance to get to know him before we ran off and got married, but you'll love him."

"And your brother? He approves?"

For the first time since walking into my parents I cringe. "I haven't told him yet. I'm introducing them Tuesday."

Mom's eyes go round behind her glasses. The only indication that she realizes how much of a train wreck that could be.

"If you could refrain from telling him until I do, that would be great."

"Of course, honey. If you are happy, we are happy. You haven't had an easy road. Love hasn't been kind to you, but I'd have to be blind not to see the way you look at each other. You found your person, and I look forward to getting to know him over the years."

Over the years. Well at least for the next year. My smile falters for half a second before I paste it back on as Dad and Nate return to the kitchen.

We FaceTime the twins at school and share the big news with them. They are shocked, but don't comment otherwise. They've always looked at me like their hippie-gypsy sister. More mythical creature than sibling. It's always been James and me and then the twins. Kind of like family A and family B. It's not right or wrong, I've just never been especially close to either of them, they've always had each other, and I've always had James.

After we hang up, my parents share all kinds of embarrassing stories about me, which Nate eats up. He smirks at me over his second piece of pie while my parents bust out old pictures. Bad haircuts, braces, the works. Hopefully he still wants to be my husband after this. After a few hours, we say our goodbyes and walk hand in hand back to my car at the farm.

Nate pulls me firmly into his side and kisses my temple. "Thanks for sharing your parents with me, Cricket. They are wonderful. I see why you're so amazing."

All I can do is smile at him. I like sharing these pieces of me.

Chapter Twenty-Eight

He's My Husband

Liz

It's Tuesday night and Nate and I are waiting beside the studio for Chloe and James. I feel stupidly excited for them to meet, but also nervous. The meeting with my parents went better than I can imagine. When we got back in the car, Nate said how much he enjoyed meeting them, how much he liked seeing where I grew up. My mom called me yesterday to tell me she and my dad really loved him.

But introducing him to James won't be like introducing him to my mom and dad. My brother can be... *a lot*. Overprotective, dramatic, easily suspicious. With good cause, I guess, after my last serious relationship.

But dropping a bomb like *Oh hey, I'm married...* I'm hoping it's going to be fine. I rub my hands together in nervous anticipation. I can't wait to watch their heads explode, but also I really want them to like him.

I bounce on my toes and do another lap in front of Nate. "You're making me dizzy. Chill out."

I shoot him a look. "You're not nervous?"

"No."

"But it's my family," I argue. "You don't feel any pressure to impress them?"

"No."

"What? Why not?" I stop, hands on hips, half-offended he doesn't care more.

"Everything went great with your parents. It'll be fine with James and Chloe too." I start to pace again.

As I pass by for the millionth time, he catches my elbow and stops me. He's leaning against the brick wall, perfectly unbothered, and he tugs me to stand between his legs. "Listen, Cricket," he says, low and even. "It's not that I don't want your brother to like me. That'll work itself out. But if he doesn't, it's all temporary anyway, right? So why are you so worked up?"

I let out a long breath. He's right. I put so much pressure on myself to meet his parents, and that went fine. *Mostly.* I mean, we're married now because of my big mouth, but it's all working out... ish. Him meeting my parents went better than fine. It'll be okay.

I give him a small smile. "You're right."

He releases my arm and I settle next to him against the wall. "Okay, this is going to be fun. No need to be worried."

He looks at me like he's bracing for impact. He should be. If I'm going to throw caution to the wind and really not care what they think, I might as well enjoy it. I can't stop my delighted giggle that slips from my mouth. I spot Chloe and James walking up hand in hand, and it's go time.

"Hey," I say as I push off the wall trying to school my face. "About time you two lovebirds showed up."

"Sorry," James says, then adds suggestively, "Chloe needed to change her earrings... three times."

Gag. Don't need to hear about that.

"Excuse me, if you're gonna lie, make it believable." Chloe chimes in. I watch James lean down and kiss her on the head. They're disgustingly cute sometimes, but they deserve all the happiness.

A laugh escapes me, and I glance back at Nate, trying to read what he thinks of James and Chloe so far. His face is as unreadable as usual, but I think he gives me an encouraging nod. Maybe I'm just seeing what I want to see.

I turn back to James to find him raising an eyebrow. "Friend of yours?"

I give a little shrug, unable to stop the blush from spreading across my face. Nerves, probably. Maybe from the atomic bomb I'm about to drop. "This is Nate."

Nate nods and pushes off the wall to extend a hand. "Hey. Heard a lot about you two." His voice sounds rougher than usual. Maybe he's a little nervous after all.

"Only the good things, I promise," I jump in, bumping my shoulder into his. We are in this together.

I watch James and Chloe share a look before we all start down the sidewalk toward the car. Chloe drops back beside me and loops her arm through mine. "So... Nate? Who is this guy?"

I can't hold back my smirk. "Yeah... Nate." I hesitate for half a second. No time like the present to rip off the bandaid. "He's... well, he's my husband. I thought it was time for you guys to meet."

Chloe stops dead in her tracks, pulling me to a stop with her. James's head whips around faster than a bullet. "What did you just say?" Nate takes a subtle step away from James. I'm assuming it's in case my brother starts throwing punches and asking questions later.

I can't help it. I laugh. It bubbles up before I can stop it. "You heard me."

Chloe blinks. "Your *husband*?"

"Yup." I pop the P and flash what I hope passes as a confident smile. "As in legally binding, signed-on-the-dotted-line, till-death-do-us-part." I flash a wink at Nate, and he kind of looks like he wants to murder me for dropping our marriage bomb this way.

James blinks once. Twice. "You're kidding, right? This is like when you went off with your girlfriends for a week and you told me you were joining a cult, but really you were sitting on the beach laughing about my freak out?"

"Wouldn't that be hilarious?" I say, pretending to consider it. "But nope, I'm totally serious." I step toward Nate and lean into him. I wonder how much physical contact I can get away with tonight in the name of convincing them? "We got married last weekend."

James's eyes narrow. "Someone better start explaining. Now."

"It's kind of a long story." I wind my fingers through Nate's and start dragging him to the car.

Chloe gives me a look that makes me feel a little guilty. It's part disbelief, part amusement, and a little hurt. "Liz. You got *married* and didn't tell us?"

"Well, it wasn't exactly a planned thing." I glance at Nate, who's doing a terrible job of helping me out. I thought this would be more fun. "It's... uh, complicated."

"Complicated?" James echoes, voice scarily calm that tells me he's two seconds away from losing it.

"Yup. Complicated. But everything's fine." I offer my brightest smile. "Better than fine, actually. We're great. Married and thriving. Isn't that right, Pumpkin?"

Nate exhales, long-suffering. "Absolutely, Cricket."

Chloe covers a laugh with her hand, and I swear I can see the moment she decides to enjoy this instead of panic. "Oh, this I cannot wait to hear," she says. "Every single detail."

James just mutters something about needing something stronger than a beer to make it through trivia night. I hook my arm through Nate's, and let out an exhale. The hard part is over, I guess, now to make them believe it.

"Buckle up," I whisper, "It's show time."

***

The four of us sit around the trivia table, drinks ordered, wrapped in awkward silence. The entire way here, no matter what I tried to chat about, work, movies, or the trivia theme, no one said much in return. The air feels thick enough to chew. I've broken out into a nervous sweat, and my knee won't stop bouncing until Nate's hand settles over it under the table, warm and grounding.

Chloe keeps smiling, but it's tight. She keeps glancing between me and James, like she's silently begging him not to make a scene. Too late. I can feel the tension radiating off my brother from across the table.

James takes a slow sip of his beer, watching Nate like he's waiting for him to screw up. Then blurts, "Are you pregnant?"

Nate chokes on his beer, spraying foam across the table. Guess I know how he feels about imaginary kids.

"No!" I groan, dabbing napkins across the table. "Not pregnant. We were in California for an event, having a good time, and decided to take the fun up a notch."

James blinks. "Liz, if you want to take the fun up a notch, get a confetti cannon. Don't get married." His voice is sharp, the undercurrent of hurt shining through. "We didn't even know you'd been seeing anyone. Do Mom and Dad know?"

"We went over on Sunday and spent the day with them."

"And, what did they say?"

"They were happy for us. Shocked, but not completely surprised. I think they know to expect the unexpected. We are going to have dinner with them soon and the twins next time they are home on break."

The conversation with my parents was easier than this, that's for sure. They've always known I do my own thing, no matter what they say or do. They've adopted a come-what-may attitude. I think it was the only way they survived raising me.

No one says anything so I keep talking. "Mom had a few questions, of course. Understandable, but all things considered they handled it like champs."

Chloe exhales softly, almost in relief, but James doesn't. He just keeps looking at Nate, like he's trying to see past his skin to whatever he's hiding. I can practically see the protective-brother alarm blaring behind his eyes.

"This is all very fast," he says finally. "And we all remember how the last relationship ended when you jumped in too quickly."

His words hit hard. My throat goes tight, my palms sweat. I can feel the sting of humiliation and fear crawl up my spine. Chloe's hand lands gently on James's arm, but it doesn't stop the ache already spreading in my chest.

"I'm not the same person I was two years ago," I say quietly, trying to steady my voice. "And Nate is a good man, James. You aren't even giving him a chance."

I feel Nate's body stiffen when he hears my voice quiver. He looks from me to James and positions himself slightly in front of me, as if he can shield me from my brother's words.

James exhales through his nose, unconvinced. "You said that before too. Then you were waking up in a hospital bed, your life in shambles around you."

The sound of my heartbeat fills my ears. The words land like a punch, knocking the air out of me. Nate tenses further beside me, his body alert. I can feel him staring, waiting for me to react. I glance up at him, ashamed of my past. The things I haven't told him. His face gives away nothing.

"James." Chloe's voice is firm, a warning. "Enough."

He sighs but doesn't apologize. The memories flash through my mind like a movie. The bruises. The broken bones. The police reports. And all the things James still doesn't know.

I clear my throat, forcing a smile, completely ignoring the bomb he just dropped. If I was married for real, my husband would know about my past. "Look, I get it. We blindsided you. But Nate and I have been seeing each other for a while. As you both know, I've been out of town for months on this movie. Nate works with me. We started spending a lot of time together."

I look at Nate, my words starting to crumble. "And it just sort of happened."

Nate gives my hand a squeeze. Reassuring me that we are in this together, he picks up the thread smoothly, his tone calm, but sure.

"I know you don't know me, James. I don't have a sister, but I appreciate your protectiveness. That's good. I'm glad Liz has you in her corner."

He slides his arm around me, solid and steady, and suddenly I can breathe again.

"I know how this looks," he continues, his gaze flicking down to me before meeting James's again. "I'm not the type of guy who jumps into anything. I don't do impulsive. I don't do messy. But then Liz happened. She's chaos and noise and color, and I didn't know I needed any of that, until she walked into my life."

He pauses long enough for the silence to stretch, for it to feel like the whole table is holding its breath.

"I didn't mean to fall so quickly for your sister," he says finally, "but now I can't picture my life without her in it. You don't have to like me, but you should know I'll spend every day making sure hers are better because I'm in them."

The table goes quiet. Chloe blinks fast like she's trying not to tear up. James looks between us, weighing every word, and I see something shift. He's still skeptical, but Nate's words landed.

I know he's just playing the part, that Nate doesn't actually mean any of that, but man, when he decides to use words, he does it so well. I look up at him and can't help but pull him to me for a quick kiss. I could lie and say it's to sell this sham, but this one is just for me.

The tension finally loosens. We settle into trivia, and to everyone's surprise, Nate is a closeted nineties sitcom fan. He nails every answer, and our team comes out on top. Without him, we wouldn't have even made top three.

Before we leave, Chloe and I hit the bathroom together. The second the door shuts, she crosses her arms and stares me down.

"Okay, now that we're alone, what in the actual F, Liz?"

I stare at my reflection, cheeks flushed, heart pounding. "It's a long story."

She leans against the counter. "We've got time. You can't just drop a marriage announcement in the middle of trivia and then act like we're talking about the weather. You got married. Is it real? Is it just one of your spontaneous, wild-Liz things?"

Her tone softens a little, curiosity edging out the irritation. "I just want to know if you're okay. This feels really impulsive even for you."

I debated earlier whether I was going to tell Chloe the truth, the real truth, but after Nate's words at the table, I don't want to. I don't know who I'm fooling, me or her, but it felt so real.

"He's the best person I know," I say, a smile lighting my face that feels more true than I expect. "Selfless. Quietly caring. Funny when he wants to be. It happened quick, and I'm sorry you guys weren't there, but it was just for us. We can celebrate still, but this is very much sticking."

Chloe studies me for a long moment, her reflection serious beside mine. Then she sighs and hugs me. "You look happy," she murmurs, pulling back. "That's all that matters to me. But Liz… if something changes, don't wait to call me. I don't need an explanation. I don't need details. Anytime, day or night, I'll come running. Okay?"

I nod, my throat tight. Chloe and James love me so much. I feel so lucky to have them both.

As we walk out of the bathroom and back to the table, what sticks with me isn't James and Chloe's love for me. It's the way Nate looked at me when he said those words. Like they weren't part of a performance. Like he might actually mean them.

Chapter Twenty-Nine
She Doesn't Need A Savior
Nate

With how the night started off, I wasn't sure how it would end. Liz dropping the fact that we got married before we ever made it to the car shouldn't have surprised me, but I thought she might wait until we ordered our drinks at least.

Once James got over his shock, he turned out to be a cool dude. I could see us hanging out with them a lot. The fact that he adores my girl and would do anything for her made me respect him. *My girl.*

Speaking of which, she was uncharacteristically quiet the entire Uber ride back to the condo. Even though the night ended up fine, I've got questions. I've given her space. I haven't pushed, but it's time she's honest with me.

I watch as she pads back into the living room, freshly changed into pajamas. Her pajamas kill me. Always tiny little shorts and a T-shirt with some ridiculous saying. Tonight's shirt says *If Unicorns Aren't Real, Neither Am I.* What does that even mean?

"So I thought that went well." I can always count on Liz to break the silence. She doesn't do well sitting in the quiet. I nod my head and sit down on the couch. Hulk leaves his resting place on the rug and jumps up to me. Every day, the little guy is growing on me more and more.

"Liz."

She sighs dramatically. "I know, I know." She flings herself on the couch beside me. Not on the other end, but right next to me, and reaches over to scratch Hulk's chin.

"What do you want to know?"

"Everything." My voice is calm, but inside I'm bracing. I want to know everything her brother hinted at tonight and more.

She swallows carefully. "Alright. I'm not a closed book, you know that. I usually don't have a problem opening up about this, but I didn't want you to see me differently. Not that you would. Or that any of it is my fault. Well, maybe part of it is my fault, but..."

I run my hand over her shin. "Land the plane, Cricket. Start at the beginning."

She nods her head like she's having a conversation that I can't hear. "Okay, so I was in a pretty serious relationship for two years. It, um, it wasn't the best. I met him at work."

I try to keep my face neutral, but the similarities to her last relationship and ours aren't starting off in my favor. No wonder her brother was pissed tonight.

"He was a production assistant. We moved in with each other really quickly."

She glances away like she can't meet my eyes. Like she doesn't want to acknowledge that so far our story matches. It causes me to grind my molars. I can feel my pulse thudding in my ears.

"Probably why you and I are even more triggering than usual for my brother. There are a lot of similarities, even though I know you are nothing like my ex."

At least she realizes that. I have a feeling I don't want to be looped in with this guy in any way, shape, or form. I nod for her to keep going.

"He was good at what he did. Charming, funny, every girl wanted to be with him. No one would have suspected the monster he actually was. When he asked me out, I was in disbelief. I felt grateful that I was who he chose. Flabbergasted that he picked me to be with over all the women fawning over him. I was a complete idiot."

"Hey, don't talk like that." I can't stand to see her put herself down.

"It's true. Just wait."

She closes her eyes, straightens her spine. Her voice takes on that faraway edge, like she's narrating something that happened to someone else.

"Like I said, we moved in together super quick. I lived with roommates, and he had his own home in the city. When he asked me, it seemed like a no-brainer. I felt like such a grown-up. Living with a man, making 'grown-up' choices. I was swept up in it all. He was really good to me at first, until he wasn't."

Her throat works around the next words. "Once we were living together, he strategically isolated me from all my friends and family. That's when things started to turn. Small things at first. Telling me I was wrong when I was right, telling me something was my fault when it wasn't. I can see now that the gaslighting was next level, but at the time it confused me. Made me doubt myself. Made me question my worth. Turned me into a shell of myself."

Her fingers start to twist the hem of her shirt, her voice shaking, but she keeps talking. "After a year it escalated from psychological and emotional abuse. The bruises on my heart suddenly became bruises on my skin."

The air leaves my lungs. The thought of someone putting hands on her, *my* sunshine girl, *my* chaos, makes something feral crawl up my throat. I clench my fists until my nails dig crescents into my palms. She looks miles away.

"It felt like it came out of nowhere. The first time he hit me with intention, it took me by complete surprise. I knew we weren't in a great place, but I would have never imagined he'd do that. He hit walls near me before or elbowed me a little too hard, squeezed my arm too tightly, threw things in my general direction, but all of those things could be justified away as accidents."

She flinches like she's remembering dodging items. "I'd never known anyone who had been hit. It was shocking, but I was so turned around at the time, I thought I deserved it. That's how he made me feel. It was my fault. If I could only stop doing this or that, he wouldn't have to hit me. Whatever his reason for laying hands on me, I justified it. Even though I knew it wasn't right. I was living in a nightmare I wasn't sure how to get out of."

I swallow hard, trying not to let my voice break when I tell her, "It was never your fault."

She nods faintly but doesn't meet my eyes. "Deep down I knew I should leave, that things were out of control, but I was so embarrassed, confused, not thinking clearly. I didn't reach out to anyone. James was beyond frustrated that this guy was making me keep him at arm's length. I think he suspected something was wrong."

Her chin starts to wobble, but she keeps going.

"The day it all came to an end, I was like a ghost of myself by then. I didn't want to be in the relationship, but I didn't know how to leave. His family is well connected in the industry, and he always told me without him I'd never have a job."

Something clicks painfully in my chest. Her marrying me, the son of Hollywood royalty, wasn't just reckless. It was *brave*. It makes what she did for me that much bigger. She doesn't notice my reaction.

"I was just five minutes later than I told him I'd be. Just five minutes. One of the girls at the studio had car trouble, and I waited with her until her boyfriend picked her up. The first blow came before my feet even crossed the threshold and I knew it was all going to be over, one way or another. He knocked me out one other time. It was one perfectly placed hit that dropped me. Unfortunately, that was not how it went down that day. Blow after blow, kick after kick, until I finally slipped under into unconsciousness. I was grateful for the black. The quiet."

I can't breathe. I want to break something, *him*, for every mark he left on her.

"Before I opened my eyes, I knew I was in the hospital. I could feel the bright lights on my skin, hear the melody of beeping."

She exhales shakily. "Lucky for me, a couple was walking past our house and saw what was happening. They called 911 and saved my life that day. But, when I woke up and realized what happened,

I didn't feel lucky. I felt mad. I was mad that he hadn't just ended it all. When I finally braved opening my eyes, my parents and James were sitting there. The twins were already away at school. Even through the pain, the busted face, the broken ribs, all I could feel was shame. How did I become this person? Why didn't I reach out? My parents didn't raise us this way. How was this my life?"

She finally looks at me. "James is the way he is because he saw me at rock bottom. He was the one that picked me up and put my life back together again. I moved in with him and he handled everything for me: gathering my things, work, medical appointments, police reports, therapists. You name it, he fixed it. I stayed with him for a month before I felt ready to be alone again."

She blinks back tears and forces a small, brittle smile. "So now you know."

I nod slowly. "And the money?"

She lets out a hollow laugh. "I should've known you'd make me spill it all."

"A few months after I was settled in my apartment, I started getting bills, then calls. Apparently my ex took out a "business loan" and I signed my name to it. I don't remember doing it, but there was my name on the documents, heart over the i, and everything. I asked a friend in law school if it would hold since he went to jail. Unfortunately, since I signed it, I was on the hook for almost one hundred grand."

A wince crosses my face that she catches. "I know, right? Since I just drained my bank account getting a new apartment and buying all new stuff, I had nothing. I don't know if you know this or not, but makeup artists don't make a lot of money."

"I sent money when I could," she finishes softly. "Especially after they sent someone to *remind* me it'd be a shame if I fell behind. He didn't touch me, but he had some creative threats."

Her voice fades to a whisper. "Just when I thought I was healing, rebuilding, a piece of the past comes clawing back. After that, I struggled with panic attacks for a while. I started seeing my therapist three times a week. Slowly but surely, the pieces of me fell back into place. The sparkle that he snuffed out came back."

I want to say something. Anything. But there aren't words for this. Not for the kind of strength it takes to survive what she just described, to still laugh the way she does, to still be light after being dragged through that kind of darkness.

My chest feels too tight, like I'm holding my breath underwater. I thought I understood what resilience looked like: the training, pain, sacrifice, but this is something else entirely. This is courage beyond what I can understand.

"I don't want you to look at me differently," she murmurs, barely audible.

I squeeze her hand. "Too late for that."

Her eyes flick up to mine, wary, searching.

"Because now," I say quietly, "I look at you and see the strongest person I've ever met."

She doesn't say anything, but her throat works like she's trying to swallow something thick. A tear slips down, and she wipes it away before it fully falls, pretending it never existed.

I want to tell her she never has to fight alone again. That whoever so much as speaks her name wrong will answer to me. But I bite it back. She doesn't need a savior. She already saved herself, but I'll be damned if she keeps doing it alone. Not anymore.

I pull her against my chest. She comes willingly, curling into me like she's run out of ways to keep herself upright.

I press my chin to the top of her head and close my eyes. The weight of what she's survived presses against my heart, heavy and humbling. I came so close to never knowing Liz, and I had no idea. A world without her in it isn't a world I want any part of.

As she settles against me, her cheek warm against my chest, something in me shifts, quiet, but seismic. Her breathing evens out slowly, like being held by me makes her feel calm. Her hand drifts down, almost absently, and her fingers find mine. She starts tracing the inside of my wrist with the softest little circles. It's not intentional. I can tell. She's not trying to flirt. She's grounding herself. And somehow, grounding me too.

Those tiny circles undo me.

I've taken hits from professionals, jumped off buildings, had bones cracked back into place, but nothing has ever wrecked me the way this woman does by simply trusting me with her touch. With letting me touch her.

She has no idea what it does to me. No idea what it means to me to be allowed this close after everything she just told me. No idea that I would burn the entire damn world down before I let anything hurt her again.

She sighs softly, curling her fingers between mine.

And all I can think is: I want to take care of her. Really take care of her. Not because she needs saving, but because she deserves to be loved in a way that she never has to worry, in a way that never asks her to shrink.

The trust money should hit my account this week. The first thing I'm doing is paying off that loan. She can be as mad at me as she wants, but I'm done letting her carry this alone. Not anymore.

Chapter Thirty
Korean Skincare
Liz

AFTER TELLING HIM EVERYTHING about my past, I expected to feel heavy and wrung-out. That is how it usually goes. But he made me feel cared for and understood. Strong, even. I feel lighter today, like nothing from my past gets to reach into this new part of my life. My ex doesn't get to steal any more of my joy. Not anymore.

We woke up this morning like we have for the past several days, with me snuggled under Nate's chin, firmly anchored into his side. You'd think it would be weird going to bed every night together. While there is sometimes the undercurrent of attraction, we don't act on it. It's comforting sleeping next to him.

I climb into the passenger seat of my car. Nate likes driving, even if it's not his car, and I don't mind being a passenger princess. He hands me the travel mug he filled for me this morning, wordlessly.

"Bless you," I whisper to the coffee.

He chuckles. It's soft. Rough from sleep. He turns the radio up on the drive in. I guess he has figured out that even if I am tired, I will start talking just to fill silence. And before caffeine, my rambling barely qualifies as English.

We pass the guard station and he gives us a knowing smile that I pretend not to see. I'm sure rumors are already flying. We still haven't told everyone we are working with that we got married. It's not against the rules or anything, but Nate isn't exactly the guy chatting it up in the break room and my close friends already know. We didn't see a point in broadcasting it to the masses, but we do ride to work together every day.

I love it. I hate being alone, so having Nate with me twenty-four hours a day is so fun. I love to annoy him. I love to coax smiles from him. I love to see him snuggled up with Hulk when he thinks I'm not paying attention. I guess what I'm saying is there are worse people I could be married to.

We park and split off toward different buildings. I'm not working on him today. When we say goodbye, something inside me tugs tight, like I'm forgetting something. There's no one around watching us. No performance needed. No kiss for show. No "love you, baby" whispered for effect.

So instead, I punch him in the arm like a middle school boy and stalk off toward my makeup trailer.

Behind me, I hear him huff a quiet laugh, that low sound he tries to hide. My stupid heart does a little happy somersault.

My morning flows like normal. I settle into work on Becket. I'm no longer uncomfortable around him, but he is still the most annoying, self-centered man on the planet.

I'm lost in the rhythm of work when Autumn trips over the steps of the trailer and enters with a bang.

"Whoa, friend. Slow down."

I catch Autumn's reflection in the mirror and the second I see her face, my stomach drops straight through the floor.

"What is it?" My breath hitches. "Autumn, what happened?"

"It's Nate," she pants.

I'm running before she finishes his name.

I don't even grab my shoes. My bare feet slap against the ground, but I don't feel a thing. My brain is already racing through every horrible possibility.

I don't have to look far. There's a crowd gathered and the on-set EMT is crouched beside him. My heart slams against my ribs. I shove my way through bodies until I see him.

Nate. On the ground. Face tight with pain. Shoulder at a wrong, awful angle.

"Hi, Cricket," he grunts, the second I drop to my knees beside him.

My hands skim over him, frantic, searching. "What happened? Where does it hurt? What do you need? Do you need blood? I'm pretty sure I'm a universal donor. Just tell me what you need."

"Ma'am, I'm going to need you to back up."

The EMT pauses his evaluation to look directly at me, then lifts his voice to the crowd. "Actually, everyone needs to back up. Give us some space. Ambulance is almost here."

Nate sucks in a sharp breath, jaw clenched. "Liz stays."

"Sir," the EMT says gently, "she can meet you at the hospital, but it's family members only in the ambulance."

"I'm his wife." The words fly out before I can think. "That counts for something, right?"

The entire group freezes. People actually stop walking. Half the crew does that not-subtle glance between me and Nate like they're trying to decide if they heard me right.

The EMT blinks. "Uh, yeah. Yeah, that qualifies."

Nate exhales, painfully but with a dash of relief.

And just like that, the secret is out.

***

WE'VE BEEN HERE HOURS now. Thank God nothing more was wrong with Nate. The doctor put his shoulder back into place, of course Nate refused the pain medicine. The scans confirmed he does have a mild concussion.

We are sitting here waiting on the discharge paperwork, when a text comes through from Autumn checking on Nate and letting me know she dropped my car in the parking lot. It's a good distraction from the worry that's coursing through my veins.

His arm is in a sling and he looks more grumpy than I've ever seen him. The curtain is half-drawn around his hospital bed, not that he's sitting in it. He's sitting next to me in a visitor's chair after declaring hospital beds were for unwell people and that he is completely fine. Sure.

The fluorescent lights hum overhead. The room smells like antiseptic and lemon disinfectant. My leg bounces uncontrollably. The last time I was in a hospital was when my ex put me here. Nate gently reaches over with his good arm to hold my hand. Stilling my leg in the process. His hand is rough against mine.

He shouldn't be comforting me though, I'm here to make his life easier. I was so scared earlier. I don't think I've ever been that worried. I look him over from head to toe again.

Nate's shoulder is back in place.

His scans are done.

He's in one piece.

He's fine. He's going to be just fine.

He is absolutely, aggressively, profoundly grumpy, but fine.

His hospital gown is in a pile on the floor next to us. He insisted on putting his own T-shirt back on one-handed. His jeans are back on but left unfastened. His jaw ticks every few seconds as he flexes his fingers, testing his arm like he's trying to will it back to full strength.

"You're supposed to be still," I remind him.

"I *am* being still," he grumbles.

"You're clenching every muscle in your body."

"I'm testing mobility."

"You're in denial."

He shoots me a look that would terrify lesser mortals. I don't budge. Finally, he sighs. "It's not that bad."

"You dislocated your shoulder."

"I've had worse."

"You have a concussion."

"It's tiny."

"You were dizzy when they stood you up."

"They moved fast."

"You are *exhausting*," I whisper.

His mouth twitches the first sign of any emotion other than annoyance. "You like me anyway."

I cross my arms. "That is still up for debate."

His eyes soften in a way that wrecks my insides. Little crinkles appear around his brown eyes, the kind he only gets when he's looking at me. Without thinking, my thumb slides over his palm, slow and silent. My mind spins with everything that could have gone wrong today. The thirty-second sprint from the trailer to reach him was the longest of my life.

We hold eye contact. Everything else, the machines, footsteps, hallway noise, fades to static.

"Nate," I whisper, "if anything would have happ..."

The curtain swishes open and I jump.

The doctor strolls in, eyes glued to his clipboard. "Alright, let's get you out of here. What do you say?"

He looks up, then turns to me like I'm the one he's actually reporting to.

"I'm releasing him into your care." He hands me a stack of paperwork. "Here are his care instructions and a prescription for pain medication."

Nate grunts beside me. That's not hard to translate. *I'm not taking that, don't even try.*

I roll the papers in my hand, biting back a smile.

***

BY THE TIME WE make it back to the condo, Nate is highly annoyed at me and pretending he isn't in pain. Lucky for him the doctor gave me some pain meds to get him through the evening. Now I just need to figure out how to get him to take them.

"Let's get you to the couch," I coo. His face scrunches.

"Liz, you drove like a geriatric patient on the way home, you haven't let me take one step by myself. I think I'm capable of making it to the couch by myself," he mutters.

"Congratulations. I'm very proud of you." I take his hand and lead him there anyway.

He shoots me a look, annoyed, impressed, a little amused, and finally eases himself down onto the cushions with a stiff exhale. I grab a pillow and gently wedge it behind his back. He glares at it.

"Comfort is not an enemy," I tell him.

"Feels like one," he grumbles.

Despite himself, he lets me fuss. I bring him water, adjust the blanket across his lap, and take the spot beside him, tucking one leg under me so I'm angled toward him and drop two pills into his open palm.

"No."

"Not up for debate. You are in pain. Both your head and your shoulder. I won't force you to take any more after this dose, but please?"

He gives me a hard stare. I'm positive he's going to say no.

"For me? Please? I can't stand to see you hurting."

He closes his eyes like *I'm* the one causing him pain, not the concussion or the shoulder, and lets out a long exhale. Then his hand curls around the pill packet and he throws them back without water.

Serial killer behavior. But whatever, he took them. My body relaxes beside him. For a minute, we sit in a quiet that feels weirdly intimate.

His jaw flexes as he takes me in. "You're still stressed."

"I'm not," I lie immediately.

"You are." He reaches out with his good arm and lightly drags his fingertip between my brows. "You've got worry lines right here."

"Ugh. My stupid face always giving me away." I flop back dramatically and drape my arm across my forehead.

I peek at him. He doesn't smile, but his eyes soften, warm and knowing. "Want me to tell you what happened?"

I nod. Maybe knowing will make the adrenaline finally settle.

He shifts, hissing under his breath when the movement pulls at his shoulder. "We were running the sequence with the new guy. Simple setup. He was supposed to tuck and roll on impact to redirect the energy."

"What does that mean in normal-person English?"

"He was supposed to make himself small." His mouth curves humorlessly. "He did not make himself small."

I wince. "What did he do?"

"He speared me," Nate says flatly. "Full body. No tuck. Just launched into me midair like we were playing football instead of filming a controlled stunt." He gestures with his good hand. "The force threw me off the crash pad. Shoulder took the hit. Head bounced after."

"Oh my gosh." My stomach tightens. "Bear."

He shrugs one-sidedly. "Concussion and a cranky shoulder. Could've been worse."

"Worse?" My voice jumps an octave. "You could've broken your neck. Or your ribs. Or..."

"Cricket," he cuts in softly.

I shut my mouth.

"I'm okay," he says, eyes holding mine. "I'm right here. And I'm okay."

Something in my chest loosens. Just enough to breathe again. I reach for his hand, not even thinking about it until our fingers thread together. Warm. Familiar. His thumb brushes my knuckles like a reflex.

"For the record," I say quietly, "you scared the bedazzle out of me."

"For the record," he replies just as quietly, "you running toward me barefoot in a panic scared me more."

My cheeks heat. "Well, don't get speared next time and I won't have to."

He huffs a soft laugh. "I'll put in a request."

His voice is already growing heavy. I shift, tucking myself into the corner of the couch, then gently pull him toward me. His eyes drift closed, slow and unfocused, and he finally settles with his head on a pillow in my lap. There are a hundred things I could be doing right now. But I don't move.

I sit there and watch him, safe and sound, right where I can touch him. My fingers thread through his hair over and over. His hair is so soft. Running my fingers through it is addicting.

He makes a small sound in his sleep, a vulnerable little whimper, and my heart caves in on itself.

I lean down and brush a kiss to his forehead. "I've got you," I whisper.

***

NATE

I wake up slowly, like I'm surfacing from the bottom of a lake, everything feels heavy and warm. My neck aches, my shoulder throbs, and there's a pillow under my head that feels weirdly alive. My stomach feels too hot.

Oh, it's not a pillow. It's Liz. And my stomach isn't on fire. It's Hulk curled up purring.

I'm curled around Liz and Hulk on the couch, arm across her waist, forehead resting against her stomach. My hand feels numb. One glance tells me why. Liz's hand is laced so tightly through my good hand it's fallen asleep. It's like she's afraid I'll vanish if she loosens her grip.

My chest squeezes.

"Cricket," I murmur, voice rough.

She stirs, blinking blearily. "Wha...? Did I drool? I probably drooled."

"No." Though honestly, I wouldn't even care if she did. "You fell asleep on me."

She squints at me. "You fell asleep first."

Fair point. I shift, groaning as my shoulder protests. Immediately, she's upright and alert like someone fired a starter pistol.

"Are you okay? Does it hurt? What do you need?"

"I'm fine," I lie. My skull is pounding. My shoulder feels like i've been run over by a truck. Unfortunately, I'm familiar with how that actually feels. She's looking at me with so much worry that the truth can burn.

She glances at her phone and gasps. "Oh my gosh, it's almost eight. You need dinner. You need real food. You need... do you want cereal?"

I stare at her. "Cereal is your version of 'real food'?"

She narrows her eyes. "Don't mock my culinary skills."

A huff of laughter escapes my lips.

"Fine, sir. I'll order something. But just know I could've made you toast and it would have been the best darn tooting toast you've ever had."

"Fancy."

"Shut up."

"As much as I love breakfast, I think I need something more than that."

She orders Thai food, something mild "because your brain is probably sensitive right now," whatever that means, and we settle back on the couch. I'm not allowed to move except to breathe. She brings me water, rearranges my pillow, scolds me for trying to sit up straighter. I usually hate sitting still, but with Liz nearby I find I don't mind.

Dinner arrives and she insists on opening everything for me, even though I can do it one-handed. Probably.

We eat. We watch some show she insists I must see. I barely follow the plot because I'm concussed and because she's distractingly pressed against me.

Halfway through the second episode, she claps her hands suddenly. "Ooh! Face mask time."

"...What?"

She returns with a shiny, chrome-looking sheet of goo plastered to her face. It's reflective. It's horrifying. It's...a jump scare.

I stare at her. "Okay. Listen."

"What?" she sounds muffled because she's barely moving her mouth. "Do I look crazy?"

"I know I suffered a head injury today," I deadpan, "but what the *fuck* am I looking at right now?"

She cackles in delight. Actually cackles. "It's a Korean face mask! They're hydrating and brightening. I picked them up at the spa when I went with the girls a few weeks ago. I have one for you too!"

"It's blinding me. I'm getting a glare off your face from the TV."

She wiggles her eyebrows behind the chrome alien nightmare. "So you're saying I'm glowing."

"That is not what I'm saying."

She bumps my knee with hers. "Seriously, is it bothering you? I can take it off." She goes to stand.

I rest my hand on her knee to keep her in place. "It's fine, babe. I was just teasing you. Leave it on and marinate however long you want, but I'm not doing one too."

She smiles so wide the mask is in danger of peeling off.

"What?"

"Who knew all it would take is a concussion to get you to tease me."

I roll my eyes at her, but she keeps going. "Do you think getting your head knocked around is going to make you more pleasant to be around?"

"Har, har, har. Watch your stupid show." I try to school my face into a scowl but the curve of my lip won't obey.

When bedtime rolls around, I try to get up on my own. Bad idea. My shoulder screams at me. My head pulses. She instantly rushes to my side.

"Okay, okay, no more macho nonsense." She leads me to our room and into the bathroom before she backs me against the counter. I think she's afraid I'll topple over. She looks up at my face evaluating.

"Alright, mister." She gently undoes my sling and grips the hem of my shirt. "Arms up."

"I can do it," I protest.

"No, you can't."

She's right. I can't. My arm is too stiff after keeping it still for so long. She lifts my shirt carefully over my head. Slowly. Careful. Her warm fingertips brush along my ribs and back as she works around my injured shoulder. My breath hitches. Her breath hitches. The air thickens.

We are inches from each other. Her blue eyes lock onto mine and then she reaches for the button of my jeans.

"Cricket."

"It's fine," she says, all business. Her pulse point in her throat betrays her. "You can't do it with one hand, so let me."

I swallow. My pulse spiking further. Her fingers are right there. She's close enough for me to feel her breath on my chest. The second she gets the button undone, the tension spikes so hard it crackles in the air.

She must feel it too because she steps back and blurts, "Do you want me to brush your teeth for you?"

I stare at her. Blinking, trying to make sense of her words.

"I think I can handle brushing my own teeth."

She snaps her fingers. "Right. Right. You can do it with your good hand. My bad."

She holds her fist out to me and I tap my good hand against hers. I guess we give each other knuckles before bed now. She pivots leaving the bathroom in a hurry. I let out a long, pained, overwhelmed breath.

If I wasn't already concussed, she'd be the reason I was confused.

Chapter Thirty-One
Biofreeze Heats Me Up
Liz

The doctor recommends Nate take off for at least three days. I take all three days off too. I can't afford it. I know I can't. My bank account knows I can't. At this point, I'm expecting a plane to fly over the condo trailing a banner that says: 'LIZ HARRISON IS BROKE, PLEASE DON'T ASK HER TO SPLIT THE CHECK.'

But the thought of Nate at home, concussed and hurting and stubborn, with no one to make sure he actually rests, makes my stomach twist. And every time I think about going in, I picture the way he looked on the ground. The way his eyes went unfocused. The way my entire body reacted like someone unplugged the world until I reached him.

So I stay. Whether I should or not.

After getting myself and him ready, we go grocery shopping because my version of caretaking apparently involves feeding him something other than granola bars and toast.

At the store entrance, I grab a basket. He takes it from me immediately.

"I've got it," he says.

"You have one functioning arm," I remind him. He refused to put his sling back on, but he's still babying his shoulder like it's a newborn.

He lifts his brows. "And you have noodle arms. What's your point."

I gasp. "Noodle arms!"

He smirks and squeezes the part of my upper arm where a bicep would be if I believed in push-ups. "Yeah. I've got this, Cricket."

We bicker the entire first aisle. There's an elderly woman grabbing soup behind us who giggles while she watches us like we're some sitcom couple she's rooting for.

Eventually we compromise: I carry the basket, and Nate grabs whatever I point at like a very muscular personal assistant.

After an hour of wandering around, we end up with a basket full of things that look easy in theory. Sandwich ingredients. Pasta. Frozen meals. And a rotisserie chicken Nate eyed like it belonged behind a beaded curtain in an adult store.

Back home, he puts on Food Network and claims he can "verbally guide" me through something simple. Spoiler alert, he cannot.

"You're chopping it wrong," he says.

"You can't even chop right now," I argue.

We argue for thirty minutes, and the dish still emerges charred. Burnt in a way that somehow feels personal. Bobby Flay's smug face pops up onscreen, and I swear he's mocking us.

We stare down at what's supposed to be dinner. Until finally I break the silence, "Wanna order dinner?"

He nods, dead serious. "We don't speak of this again."

***

THE NEXT DAY WE do nothing. He naps off and on, always ending up with his head on my lap or shoulder like his subconscious magnetizes him to me. Every time he shifts closer, something in my chest tightens. I don't hate it.

While he naps, I bedazzle a snuggie for him. It reads *Number One Cat Daddy* in rhinestones. He wakes, sees it, refuses to wear it, but I force it on him and snap a thousand pictures.

We watch three episodes of a show he claims to hate but laughs at more than I've ever heard him laugh at anything. At one point, I catch him looking at me instead of the TV. His gaze is serious. I quirk a brow. He shakes his head like it's nothing, but his gaze lingers searching my face until he eventually looks back at the TV.

By Tuesday morning, we've fallen into a rhythm. A simple breakfast that I don't ruin on the outdoor patio together. Slow walks around the neighborhood with Hulk when his headache eases. He hasn't had a headache in the last twelve hours, so I know he's going to insist on going into work tomorrow.

Today we reorganized our closet just because we're bored. I ran down to the store and printed a bunch of pictures of us, scattered them all around the apartment, and surprised him when he woke up from a nap. I can't tell if he likes it or hates it, but he got a funny look on his face when he saw them all, kind of like heartburn.

Whatever, I like them.

After cleaning the kitchen that evening, it's bedtime. He's been pushing himself all day, whether he admits it or not, and I see the grimace as he grabs his shoulder.

"Need help?"

"No." He pauses and lets out a long sigh. "Actually, yes. Can you put that Biofreeze numbing stuff on my shoulder? The one the doctor sent home? I think it'll help."

"Sure."

I go to our bathroom to grab the tube and return to the living room.

And stop in my tracks.

The evening light stretches across the hardwoods, bathing everything in gold. Nate is sitting shirtless on the couch, head bowed slightly, the muscles in his back and shoulders sharp and sculpted like someone carved him out of a marble slab.

Holy muscles, Batman.

I've seen him shirtless before, quick glimpses, fast moments, but never this long. Never like this. And my suspicion was right:

he has a small tattoo on his ribcage. A bird in flight. Beautiful. Unexpected.

He glances over his shoulder with a smirk. "You just gonna stand there or are you actually planning on rubbing that on my shoulder?"

My body flames all the way from my face to my toes, but I force myself forward and slide onto the couch behind him. My knees bracket his hips as I settle in close, closer than necessary, closer than is safe for my sanity.

I squeeze the Biofreeze into my palms. And the second my hands hover over his bare skin, my heart starts pounding in my throat.

Shizzlefritz. He's warm. All muscle. I swallow hard and place my hands gently on his shoulders. He tenses. Just for a second. Barely visible, but I feel it beneath my fingertips.

"You okay?" I don't know why I'm whispering. It feels like this moment is wrapped in a fragile bubble and I don't want to burst it.

A beat.

Two.

"Yeah," he says softly, "just...cold hands."

I know that's not the reason, but I let it slide. I start working the gel into the tight muscle along his shoulder. Beneath my fingers, he's heat and strength and coiled tension. His breathing shifts, slower, deeper, as I follow the ridge of muscle up toward his neck, careful around the bruising.

He lets out a quiet, strangled breath.

"You're hurting," I murmur.

"I'm fine." His voice is low and rough. "Keep going."

I keep working the ointment into his shoulder, my thumbs brushing along the slope of muscle. The minty smell fills the room. My fingers glide down the length of his shoulder blade, and his head tips forward, just slightly.

"You can press harder," he mumbles.

"Tell me if anything hurts."

"Nothing hurts."

The way he says it runs straight through my entire nervous system. I shift a little, leaning closer so I can reach the top of his shoulder. My chest brushes his spine. I freeze. He does, too.

"Sorry," I whisper.

"It's okay," he whispers back.

I move slowly, carefully, trying to pretend the air between us isn't getting heavier by the second. My hands drift lower, over the curve of his ribs, just far enough to spread the ointment without crossing any lines.

He makes a low sound. Barely audible. Almost a groan.

My hands stop. "Was that good or bad?"

His breath shudders. "You're killing me," he says under his breath, so quiet I almost miss it.

My pulse spikes. "What?"

"Nothing." He clears his throat and lifts his head again. "You can keep going."

I rub along the top of his shoulder one more time, softer now. The tension in him eases under my hands, slow and gradual. His breathing evens out.

"Better?" I ask.

He nods once. "Yeah. Feels really good."

My cheeks heat at the way he says it. "All done," I say, my voice embarrassingly breathless.

I wipe my hands on a towel and shift back to give him space, but before I can move too far, his hand shoots out and grabs mine.

"Thank you," he says quietly.

It's the softness that ruins me. The sincerity. The way he's looking at our hands like they're something he's afraid to break.

"You're welcome," I whisper.

He doesn't let go. Not for a long, long moment. And then he finally clears his throat, releases my fingers, and stands, slowly, still shirtless, still beautiful.

He rolls his shoulder experimentally. "Definitely better."

"Good." I tuck a strand of hair behind my ear, still buzzing. "You wore yourself out today."

"I didn't overdo," he mutters after a moment, almost defensive.

"You don't need to be at one hundred percent. You got speared. Your body is allowed to be mad about it."

A soft huff of a laugh. Barely there. "Okay," he says, voice low and uneven. "I, uh... we better get ready for bed."

"We should," I say, even though I'm not sure I remember how walking works.

He nods once, quick, like any more movement might break whatever this is. He grabs his shirt off the back of the couch and moves toward our room. I clear my throat as I follow behind him. "Well, you've got to sleep on your back again tonight. Don't let me catch you trying to roll onto your shoulder."

The corner of his mouth lifts. "You planning on policing my sleep?"

"Obviously."

"Bossy." I smirk at him and nod my head like, if the shoe fits. His eyes warm in that quiet, devastating way that makes my ribs tighten. He grabs the water bottle from the kitchen, takes a long sip, then turns off the living room light. Suddenly the only illumination is the soft glow coming from the hallway.

He stands there a moment, thoughtful, like he's checking in with himself. Or like he's checking in with *me*.

"Ready?" he asks finally.

Ready? No. Absolutely not. Having my hands run all over his body has made me a marshmallow in human form. My brain is soup. But I nod anyway.

We walk down the hall together, side by side, not touching but close enough that our arms brush every few steps. Each brush sends a tight little zing up my spine.

The walk from the kitchen to the bedroom is only a few steps but it feels like a mile. When we finally reach the entrance, he pauses. Just a beat. Barely anything. I hold my breath waiting for him to say or do something. Anything.

He nudges me forward. "After you."

I step inside, trying not to analyze the way his voice dipped. The room is dim and quiet, the kind of quiet that amplifies everything. The sound of his breath. The flicker of one of my candles. The soft creak of the bed when he sits. My heartbeat punching the inside of my ribs like it's trying to make an escape.

I go to my side of the bed, pull back the blankets, and slide in. He does the same on his side, but slower, more carefully. We end up lying there, staring at the ceiling.

It feels like the closest we've ever been to crossing a line.

His voice breaks the silence first, quiet enough that I almost think I imagined it. "Thanks for staying home with me." A pause. "I know you didn't have to."

"There's nowhere else I'd rather be."

I don't know if he hears the real meaning underneath, but I hope he does. He turns his head, eyes finding mine in the dark.

"Goodnight, Cricket," he whispers.

"Goodnight, Bear."

We're inches apart. Neither of us moves. Neither of us sleeps right away. Because for the first time, the tension doesn't disappear when we crawl into bed. It settles beside us. Ramps up.

And I think we're both in trouble.

Chapter Thirty-Two
The Dark Lords
Liz

Mornings shouldn't be allowed to hit this hard. Especially after nights like last night, where the air between us felt thick enough to stand on and I went to bed convinced we'd accidentally start making out in our sleep.

Instead, we wake up like we do every morning, a warm tangle of limbs, my face pressed to his chest, his arm wrapped around me.

I've tried, really tried, not to sleep on Nate these past three days. I didn't want to accidentally hurt him, but sometime in the middle of the night my body betrays me like, "Shh, girl, it's fine. This six-foot wall of muscle is comfortable," and curls straight into him. And every night, without fail, he pulls me closer like he was waiting for me.

For a beat, I stay there, blinking into the soft morning quiet, listening to his slow breathing, the steady rise and fall of his chest under my cheek. There's a comfort in it I can't explain.

I try to extract myself from him before he realizes I've been clinging to him like a spider monkey all night and things get awkward. But Nate only tightens his hold for a sleepy second, like he's not ready to let me go yet, before releasing me with a quiet, "Morning, Cricket."

Nothing is awkward. Nothing is weird. If anything, he seems gentler this morning. When we climb into my car, he wordlessly hands me the coffee he made me, the exact way I like it, and that tiny, normal gesture erases any of the unease I had about us being awkward today. We drive to work in a quiet that feels warm instead of tense.

I'm in the trailer, halfway through unpacking brushes when I hear it. A hum of excitement rolling through the set outside. Quick footsteps. Loud whispering. The unmistakable vibe of celebrity-level chaos.

The trailer door slams open and Autumn rushes in like a tornado. She looks wild. "Do not panic."

"You can't bust in here all wild-eyed and tell me not to panic. You know that's exactly what I'm going to do! Is it Nate? Is he hurting?"

She grips my shoulders. "Nate's parents are here."

I feel my entire body go still. Like I'm a squirrel that just made eye contact with a car and I don't know which way to run.

When we came back from California, I told the girls an abbreviated version of what went down with his parents. How they are basically the dark lords of hell. Why are they here? In Georgia. Nate told me they rarely visit.

"Well, shizzzzz." All the air escapes my lungs. "What do you mean his parents are here? I just walked in with him. We didn't see them anywhere."

"I don't know what to tell you babe, they just breezed onto set like the King and Queen of the world."

"Can you tell what they want? What they are doing here?" I'm holding out hope that maybe they are here for some other reason other than me and Nate.

"They found the first PA they could and requested to see their son, Nathaniel and his wife, *Elizabeth*."

I cringe. "Any chance people haven't connected who they are? Or that they are Nate's parents?"

"Basically zero."

Nate barges into the trailer. He looks like he sprinted to get here. He looks frazzled, like someone told him his childhood nightmare crawled out of the closet and wants a hug. Which is kind of accurate.

His eyes land on me instantly, relief punching through the panic. Autumn backs into the corner like she's watching a nature documentary about two antelopes being stalked by lions.

I clutch my brushes like a weapon. "How bad is it?"

He scrubs a hand over his jaw. "It could be bad. They have one of the lawyers with them."

"Nathaniel?" The voice floats from outside the trailer.

Nate closes his eyes for one second, one long suffering second, then opens them again. "Well, it didn't take long for them to find us."

I shoot a pleading look at Autumn. "Spread the word to anyone who didn't hear earlier this week that we are married. Maybe getting slightly ahead of it will give people time to adjust."

She gives me a serious head nod like she's accepting orders to go behind enemy lines. "I'll pray for you," and slips out the back door.

I stare at him. "What do we do?"

He steps closer, eyes locked on mine. Controlled. Steady. Bracing for impact. "We act married."

My pulse jumps. "Well good thing we are married."

"Exactly." He tips his chin up, determination settling over him like armor. "We stick together. No distance. No hesitation. We're a team, just like California."

My insides do a nervous little electric shimmy. "Okay." There is no time to discuss anything else because suddenly his parents fill the doorway.

"There's the newlyweds!" Nate's mom declares. She and his dad file in, but before the door closes, another man in a suit trails in behind them. He must be the lawyer. I can only hope that Autumn and Jenn make the rounds and spread the word to those that don't know that we are married while we are trapped in here. And for the love of all things, that everyone acts cool about it.

"Here we are." I say with false brightness. I haven't even finished my coffee yet, it's too early for this level of emotional warfare. Nate slips his arm around my side pulling me flush against him.

"Mom, Dad, didn't think we'd be seeing you again this soon."

Before his dad can say anything, Nate's mom answers, "Well, darling, once the lawyers got your marriage paperwork," she gestures to the man behind them. "They reached out to us. Of course, I couldn't lie to a man of the law, so when they asked us about your marriage," she pauses to look me up and down, "we expressed our concerns. They share our worries after receiving the papers out of the blue. I told them we'd all just come down here and make sure everything is on the up and up."

"How thoughtful of you, mother. Plan to put us through another game show to prove we're really together?"

Her face tightens in displeasure. "Of course not, darling. I told them since you two work together, we could all stop by here and then come by the condo for dinner. Mr. Harrington will ask a few simple questions, if you have nothing to hide, it shouldn't be a problem. I'll call and have something catered in."

Nate's jaw flexes. "We *don't* have anything to hide."

His mother smiles, but it is the kind of smile you give the waiter when he brings you the wrong order. "Wonderful. Then today will be easy."

It will not be easy. Not even a little. His father steps farther into the trailer, hands clasped behind his back like he is inspecting a real estate investment. "We were hoping to meet everyone you two work with now." He looks back at the lawyer. I don't get great vibes from him. "People tend to reveal their truest selves through the company they keep."

Translation: We want to interrogate your coworkers and see who cracks. I try to keep my smile in place, but it feels like my teeth are going to fall out from the tension.

His mother glances at the clock on the wall. "We should get moving. I can't imagine production wants us to hold up the day."

She says it like she is trying to be polite, but she absolutely knows she has already held up the day. This is her area of expertise after all. Nate steps back, his hand staying firmly at my waist. "Alright. Let's go."

They turn to leave, and we follow them out of the trailer hand-in-hand.

The second the door swings open, the set goes suspiciously still. Jenn and Autumn stand twenty feet away, trying to look casual and absolutely failing. Their faces are flushed, hair frizzy, breathing like they sprinted a marathon. Jenn has a clipboard turned upside down in her hand. Autumn is holding a powder puff like a weapon.

Every crew member in sight pretends to be extremely busy. But they are all doing the same thing. Staring at us. At Nate's hand on my waist. At his parents walking in front of us.

Everyone immediately tries to pretend they weren't staring. Autumn gives me a thumbs-up as big as her entire face, then mouths, "We told everyone," like she is announcing the birth of a royal baby. Jenn tries to wink discreetly but only manages to blink with her whole face.

Someone whispers, "I knew it," which is hilarious because no one knew anything. Someone else whispers, "He got married? Like for real?" followed by, "Wait, those are Nate's parents, I thought his last name was Jones?" A prop guy tries to bow as we walk past him. Why? Why is that happening? Nate's parents look around, bewildered by the sudden bustle of chaos.

The producer and the director of the production hustle over to us. It's clear that word got out that the Sterlings were on set. The Director shakes Nate's dad's hand firmly. "George, Isabelle, what a surprise, we didn't expect to see you today."

Once again Nate's mom answers. "We just stopped by to pay our son and his wife a little visit."

I watch as both the producer and the director's eyes bug out. Not at the mention of wife, but because they called Nate their son. I can feel his huff of frustration. He's worked so hard to not be associated with them and she's ruined it.

They turn to Nate. "These are your parents?"

He winces. "Guilty."

They turn back as a unit. "George, Isabelle, we had no idea. None at all."

Nate interrupts them. "Don't worry about it. Mom and dad just popped in to say hello. They came into town to congratulate Liz and me on getting married."

He says it with such confidence. Like it's a fact. Neither of them bat an eye. They pretend like they already knew we were together. That we got married. "Of course, of course. Well we are so glad you stopped by, please let us know if you need anything while you are on set." He snaps at a PA and assigns them to stay with the Sterlings until they exit the lot.

Satan, I mean Nate's mom, turns a raised brow toward us just as Becket strolls up, all smug swagger perfectly timed to ruin our day.

Mother-trucker.

He greets Nate's parents like they're old friends, which apparently they are. "George, Isabelle, so good to see you. It's about time you made it out here."

My stomach drops. What is happening? Is this good? Or terrible? Probably terrible. Ninety percent chance this is terrible.

"It's good to see you, son," George says, giving Becket a hearty handshake and a slap on the back. The amount of bro energy radiating off the two of them could power a small city.

Becket's smirk flicks to Nate, then to me, then back to Nate. He knows exactly what he's doing. "I heard congratulations are in order," he says casually, eyes narrowing like he's trying to peel back our marriage with his gaze alone. If the next thing he says is I didn't know you were together, I'll murder him.

"I didn't reali..." Luckily, Jenn and Autumn swoop in, cutting him off. I haven't told them that we got married under less than truthful intentions, but they've picked up enough.

"Will we see you two tonight for our weekly trivia, right?" Jenn asks brightly.

Autumn looks right at his parents, "Ever since Liz started bringing Nate, our team is undefeated. What's our streak now? Five, six months?"

Oh bless you, sweet angels.

"Not tonight," I answer. "Nate's parents are coming over for dinner."

Jenn pretends to pout. "Next week then. Are you going to make them your famous chicken pot pie?"

We, in fact, do not have a famous chicken pot pie. My eyes widen. I silently beg her to abort mission.

"Nathaniel, you cook?" his mother asks in disbelief.

His grip tightens on my waist. His scowl at Jenn is pure warning. Becket snickers. "Sometimes Liz and I cook to unwind after a long day on set."

Lie. We have only ever made breakfast successfully. Everything else we burn and then have to order in. I am not sure either of us could make a chicken pot pie without summoning the fire department.

"Perfect. We will have that. See you tonight." The three of them march past us, none of them sparing us another glance.

Becket calls after them jogging to catch up, "Let me walk you out."

Looks like we are cooking for five tonight. This should be fun.

Chapter Thirty-Three
Chicken Pot Pie
Nate

The set never recovers after my parents drop in. Both the producer and director call me into their offices. I feel like I'm a teenager caught sneaking out past curfew. They're understandably irritated they didn't know who my parents are. I explain, for what feels like the millionth time in my life, that I don't tell people because I don't want special treatment. Once they realize I'm not some undercover Sterling spy sent to audit the production, they relax.

Movie people love to dramatize everything. If there's a way to turn a normal situation into a conspiracy theory, they'll find it. Me? A spy? I barely talk to anyone unless it's absolutely necessary. Outside of Liz or her friends, I keep to myself. I would be the worst candidate for espionage in the world.

After the excitement dies down, they manage to reshoot a few scenes from yesterday, but the day is basically a wash. Thank God we wrap early. My shoulder is killing me, and if one more person asks what it was like growing up with my parents, or pries about Liz and me, I'm going to blow.

I quickly snatch Liz away from Jenn and Autumn, flipping them off in the process as thanks for getting us into this debacle. They couldn't have chosen a dish I actually know how to make? Or at least something simpler?

On the way home, we stop by Whole Foods to get supplies. Liz is locked onto Pinterest like it's a life-or-death mission, calling out ingredients from half a dozen different recipes as we walk down the aisles.

"Baby," I groan in frustration, "just choose one. We don't have all night and we can't mash a bunch of different recipes up to make our own creation."

What is it about the grocery store that makes us fight?

Liz stops mid-aisle, mid-scroll and gives me a small smile, a blush creeping over her pretty cheeks. I try to figure out why she's looking at me like that and replay what I just said. *Baby.* I called her baby. Pretty sure she likes it. The crazy part is, I didn't even think about it. It just slipped out.

"Alright, Bear. This one." She thrusts her phone in my face. She's changed the phone cover on it in the last day. It looks like her phone is being hugged by a bear. His head and ears pop out over the top. It's ridiculous and very Liz. I wonder if she was thinking of me when she ordered it.

I grab her phone and squint at the screen, wishing I had my glasses with me. Liz starts to babble while I read over the list. "It has a four-point-seven-five rating. It's on a blog called *Busy moms who cook delicious meals with their kids that everyone in your home will love.*"

"That's a stupid name for a blog. It's too long." She rolls her eyes and snatches her phone back.

"The point is, the blog is all about cooking simple meals with kids. All the reviews all say that their children helped them make it and it was successful. Surely if children can do it, we can." She looks up at me with hopeful eyes.

"I'm sure we'll be able to do it." After that we buckle down and split the list, grabbing everything that we need in record time. We get back to my condo two and a half hours before they are set to arrive. It's time to get down to business.

"This is child abuse," I mutter, hacking at another carrot chunk.

Liz flicks flour at me. "It's therapeutic."

"For who? The vegetables?"

She points her rolling pin at me. "It says busy moms can do this."

"Those busy moms are lying."

"You take that back." She holds up her phone showing me an image of two perfectly put together mothers. "Do you think these look like the faces of women who would lie?"

"Considering their whole faces are frozen with Botox, yes I do." I hold up my carrot-crippled hand. "Liz, I would rather take a punch from a heavyweight than dice one more of these demon carrots."

She snorts, then immediately tries to hide it behind a cough. "You're being ridiculous."

"You're being lied to by a blog called *Busy Moms Who Cook Delicious Meals With Their Kids That Everyone In Your Home Will Love.* Which is false advertising on at least four separate fronts."

Before she can defend her imaginary mom-friends again, the timer goes off. Liz stops rolling the dough, pulls the chicken from the oven, and puts the pan between us.

We both stare down at it in silent horror.

"That's not the color it's supposed to be," she whispers.

I lean in. "Maybe it finishes cooking and changes colors once everything is combined?"

She gives me a helpless shrug. "The blogger said nothing about that."

"Yeah, well the blogger also acts like toddlers can dice parsley."

She pinches her lips to keep from laughing, then wordlessly turns back to her dough and adds water, reworking the whole thing. From here it looks like some sort of glue paste, but I wisely refrain from telling her.

Zero chance this turns out edible.

We somehow manage to get it all assembled, shove the thing in the oven, and slam the door shut like we're capturing a wild animal. Unfortunately, we don't have time to clean anything before there's a knock on the door. I survey the kitchen. It certainly *looks* like toddlers prepared this meal.

"Shizzle," I mutter under my breath.

Liz blinks at me. "Is that mine? Did you just use one of my cuss words?"

"They're contagious." I groan. She grins like that's the best compliment she's ever received.

"Why don't you just say the real thing anyway?"

"Anyone could say the real thing. It takes an extra layer of creativity to come up with something else." She shrugs as we walk down the hall to the front door. "It never felt natural having a bad word come out of my mouth."

I believe that. She's too pure. Another knock. We exchange a look that says *we're screwed*.

We stand in front of the door together, shoulder to shoulder, a united front marching into battle. Opening it feels like pulling back the curtain to our own personal hell. Liz inhales sharply and pastes on a fake smile. When my parents get a good look at us, they both visibly recoil. Full-body flinch. Fantastic start.

"Mom, Dad, sir," I nod at their lawyer and step aside. "Come in."

The trio files past us into the absolute war zone that used to be my kitchen.

"Can I get anyone a drink?" Liz asks brightly.

She still has flour on her face, cream sauce on her shirt, and her hair that looks like a family of squirrels held a rave in it. She's perfect. My mother clearly disagrees. Mom takes in the kitchen, the overflowing sink, the overturned measuring cup, the vegetables that didn't make the cut, the flour drift on the floor, before pinning us with a look. "I can *see* how this is a relaxing activity for the two of you." Her voice drips with condescension.

That's when Hulk chooses to make his entrance. He trots out, sniffs our guests, determines they're not worthy to be in his presence and immediately retreats to the bedroom to hide. Smart cat. I wish I could follow him.

"You have an *animal*?" my mother asks, as if we've just unleashed a rabid boar into the living room. Although, knowing Liz's history with bringing home wild animals, it wouldn't be the weirdest thing if we owned a pig.

"Yup."

"In your *home*?"

"Yup."

Liz uncorks a wine bottle, the cork shoots across the kitchen, narrowly missing the tip of my dad's nose. Liz's eyes widen to the size of small plates, but no one else reacts. Which tells you everything you need to know about this dinner with my family.

Liz recovers and holds up the bottle, giving it a little shake. "Hope everyone likes red!"

She pours the wine with a heavy hand. Good thinking. We're going to need it if we're going to survive the night.

After the silence gets too heavy Liz breaks the tension, "Feel free to get comfortable on the couch or take a look around. We're about twenty minutes from everything being ready."

Our three unwelcome guests take that as an open invitation to fan out and snoop through all of our things.

I scan my condo trying to see it through their eyes. Liz's colorful pillows and blankets scatter along the couch. Her living wall of plants behind the couches. Liz is a selfie queen. Her own proclamation, not mine. I didn't feel very grateful when she was making me stop every five minutes on our walks to snap pictures of me, her, and Hulk. But, suddenly I feel very lucky that she did and we have pictures throughout our home of the two of us.

There's even a picture of our wedding night. The photographer emailed it to us the morning after we got married. Liz blew it up, framed it, and hung it near the shelves I installed for her. When I noticed it, it took my breath away. I look happy. Liz looks incredible.

Liz snuggles up to my side and talks out of the side of her mouth. "What do you think they are whispering about?"

In our bedroom, the lawyer and my parents are whisper-fighting like their lives depend on it. Mom looks furious, Dad looks like he'd rather be at the DMV, and the lawyer keeps lifting his hands in a helpless little *what do you want me to do* gesture.

"Hard to say," I answer, because it *is* hard to say and also because I don't want Liz stressing before we're forced to sit at a table with them.

They make their way back to the kitchen. Mom's eyes sweep the room like she's appraising a crime scene. "The place certainly has changed since we were last here."

"Well," I pause, "considering the last, and only, time you were here was five years ago, and Liz didn't live here yet, that makes sense."

My mom huffs just as the oven timer goes off. Liz meets my eyes, wide and terrified, before taking a hesitant step toward the oven. When she slowly lowers the door, I take it as a good sign that smoke doesn't billow out and choke the room. I wouldn't say it smells good, but the absence of smoke feels like a win.

Liz carries the dish over to the table and sets it carefully on the oven mitts we laid out, like it's a bomb we're hoping won't detonate. Everyone takes their seats wordlessly.

I don't know how Liz has managed to stay silent this long. It's a world record. Honestly, I almost find myself wishing she'd start rambling about literally anything, her plants, Hulk's emotional support needs, the documentary she made me watch about crows stealing muffins, something to break up the suffocating awkwardness sitting at this table with us.

I serve everyone a generous helping. Nothing left to do now but face the music.

Before I take my first bite, Liz clamps a death grip on my knee under the table. I look at her, and she jerks her chin down. I follow her gaze to her hand. Her nails look great. Bright green. Shiny. Fresh.

All nine of them.

Her pointer finger is... naked. Oh fuck.

I scan the table, trying to determine whose portion contains the missing fingernail. Impossible. The color she picked is the exact shade of the peas and green beans. Of course it is. Of course she'd accidentally garnish our meal with camouflaged fake nail.

I give her the tiniest head shake, trying to telepathically communicate do not say one word because the only thing worse than someone finding a nail in their food is Liz announcing that someone *might* find a nail in their food.

I take a bite.

I chew.

And chew.

And chew.

The taste isn't awful, but the consistency is concerning. Like the glue-slime kids make when their parents aren't watching. Mr. Harrington clears his throat like he's about to conduct a deposition, not choke down our Franken-pie. He offers a polite smile and gently places his fork beside his plate.

"So," he begins, adjusting his glasses, "why don't you tell me how you two met?"

Liz perks up immediately. "On the side of the road," she says. "He was grumpy. I was chatty."

I stab another forkful just to keep from snorting. "Liz had a flat tire on the way home from an out of town shoot. I stopped to help her."

Liz bumps my shoulder. "I didn't know who he was, but he knew who I was. He admitted later he had been watching me for weeks. "

Mr. Harrington nods like this is all perfectly normal. "And living together? Getting married? Those transitions have been smooth?"

Liz answers without missing a beat. "He hogs the blankets."

"She steals my hoodies."

The lawyer's smile grows, and he glances, almost knowingly, toward the bedroom where my parents were whisper-fighting minutes ago. "And would you say you spend a significant amount of time together outside of work?"

Liz squeezes my knee again. This time much more gentle. "Pretty much all of it," she says softly.

"Right," he murmurs. He looks down at his dinner like it's his last meal, then back up at us. "Well. Seems real enough to me."

My dad stiffens. My mom's eye twitches and she aggressively slams a bite of food into her mouth. There's a crunch. A loud one. Too loud.

Liz and I freeze at the same time. Our hands find each other and she squeezes with enough force to sever circulation. My mother's chewing slows, then stops entirely. She reaches up, touches her jaw, and winces.

"Oh," she says sharply. "Something is, something is very wrong with this." She prods at her molar. "I think I've chipped a tooth."

Liz inhales like she's about to pass out. I choke on air.

My dad squints at her plate. "What did you bite down on?"

She pokes through the casserole with her fork, and then, horror of horrors, lifts something green and curved. A broken acrylic nail. Liz lets out the tiniest squeak.

My mother holds it up like evidence in a murder trial. "What," she demands, "is this?"

Mr. Harrington stands very carefully, as if sudden movements might trigger a catastrophic event. "Well," he says under his breath, "this concludes my questions."

My mom screeches. I pinch the bridge of my nose. Liz grabs her wine and takes a giant gulp.

My dad rises too. "Tonight didn't prove or disprove anything."

The lawyer clearly decides this is his moment to escape. "Right! Well! I'll just review the paperwork and transfer the money early next week."

He turns, but my parents move faster than I've seen either of them move in a decade.

"Mr. Harrington," my dad calls, practically lunging for the poor man's briefcase. "We need a full evaluation."

"We are *not* finished here," my mother adds, stalking after him with the nail still in her hand like she's brandishing a cursed artifact.

Liz and I sit frozen as the three of them bottleneck in the doorway, their voices rising:

"You didn't ask them enough questions!"

"There is nothing suspicious here!"

"You barely even looked at the apartment!"

"What else do you want me to do, search for love letters?!"

"We should have done a lie detector!"

"This isn't an interrogation!" Mr. Harrington's voice cracks. "I just spent the last hour watching two people who, by all accounts, are very much in love, be made to feel uncomfortable and less than in their own home. I assure you after spending one evening with them, this is not fraud!"

My parents push after him, still arguing, still demanding explanations and stronger evaluations and more questions, their voices fading as they chase him down the hallway like two deranged seagulls after a french fry.

The door closes. It's suddenly quiet. I exhale hard, run a hand through my hair, and slump onto the couch.

"Well, we survived."

"Barely," Liz croaks.

I glance over at her, my stance softening. "You okay?"

"I served your mother my fingernail," she whispers. "I'm going to be thinking about that until I die."

My mouth twitches, then my laughter escapes. It starts low, exhausted, and quickly turns into real laugh. And thankfully, Liz starts laughing too and collapses on the couch next to me, both of us laughing like lunatics who just escaped a hostage situation. Hulk climbs onto my lap, licking some of the sauce off of Liz's arm next to me.

I lean back, closing my eyes. "We are never making pot pie again."

"Never."

When her hand finds mine and she squeezes like she never wants to let go, my chest aches. I can't stop replaying what the lawyer said. *"Two people who, by all accounts, are very much in love."*

I'm starting to wish that was actually true. Even in the middle of a disaster, there's no one else I'd rather have next to me.

Chapter Thirty-Four
Cheering Section
Nate

A FEW DAYS AFTER the nightmare of a visit from my parents, things on set settle down. People stopped asking me what it's like to be George and Isabel's son. Probably because they realized I wasn't going to give them anything besides a blank stare and a grunt.

They moved on to Liz instead. They all ask *her* what it's like being married to a man who is basically a mute. And every time she gives the same answer, soft mouth tilt, eyes bright even when she's pretending to be annoyed.

"He talks to me."

Every damn time, it hits me. Somewhere deep. Somewhere unguarded. It feels like we're a real team. Tonight, we wrapped after four in the morning. Everyone is dragging, half-dead, walking corpses. Except Liz.

Liz is slap happy. Which is apparently a setting I didn't know she had. If you asked me to describe it, I'd say it's like watching a bouncy ball hit concrete for the first time. Chaotic. Unpredictable. Impossible to control.

I herd her to the car like I'm corralling a five-year-old who has had too much sugar or a drunk college student. Actually, when I look at her closer, maybe she is overly tired *and* drunk. I grab her by the shoulders to look in her eyes. "Are you drunk?"

"We got done so much long before you. The girls and I did the, uh, few shots while we were waiting. So much long? So longer much?"

I groan and look up at the sky.

"Bear," she giggles as she misses the open car door entirely and bumps into the side of it. "Why are there three of you?"

"There aren't," I mutter, steadying her.

She gasps dramatically. "Oh my gosh. Did you clone yourself? Bear one, Bear two, Bear three. That's, that's too many Bears. I can't handle that many muscles."

I try to glare at her. I do. But she's so damn pleased with herself she starts laughing before I manage it. Not a normal laugh. A full-body, wheezing, tears-in-her-eyes laugh.

"Liz," I warn, "get in the car."

"Bossy," she sing-songs, poking my chest with one finger. "Bossy Bear. Bear-sy. Bossy Bear-sy. Ooo that's fun to say."

"Get. In. The. Car." It's too damn late for this.

"Okay, okay, okay," she says and dances her way into the car.

I pinch the bridge of my nose. "For the love of all things, Liz, sit down."

She salutes me. Actually salutes. "Yes, Captain Bossy Bear-sy, sir." She misses the seat completely and ends up on the ground in the parking lot.

"Bear," she giggles as I pick her up off the ground and place her in the car, "did you know humans have, like... twenty toes?"

"Ten," I correct automatically.

"Noooo," she whispers, extremely offended. "I have ten. You have ten. That's twenty." She wags a finger between us. "Our toes are married too."

"Why me?"

She gasps. "Wait, do you think our toes like each other? Or are they like, 'ugh, my partner is so sweaty?' Your toes are probably sweaty. You look like someone whose toes work too hard."

I blink at her. "What does that even mean?"

She nods, deadly serious. "You walk like a man with important ankles."

"...What?"

"POWER ANKLES," she shouts, startling a bird from a nearby tree. "You have power ankles, Bear."

I give up and round the hood to drive us home. When we pull into the lot, she leans forward and gasps like she's witnessed a miracle.

"Look!" She points dramatically at absolutely nothing. "The moon is following us."

"That tends to happen."

She smacks my arm. "Don't ruin the magic."

"It's the moon, Liz."

"It's our moon," she insists. "He knows we're married."

"He?"

"The moon is a boy," she huffs, as if this is obvious. "The sun is a girl."

I'm too tired to argue. "Sure."

"He's cheering for us," she whispers. "He's like, 'Go, Bear and Cricket, fall in loooove.'" She beams. "He shipped us."

I groan into my hands. "Inside. Now." She slumps forward and I easily catch her lifting her from the car.

"Whoa," she mumbles into my chest, voice muffled. "You're warm. You're always warm. Why are you always warm? You're like a human space heater. Like a like a heated blanket. A hot, heated blanket."

I try to be annoyed. It lasts two seconds. She's too adorable when she's out of her mind from lack of sleep and one too many shots.

"Come on," I mutter, hooking an arm under her legs and lifting her.

She squeaks. "Nate! Put me down! You're hurt! You're concussed! You're shoulder-y!"

"Shoulder-y?"

"Yes! Shoulder-y! You have shoulders! And they're injured! And I'm heavy!"

"You're not heavy."

She squirms for half a second before her body gives out and I carry her to the elevator. It's moving at a snail's pace tonight. Or this morning rather.

"Do you think elevators get bored?"

She startles me, I thought she passed out on my shoulder. "No."

"They just go up, then down, then up again, like a very sad yo-yo."

"Liz."

She looks at me with tragic sincerity. "Bear, I think our elevator needs a hobby."

"Liz."

"Maybe knitting?"

"Liz."

"Or pottery, can elevators do pottery?"

"Fuckin' hell."

She pats my cheek. "Language."

We exit the elevator. "You're going to hurt yourself," she mumbles, head dropping onto my shoulder. "Then I'll have to carry you and I can't do that because you're like biceps with legs. And I'm small."

"You're fine," I say, nudging the door open with my foot.

"I'm not fine," she whispers dramatically. "I'm sleepy." She yawns dramatically before loudly declaring, "TUCK ME IN, POWER ANKLES."

She knocks out instantly. I mean instantly. Her head touches the pillow, and she's gone, breathing slow and even, lips parted the tiniest bit, hair spilling across her cheek.

I stand there for a long moment, just staring. If I attempted to explain the last half hour to anyone, they wouldn't believe me. She's insane in the best way possible. She's curled toward my side of the bed, one hand fisted in the blanket like she's holding onto something. Even unconsciously, she reaches for me.

She's so small in our bed, so soft. The room is dim, quiet except for her slow breathing, and I feel this, sting? Tug? Squeeze? I don't know. It's not physical pain but something deeper. Something I can't stretch or ice or Biofreeze away.

I reach out and brush a piece of hair off her cheek. My fingers barely graze her skin. She doesn't stir. She trusts me. She really, completely trusts me. It warms my soul as much as it scares me.

There's nothing rational about the way my chest aches looking at her sleep in my bed like she belongs there for forever. There's nothing calm about the way my hand shakes when I think about waking up tomorrow and knowing her, here, like this, won't last forever unless I do something about it.

We haven't crossed any lines that we can't come back from. Yet. We haven't broken any of our stupid rules too badly. But every day with her, those lines blur a little more.

She shifts in her sleep, burrowing deeper into the blankets, and a soft noise escapes her throat, somewhere between a sigh and a hum. It lights my blood on fire. My heart hits my ribs so hard it actually hurts.

This is bad. This is so, so bad. I sit on the edge of the bed and just watch her for a minute longer, my elbows on my knees, hands clasped.

"I'm screwed," I whisper to the dark room. Eventually, I stretch out beside her carefully, not touching, not crowding the way I want to. But she senses me anyway and inches closer, her forehead bumping my arm like it's instinct.

I wrap my arm around her and she settles her head on my chest. Yeah. I'm completely, absolutely screwed. How do I go about convincing my wife that I want her to stay my wife?

***

THE NEXT MORNING I wake before Liz. No surprise there. Even with a full eight hours, I've learned she'd rather be in bed than join the land of the living. I slowly slide myself out from beneath her. Hulk immediately takes my spot and curls into Liz's hair.

We have half the day off before we need to drive South for the last on location shoot tonight, but there a few things I need to take care of this morning before she wakes.

First up, changing the locks.

My mom has been blowing up my phone ever since she and my dad walked out of here the other night. It is insane that she thinks I will forgive her so quickly after how she treated me. How she treated Liz.

I should have changed these locks a long time ago, but until now they had never shown up uninvited. They just sent their cleaning crews, which I now realize actually were spies, or arranged grocery deliveries under the guise of helping. I see it clearly now for what it is. Control dressed up as concern.

I'll eventually talk to them. I don't think they will ever understand my life here, and I am finally making peace with the fact that I may never get the easy, loving acceptance Liz has always had from her parents. And that is okay. I'll talk to them a few times a month, see them once a year, and let that be that.

I hear Liz stirring in the room. I made sure to get the coffee brewing and the canned biscuits in the oven before I started my projects. I figured Liz would be in desperate need of caffeine after last night.

After some shuffling around, she emerges in last night's clothes as I'm closing my laptop. I debated changing her into pajamas, but decided that would definitely break one of our rules.

"Morning, Cricket."

Her eyes narrow and she makes grabby hands at the cup of coffee I hold out to her.

"Feeling okay today?"

She takes a deep inhale of her cup, pleasure lighting her face. Damn it. That's going to be a problem for me if she keeps doing that. I watch her slowly take a sip and melt into the couch.

"I feel fine. Just still tired. Too many late nights in a row wore me out."

"The shots of tequila probably didn't help."

Her face scrunches. "Yeah. That too. I hope I wasn't too much last night. When I'm that tired I tend to just black out."

"You should have just come home when you got off work. You didn't have to wait on me."

"I like coming home at the same time you do. I didn't mind waiting." She pauses to take another sip. "Besides, I haven't hung out with Jenn and Autumn in a while. Once they realized I was waiting on you, Autumn pulled out her emergency tequila stash from her purse and that was that."

I walk a plate with a biscuit over to her and settle in.

"Feeling up to going somewhere with me today?"

"Always." She mumbles around a big bite. I love that she didn't hesitate or ask questions. She just jumps in head first. Sometimes I wish I was more like that. Maybe I am, since meeting Liz. Hell, I did marry her after only knowing her a few weeks.

"Cool. We'll take my bike." Her eyes light up with excitement. Even wearing last night's clothes, her make up running beneath her eyes, and her hair a mess, she's beautiful. I can't believe she said yes to me. Even if it was under the guise of helping me. I can't believe she signed up to marry me.

***

Liz claps in delight as I sink a three-pointer to win the game. She jumps to her feet like this is the NBA championship, not a pickup basketball game in a musty gym with flickering lights. The guys give me endless shit about bringing my own cheering section, but I can't wipe the grin off my face. She's been loud the entire time, gasping, cheering, shouting "THAT'S MY HUSBAND!" The word husband makes me puff up with pride.

She met Lane and Joseph the day they helped me move, but none of the other guys have met her yet. The second they learned I'd gotten married, they acted like I'd confessed to robbing a bank. Before tip-off, I wanted to introduce her to Joe, but he wasn't here yet. I saw him slip in sometime during the second half. Hard to miss the guy, bald, broad, quiet, always watching.

He sits two rows behind Liz, diagonally over her shoulder. Watching the game. Watching her. Watching us.

When the game ends, I yell to Liz that I'll be out of the locker room in five and sprint to shower. Fastest I've ever moved. By the time I walk back out, she's on her phone, swinging her legs, completely unaware of the way she looks sitting there, a bright spot, entirely too pretty for a dingy gym.

But her head snaps up the second I appear. Like she sensed me. Her whole face lights up. She rises slowly to her feet, legs impossibly long. I've gotten used to her boho skirts and floaty dresses, but today she's in pale pink shorts and a tank top so she could ride with me on the bike. I thought she'd be scared, but the woman let out a full-throttle whoop when we took off. I felt that sound all the way through my ribs.

Joe starts making his way down the bleachers toward us.

"Son, good game out there." He rests his hand on my shoulder. "Not sure it was smart to be playing this close to an injury." He lets the reprimand land, then turns to Liz. "And who do we have here?"

The old bastard smiles. If people think I'm grumpy, Joe puts me to shame. Seeing him smile is like catching sight of one of Liz's unicorns.

"I'm Liz!" She hits him with full sunshine. "I've heard a lot about you."

And instead of shaking his hand, she wraps her arms around him in this enormous, enthusiastic hug. Joe stiffens like he's being attacked by a rabid dog, then, slowly, hesitantly, hugs her back. His eyes meet mine over her shoulder, eyebrows raised in disbelief.

"Sorry," she says when she pulls back. "I'm a hugger. And I'm just so thankful Bear had you growing up."

Joe's cheeks flush. He coughs. "He would've been just fine."

He turns to me. "So I got an interesting call a few days ago." Dramatic pause, he lives for those. "Your father called. Thankfully I haven't heard from him in years."

I grunt.

"He wanted to ask me about your marriage. If I knew Liz. What I thought."

"And?" I ask tightly.

"Seeing as how I didn't know you were married, and didn't think I should tell him that, I told him my thoughts were none of his damn business."

My jaw ticks. "And then?"

"He said if I noticed anything off to give him a call. Day or night." Joe looks at Liz. "Anything I'm supposed to be worried about?"

Liz loops her arm through mine and looks up at me with such pure, unfiltered adoration I swear my heart stops. "I don't know," she says sweetly, "what do you think, Boo-bear? Anything Joe needs to worry about?"

I lean down and brush my lips against hers. Barely there, but enough to short-circuit us both. Without looking away from her, I answer Joe.

"Nope. Nothing to worry about here."

Joe nods. "Good. Glad you're making time in your life for more important things. Call me if you need me, kid."

He leaves the gym, but Liz and I stand rooted, eyes locked, like neither of us is ready to break whatever is humming between us.

"Alright," I murmur, "let's go get brunch."

Liz squeals at a decimal only dogs should be able to hear. "Brunch?"

"I heard you mention the place a mile from the condo enough this week," I say, fighting a smile. "I can take a hint."

The sunlight hits her face and streaks through her hair like the damn universe is spotlighting her. The joy pouring out of her at the promise of brunch is enough to make me wonder if I'd eat froufrou meals every day of my life just to keep that look on her face.

We reach my bike, but before she can put her helmet on, I hook an arm around her waist and pull her to me. Her eyes go wide, startled, lips parting. There are strands of hair stuck to her lip gloss, so I tuck them gently behind her ear.

"Joe hasn't left the parking lot yet," I say quietly.

She peeks over my shoulder. Joe's in his car, not even glancing our way, but sometimes a man has to get creative when he wants an excuse to touch his wife.

"We should probably give him something to report back," she murmurs. "Just in case your parents call him again."

I smile. Slow. Deep. Hungry.

"Took the words right out of my mouth, Cricket."

I can't wait another second. The kisses we shared in California feel like another lifetime, and the moment our lips meet, everything in me detonates. She tastes like sugar. She tastes like she's mine, even though she isn't.

She moans softly into my mouth and it destroys me. My control shatters. I back her against the brick wall, and she breaks the kiss just long enough to jump up, legs wrapping around my waist like she was made to fit there.

Oh, hell yes.

I lock one arm around her waist; the other dives into her hair, tilting her head so I can kiss my way down her throat, along her jaw, back to her mouth. I take my time. Mapping her. Memorizing her.

Her pulse is racing beneath my tongue. I nip at the skin there. She lets out a sound, soft, desperate, and it damn near undoes me. When I finally reach her lips again, she drags her hands up my chest and into my hair, taking over the kiss, deepening it, wrecking me cell by cell.

This kiss isn't just heat. It's hunger. It's possession. It's a line being crossed and burned straight to ash. Rules destroyed. This kiss is rewriting my DNA. And I know one thing with absolute certainty: I will not survive losing her.

Chapter Thirty-Five
Good Practice
Liz

I'M SITTING IN THE passenger seat of my car after the most perfect day. I'm floating. My whole body feels like it's levitating. If this is what being high feels like, I finally understand why people get addicted.

After the kiss that scrambled my brain and left me begging for more, we got brunch at the cutest place on the planet. Nate and I have never struggled with touching each other, in public, or at home, whatever, but today? Today our affection was feral. I couldn't stop reaching for him, sliding my hand into his, leaning over to kiss his cheek, his jaw.

And he was just as bad. When the waiter lingered too long dropping off our drinks and chatting with me, I genuinely thought Nate might remove his head from his shoulders.

The way he touched me, brushed hair out of my face, slid his calloused hand up my thigh and squeezed gently under the table, it melted me. I was Mid–happy-food-dance after taking a massive bite of French toast when he chuckled, leaned over, and kissed my shoulder. Full stop.

Shoulder kisses are hot. Shoulder kisses should be illegal. Shoulder kisses should come with a warning label because I almost dissolved into a sticky puddle right then and there.

We wandered a farmer's market afterward, strolling hand in hand, tasting samples, laughing at nothing. We've had glimpses of normal married life, but today was different. Today neither of us pulled back. Neither of us pretended.

And I don't know what that means.

I need a few days to unscramble how I'm feeling, to try and figure out what he's thinking. It's a good thing we are out of town for a few days. I don't know if I could handle laying in bed next to him and not continuing what we started earlier. A few days will be good for me to clear my head. He's probably relieved to have some space, a break from my constant orbiting.

Hulk lets out a tiny mewl in my lap, head butting my hand. I'm so glad Nate agreed to help me sneak Hulk in. My sweet boy has been alone enough lately. We've been driving in silence for a while, but for once I don't feel the need to break it. It's comfortable. I'm relaxed. I can't stop touching my lips and reliving this morning all over again. Every time I look over, Nate has that smug, satisfied smirk that makes my stomach flip.

He reaches over and grabs my hand, threading our fingers together. My stomach swoops.

His thumb rubs slow circles over my knuckles, like he's grounding himself. Like he's about to say something important.

"So," he says casually, eyes still on the road, "the money hit yesterday."

I blink. "What money?"

"My trust," he says, like he's telling me the weather. "I paid off the loan this morning. Before you woke up."

The world tilts.

"Oh." The word comes out small. Useless. My chest tightens and then loosens all at once, relief rushing through me so fast it makes my eyes sting. The weight that's been sitting between my shoulders lifts. I always knew he planned to pay it off. There was no stopping him, it was a part of our deal after all.

"That's..." I swallow. "Thank you." I don't know how else to express my gratitude. This is huge.

He squeezes my hand once. "I told you I would."

Gratitude floods. Then relief. Then the quieter thing underneath it. That small reminder. He upheld his end of the deal, just like he promised. Just like this arrangement has always been.

Temporary. Transactional. An expiration date baked right into it.

I force a smile and stare out the window, watching the trees blur past. I should feel nothing but grateful. I do feel grateful. But it's tangled up with the awareness that this all started as a way to help each other out. He pays my loan. His parents leave him alone. We stay married for a year.

"So," I say, needing to move us somewhere safer before my thoughts spiral. "What's your next project?" The lamest possible question. But instead of asking what I want to ask: *What are we? What did today mean? You upheld your end, does this really have to end?* I pick work. It's safer.

"I don't know," he says. "What were you thinking? What do you want to do?"

"Well, if you are tired of seeing me so much, we can try and get different contracts." He gives me a look I can't decipher so I keep rambling.

"Totally understandable if you *are* tired of me. We see each other at work and at home, I can be a lot I know. I get it if you want a break. Actually tonight in different hotel rooms will probably be a good thing, right? You probably are tired of me being wrapped around you every night. I'm sorry by the way, but I'm a people person. I love being with people. Any people. I don't mean to gravitate to you every night. That's probably not fun for you, huh? After all, you're just doing this as a favor to me. You didn't really sign up for a bed buddy."

He gives me another funny look. His grip loosens. My heart stops.

"Okay, cool. When we get there, we will go to our own rooms and it'll be a good break from your fake wife. Practice for when this is all over in a year. Right?"

His hand slips from mine and grips the steering wheel, his knuckles turning white.

"Nate?"

He clears his throat. "Right, good practice." Under his breath he mutters, "Good reminder."

The air in the car shifts instantly. Heavy. Wrong. Hulk mewls again, crawling into my lap like he feels the storm brewing.

Thank every star in the sky that we pull into the hotel, the same one we stayed in at the beginning of filming. The hot tub glows through the windows, and the memory of sitting there with Nate in the middle of the night slams into me. It feels like a lifetime ago.

Nate gets out and slams his door without a word. Okay. Cool. We're fine. Everything's fine. Totally normal to go from kissing-on-walls to slamming car doors. Totally fine.

I leave Hulk in the car and follow him in to get my room key. I get to the desk as the attendant says, "Here you go Mr. and Mrs. Jones, your two keys." Nate freezes, I freeze.

"Excuse me?" I squeak.

The front desk guy looks down at his paperwork and back at us. "Yup right here, Mr. and Mrs. Jones room one-oh-eight. Is there a problem?"

Nate grabs the keys and turns to walk away. "No, no problem."

I scurry after him and help unload our bags, while he wordlessly fumes. I guess it makes sense we would be in the same room this time. Everyone knows we are married and married people usually want to stay together. It's silly it never crossed my mind that the office would call and change our arrangements.

Guess Nate won't be getting a break from me after all.

***

NATE

A break from her? Is she not feeling the same thing I am? Was today not a turning point for us? Because I thought it was. I *really* thought it was. The joy I felt paying off her debt this morning, knowing she wouldn't have that burden anymore and we could put it behind us. We could focus on us. Brunch. The way she looked at me. The way she touched me. The way she wrapped her legs around me like she couldn't get close enough. She kissed me like she wanted more.

And I let myself believe, just for a minute, that we were on the same page. That maybe she felt the shift too. That maybe this thing between us was turning into something real. Then she said she thought I needed a break from her.

From *her*.

Like being with her isn't the best part of every day. I feel something sour climb up my chest. It's not anger. Not exactly. More like disappointment twisting into something sharp. Every word she said chipped away at what I thought we were building.

Do I make her feel unwanted? Unwelcome? Did I screw this up that badly? Does she think everything today was fake? Everything the past few weeks has been the realest thing I've ever experienced.

The idea that she doesn't feel the same makes my stomach drop. I suddenly can't be in this room anymore.

"I'm headed to set. Can you catch a ride with the girls?"

She wordlessly nods her head and I walk out the door without looking back. I arrive at set and run straight into Becket. He's the last person I want to see right now.

"Woah, pal. What's got your panties in a twist." His hand rests on my shoulder stopping me in place. I stare at him and then down at his hand. He takes the hint and releases me and I blow past him. A normal person would take the hint and back off, but not Beck.

"Honeymoon over?"

I stalk over to the crew member in charge of my rigging to get set up. Thankfully, I don't need to spend anytime in hair and makeup tonight. That might send me over the edge.

I ignore Becket the best I can as he spews marital advice. As if I would take advice from Hollywood's biggest playboy. I've personally witnessed him hooking up with four different women, just during this project. He's a real treat.

Thankfully the director is ready for me and I can jump into work and bury my raging thoughts for a few hours. We shoot well into the morning. I never see Liz, but I know she's here. I see her handy work when I look into the faces of the actresses.

I don't look for her before I leave, she made her way here without me, I'm sure she can make her way back. I wish I had my motorcycle with me. A few hours ripping down these back roads would help clear my head.

By the time I get back to the hotel room I see Liz is already there and sleeping. She's curled into the tiniest ball possible. It's like she's curled into herself, trying to take up the least amount of space possible.

Hulk lifts his head eyeing me and promptly closes his eyes again. Dismissing me. I sit on the edge of the bed, elbow braced on my knees. I haven't let myself mull over everything she said in the car while I was working, but now I replay her words over and over.

You're probably tired of me.
It'll be a good break.
I know I'm a lot.
That's probably not fun for you.
We should practice being apart before the year is up.
Every sentence sharpens the ache.

I thought stupidly, that she liked being around me. That she felt safe with me. That she wanted me the way I want her. Maybe I read everything wrong. Maybe earlier today, or yesterday rather, meant nothing more to her than playing a part. Maybe I'm the only one falling.

My jaw tightens. As I sit there, something slowly, painfully, clicks into place. Her ramble was never about me. It wasn't about her feelings for me either. It was about *her*. Her insecurities. Her fear. The way she probably thinks she's a burden to everyone, not just me. She's not trying to push me away. She's bracing for me to walk away. Preparing herself.

My chest pulls tight, all the frustration draining out of me until only worry remains. She thinks *she's* the problem. She couldn't be more wrong. There's nothing I can do about it now. I fall into bed beside her. I'm exhausted. I should fall right to sleep, but my side feels hollow. I gently pull Liz to my chest. In her sleep she uncurls from her ball and drapes herself around me like a second skin. I drift off to sleep with her head resting on my heart, just the way it should be.

I wake to see Liz quietly moving around the room like a ghost. Her features are turned down. Her sparkle is missing. A glance at the clock tells me I need to be on set in less than an hour. I clear my throat to alert her I'm awake.

She stiffens like she's bracing for whatever I'm about to say. Like she's scared. And that thought? That thought hits me harder than getting speared off a crash pad.

I slowly sit up and wipe the sleep from my face. "Liz, stop." She pauses, fiddling with the snacks on the bar, and turns her head to look at me. Her eyes shine with tears that she's holding back from falling. I hold out my hand to her. "Come here."

I watch her throat bobble, but she walks over to me and sits down. I turn to her, pull her legs into my lap, and make sure she's looking in my eyes when I say, "I'm not tired of you." Her chin wobbles. "You aren't too much."

I thread my hands through her hair. "I like when you wrap yourself around me at night. If you didn't, I'd pull you to my side of the bed anyway."

The first tear spills over. "I like spending time with you. I like being with you. Liz, I just like you." She sucks in a small breath of air. "I don't need or want a break, but I need you to be very clear and tell me if that's what you want from me. Do you want me to back off? Is this just a game to you?"

She doesn't even wait a beat.

"No." Her voice is small, her eyes focused on her lap. I gently lift her chin so her eyes meet mine.

"I know we have to get to set soon," I murmur. "And we don't have time to get into all of this the way we should. But hear me. Let me be very, very clear."

I hold her face between my palms. "Just because I paid off the loan doesn't mean I want a break from you. It doesn't change how I'm feeling. Not now. Not ever."

Her wide eyes search mine for the lie, but only see the truth shining through before a small timid smile breaks across her face. I gently kiss her lips. Not how I really want to, but we don't have time for that now.

***

Liz

The next two days we work round the clock to get the final shots for the movie. We work long, odd hours and make it back to our hotel to crash for a few hours and do it again. We haven't talked about anything serious, there hasn't been time, but we are sharing more looks, more touches through the day. I can't wait to get home and figure out what our life together means.

We wrapped early this morning. Finally. This movie felt longer than the others. Not because the lead was a jerk, though he absolutely was, but because filming in the swampy southern humidity for weeks on end slowly melted my will to live. The only saving grace was having Nate with me.

Normally I survive set life on girl time. Usually Jenn, Autumn, and I have a great time on location. We stick together and keep each other sane. But once Nate and I started hanging more, they drifted toward the single crowd. They are currently both aggressively single, which is why we are all going out tonight when we get home.

Celebrating the project's completion seems like a good excuse for Jenn and Autumn to go on the hunt, and for Nate and me to celebrate being out from under the thumb of our oppressors. His parents and my giant loan.

I've never gone out to a bar with Nate. The thought of his grumpy face with pop music playing in the background makes me giggle. It should be fun. Now that my mind is on Nate and I have time to breathe after our hectic schedule, my brain does circles. Are we dating even though we are married?

My thoughts are interrupted by Nate coming in the room. "They just cut me. We are good to head home." He tosses me a bag of gummy bears as he walks toward me. "Snacks for the road."

He wraps me in a hug before gathering our stuff to load the car. I stand there mutely staring down at a bag of my favorite snacks from my favorite person.

Real life, here we come. I couldn't be more excited.

Chapter Thirty-Six
Defibrillator Needed
Liz

I ended up napping most of the way home today, and when we arrived, we both crashed for a few hours. We woke snuggled on the couch, Hulk curled on top of Nate's head. It was ridiculously cute. We still haven't had a serious talk about our future, but I'm hoping we can tonight when we get back from the bar.

We are running late, scrambling to get ready to meet everyone out to celebrate wrapping. Going out is an excuse for Autumn and Jenn to troll for their next victims. I mean dates. Chloe and James are meeting us out with a few of their friends too. It feels just like old times, except better because Nate is with me.

Miracle upon miracles, Nate and I walk into the bar just a few minutes late. Major perk of moving in with him: his place is close to everything. No more suburban exile. It also helps that he keeps me focused and on task. No more arriving thirty minutes late for me.

This place straddles the line between bar and nightclub. The later it gets, the more bumping and grinding, and the less catching up over drinks. We arrive as the crowd shifts from "after-work drinks" to "chaotic college reunion" energy. I glance at Nate and he doesn't even try to hide his grimace.

"Wow," I say, lips twitching. "You look thrilled."

He deadpans, "This is my nightmare."

"Come on. It's not that bad."

A group of girls shriek over by the bar. A guy bumps into Nate and doesn't apologize. Someone sloshes a drink onto the floor. Nate levels me with a flat stare. "Cricket."

I snort. "Okay, fine. It's a little bad."

"If we weren't meeting your friends, we'd already be back home in bed."

Us. In bed. Together.

Every night ends with us falling asleep inches apart, and after our brief conversation the other day, the thought of us in bed holds new meaning. New potential.

I play it cool, even though my insides are tap dancing. "Well, we're not in bed. We're here. So let's try to survive this together."

He leans down, voice low in my ear. "But I'd rather be in bed with you."

My cheeks turn red, heat shoots straight down my spine. And he knows it. Oh, he definitely knows it, because a slow smirk forms on his stupidly handsome face.

"I hate you," I mutter.

"Liar."

I grab his hand before he can see me melt. "Come on, let's find the girls and Chloe and James before you bolt."

He squeezes my hand once, firm, warm, grounding, and follows me deeper into the crowd. It's ridiculous, but the simple act of holding his hand in a place this loud, this chaotic, makes my chest feel warm and full and safe. Like I'm tethered to him.

I spot our group near the back. The moment they see us, Chloe waves wildly, and James gives Nate a chin-lift that's basically the male version of a hug. I do the introductions for those that Nate hasn't met yet, and he actually relaxes a little. He stands closer to me than necessary, one hand brushing the small of my back like he can't help himself. Every time, my breath catches.

Autumn leans in. "Your husband looks stupid hot tonight."

I whisper back, "Right? The shirt should be illegal."

Autumn grins like someone who knows things and singsongs, "Someone's getting lucky tonight."

Nate glances down at us, suspicious. "What are you two whispering about?"

"Nothing," we say in unison.

His brows raise. "Uh-huh."

Before I can come up with something, he steps close, our bodies molding together, and tucks a strand of hair behind my ear. "Want a drink?"

He didn't need to lean into me like that. He didn't need to touch me. But he did. "Y-yeah," I manage. "Something light."

His lips twitch. "I've got you."

His hand glides over my lower back again as he passes, it leaves a trail of heat behind. He disappears toward the bar, shoulders cutting through the crowd, people part for him instinctively. I watch him walk away and sigh. Autumn laughs at me and downs another shot.

I don't drink a lot when we are out in public. After everything with my ex, losing control in public doesn't feel fun, it feels dangerous. My friends never notice when my "shots" are just lime water. I'm pretty sure James has picked up on the fact that I don't drink in public as often. Especially after last year when everyone but me ended up draped over strangers and needing to be carried home.

I feel Nate's return before I see him. He slides up behind me, his scent wrapping around me, his arm looping around my waist as he hands me my drink over my shoulder. With Nate beside me, I could get drunk if I wanted. With Nate beside me, I'm safe.

Nate's fingers brush mine as I take the drink. "Drink it slow, Cricket. Power ankles doesn't want to carry you home again tonight." He smirks at me.

I squint up at him. "Power ankles?

"You know what, never mind." He laughs and takes a sip of his drink.

"You think I can't handle my liquor?"

"Not if you're drinking all the shots Jenn is pushing." He glances over at her, amusement coloring his features. "She's going to feel like shit tomorrow."

I giggle and press my back into his chest. He tightens his arms around me, dropping a kiss to the top of my head. I love how affectionate he is being.

My whole body goes warm. He pulls back like he didn't just set my bloodstream on fire and casually asks, "You need anything else?"

Just air. Possibly CPR. Maybe a defibrillator. "No," I breathe and give my drink a little shake. "This is good."

He kisses my temple lingering for a breath, gives me a wink that destroys my brain chemistry, and turns to talk to James. I down my drink, quickly catching a buzz. I feel happy. And after our conversation tonight, I know I'll feel happy and settled. I can feel it in my bones. My body does a happy shiver and Nate looks down catching my eye.

You good?

It's a silent question.

I nod happy in our little bubble. A few minutes later the girls drag me to the dance floor. Nate watches from the outskirts with the other guys. Knowing his eyes are on me? It does something to me. Makes me feel bold. Wanted. I let myself get lost in the music and the laughter. It's been too long since we've had a night like this. Halfway through song two, Jenn dances by, passing out shots like she works here. For once, I let myself partake.

Four, maybe five songs later, I'm sweaty and need to go to the bathroom. Chloe offers to go with me, but I wave her off. Dancing is one of her favorite things in the world, but she hasn't had as much time lately to come dancing with us. I'd never pull her away.

I make eye contact with Nate and point to the bathroom. He gives me a subtle head nod.

Washing my hands I stare at the girl looking back at me in the bathroom mirror. I'm flushed, joy radiating from every pore. Can I still see the scars staring back at me if I look hard enough? Sure. But I'm not ashamed of them anymore. Nate reminds me every time he sees me staring, or absently running my finger over one, that they are proof of how strong I am. I'm starting to believe him.

I think I'm smitten with my husband. I think it's time to pull my man on the dance floor with me. Giddy with the thought of Nate dancing, I don't pay attention as I leave the bathroom and knock right into someone.

"Oh my goodness, I didn't see you ther..."

My apology dies on the tip of my tongue, my blood turns to ice, as I come face to face with my actual nightmare.

Colby.

My ex. In the bar. Standing in front of me like a demon summoned from the past. He shouldn't be here. He shouldn't be *anywhere*. When did he get out? How?

I glance around, my pulse rising even higher as I realize the bathroom hallway is cut off from Nate's view.

Fuck.

No other word will do. Only the real one.

He still hasn't said anything. "Excuse me." I try to sidestep him, but he blocks my path.

"I thought I saw you," he slurs. "Putting on quite the show out there with your little whore friends."

"I need to go." I move again. He grabs my arm. Hard enough to leave marks.

"I don't think you do." He pauses and slowly looks me up and down. It doesn't feel like when Nate looks at me at all. I feel exposed. Scared.

"I've had a lot of time to think about what I'd do if I ever saw you again."

"Let me go."

"No, I don't think I will." He steps closer. His breath hot and sour with whiskey hits my face. I swallow down a wave of nausea as he shoves me against the wall.

I should scream. I should fight. I should knee him. I should do something. Instead I'm paralyzed with fear. Right back to the shell of a girl who woke up in the hospital after this same man almost killed me.

Until I remember I am *not* that same girl and I fight like hell.

He's not expecting me to actually fight back. My elbow barely connects and my knee hits his thigh instead of his groin, but his grip slips momentarily. We struggle as I fight to escape him. His hand strikes high on my cheekbone, momentarily dazing me. It slows me enough that he regains control trapping me in his grip again. He slams me back against the wall so hard my teeth clack together.

"Please," I gasp. "Let me..."

Suddenly he's gone, ripped from me like a rag doll, and Nate has him by the throat.

Colby's feet barely touch the ground as Nate pins him to the opposite wall. Nate is calm, terrifyingly calm, his jaw clenched, eyes blazing with a fury I've never seen.

"N...Nate," I whisper.

He doesn't look at me. His focus is locked on Colby like a predator deciding the most efficient way to end something.

"You put your hands on *my* wife." The words are low. Deadly.

Colby's face purples. He claws at Nate's wrist, heels scraping uselessly against the floor.

Nate leans in, voice so low it feels like it reverberates through the walls. "Do it again, and I'll bury you somewhere no one will ever find you. I won't lose a single night of sleep over it."

He tightens his grip just long enough to make Colby's eyes bulge, a silent promise of exactly how far he could go, then releases. Colby collapses to the floor, wheezing, slobber dribbling from his mouth, trying to scramble upright.

Nate immediately steps between us, shielding me with his entire body. His hands come up, framing my face with a gentleness that makes my throat close.

"Liz," he breathes, scanning me, touching my shoulders, my arms, like he's scared to miss an injury. "Are you hurt?"

I shake my head, but my knees give out. Nate catches me before I hit the ground. A growl rumbles out of him when Colby staggers past us, but Nate doesn't turn. He doesn't need to. Colby flees. Footsteps pound toward us.

"Liz!" Chloe's voice is high, panicked.

"What the hell happened?" James demands, already stepping in front of Nate like he's ready to fight whoever is behind this.

Nate doesn't answer them. His eyes are locked on me as he clocks my reddening cheek, the purpling on my upper arms. He pulls me tighter into his chest, one hand cradling the back of my head, the other gripping my waist like he's afraid someone might try to take me from him.

"I'm taking her home," Nate says, voice hard.

James looks past Nate at the hallway, at the panic on my face, and his expression turns murderous.

"Who was it?" he asks, tone deadly calm.

Nate's jaw flexes, but it's like he can't bring himself to say his name. I answer, my voice sounding small. "Colby was here."

Chloe's eyes go wide. James's whole body freezes like maybe he didn't hear me correctly.

"If he's smart, he'll never come near her again." Nate growls.

Chloe steps closer and touches my arm gently. "Do you want us to come with you? I can grab your purse, your jacket."

I swallow, still shaking, still clinging to Nate. "I just... I want to go home."

"Then we're leaving." Nate presses a kiss to the top of my head, protective before slowly lowering me to my feet. He holds onto me another moment searching my face, then gathers me against him, one arm around my waist, one hand holding my hand, and leads me out of the bar with James and Chloe forming a silent wall behind us.

As the cool night air hits my face, Nate pulls me even closer, his voice rough, breaking, furious, loving, all at once. "He's never touching you again," he whispers. "Not ever again."

Chapter Thirty-Seven
Not Fragile
Nate

Liz is silent on the way home. It's only a few blocks, but James and Chloe drove us home. Liz wasn't in any shape to walk the ten minutes. James and I shared a look before I carry Liz inside. I know he'll take care of Colby, my job is to take care of Liz.

As soon as we cross the threshold Liz's body relaxes. I stand next to her, touching her the entire time she gets ready for bed. As soon as we climb into bed, Liz crashes. Not gradually. Not slowly. She folds into me like her body finally understands she's safe, and the second her head touches my chest, she's out.

I lay beside her, watching her breathe, trying to calm my racing heart. The moment I rounded the corner and saw Colby's hands on her a rage that I've never experienced before coursed through my body. My jaw still aches from how hard I ground my teeth.

I've taken hits before. I've been slammed, kicked, tackled, and thrown off buildings. I've had stunt rigs snap and send me flying. Nothing, *nothing*, has ever hit me as hard as the sight of Liz pinned against that hallway wall. Her eyes terrified. Her whole body frozen. And that piece of shit touching her.

My hands curl into fists even now. I stretch them out before the rage crawls back up my throat.

She stirs, eyelashes fluttering. "Nate?" Her voice cracks. Small. Wrecked.

I hold her tighter. "I'm here."

Her fingers tighten around mine, tugging me closer. "I'm sorry," she whispers. "I didn't do anything. I should've screamed. I froze. I'm so sorry."

I cup her cheek gently. "You don't need to apologize. You did nothing wrong. Nothing."

She closes her eyes. A tear slips out.

"I hate that I froze," she whispers. "I hate that he touched me."

"Liz," I say, and my voice comes out darker than I intend. "I will never allow him to touch you again. Do you understand? He won't ever get to you."

Her breath shudders. "You scared me," she admits softly.

The quiet admission tears me apart, but she adds, "I wasn't afraid of you. I was scared for you. I thought you were going to kill him."

I swallow hard. "I've never *felt* like that."

She brushes her thumb along my jaw. "I'm glad you were there. You always make me feel safe."

I bend down and press a kiss to her forehead, gentle, in complete opposition to the violence that I still feel coursing through my veins. Her breathing slowly evens out again. Within moments, she's drifted off again. Her grip loosens only enough that she's resting on my chest rather than holding me like a lifeline.

I stay awake long after she's fallen asleep. I can't let myself relax. Not yet. Not while that bastard is still breathing free air.

***

I BARELY SLEEP. MAYBE an hour, maybe less. Every time I shut my eyes, I see Liz pinned against that wall, fear in her eyes, his hands on her like he had the right.

By the time the sun nudges the horizon, my blood is running too hot to breathe normally. Liz is curled against my side, face tucked under my chin. I brush a thumb along her shoulder and ease out of bed carefully so I don't wake her.

My phone buzzes on the counter.

James: Called last night to report it. Followed up this morning. They'll need Liz to sign a statement today. He violated parole ×4. They're picking him up.

I stare at the message, emotion bubbling up my throat. I'm not surprised he did it, James would walk across fire for her, but tears threaten to spill with relief that sweeps through me.

I text back: **Thank you. I'll take her in this morning after she wakes up.**

Three dots appear immediately. **Let me know if she needs anything. Take care of my sister.**

My throat tightens further. I set the phone down and lean both hands on the counter wide, my head hangs, and I breathe through the mix of fury and gratitude.

Liz has people who show up for her. A brother who watches without hovering. Friends who love her fiercely. She doesn't need me, but she has me. Not because she asked, but because there is no universe where I let her face any of this alone.

I walk back to the bed, she's shifted, curled into herself, smaller than she ever sleeps, like her body is still bracing even unconscious. I sit down gently, and her eyes flutter open, groggy and soft.

"Nate?" Her voice tentative.

"I'm here," I say, brushing her hair from her cheek.

She sits up slowly, confusion flickering. "What's wrong?"

"Nothing," I say quickly. "Nothing bad has happened. James texted. He filed a report last night. The police are already on it. They just need you to come in today and sign the statement."

Her whole body deflates on a shaky exhale.

"He already took care of it?" she whispers.

"Yeah," I murmur. "He did."

She nods, blinking fast. I reach for her hand.

"The police station will be quick, we don't have to stay long. I'll be with you the entire time."

Her eyes lift to mine, glassy in the morning light.

"Don't worry, I'm not going anywhere, Cricket."

She swallows hard, then inches closer, tucking herself beneath my arm. For the first time since last night, the fury subsides, the knot in my chest loosens, and I let myself enjoy comforting her.

***

Liz

The police station didn't take long. That surprised me. I thought recounting everything would feel awful, but somehow the worst parts of the night were already softened in my memory, like my brain decided the only thing worth remembering clearly was Nate's arms around me afterward.

James already did most of the work. I know it must be killing him to not be the one handling everything, but I'm grateful he recognizes Nate's role in my life.

Nate's body relaxed when the officer said Colby had already been picked up and was in custody for parole violation. We ducked out of there after they took pictures and documented our statements. Since I got out of bed this morning, Nate hasn't been more than a few feet away. He keeps brushing his thumb along the back of my hand like he's reminding himself I'm still here.

It's Saturday evening, and for the first time in a while nothing has been required of us all day. If we would have had plans, Nate would have insisted I take it easy. All day he has been taking care of me. Making sure that I rest. So I do. Or I attempt to anyway.

I put on one of my stupidly expensive hydrating face masks, the kind that makes me look like a shiny ghost. Nate checks in with me before he runs out to grab dinner to make sure I'm okay by myself. I'm totally fine, but I love his care and attention.

While he's gone, I sit on the couch with Hulk curled on my lap and let my mind replay last night one last time. Colby's hands on me. The shove against the wall. The way the air felt tight and thin. The panic clawing its way up my throat. And then, Nate.

Nate's voice. Nate's arms. Nate's steadiness. Nate's anger, not directed at me, but for me. I press a hand to my chest. I'm not fragile. I know that. I survived worse. But last night, the second I felt safe again, it wasn't because of *my* strength. It was because of his.

When Nate returns, he's balancing takeout bags and a milkshake.

"You're supposed to be horizontal," he grumbles, nudging my knee with his when he sees me sitting up.

"I was. Hulk needed emotional support."

He cracks half a smile at that, then sets the food out on the little table. He keeps glancing at me, checking in without asking out loud. It's strange having someone do that.

We eat dinner on the couch together. He doesn't press me to talk about it and I'm grateful. I don't want to spend any more of my life talking about it. After we finish our meal Nate suggests I take a bubble bath. He got all the stuff while he was out. The good bubbles, expensive salts. And by suggests, I mean he insists. He even runs it for me, lighting tiny candles all around the edges. My heart overflows at his display of tenderness.

When I undress, the marks on my arms, the small bruise on my cheekbone stand out in the mirror. Outlines where Colby grabbed too hard, where he struck me. The sight doesn't affect me how it used to. They'll fade. He can't hurt me anymore.

I turn away from the mirror determined to forget it all.

I sink into the bath. Let the warmth wrap around my body until my shoulders loosen and I'm pruney. I finally drag myself from the tub and get ready for bed.

When I open the bathroom door, steam billows out behind me. I feel my hair dripping through my tank top. Nate is leaning against the headboard, already undressed and ready for bed even though it's early. It's like he couldn't stand to be more than ten feet away, so there he sits, scrolling his phone. I clear my throat, he looks up and he freezes.

I realize that my shirt is plastered to my still damp skin. Almost see-through. Hugging every curve. I feel a drop of water slide down my collarbone and disappear into the fabric. His eyes track that drop, darkening.

His throat works. His jaw clenches. His eyes drag over me and stop on the faint bruising on my face, then my arms, before quickly shifting away from them. I take a tentative step.

"Nate," I whisper, because the air feels too thick to speak regularly. "I know you've seen them." I gesture to the bruises. "And I know you keep pretending you're not staring."

His jaw tightens again. "Liz."

"I'm not fragile." My voice comes out soft but steady. Stronger than I expected.

He nods slowly, like he's afraid to spook me.

"I know you're not," he says. "You're the toughest person I know."

"Then why are you treating me like I might break?"

I slide into bed, propping myself up slightly against the headboard, and face him. He turns off the lights, shifting closer, until his chest is inches from mine.

"I'm not," he says, and this time his voice cracks in a way that destroys me. "I just want to take care of you."

Oh.

The tension that's been circling for weeks rises up like a tide, unstoppable. I don't want distance. I don't want space. I don't want caution.

I want him.

My fingers tremble as I reach for him. He still doesn't move, not an inch, eyes locked on mine, waiting for the smallest sign of hesitation.

"Nate," I breathe, "I want you to touch me."

Something shifts behind his eyes, uncertain at first then, almost reverent. His hand lifts to gently cup my face. His fingertips trace from my temple, to my eyelids, down to my lips, further to the hollow of my throat. He follows the strap on my shoulder with a barely there touch.

His pace is killing me, but still he doesn't hurry. His hand traces down my arm until he reaches my finger tips. He grabs my hand and brings it between us. Leaning down, he places a hot kiss on my palm. He releases me, his hands moving to trail down my side, hovering near my waist, but he doesn't let himself touch me further.

"You sure?" I nod. "Liz, we don't need to do this today. Not after everything."

"I'm sure. I want to. I want you in every way. No more fooling ourselves. No more performances for other people. Just me and you. There's nothing I've been more sure of."

His breath leaves him in a shudder. One of his hands immediately finds my waist with a firm grip. The other moves with purpose up my ribcage, not stopping until his fist tangles in my hair. He lowers his forehead to mine, eyes closing like he's overwhelmed.

"There's nothing I want more," he murmurs. "Not just tonight. Not just this moment." His thumb presses into my waist like he needs the contact to anchor himself. "I want whatever comes after it too. The quiet mornings. The messy parts. The hard ones we don't know how to name yet." His voice drops, sure and unwavering. "All of it. With you."

And then he kisses me. It's not hungry or rushed or frantic. It's a promise. Soft. Deep. Steady. The kind of kiss that steals oxygen. That's rebuilding something inside me brick by brick.

"Nate." My fingers dig into his shoulders.

His lips trail down my jaw, slow, deliberate, reverent.

"You tell me if you want to stop," he murmurs against my skin. "Any time."

"Don't you dare," I breathe.

He groans, low, quiet, wrecked, and in one smooth motion, he flips us and looks down at me with so much love in his eyes, I have zero doubt about how he feels about me. My hands instinctively slide up around his neck, my legs lock around his waist.

His mouth returns to mine, deeper this time, less restrained. Heat pools low in my stomach. I've never felt safer. I've never felt more wanted. I've never wanted someone back this intensely. This moment belongs entirely to us. Only us.

Chapter Thirty-Eight
Bomb Shells
Nate

Liz is still asleep when I wake, and thank God for that, because it gives me a minute to just take her in.

She's sprawled half on top of me, one leg slung over mine, her cheek pressed to my chest, her palm resting over my heart. Her hair is a mess, stretching across my collarbone. Her breathing is slow, steady, soft. And she is naked. Very, very naked. A fact that I *have* to acknowledge before I try to quickly move past it.

She looks peaceful. Somewhere in my caveman brain it's screaming: mine.

My arm tightens around her automatically. I don't mean to do it, but my body acts faster than my mind. Everything about last night replays in warm flashes, her hands shaking, but still reaching for me, her whisper of *I want you to touch me*, the way she opened for me, trusted me, let me take my time with her. The way she held onto me afterward, not letting me move more than an inch away.

I'd imagined being with her before, hell, I'd imagined it more times than I should admit, but nothing I ever pictured came close to the real thing. To her.

My wife.

Her leg shifts against mine, tightening around my hip for a split second before she relaxes again. I stare up at the ceiling and try not to grin like an idiot.

Because, yeah. Last night was perfect. But it wasn't just that. It wasn't just physical. It was everything underneath it, our trust, the tenderness, the way she looked at me like I was something good.

I'm not letting this go. I'm not letting *her* go. Not in a year. Not ever. Liz stirs again, this time with a tiny groan, her nose nuzzling into my skin searching for warmth.

"Mmm," she mumbles, "You're comfy."

My chest turns to goo, but I grunt out, "Good. Stay there."

She cracks one eye open, blinking up at me. And damn it, her morning face is lethal, soft, flushed, lips swollen from sleep and from me.

"Hey," she whispers.

"Hey." My hand dances down her spine before I can stop it. "How do you feel?"

She smiles against my skin, slow and shy in a way that makes my ribs ache. "Really good."

Same.

We stay like that for a long quiet minute, listening to the soft hum of the air vent and Hulk snoring from somewhere near our feet. She traces small absent circles over my chest, right above my heart, and it's stupid how much that one little movement wrecks me.

I clear my throat. Now or never.

"Liz," I say quietly, cupping the back of her head so she has to look at me. "In case anything wasn't clear last night, I'm in this. For real."

Her breath catches.

"I've been in this for a long time," I continue. "I don't want an expiration date. I don't want to call this fake anymore." My thumb strokes her cheek. "I want you to be my wife. My real wife. No end to it."

For a second, she doesn't speak. Just looks at me like she's memorizing every detail of my face. Of this moment. Then her lips tremble. "Nate."

"You don't have to say anything yet," I tell her gently. "I just needed you to know where I stand. Where I've stood for weeks."

My fingers drag gently along her jaw. "I'm not going anywhere unless you tell me to."

Her eyes fill, not with fear, but something deeper. Something that looks a lot like relief.

"I thought," She swallows hard. "I thought I'd scare you off if I said how I felt."

"Cricket." I tip her chin up. "You couldn't scare me off if you tried."

She makes a shaky little noise and pushes herself up to kiss me. My hand slides into her hair as I kiss her back, slow and sure. When she pulls back, her forehead rests against mine.

"I want that too," she whispers. "I want all of that."

My eyes close as the words hit, solid and deep. "Good," I murmur, pulling her fully onto my chest again. "Because you've been mine since the moment you talked my ear off when I was changing your tire."

She snorts against my skin. "Yes, I'm sure that's when you fell for me."

I grin into her hair. "Of course it was."

She laughs softly, that quiet, sleepy laugh I've grown addicted to. And for a moment, everything is exactly how it should be: Her in my arms. My future in front of me. Our life finally beginning for real.

***

Liz

Rosebud, my favorite place to brunch with James and Chloe, is packed today. Clinking silverware, people shouting greetings across tables, waitresses weaving between booths like over-caffeinated ballerinas. It smells like pancakes, butter, and happiness.

Nate's hand hasn't left mine since we walked in. He says it's so he doesn't "lose me in the crowd." I strongly suspect it's because last night shifted something between us and he hasn't figured out how to exist without touching me every four seconds.

I hope he never figures it out.

We spot Chloe and James in a corner booth. Chloe is waving both arms like she's landing a plane; James gives a more restrained nod, his eyes doing a subtle head-to-toe scan of me, checking for any lingering signs of what happened with Colby.

We slide in the booth together. A beat of silence settles over the table, the kind that feels like a pressure cooker about to hiss.

James clears his throat. "Before anything else, how are you? Really."

I answer honestly. "Better today. Still shaken, but y'all took care of everything. And Colby's gone." My voice wavers on the last word. Chloe squeezes my arm across the table. James nods, jaw tight with protective fury.

Then James looks at Nate. "I owe you a beer." A beat passes. "And a thank you."

Nate waves him off. "You don't owe me anything. I'd do anything for your sister."

Chloe has hearts in her eyes. "I can't tell you how relieved I am that you're okay, Liz." Then her eyes narrow, sparkling like she just scented gossip. "Now that we know you are okay... What else do you two need to tell us?"

A snort escapes my nose. Nate stiffens. James squints. Of course Chloe can sense a secret from a different zip code.

She leans in conspiratorially. "Liz is doing the face."

James frowns. "What face?"

Chloe beams. "The face she gets before she confesses something huge. Like when she backed my 4Runner into that boulder *she* painted and then blamed raccoons."

"It *was* raccoons," I mutter. Nate stares at me, stunned. Great. Add that to the list of things I'll have to explain later.

I guess it's time to come clean. I clear my throat. "I, uh, funny story. Actually hilarious, depending on your perspective."

James arches a brow. "You're stalling. Spill."

"So you know how Nate and I are married?"

They both nod.

"Well, that wasn't totally real. I mean, the marriage is real, we signed things, but it didn't start because we were in love. I was helping him out. He was helping me out. It was supposed to last one year before we divorced and went our separate ways."

Chloe gasps so loudly the couple behind us jumps. James doesn't blink. He just stares at Nate with the kind of stillness you see right before a coastal town gets obliterated by a hurricane.

"Explain," James says.

Nate opens his mouth.

"Nope," I cut in quickly, holding up a finger. "Let me. You'll make it sound like a hostage situation."

I tell them everything, the parents situation, my debt (James is understandably upset that I never told him), the impulsive courthouse marriage, how we planned for it to be temporary and how somewhere along the way, pretending became building a real marriage.

"So let me get this straight," James says finally. "You married my sister, whatever your reasons. You stood up for her. Looked out for her. And then you paid off her debt. Debt I didn't even know she had." He gives me a hard stare.

Nate nods once. "Yes."

James eyes lock on mine. "Did he pressure you into marrying him?"

"What? No!" I grab Nate's forearm instinctively. "If anything, he's been a walking consent form. Everything we've done has been my choice."

Nate's hand slides over mine and squeezes.

"Didn't need to know about all that." James grimaces.

Chloe sighs dreamily. "Oh my gosh, I love love."

James ignores her entirely and faces Nate. "Do you care about her?"

"More than anything." Zero hesitation. It knocks the air out of my lungs.

James absorbs that. Then he nods once, decisive. "Then we're good."

Just like that, the storm passes. I really built this up in my head to be a bigger deal, but I guess they can both see how much we care about each other.

We order brunch, and the whole booth shifts lighter, easier. Chloe kicks my shin under the table every five minutes. Nate can't keep his hands off of me. He's constantly running a hand over mine, squeezing my knee, dropping a kiss on my head. I don't know when I'll get used to it but for now, my pulse might be clinically concerning.

At one point Chloe leans over and whispers, "Your husband is staring at you like you hung the moon."

I glance at him. He doesn't look away. My face heats. "Shut up."

When the check comes, Nate and James both grab it at the same time. Their hands collide. They glare.

Chloe sighs dramatically. "Men."

James pays while Nate mutters something about *next time*. We stand to leave. Chloe gives Nate a congratulatory hug. Then James steps beside me.

"You really okay?" he asks quietly.

I nod. "Yeah. Better than okay."

He bumps his shoulder against mine. Big-brother affection in its purest form. His gaze shifts to Nate, who's waiting near the exit, hands in his pockets, expression softening the second he looks at me.

"About time you had someone who actually shows up for you," James says, wrapping me in a hug.

I swallow past the lump in my throat. "Yeah," I whisper. "It is."

***

We get home from Rosebuds and I feel floaty. Like I'm wrapped in a warm bubble that only happens when everything feels right. Nate's hand stays tangled with mine until I flop on the couch. Exhausted from the emotions of the past few days. Hulk immediately curls up on my stomach like a weighted blanket. My eyes grow heavy, the good kind of tired, the peaceful kind, so I close them just for a second.

As I'm drifting between sleep and awake, I hear Nate answer his phone in the kitchen. His voice drops low while he's talking, that gravelly tone he uses when he is trying not to disturb me. I smile into the pillow.

I hear his footsteps moving down the hall. He must think I am asleep, which I guess I kind of was, but I'm wide awake now. I keep still, not meaning to eavesdrop, but the words reach me anyway.

"Yeah, this is Nate Jones. Yes, I got your email last week. I looked everything over. I want the contract."

Contract? Whoever is on the other line must be speaking. Nate's quiet as he listens.

"Yup, three months in Colorado won't be a problem."

My stomach dips. He keeps talking, I hear him pacing lightly across the hardwood.

My brain feels muddled. After everything we've gone through, how is he just accepting a new contract without talking to me in Colorado? Is he leaving me? Surely he hasn't already changed his mind about everything.

Why didn't he tell me? Why did I hear about it like this? I sit up slowly, Hulk protesting with a squeak. Nate hangs up and steps back into the living room the same time I stand. His hand freezes halfway through sliding his phone into his pocket.

"Liz." He looks at my face and rushes to my side. "What's wrong?"

My voice comes out confused, hurt. "Colorado. Three months."

Nate blinks at me like he was expecting excitement and instead got... this.

"Baby, it's not what you think."

I wrap my arms around myself because my voice is wobbling. "I don't know what to think because you didn't tell me. You accepted a contract in another state, Nate. Without me."

His eyes widen. "No. No, Cricket. Not without you."

I open my mouth but nothing comes out. He steps closer, careful, like I am something breakable even though I told him yesterday I'm not. His palms hover at my elbows before he drops his hands to his side like he's afraid to touch me.

"I thought you were asleep so I took the call in the hallway," he says gently. "And I was going to tell you. I wanted to sit you down and explain everything."

He drags a hand through his hair, exhaling hard.

"After everything with Colby, I thought getting out of town for a few months might help you breathe. I thought a change of scenery would feel good. Safer. Calmer. And I wanted something we could do together. Away from Atlanta. Away from the noise. I wanted to give you space to heal, not space from me."

My throat tightens. He keeps going, voice steadier. "That contract is for *us*. Not for me. I already told them you would be coming with me. That we are a package deal. I made sure to ask if they needed other makeup artists. I made it known that we would like them to offer contracts to Jenn and Autumn too. I was thinking of you in every line of that contract. I swear."

My knees go soft and my voice comes out small. "You negotiated all of that before you told me?"

"Yeah." He winces. "Because I am an idiot who thought surprising you with a paid mountain getaway was romantic."

I let out a watery laugh that breaks halfway through. His shoulders loosen like he was bracing for me to walk out the door. He steps closer. This time his hands touch my arms and glide down to my finger tips.

"Liz, I am not leaving you behind. I would never do that. I accepted because I thought it would be good for you. For us. I want a life with you. I want..."

He swallows hard, searching my face for something.

"I want every version of our future. Even the ones we have not talked about yet."

My body goes still while my brain races ahead, cataloging the moment. He would never do anything to harm me. I pull back just enough to look at him.

"I thought you changed your mind," I say, because I need to hear him say it again. I need to hear it out loud.

"Not even for a second," he says immediately.

The truth of it settles slowly, my nervous system calming before going haywire all over again with Nate's next words.

"Liz, I love you."

I freeze, not because I don't feel it, but because this is the first time love hasn't come with conditions. With expectations. With the quiet threat of what happens if I disappoint.

"I love you," he repeats, steady and sure. "I'm in this for real. Just like I said this morning." The words spill out like he has been holding them in, like they burned a hole through him on their way out.

Something in me unclenches. "I love you too."

His breath shudders out of him, a smile breaking through that looks like relief, like awe, like he cannot believe this is happening. He pulls me into his chest, his lips pressing to the top of my head.

"Colorado will be amazing," he murmurs. "But even if it was three months in a cardboard box, I would want you there with me."

I rest my cheek against him, sinking into the safety of his arms. "We should probably call and tell Jenn and Autumn they need to pack."

He laughs softly. "God help Colorado."

I laugh too, the hurt from moments ago dissolves into something warm and certain. Because he is not leaving me.

He's always thinking of me. Always choosing us. Every time.

Chapter Thirty-Nine
Six Months Later
Liz

The beach is perfect. Soft waves, pale blue sky, white chairs lined in neat little rows. Everything smells like saltwater and flowers and the kind of happiness that makes your chest feel full.

I've been running around all afternoon making sure every detail is perfect, but now it's time. Jenn, Autumn, my little sister, take turns walking down the aisle. Before it's my turn, I reach around and grab Chloe's hand, pulling her in for one more hug.

Five months ago, when James and Chloe FaceTimed us in Colorado to tell us they were engaged, they did not even get the words out before I pounced on the screen. Between their smiles and the ring flashing so bright it nearly blinded me, I knew instantly my brother popped the question.

Nate said I nearly deafened him with my squeals, but I could not help it. How was I supposed to keep that much joy sealed inside? It had to come out somehow. That day I thought there was no way my heart could hold any more happiness. I was wrong. Standing here with sand between my toes and my brother about to marry my best friend, it feels like this joy has weight, like it might split me in two if I breathe too deep.

"I cannot believe that when we met in our apartment parking lot we were two broken strangers, and now I get to call you my sister," I whisper. "I love you so much, Chlo. I am so proud of you. I am so happy for you."

I pull back after one final squeeze and we both dab our eyes before I head down the aisle leaving Chloe with her dad. I feel Nate's eyes running over every inch of my body as he stands with the other groomsmen. Chloe chose blue for her bridesmaid dresses to match James's eyes. Lucky for me they match mine too.

I turn and take my spot in time for the music to change as Chloe and her dad march toward us. She looks like a dream walking down the aisle. Sunlight glints off her bouquet and catches the tiny crystals in her veil. Watching her walk toward my brother, so sure and steady, I think about how far we've all come. How love didn't rescue any of us, it just met us where we were and stayed.

I pull my eyes from Chloe to watch James. When he sees her, his face crumples in that way that makes everyone with a soul start crying too, including me. Nate mouths across the aisle. "Called it."

I smile so wide my cheeks ache. My brother is moments away from marrying my best friend and the love of his life, the ocean is shimmering behind them. My husband is eyeing me from across the aisle like he can't wait to rip this silk bridesmaid dress off later.

Chloe reaches James and he lifts her veil with shaking hands. He mouths, "You look perfect."

She mouths back, "You better not ruin your suit by crying on it."

It makes him full body laugh. Just what he needed to pull himself together. The ceremony starts, but I barely hear the words. My heart is full. Nate's eyes locked on mine. My husband. My real husband. Not temporary. Not pretend.

Watching my brother and my best friend promise forever feels like standing at the edge of something. Like love doesn't stop growing just because you think you've reached the ending.

When Chloe and James finally kiss, cheering breaks out across the beach. Jenn and Autumn scream loud enough to scare the seagulls, and Chloe's brothers glance at the two of them with matching grins that say trouble is coming.

At the reception, the white tent is lit with thousands upon thousands of twinkle lights, everyone is barefoot dancing, and champagne is flowing in every corner. I watch my brother twirl his new bride and feel a tug in my chest that is sweet and soft. What a gift they are to each other.

Nate slides up behind me and wraps his arms around my waist. "You look happy."

"I am," I say.

His lips brush my cheek. "I love you."

"Mmm," I hum.

He turns me gently, one hand warm against my back. His face is tender, the way it only gets when it is just us. He pulls us on the dance floor. I'm shocked he's willingly dancing, but I'm not about to complain.

I loop my arms around his neck as the song *I Don't Dance* by Lee Brice comes on. My eyebrows rise.

"Is this the song you said described our relationship in that stupid game your mother made us play?"

He nods and spins me as I listen to a man sing about how he didn't think he was meant to settle down. That love wasn't in the cards for him. How he doesn't dance, but he dances for her because he's so in love. How she has him wrapped around her finger.

I'm amazed at what he was telling me, even before we were married. Even before we truly fell for each other.

The song comes to an end and I wipe the tears from my eyes. I pull Nate from the dance floor, a slow smirk spreading across my face. "So Mr. Grump Pants, are you ready for our next adventure?"

He groans. "Cricket, we just got back from three months in Colorado. I thought we agreed our next adventure was taking it easy for a while."

I give him a small smile, "But this is a different kind of adventure."

He lifts my hand, pressing a kiss to my knuckles. "Okay, Cricket. You know I love our life. I love coming home to you. I love waking up with you on my chest. I love everything we have built. I'm up for any adventure you want to go on."

"Good," I whisper.

He gives me the softest smile, the one that melts my bones. "What kind of adventure are we talking about? Do I need a passport? A fake name?"

My heart hammers so hard I think he can hear it. "The kind where there are three of us instead of two."

He blinks at me. Slow. Then his eyes drop to my stomach for one careful second before meeting my eyes again. He lets out a shaky laugh and pulls me into him, forehead to forehead. "You're pregnant?"

"Yes." My hands slide up to cup his face. "We're having a baby."

His breath hitches, then he kisses me. Not rushed. Not careful. Just full of awe. Full of love. When he pulls back, his eyes are shining.

"You have no idea how happy you just made me," he whispers. "You are my greatest adventure. This baby is just a bonus."

I feel the truth in his words all the way to my toes. Behind us, music swells. Someone shouts that it's time to toss the bouquet. Jenn and Autumn sprint toward Chloe like competitive wild animals. People laugh. Waves crash. Fairy lights glow in the fading sunset.

Nate rests his hand gently over my stomach.

"We are going to be parents," he murmurs.

"We are."

Standing there in the middle of the most beautiful reception, with the man I love and the life we're building unfolding in front of us, I know this with absolute certainty: love isn't something I have to endure. It's something you choose. Something you build. Side by side, with the person you want forever with.

And our love story is only getting started.

The End.

Acknowledgements

So many people deserve thanks, but I will try to keep this brief.

First, a huge shout-out to **Rendezvous Cafe** for letting me camp out at your tables day after day while I wrote my little heart out. Your decaf lattes, food, and kindness helped me write this book.

To my husband, thank you for being my biggest supporter and cheerleader, even if you still have not read one of my books. I see everything you do for our family and I could not do this without you.

To my boys, thank you for telling everyone you meet that your mom is an author. Thank you for believing in me without wavering and for reminding me every day why chasing big dreams matters.

To my beta team, thank you for helping me hammer out plot holes, grammar problems, made-up words, editing, and all the messy parts in between.

To my ARC team, thank you for reading, reviewing, and shouting your love for Liz's story from the rooftops. You are the reason this book has a chance to find its people.

Finally, to the readers, thank you for giving this indie author a chance. Every page you read is a gift I will never take for granted.

About the Author

Katie King was raised in Tennessee and moved to Georgia shortly after graduating college, where she still lives with her husband, two adventurous boys, and two chaotic dogs.

She spent her childhood reading, writing, or crafting stories in her head—and not much has changed. Reading remains her favorite escape, and fiction has always been where she turns for comfort and inspiration. Now, she hopes her books can offer readers the same kind of joy and escape her favorite authors have given her over the years.

Also By

Katie King's debut contemporary romance, *Rules for Starting Over*, follows Chloe and James through a story filled with warmth, humor, and Katie's signature slow burn. *Rules for Starting Over* introduced readers to the cozy, interconnected world Liz and Nate are now a part of.